SAINTS AND SINNERS

BLOODY JOE MANNION BOOK THREE

PETER BRANDVOLD

WOLFPACK PUBLISHING
— EST 2013 —

Saints and Sinners
Paperback Edition
Copyright © 2022 Peter Brandvold

Wolfpack Publishing
5130 S. Fort Apache Rd. 215-380
Las Vegas, NV 89148

wolfpackpublishing.com

Paperback ISBN 978-1-63977-252-0
Large Print Hardcover ISBN 978-1-63977-503-3
eBook ISBN 978-1-63977-251-3

SAINTS AND SINNERS

CHAPTER 1

SAND AND GRAVEL RAINED DOWN ON THE BRIM OF "Bloody" Joe Mannion's high-crowned, black Stetson.

He saw a man-shaped shadow wielding a rifle on the gravelly ground straight out away from him and threw himself forward just as a rifle thundered from above. The wicked report echoed around inside Mannion's head as the bullet tore into the ground where he'd been standing half an eye blink before.

He hit the ground, losing his hat, and rolled onto his back and raised his prized Winchester Yellowboy, cocking it. He took hasty aim at the hulking, duster-clad figure standing atop the escarpment thirty feet above him.

He fired a hair too late.

The man gave a startled grunt and threw himself back out of sight as Mannion's bullet sailed toward the vaulting cobalt arch of the Colorado sky.

Another bullet sailed in from Mannion's right to plow into the ground just inches from his right elbow. Joe grabbed his hat then rolled to his left and scrambled to his feet, his forty-six-year-old knees barking out their complaints. He ran into a notch between two more escarpments in the craggy badlands area in the San Juan Mountains south of Del Norte, where Mannion was town marshal, in the south-central part of the territory.

Two more bullets tore into the ground just behind his running feet, and two more screeching reports echoed loudly.

Just inside the notch, Mannion stopped and pressed his back against the stone wall on his left, gritting his teeth, squeezing the smoking Yellowboy, which he held up high across his broad chest. He brushed a gloved fist across his salt-and-pepper mustache then shook his head to shake the grit and sand and pine needles from his neck-length, salt-and-pepper hair.

Joe edged a look around the corner of the notch to see a man kneeling on yet another escarpment maybe a hundred and fifty feet away. The man, whose small size identified him as Billy Lord, the gutless, young killer Mannion had followed out of Del Norte late the previous afternoon. Lord had ridden out with his partner, Hector Hagness, a half-wit half-breed cut from the same cross as Lord.

A back-shooting no-account killer for hire.

A lucky one. He was the one whose bullet Mannion had just missed.

Lord and Hagness had killed a liveryman in Del Norte. As far as Joe Mannion knew, no one had hired the job done. Lord and Hagness had just been both drunk and piss-burned that the liveryman, Cletus Alvarez, had cleaned them both out during a poker game in the San Juan Hotel & Saloon in downtown Del Norte.

That was the establishment, the best of its lot in town if not in the entire southern Colorado Territory, that Joe Mannion's new bride, Jane Ford, owned and operated. Joe had heard about the liveryman emptying Lord and Hagness's pockets from Jane herself after a couple of townsmen had heard the shots fired in Alvarez's Livery and seen Lord and Hagness galloping away as though their mounts had had firecrackers tied to their tails.

Laughing as they had, too, it had been reported to Joe.

Mannion pulled his head back into the notch just as Lord, aiming down the barrel of his Winchester, stretched his lips back from his teeth. The rifle roared; the bullet smashed into the rock wall where Mannion's head had just been, kicking up rock dust and spitting stone shards into the notch and onto the brim of Mannion's down-canted hat.

"You're a dead man, Mannion!" the rat-faced killer screeched out from atop the scarp. "We led you in here to kill you, Bloody Joe!"

He whooped a laughed, his cries laced with lunacy.

"Going to kill you slowww, amigo!"

He laughed again.

Mannion grinned. He cocked and jerked the Yellowboy out of the mouth of the notch, aimed at where the snake-like, little yellow-haired killer knelt atop the scarp, and fired.

Billy yelped as he ducked and rolled out of Mannion's sight but not before Joe's bullet blew through the crown of the killer's shabby gray Stetson, blowing it off his head.

"Damn, Joe!" the killer yelled. "Some say you lost your edge, but you came purty dang close to blowin' my head right off my galldarn shoulders!" A squeal of jeering laughter. "Close don't count, though, Joe!"

Mannion ejected the smoking cartridge casing from the Winchester's action. It clanked onto the gravel at his feet. He seated a fresh round in the chamber then turned his head to peer through the notch to his left.

Time to leave Lord. For the time being, anyway.

A lawman's sixth sense told him the half-breed, Hec Hagness, was repositioning to put Joe in a whipsaw between himself and Billy.

Mannion turned and strode through the notch, taking a right where yet another notch in the stone canyon carved by an ancient river opened off the first one. Joe removed his hat to crouch under the low-slanting ceiling —too low to accommodate Mannion's six-foot-four-inch frame—then made his way through the twisting corridor that angled downward.

A high screech sounded on Mannion's left.

He stopped suddenly and aimed the Yellowboy into a small cavern. He eased the tension on his trigger finger. His hawk-like gray eyes narrowed. A human skeleton lay in the cave, sitting up against the cave's back wall. Tufts of leathery skin and clothing—canvas and buckskin— remained on the dead man's body. Tattered boots rose nearly to the dead man's knees. The skeleton was slumped to one side. It had lost its head. Gravity had likely removed it over the many years the poor soul had been here, somehow overlooked by the larger carrion eaters. The skull lay in the dirt beside the rest of the man, staring at Joe through its large, dark, empty sockets.

The man had likely taken a bullet or two—Mannion spied some splintered ribs and a bullet-shaped hole in the right leg bone—and had crawled in here to recover...or to die, as the case had been.

An outlaw on the run, most likely. Maybe a lawman caught in a whipsaw between two killers like the one Joe was in danger of getting caught in now. Never to be heard or seen from again. These badlands had their secrets. A man could die here and even be over-looked by the carrion eaters.

Something moved in the shadows behind the skeleton. Two little, yellow eyes peered out of the darkness. The rat gave another shrill screech then skittered along the base of the back wall, flicking its hairless tail, and out through a V-shaped crack bleeding daylight into the cavern.

Mannion continued forward. He stopped at the base of the declivity and surveyed the rocks and cedars around him. They were backed by the tall, red crags known as the Devil's Anvil. Beyond the Anvil and down the pass lay the little town of Fury.

As harshly pristine as it all was, this rocky, forested, canyon-gouged country southwest of Del Norte was stitched with men like Lord and Hagness—men on the run. Desperate men. Wolf-like killers.

Mannion would be glad to rid the world of Lord and Hagness, he thought now as he closely scanned the nooks and crannies between rocks around him. They'd been an annoyance for long enough. Mannion had never been able to pin anything concrete on them; at least, not concrete enough for a judge. Now he had enough on them that he wouldn't waste time throwing the bracelets on them and taking them back to Del Norte for trial. No point in wasting a judge's time.

Mannion would put a bullet through their heads whether he had to or not.

Who would know if he followed the book or not? Lonely country, this. A man could die and not even have the carrion eaters for company.

Joe stepped forward, intending to climb an escarpment jutting before him. Up there, he'd have a better view of the rocks around him. When he reached the base of the crag, he looked around carefully. Lord and Hagness were closing on him. He could sense them skulking around in the rocks around him, waiting to plant a bead, fire a bullet he wouldn't hear.

Joe grinned.

He took the Yellowboy in one hand and climbed natural stone rungs up the side of the crag. After a twenty-foot ascent, he gained the crest of the rock and looked around at the natural stone shelf before him. It was backed by another twenty-foot height of stone wall beyond the top of which a lone golden eagle wheeled slowly on a thermal against the sky dimming toward dusk.

Seeing no one in the rocks around him, Mannion stepped up onto the shelf.

He'd just taken the Yellowboy in both hands when sunlight glinted in the upper periphery of his vision.

He levered a round into the Yellowboy's chamber, snapped the rifle to his shoulder, and fired at the hulking, bearded figure just then bearing down on him from a notch in the stone wall with a Henry repeater whose brass breech a ray of the westering sun had found.

The Yellowboy spoke loudly, the ejected cartridges pinging onto the stone floor around Mannion's black boots.

Hector Hagness's Henry roared, stabbing smoke and flames, the bullet caroming skyward as the big half-breed fell back against the stone wall. He dropped the rifle and slapped his hands over his eyes, giving an agonized howl.

Mannion had shot the man at least once. He saw the red on the man's left shoulder. But the third shot had clipped the edge of a stone thumb from behind which Hagness had been hunkered. The rock shards had peppered his face.

He bellowed again, his deep voice crackling. *"My eyes!"*

He stumbled forward, clawing at his face. He took one step too many and dropped down over the edge of the rock. His hat sailed off his head and his long hair flew up like a crow's wings as he plunged down toward Mannion, turning a single, oddly graceful somersault halfway between his previous position and the ground.

He struck the floor of the shelf ten feet in front of Joe. He lay on his back, blinking his bloody eyes.

He threw his arms out to both sides of his thick body clad in buckskin and sweat-fetid wool, ground his spurred boots into the floor of the shelf, and arched his back, his belly expanding and contracting rapidly. His long, greasy, gray-brown hair lay in tangles on the ground beneath his head, curling onto his shoulders.

Mannion racked a fresh round into the Yellowboy's chamber and shot the man through the head. Hagness dropped his back to the ground and lay shivering, spurs jingling.

A veteran lawman, Mannion felt more than saw the danger now flanking him. He abruptly half-turned and dropped to a knee behind a thumb of rock jutting from the outside edge of the stone shelf.

As he did, he heard the high-pitched wail of displaced air as the bullet raced over and just behind him to bark into the stone ridge from which Hagness had tumbled.

The roar of Billy Lord's rifle followed.

Mannion peered over his covering thumb of rock, saw Lord kneeling on a ridge maybe a hundred and fifty feet beyond. He was hunkered between two rocks. His pale powder smoke wafted in the gathering evening shadows.

Mannion returned fire then, seeing that his ridge was connected to Lord's ridge, both of which together seemed to form a horseshoe of solid rock and boulders with a few gnarled cedars here and there. Mannion gained his feet and ran to his right along the narrow shelf.

As he did, Lord's rifle wailed. Bullets slammed into the rocks jutting around Joe's running feet.

Nine...ten times the killer's rifle wailed, the little killer himself whooping and hollering like a moon-crazed lobo.

Silence.

Mannion climbed the rise of rock that formed the closed end of the horseshoe and then followed the bow in the escarpment back toward where Lord hunkered in silence, probably reloading his empty repeater.

Mannion was above the killer now, closing on him. Lord poked his head up suddenly. When his eyes found Joe, they grew bright with fear beneath the brim of his battered, bullet-torn hat.

"Shit!" Billy leaped to his feet. The clinks of dropped bullets sounded as he ran along the shoulder of the stone rise, away from Mannion.

Joe dropped to a knee and sent two slugs hurling toward the fleeing kid. Billy followed a serpentine course, twisting around rocks and cedars growing up from cracks in the stone scarp, making a hard target. The Yellowboy barked a second and the kid gave a yell and dropped down over the side of the escarpment and out of Mannion's sight.

Joe took the Yellowboy in one hand and hurried down the side of the scarp, following the kid's course.

He stopped at the edge of the scarp, cocked the Yellowboy loudly, and aimed down the side.

Billy Lord—a yellow-headed squirrel of a man with a soot-smudge of a mustache mantling his upper lip—lay on the ground ten feet below Mannion. He lay on his back, his black denim jacket winged out to both sides to reveal his Spanish-cut red shirt with green piping on the breasts. One black denim clad leg was curled beneath the other. A dirty white sock shone through a hole in the toe of his right boot.

Billy sat up on his elbows.

"Oh," he said. "Oh...mercy..."

His eyes found Mannion bearing down on him from above. They widened anxiously.

"Don't kill me, Joe!"

The fear in his eyes was surprising to Mannion.

Even more surprising to Joe was the fact that Mannion himself seemed to hesitate, his finger not drawing back against the Winchester's trigger like it usually would in such a situation.

Usually by now a cold-blooded little squirrel of a spineless killer like Billy Lord would be coyote bait.

Worm food.

A gift to the carrion eaters, if any would bother with him. He couldn't have weighed much over a hundred and twenty pounds soaking wet from a bath in a horse trough.

He'd be lying there staring up unseeing at Joe with a quarter-sized hole between his eyes.

Why was he not?

Mannion frowned down at the kid.

Billy continued to stare up at Mannion, pleading in his eyes. He shook his head, grimacing as he awaited the bullet. "Don't, Joe! Come on, pard! I'm beggin' ya, now!"

Mannion had no idea why he did what he did next.

But do it, he did.

He gestured with the Yellowboy. "Pull that hogleg from your holster, toss it away. A good ways away. Any fast moves, Billy-boy, and you'll be shaking hands with Ol' Scratch."

"All right, all right."

Staring up at Mannion, skeptically, suspiciously, the kid did as he'd been told.

The Colt thumped onto the ground fifteen feet away.

Just after it did, hoof thuds rose in the distance.

Mannion glanced up a distant rise painted pink and salmon by the west-falling sun at the edge of the badlands. A horse and rider were galloping off to the east, an ink smudge in the distance, the rider turning a look back over his right shoulder then turning his head back forward. Horse and rider were a long ways out, but Mannion thought he saw a black hat, maybe a dun horse. Horse and rider disappeared down the other side of the boulder-strewn rise.

"Who was that?" Mannion asked Billy, keeping his rifle aimed at the kid. He'd followed only two men out from town—Lord and Hagness.

Billy had heard the hoof thuds. He, too, had turned his head to look toward the fleeing rider.

He turned back to Mannion. "Beats me."

The kid seemed to be telling the truth.

The fast-fleeing rider was probably just another raggedy-assed outlaw scared out of the rocks by the gunfire.

"Stay right where you are, kid," he said, lowering the Yellowboy in disgust with himself. "I'm comin' down."

CHAPTER 2

WELL AFTER GOOD DARK, A PIANO PATTERED IN THE distance straight ahead along the trail.

Mannion and the kid, riding with his hands cuffed behind his back on his coyote dun, which Mannion led by its bridle reins, rode along the two-track trail between high, shelving mesas that loomed blackly against the starlit sky. The kid's chin lolled against his chest. He was snoring, sound asleep.

The midsummer air was perfumed with mountain honeysuckle blooming along the creek that murmured over rocks to Joe's right. The dark, rippling waters shimmered in the starlight.

"Who in hell's playin' a piano way out here?" the kid wanted to know, jerking his head up suddenly.

His tone had grown obstinate as well as belligerent not long after Mannion had lowered his Yellowboy and, instead of giving the killer a pill he couldn't digest, had cuffed his hands and tossed him onto his horse, which the kid had tethered along with Hagness's mount in a grove of pines.

Mannion had tethered his prized bay, Red, in some

rocks after he'd seen his quarry through his spyglass scuttling around in the canyon, hurriedly and nervously setting up an ambush.

Mannion had had too much experience to ride into the bushwhack. Now Billy Lord was in custody, Hagness was dead, his horse unsaddled and free, and Joe was looking forward to enjoying a whiskey or two with his old friend, Jeremiah Claggett.

He did have to admit feeling a bit regretful for not having given the nasty little killer that indigestible pill, however. Now it was too late. Not even he could kill him now, all trussed up as he was, though he wished he could.

"Hey, Joe," the kid said now, urgently. "Where's that music comin' from? Where you takin' me?"

Mannion glanced over his shoulder at the kid looking around anxiously.

"Fury," Mannion said as he and the kid climbed toward the crest of a low rise.

"Fury?"

"Yeah, you know Fury." Mannion grinned.

"What're you takin' me there for? Come on, Joe. Anywhere but there!"

"Shut up, Billy."

"Come on, Joe!"

"Shut up, Billy," Mannion said again, smiling to himself.

The Lord family, including Billy and his older brother, Frank, as well as their old man, Delbert, and the boy's half-sister, Eloise, had been kicked out of town by the good citizens of Fury, who'd tired of the low-rent family's thievery and other sundry sins, as well as Eloise's "corrupting of otherwise good men," and sent running for their lives with only the clothes on their backs, one mule, and their buckboard wagon. Behind them, their old wooden shack, hunched in the rocks of Two Hawks Creek, where the family had prospected when they hadn't been shaking down other prospectors or venting brands and reselling beef, had been burned.

It had fairly lit up the night sky over Fury, so Mannion had heard. That had been five, six years ago now.

"Anywhere but there, Joe," Billy pleaded now.

"Shut up, Billy," Mannion said with a sigh of disgust—with himself as well as with the kid, for not having drilled a .44 round through the kid's brain plate. "You got nothing to worry about. Much has changed in Fury since you last saw it."

Ahead and below the rise Mannion and his charge had just crested, a soft orange light shimmered in a pine forest that stretched through a deep canyon. Those were the lights of Fury, the little mountain mining town which had boomed briefly ten years ago when a hoard of prospectors had swarmed into the area and soon depleted the nearby creeks and canyons of all that wonderful gold that had been waiting to fill their pockets since the earth had become more than just a shimmer in God's eye.

Mannion and the kid entered the forest and passed the mostly abandoned, gray log cabins that lay strewn among the pines, most hugging the secondary creeks that scored the canyon and met the larger creek, Skeleton Creek, running along the high, southern ridge. The tipple of the old Fury Mine, five years defunct, could still be seen shimmering in the starlight where it jutted out of the side of the slag-littered ridge.

The piano music had grown louder as Mannion and the kid had entered the town.

It was coming from one of the only two saloons that appeared still open for business, just ahead and on the north side of the narrow main street. Three or four bearded gents stood outside the place, fittingly called the North Side, chinning and drinking beer, a few smoking cigars or cigarettes, the smoke drifting over the street lit by two oil pots, one sitting on the street fronting each saloon. Wan lamplight flickered behind the plate glass windows.

As Mannion rode past the North Side, one of the bearded gents raised his mug and gave his gray-bearded chin a cordial dip. "Evenin' to ya, Marshal," he said with a heavy Irish accent. "See you been busy, as usual. But why bring that vermin back to town?"

Mannion didn't answer.

But Billy did. He spat and told the man he could do something physically impossible to himself.

That man and the others laughed derisively.

"Yep, that's Billy Lord, all right," one of them said as Mannion and the kid drifted off down the street.

"How come you're bringin' him in upright, Joe?" yet another gent called behind them. "That just ain't *like* you!"

Again, they all laughed.

Mannion didn't know any of the men out there by name though he'd probably seen them around a time or two. His dogged reputation preceded him pretty much everywhere he went in this neck of the western frontier.

He and the kid passed the only other open saloon— the Parthenon, owned by a stocky Chinaman the last time Joe had been through Fury—on the street's south side. It lay three doors up from the North Side, on the south side of the street. Mannion could see a few man-shaped shadows slumped at the bar beyond the windows to each side of the batwings, but there was no sizable crowd in the Parthenon, just as there hadn't been in the North Side.

A few shops appeared to still be doing business though it was hard to tell at this late hour when everything except the saloons were closed. Most of the other businesses had the shabby look of abandonment.

A light shone in yet another window up the street, on the north side. This was a long, low, shake-shingled log cabin. A badly faded sign stretching into the street on peeled pine poles read: JEREMIAH CLAGGETT, CONSTABLE.

Several bullet holes marred the sign, attesting to Fury's wilder days. Mannion wasn't sure how Claggett held on here as marshal. The town couldn't be paying him much anymore. On the other hand, Claggett was mostly part-time these days. At least he had been last time Joe had ridden through. The old constable, who still had a case of the gold fever, maintained a small digging a mile out of town to the southwest.

Jeremiah claimed to even find some color on occasion —enough to buy himself a good bottle of whiskey and steaks for himself and the granddaughter who lived with him and didn't seem to mind living this far out in the high and rocky. In fact, Mannion thought that Justy Claggett, short for "Justina," liked it just fine out here off the beaten path as much as her grandfather did. Last time he'd seen her she'd seemed as wild as the cats that roamed these mountains.

As though to corroborate Mannion's opinion:

"Name yourselves!" came a harsh female voice from the shadows fronting the constable's office.

There was the thud of booted feet dropping to the floor of the small veranda that fronted the shack.

Mannion checked his horses down and peered into

the shadows under the awning that covered the stoop. "Joe Mannion, Del Norte town marshal." He saw a slender figure rise from a chair to the right of the door and set a rifle on her shoulder. *Her* shoulder, sure enough. Judging by the curves Mannion could see even in the shadows, silhouetted against a lamplit window behind her, the figure on the porch was a girl all right.

No doubt about that.

Young woman, rather.

Joe smiled. "Hi, Justy. Did that old scudder deputize you now?"

The girl stepped forward, opening and closing her hand around the neck of the rifle on her shoulder. "Marshal Mannion, what're you doin' out in this neck of the woods so late?"

A silver star glinted on the breast of her men's wool shirt.

"Brought in a prisoner." Mannion glanced at the sullen, angry Billy Lord. "I was hoping to leave him with your grandfather while I ride over to Forsythe to pick up another one instead of having to make another trip out from Del Norte."

The prisoner he'd been summoned to retrieve by the Forsythe town marshal was wanted in Denver on federal charges. A deputy U.S. marshal would be sent from Gunnison to fetch the prisoner out of Mannion's jail as soon as Mannion had the man locked up in Del Norte. This system cut down on travel time for individual lawmen. It was sort of a pony express-style relay "you scratch my back, I'll scratch yours" arrangement.

Lawmen in the area, regardless of jurisdiction, helped each other out. Mountain travel was time consuming, not to mention dangerous, for bad men badly outnumbered lawmen out here in this still mostly lawless country. Del

Norte was abutted on three sides by large, high, sprawling mountains ranges—the Sangre de Christos, the Sawatch, and the San Juan. Mannion had the authority to work in the country beyond Del Norte's jurisdictional boundaries due to the fact he'd been deputized by the county sheriff.

As Justy Claggett stepped up to the edge of the porch steps, she looked at Mannion's prisoner. Her eyes held on Billy. She drew a slow, deep breath then looked at Joe.

"I'm sure that'd be right fine, Marshal," she said, tonelessly.

Mannion hadn't seen Justy Claggett in well over a year, but in that time, she'd filled out in all the right places to make a woman, and she'd grown straight and tall. A pretty but tough-looking young woman with long, straight, dark-brown hair attesting to her half-Mexican blood. Her mother had been from a little town in Sonora. Both parents, her father having been a soldier during the Apache Wars and had ridden with General Crook, were dead—killed by desperadoes in Arizona. Justina had come to Fury to live with her grandfather when she'd been only eight years old.

She wore a wool plaid work shirt that likely fit her too tightly for her grandfather's comfort—Mannion knew it would for his having a daughter only a couple of years younger than Justy—and tight black denim trousers and brown leather boots. Her long, unbrushed hair as well as the trail gear and the rifle on her shoulder gave her a wild, sexy look.

"He should be back soon. He just walked over to the Widow Khun's place, left me to man the shop. The Widow thought she heard intruders again." Justy smiled. "Her memory is slipping; she still thinks these are Fury's wild old times. She's called Pops to her old shack by the mine a half dozen times already this month and all he's managed to find was a wild cat living in her buggy shed."

Mannion chuckled.

The girl—she must be twenty by now, Joe thought—looked at Mannion's prisoner again, and her smile faded. A grave, pensive expression replaced it. She reminded Joe of his own half-wild daughter, Vangie, who dressed the same and preferred the company of horses to people.

"How-do, Miss Claggett?" Billy said, grinning at her. "I'd remove my hat but as you can see, my hands are cuffed."

"As they should be," Justy said, again tonelessly.

Billy ran his lusty gaze up and down the girl's tall, busty frame, and whistled. "Why, look at you! You always was purty, but now...now you're a wakin' dream, sure enough!"

"Shut up, Lord," Mannion said. "Any more of that kinda talk—"

"Oh, no, no, no, Marshal Mannion. I can handle men...er, *boys*...like Billy Lord."

Again, Billy grinned, lustily. "Like you handled my brother Frank?"

In the lamplight from the window behind her, Mannion thought he saw the girl's pretty face blanch.

Frank Lord may have left Fury in disgrace five or six years before, with the rest of his no-account family. But in the years since, he'd made quite a name for himself. He was now the infamous leader of a gang of a dozen outlaws that ran wild in New Mexico and Arizona Territories. Lord and his hardtails including two tough lieutenants, two Mexicans, and a full-blood Apache scout and tracker would occasionally drift into the mining camps in southern Colorado to prey on stagecoaches hauling gold ingots or freshly minted gold coins. They were feared for their savagery. Bounty hunters and lawmen had tried to take them down for years, but the cagey Lord always managed to give them the slip.

Tightly, Justy said, "Frank is and always will be scum. Just like you, Billy."

Billy leaned toward her. "You best be careful what you say about ol' Frank. He's not that far away. In fact, I was fixin' to meet up with him and his gang when Bloody Joe here"—he turned to Mannion with a sneer—"got lucky."

"Hah," the girl laughed. "Bloody Joe never gets lucky."

"How 'bout you, little girl?" Billy's eyes drifted again to the girl's well-filled shirt. "You wanna get lucky? With me this time?"

"Billy," Mannion said, "I told you—"

"Don't worry, Marshal," the girl said, coming down off the porch and walking up to the side of the little killer's horse. "I'm used to such vermin as little Billy Lord."

"You tell the marshal to get lost, little girl," Lord said through a grin, his eyes continuing to brazenly ogle her, "and I'll show you how little I am."

He leaned his head far down to cackle in the girl's face.

She moved so fast, bringing her Winchester carbine down off her shoulder, that Mannion didn't realize what had happened until after he had heard the sharp smacking sound followed by Billy's screech.

"*Ow!*" he cried, leaning back in his saddle, blood glistening on his lips. He spat to one side, ran his tongue across his lips then glared down at the girl who was smiling up at him now. "Why, you smashed my mouth an' all I done was pay you a compliment!"

Justy threw her pretty head back and laughed throatily, sliding her cagey gaze to Mannion. She had a lovely, savage, south of the border look about her. "See, Marshal

Mannion? I told you I could handle little javelinas like Billy Lord. You leave him with me an' abuelito, and we'll see how much of him you'll have left to pick up on your return from Forsythe."

Mannion laughed and was about to respond but stopped when another man's voice called from up the street: "Justina Claggett, are you causin' trouble again, you fiery little Mescin catamount?"

Mannion turned to see the pot-bellied, bandy-legged Jeremiah Claggett ambling toward him from along the street to the north. Claggett wore a cream sugarloaf sombrero, a gray beard that hung halfway down his chest, and a single Colt low-slung on his right thigh. The mule ears of his high-topped boots jostled as he strode in his bull-legged fashion.

"She's not the one causin' trouble here, Jeremiah," Mannion said, swinging down from Red's back. "But she sure is good at meetin' it head on. You've obviously trained her well."

Claggett chuckled as he approached. "Oh, she didn't take no trainin'. She's a natural. Then, again, in the last year or so, she's gotten right good at puttin' men in their places." He stopped before Joe, nudged his hat down low on his forehead to scratch the back of his head. "Can't quite figure how that came about."

Mannion chuckled. "I got a feelin' I do, but I'll leave it at that." He glanced at Justy and saw a blush rise in her cheeks. Joe stuck his hand out to his old friend. "How you doin', Jeremiah?"

Shaking Joe's hand, Claggett said, "My bursitis an' chilblains is actin' up, and some mornins I feel like I'm comin' apart at every joint, but I'm here so I ain't complainin'...overmuch."

"Overmuch," Justy good-naturedly teased her grandfather, winking at Joe.

Lord said in a high, screechy voice to Mannion, "Would you free my hands, you old devil, so I can dig out my hanky and wipe the blood off my mouth?"

Mannion ignored him.

Claggett frowned up at the little killer. Quietly, scowling, he said, "Is that Billy Lord?"

"One an' the same."

"Ah," Claggett said, fingering his beard, staring at the kid. Deep, pensive lines cut across his leathery forehead beneath the brim of his big hat.

"I got him on a murder charge," Mannion said. "I was hopin' you'd hold him for me while I ride up to Forsythe to fetch Jasper Neal." Joe stretched his lips back from his teeth as he glanced at Billy. "I'm havin' second thoughts about it now, though."

Claggett turned to him, one gray brow arched. "Jasper Neal, the train robber?"

"One and the same. The federals want him in Gunnison an' you know how those suits don't like riding into these mountains. Too many men up here they put away at one time or another. I'd take Billy back to Del Norte and make a special trip for him, but Neal's trial is coming up soon." He smiled and shook his head. "Wouldn't want that viper to miss his date with Sawyer Grange."

Grange was the hangman in this part of the territory, a local bogeyman. "You be good," parents warned their children, "or Sawyer Grange will come acallin'!"

"Speakin' of too many men put away at one time or another, I could say the same thing about you, Joe," Claggett said with a coyote grin. "You know how your reputation precedes you."

The old constable winked.

"Yeah, but I'm not afraid of a tussle. Those federal boys don't like gettin' their suits dirty."

"Ain't that a fact?" Claggett laughed and looked up at Billy again. "Sure, sure. I'd be right honored to have the kid spend a night or two in my hotel. The rats in the cellblock get lonesome, don't ya know."

Billy Lord told the old lawman what he could do. He'd no sooner gotten the last word out than Justy rammed the butt of her carbine against his bloody mouth again, bloodying it further.

Billy howled and sagged back in his saddle.

"That's no way to talk to mi abuelito, you fork-tailed little urchin'!"

Claggett clapped his hands and roared. "I think we'll all get along just fine, Joe. Just fine!"

"Like I said, I'm havin' second thoughts, though, Jeremiah. It sounds like his brother might be on the lurk. Billy said he was ridin' up to meet Frank when I took him down."

Claggett turned his head quickly to Justy. Justy returned her grandfather's gaze then, blood again rising in her cheeks and looked down at the toes of her boots.

What the hell's going on here? Mannion wondered. *What kind of history could Justy Claggett possibly have with Frank Lord? Frank had to a good six or seven years her senior.*

Jeremiah tugged at his beard, frowning at Billy. "I see, I see..."

Mannion looked at the kid leaning out from his saddle to spit blood into the street. "Where were you gonna meet Frank, Billy?"

"Go to hell, you bloody bastard!"

Claggett turned to Mannion and drew a deep breath, puffing up his broad, lumpy chest. "I ain't afraid of no Frank Lord, Joe. Hell, no." He glanced at Justy, who was still looking at her boots. "Frank Lord oughta be afraid of *me*!"

Justy raised her gaze to her grandfather, gave a weak smile.

"I don't know...given your history, Jeremiah..." Mannion didn't like it. As town constable, Claggett had likely led up the citizens who'd run the Lords out of town on the proverbial long, greased pole.

"Nonsense!" Claggett intoned. "Don't insult this old bushwhacker, Mannion. If Frank Lord's foolish enough to ride into Fury to free his pipsqueak brother, Justy an' me an' the remaining good citizens of Fury will kick him and them curly wolves of his out with cold shovels!"

Justy didn't look as confident as the old man. "Abuelito," she said, warningly.

To Mannion, Jeremiah said, "If Frank Lord thought he had a chance against Fury, he'd have come callin' long before now." The old lawman turned to his granddaughter. "Pull your prisoner down from there an' haul him inside, Deputy," Claggett ordered. "I've had about enough of this nonsense!"

In a huff, he turned and stomped up the jailhouse's porch steps, the mule ears of his boots jostling violently.

Justy turned to Mannion. She had a dark look.

"Justy..." Mannion started.

Claggett interrupted him with, "Justy!"

Still looking at Mannion, Justy shrugged.

"All right, then." Mannion didn't like it, but he didn't want to further damage his old friend's pride. He reached up to pull the kid down from his horse. "I'll get him inside then buy ya a drink, Jeremiah."

Claggett smiled over his shoulder.

"Ain't seen ya in a whole year, Joe!" he said, opening the jailhouse door. "You'll buy me two!"

CHAPTER 3

EDGAR "HARD TIME" LAWTON PULLED HIS SLOUCH HAT down low lest the night breeze should blow it off his head.

"Come on, Buster!" he wheezed into the left ear of his galloping gelding. "There's enough light out here to steer by—stretch it out, boy! We gotta get back to town fast!"

The zebra dun shook its head as though in defiance of the order but, feeling the sharp spurs cut into its flanks, it laid its ears back and increased its speed along the trail twisting through the pine forest on this high-mountain plateau, just north of the Devil's Anvil.

Hard Time saw the lights of the mining camp of Hardville dead ahead through the pines. He smiled and gave his hat one more, unnecessary tug. He was excited.

Frank Lord was in Hardville. All dozen of his gang were there, stomping with their tails up. Hard Time had information Lord would likely pay a hefty amount for. Yessir, a hefty amount. Lord might even make Hard Time a member of his formidable gang.

That alone would be more than enough pay for Hard Time.

Hard Time had seen Frank Lord and his impressive, stony-eyed gang throughout the west on several occasions—mostly by chance but Hard Time had followed the gang from a distance a time or two. He had to admit that. They were damned impressive, and Hard Time was fascinated. Though he'd been raptly attentive to Frank Lord's savage exploits for the last several years, since he'd formed the gang, his unexpected meetings with the man and his gang had mostly been—what would you call it?

Coincidence?

They'd surely been that, but there was another word Hard Time was looking for. He was not a fellow who collected words or had had much by way of learning. He'd never learned to read, and he used an *X* to make his name. He was a twenty-two-year-old, short, bandy-legged saddle tramp who was still looking for his place in the world though a voice deep inside his head kept telling him that he, like his father and most others who'd come before him, would never amount to much more than what he was—a saddle tramp.

From childhood, he'd been on hard times, thus the nickname he couldn't even remember who'd planted on him. Maybe one of the poor farmers or ranchers who'd taken him in for as long as they'd been able to afford him after his mother had died in a typhoon in Oklahoma, when she'd been hoeing their garden patch...after his father had been shot by a deputy sheriff in Conrad when he'd been caught busting into a drugstore looking for Dr. Percival McSweeney's Liver Tonic—gunpowder and laudanum—after a three-day bender, three sheets to the wind.

Hard Time had worked on a few good-sized spreads but mostly he drifted from year to year to one hard-time shotgun ranch after another, working for not much more than pennies and piss water.

Eating foul grub and getting bit by ranchers' curs.

He felt an old man now, at twenty-two.

At least, he thought he was twenty-two. Maybe twenty-three?

No, Hard Time hadn't amounted to much but every time he'd seen Frank Lord's impressive bunch of tough nuts, he'd yearned to be part of such a gang. To ride hell for leather from one town after another, robbing banks or stagecoaches or mine payrolls, and just generally raising hell. They were all tough, young men, like Frank— only a few years older than Frank himself—and they were hellions, for sure!

Oh, to be respected as much as Lord's bunch was respected. To be feared as much.

Even hated.

As far as he knew, no one hated Hard Time unless you took into account a couple of small-time ranchers' flea-bit curs who'd hated him just because they'd hated every-body. Oh, and there was that rancher in New Mexico who'd caught Hard Time with his pants down in the woodshed with the rancher's dim-witted daughter, Verna. Yeah, that fella hated him for sure. Likely would have shotgunned Hard Time out of his boots if Hard Time hadn't been fleet of foot.

Other than that fella, however, Hard Time had never left enough of an impression to be hated. Certainly, never feared.

Nor respected.

Oh, to be one of Frank Lord's men. Each one had at least a thousand-dollar bounty on his head. Frank himself was worth fifteen hundred! No one had so far collected because Frank's bunch was just so dang slippery.

Even Pinkertons and federal lawmen hadn't been able to track them down.

Hard Time had tried to throw in with Frank a couple of times in the past only to be laughed at, to be made to feel the fool.

Well, see if ol' Hard Time gets laughed at tonight when he rides hell for leather into Hardville and imparts an important bit of information ol' Frank his lordship will be mighty thankful to get.

Hard Time knew Lord and his bunch were in Hardville because he'd followed them there when they'd passed through Gunnison farther west, where Hard Time had been stocking up on trail supplies. Hard Time had lurked around Hardville for a time, watching the gang as they drank, gambled, and generally caroused, one by one and two by two heading upstairs with painted ladies. Hard Time was fascinated by the tough nuts' guns and sleek ponies built for speed and the hard look in the gang members' eyes.

An impressive, uncompromising bunch!

Hard Time got a little nervous when he saw Frank himself cast him a suspicious look in a backbar mirror. Hard Time quickly averted his gaze then finished his drink and lit out toward the Devil's Anvil, where he thought he'd do some prospecting. It was near the Devil's Anvil that he'd heard the shooting. He'd hunkered down and seen through his spy glass who'd been swapping lead.

None other than Billy Lord and Bloody Joe Mannion himself!

Sure enough, Bloody Joe had been swapping lead with Frank's beloved kid brother, Billy, who must have been on his way to visit Frank in Hardville.

Bloody Joe had been exchanging gunfire with Billy until the notorious, uncompromising lawdog had—and this was noteworthy because it was so unusual for Bloody Joe—taken the man prisoner instead of killing him and kicking his carcass into the nearest ravine.

Billy was Frank's kid brother whom Frank had more or less raised, along with their half-sister Eloise, when their father, Delbert Lord, had been drinking himself blind in Del Norte. Until the entire family was kicked out of town, that was. It was said—and Hard Time listened closely to any scrap of information he could get about the legendary Frank Lord and his men—that Lord was more of a father to Billy than a brother.

In fact, not long after the Lords had been kicked out of town, Frank had killed their father in a fit of rage. Leastways, that's the story the deeply inquisitive Hard Time had been told.

Frank's story wasn't really all that far from Hard Times'. Leastways, if you cut out the part about Frank overcoming his humble past and becoming an outlaw of renown, with his long, dark-eyed, handsome face splashed across wanted dodgers throughout the Southwest...

Predestined!

That was the word Hard Time had been looking for.

He'd learned the word from an educated whore he'd once been flush enough to spend the whole evening with in Tucson after he'd taken part in a cattle drive from Las Cruces. Hard Time didn't normally take note of words but that one, "predestined," had touched his fancy for some reason.

Since hearing it, he'd tried to find a way to use it in casual conversation, so he could sound a little more educated than he was and maybe make a favorable impression on someone. But he'd never been able to swing it. He'd never had occasion to tag an experience with the word.

Predestined. As in *predestination*, the whore had told him, explaining the definition of the word.

He'd never had occasion to use it until now.

His meeting with Frank Lord at several different places around the wild western frontier had purely been an example of predestination. His and Frank's paths had been meant to cross.

Because Hard Time Lawton, galldarnit, belonged in Frank's gang!

Tonight, in just a few minutes, in fact—if Frank was still gambling at the Continental, which he likely was, as Frank was known to gamble for several nights in a row, taking breaks from the baize only for dalliances with the prettiest whores in the house—Frank would realize that himself.

That Hard Time Lawton was meant to ride in Frank's gang of stone-eyed killers!

Knowing that Mannion had arrested his beloved kid brother—who was really more like a son to Frank than a brother—whom it was said Frank felt especially protective of since Billy was known to be sort of soft in his thinker box, would piss-burn Frank something fierce.

He'd recognize the value of the information. He'd likely buy Hard Time a drink. Maybe even a poke with Frank's own favorite whore. He'd likely pull Hard Time aside and tell him to be saddled and ready to ride at first light the next morning, because Hard Time was now one of Frank's impressive bunch of hardtails!

Predestination. That's what it was.

Hard Time and Buster galloped into Hardville, nearly running over several drunk prospectors in the process as the men were making their uncertain ways across the main street, between saloons and evoking more than a few bellowing curses and fist shakes.

The tinny pattering of several pianos rattled out from several saloons at once, and bearded men—prospectors as well as freighters and game hunters—were clumped here and there in front of saloons, and doxies milled on boardwalks or flounced on second-story whorehouse balconies, yelling lewd enticements to potential clients.

Hard Time reined Buster up in front of the Continental Saloon, leaped down from the saddle, tied the dun at the hitchrack with a dozen other horses, and strode with rare confidence up onto the boardwalk.

He long-strode toward the batwings and stopped suddenly when a man's deep voice bellowed from within, "If you think I'm a cheater, go ahead and call me a cheater, sir. Don't just sit there givin' me the woolly damn eyeball through those rose-colored glasses. I...don't...like... it! Worse, Miss Sonja don't like it. It's makin' her *nervous*!"

There'd been a low roar of conversation from inside the Continental. Now in the wake of the shouted remonstration, that roar suddenly fell to silence.

Then only Frank Lord's voice—Hard Time had heard Frank's voice enough times to recognize it anywhere— said softly but not too softly to hear him clearly from within the now suddenly, eerily silent saloon: "Don't it, Miss Sonja?"

Hard Time stepped slowly, on the balls of his feet, up to the batwings to peer over them. It wasn't hard to pick Frank out of the crowd. Not only was Frank one distinctive looking cuss in his black suit, high-crowned cream Stetson, and thick, yellow, walrus mustache, but all heads in the smoky room were turned toward him.

He sat at a long table in the middle of the crowded room with maybe ten other men around him, all looking a might nervous. They all held playing cards. Play had ceased, however. Now they were all sliding their edgy gazes between Frank and the man clad in a green suit including an outlandish green top hat sitting directly across the table from him.

Top Hat was tall, thin, long faced, and pale. He wore rectangular, rose-colored glasses.

Frank had a slender brunette clad in next to nothing on his lap, one arm around his neck. She was looking at Top Hat and, yeah, Hard Time decided, she did look nervous even though with the way she was sitting he could see only her profile. Her cheek was pale beneath the face paint she wore.

"Don't he make you nervous, Miss Sonja?" Frank said again, giving the girl a little nudge.

She turned stiffly to Frank. She had brown eyes, and her brown hair was coiled atop her head and stitched with little feathers. She gave a nervous dip of her chin.

"See there?" Frank said to Top Hat. "You and your stink eye is makin' the girl nervous. I don't want her nervous. She's gonna have to perform for me again later, after I kill you, sir," he added, lowering his voice and dipping his chin and sending his own one-of-a-kind glare across the table at Top Hat.

Hard Time couldn't see Frank's face, because Frank sat with his back to the batwings, but Hard Time knew the expression on the killer's face, all right. Hard Time had seen that flat, cold, soulless expression in a couple of other similar situations—one time in Alamogordo and once in Tombstone.

Hard Time never wanted that cold, dark stare directed at him.

Each man he'd seen Frank use it on in the past had died hard.

Damned hard.

Top Hat dipped his own chin and grinned back at

Frank, his rose-colored glasses glinting in the light of a sooty lamp hanging low over the table. "I'm not afraid of you, Lord."

"You're not?"

Top Hat carefully laid his cards down on the baize-covered table, slid his chair back, and rose. Hard Time's eyes widened, impressed by the man's height. He must have stood nearly seven feet tall and was as thin as a bullwhip.

"You may think you're fast, Lord. In fact," Top Hat said levelly, sort of flaring his nostrils with each word and making the rose-colored glasses rise up and down on his long, thin nose, "you may be fast." He grinned, showing two silver front teeth. "But I'm faster."

"Oh, you think so—do you, Long Ken?" Frank asked. He was smiling now. Hard Time knew he was smiling. That made Hard Time smile.

It was about to happen. Long Ken was about to die. Hard Time didn't know how, but Long Ken was going to die, all right.

Suddenly, by ones and twos and even threes and fours, the men gathered at tables flanking Frank and Long Ken grabbed their beers or whiskey shots, rose from their tables, and scurried out of the line of fire. A low rumble of shocked conversation rose in the room.

It soon died.

Standing, Top Hat stared across the table at Frank, who sat as before, with the whore on his lap. She seemed frozen in place, too scared to move. The cheek that Hard Time could see from his angle looked waxy in spite of the garish face paint.

Top Hat said, "Do you want it sitting down, Lord? Or standing up?" Slowly, he peeled both flaps of his green, cutaway coat back behind the pearl-gripped Colt .45s thonged low on his long, thin thighs. "Makes no difference to me."

"You sure seem confident," Frank said.

"I am that."

"Bein' fast with the cold steel, you know, Long Ken," Lord said, "don't necessarily mean you're gonna make it out of here alive."

"Of course, it does." Again, Long Ken smiled, showing the ends of those two silver front teeth.

There was a sudden blur of fast movement, and Hard Time jerked with a start. He frowned, puzzled. One of the men sitting near Long Ken gasped.

"Dear...*God!*" said another man in a hushed voice, raising ringed fingers to his mustached mouth.

Hard Time returned his gaze to Long Ken and then he gave an involuntary gasp of his own. His lower jaw dropped as he said softly, "Well...I'll be a monkey's uncle..."

All the color seemed to bleed out of Long Ken's face as the gambler stared down at Frank. He swallowed, making the black handle of the short-bladed knife impaling his throat move up and down.

Hard Time was flabbergasted. He'd be damned if Frank hadn't reached up and pulled that Arkansas toothpick from a sheath he must have hidden away behind his right shoulder and given it a quick little flip just off the side of his right ear. Frank had moved so quick—quick and graceful as a cat!—that Hard Time's eyes hadn't been able to follow it.

Likely, Long Ken hadn't been able to follow it either.

That's why as he lowered his chin just now to look down at the obsidian handle protruding from his throat, his eyes widened behind the rose-colored glasses in astonishment. He raised both of his pale, long-fingered hands to his throat and closed the right one around the handle.

"Oh!" he croaked out, dropping his hands to his sides and taking two stumbling steps backward.

The rose-colored glasses slid down his nose to reveal his shocked eyes.

The whore on Frank's lap raised her hand to her mouth as she stared across the table at Long Ken in shock.

"Now, do you see your mistake, Long Ken? You might be faster than me. Hell, many are. I've never bragged about bein' fast. Not with the smoke wagons." Frank smiled that smile Hard Time couldn't see but knew was there. "But a knife? Now, that's another thing altogether!"

"Oh," Long Ken croaked again.

He tried to raise his hands to the knife again but got them only halfway before he dropped them and took another few panicked, stumbling steps backward before falling back across a large, round table away from where card players had already scrambled.

Long Ken shivered as though he'd been struck by lightning for a long time, making the coins and the glasses on the table clink and rattle, before he finally settled down and died.

Everyone in the room seemed relieved. That was a hard way for a man to die.

Hell, it was a hard way to *watch* a man die!

Hard Time grinned over the batwings.

That was Frank, all right.

Oh, to ride with such a man...

CHAPTER 4

"UM...UM...MR. LORD?" HARD TIME SAID, HAVING walked up behind the outlaw leader as the dead gambler was being hauled out of the saloon by two beefy, sweating Germans and the conversations in the room had resumed, sounding sort of giddy in the aftermath of the anxiety-producing killing the house had just watched.

Everyone was still talking about it. All heads kept turning to where Frank had resumed his poker game, casually puffing a cigar. A minute ago, the whore had whispered into Frank's ear and then slid down off his lap and slowly, a little shakily climbed the stairs that rose against the saloon's right. A red-and-gold-papered wall stood against a bullet-pocked player piano atop which a man currently slept, hat pulled down over his eyes, hands entwined on his belly.

So drunk he hadn't even stirred at the foo-foo-rah.

Likewise, Frank hadn't heard Hard Time. He was talking and laughing jovially with his fellow poker players.

Slowly, Hard Time lifted his hand, wondering if it was wise to place his hand on a man like Frank Lord's shoulder. Would Frank shoot him or—more likely, Hard Time feared now—flick that nasty knife out of the sheath he'd returned it to after ordering one of his fellow players to pull it out of the dead man's throat and clean it off, and give Hard Time the same treatment he'd given the gambler?

Hard Time decided he'd better not touch the unpredictable man. Besides, it didn't seem fitting for anyone to touch Frank Lord. Except for the whore, of course.

He stepped up to Frank's left ear, cleared his throat, and said louder than before: "Ex-excuse me, Mr. Lord. But...but...could I have a word?"

Remember, Hard Time told himself, trying to steel his nerve:

Predestination.

Frank turned his big, hard, crudely handsome face toward Hard Time, thick brows stitching over the bridge of his lumpy, hatchet nose. His eyes were a startling baby blue in such sharp, startling contrast to the otherwise severity of his features. He was the sort of man who always wore an angry scowl tempered somewhat by a vaguely jeering, not so vaguely arrogant glint in those unnaturally blue eyes.

He ran those eyes slowly down Hard Time's lean frame to his humble boots, worn as ancient Indian moccasins, the spurs rusty. He ran them back up again. As he did, a look of incredulity and possibly even of revulsion intensified.

"What the hell do *you* want?" he said, spitting the words out like tobacco juice. "I told you if I saw you again, I'd kill you."

Hard Time's heart quickened. His hands felt slick inside his gloves. He steeled himself for that toothpick.

"Uh...a word, Mister Lord?"

"A word, Mister Lord?" Frank mocked him. "Just who

in the hell are you and why are you shadowin' me, sonny?"
His heavy yellow brows stitched, a throbbing bulge
forming between them, more severely.

"Uh...it's about your b-brother, Mister Lord."

"What?"

"It's about Billy."

Frank stared at him. Then he glanced at the other
players at the table regarding him impatiently then laid
his cards face down next to his shot glass and a black
cheroot smoldering in an ashtray. "Outside."

Frank rose from his chair and headed for the
batwings, the flaps of the long, spruce green duster he
wore over his three-piece black suit, winging out around
him, brushing men and furniture.

Heart beating even faster, Hard Time swung around
and meandered through the tables, flushing when he saw
eyes on him, behind those eyes folks maybe thinking
Hard Time was already a member of Frank's gang and had
summoned the gang's notorious leader for a consultation.

Hard Time might even be an important member of
the gang, no less. Maybe even one of Lord's lieutenants.

Hard Time knew he didn't look much like one of
Frank's notorious lieutenants. But looks didn't mean
much, really. Most folks knew that. Hard Time might
dress and carry himself humbly to avoid being taken for a
trail-hardened outlaw by some bounty hunter wanting to
cash in on the thousand-dollar bounty on his head. Of
course, he wasn't wearing a duster like all the others in
Lord's gang, but he could remedy that soon enough.

Hard Time pushed through the batwings and stepped
out onto the boardwalk fronting the saloon.

"All right—what's this about my brother?" Frank said,
pushing through the doors.

Hard Time was about to speak but stopped when two

more men roughly Ford's size and age—over six-feet and broad-shouldered, eyes all business if a little drink-glazed —pushed out through the batwings behind him.

"What's this about, Frank? What's the dilberry want?"

Dilberry, eh? Hard Time thought with a sneer. *You'll see what a dilberry I am when you hear the important information I have, you cork-headed fool.*

The man standing beside the man who'd spoken elbowed him and said with a shrewd grin, "Careful—I think you riled the dilberry, Bronco."

Bronco Ford, one of Frank's two lieutenants, as Frank called them, anyway. The other man was Bryce Sager, who was too young to have fought in the War of Southern Rebellion but was enamored enough of his home territory, Dixie, to wear an ancient gray Cavalry kepi and to have had a collarless shirt, worn beneath his suit and vest, fashioned out of the old Stars and Bars Confederate flag, with gold buckles running down the front.

Bronco Ford was big and beefy, grim-faced. Bryce Sager was slender and sharp-featured, with bright, leering, crazy eyes...

"Shut up, both of you," Frank said, keeping his gaze on Hard Time. "What's this about my brother?"

"Well, I was ridin' out to the Devil's An—"

"Cut to it," Frank said, scowling down at the much shorter Hard Time, who hadn't realized how tall Frank was...nor how short and downright small he himself was...until he'd found himself standing before the man once again—for the third time in his life.

Predestination.

"Bloody Joe Mannion, town marsha—"

"I know who Mannion is. What about him and what about Billy?"

"Mannion has him. Billy, I mean. They had a shoot-out in—"

"Mannion arrested my brother?" Frank's tone was growing angrier by the second, those baby blue eyes looking stranger and stranger and more and more menacing.

"Yes, sir."

"What for?"

Hard Time shrugged. "I don't know. I just heard the shootin' an' stopped and looked over the situat—"

"Where did Mannion take Billy?"

Hard Time shrugged. "Hard to tell. I figured back to Del Norte, since that's where Mannion's from. But when I stopped on a pass and glassed 'em, it looked like they were headed north toward"—he smiled—"Fury."

Again, Hard Time shrugged and added quickly, "I can't say for sure, though."

He didn't want Frank to know he knew so much about him. That might look odd. Downright suspicious.

"Fury?" Frank said, incredulous, the sharp planes of his face coloring a little. "I heard there weren't nothin' left in Fury."

Again, Hard Time shrugged. "Like I said, I don't know for sure. Leastways, that was the direction they were headin'. Nothin' much else out that way except Forsythe higher up."

"Where did you see this shoot-out and Mannion arresting Billy?"

"Well, like I tried to tell you—"

"Cut to it!"

"In that canyon beneath the Devil's Anvil."

"When?"

"Just before sundown."

Frank turned to the two men standing beside him.

"Bronco, Sager—gather up the boys, send 'em to bed right now, no more whorin' or drinkin' or card playin'. We ride at first light. The party's over!"

"You got it, Frank," said Sager, eyes flashing like some hunting hawk's.

Lou Bronco just nodded, characteristically grim.

Both lieutenants swung around and strode back into the Continental.

"What in the hell's goin' over here?" came a voice on the street to the north of the saloon.

Hard Time turned to see a stocky man in a three-piece suit striding toward him and Frank. A town marshal's badge glinted on the man's broadcloth coat. He wore a bowler hat from which long, gray-silver hair hung down nearly to his shoulders. "I heard a man was..."

The lawman let his voice trail off when he saw the tall, suited, yellow-haired man standing next to Hard Time. "Oh," the lawman said, instantly cowed. "It's you, Frank..."

With that, he pinched the narrow brim of his hat, turned around, and made a beeline back in the direction from which he'd come, spurs jangling.

Frank gave an insolent sneer then turned toward the batwings.

"Uh, Mr. Lord..." Hard Time said.

"Go to hell, dilberry," Frank said, not even bothering to glance over his shoulder as he added, "An' quit followin' me or I'll gut ya."

Frank pushed through the batwings, disappeared inside, and left Hard Time standing on the boardwalk behind him, hang-jawed, fury building in him until he heard himself snap out, "You're the dilberry, ya low-down, dirty privy snake!"

Instantly regretting his loss of control, Hard Time

stepped forward to peer over the batwings. He heaved a relieved sigh when Frank, apparently not having heard him, did not turn around but continued heading toward the stairs rising along the saloon's papered wall, just beyond the bullet-pocked player piano where the cowboy still slept, though now he'd curled onto his side.

Frank was probably heading for the room of the nervous whore with the feathers in her hair.

Hard Time knew the only reason he was still alive was because, despite his demeanor, Frank had felt beholden about the information Hard Time had imparted. Otherwise, Frank likely would have killed him for the mere reason he found Hard Time annoying.

Hard Time flooded with disappointment and rage to the point he clenched his fists at his sides and almost sobbed.

Hard times continue...

————

AT THE SAME TIME BUT ROUGHLY FIFTY MOUNTAIN miles away, in the North Side Saloon in Fury, Constable Jeremiah Claggett refilled his and Mannion's shot glasses, set the bottle down on the table, and sat back in his chair, scowling.

"What's your problem all of a sudden, Jeremiah?" Mannion asked his old friend—one of the very few men on the planet he, indeed, called a friend.

A man like Bloody Joe didn't get along well enough with others to build many friendships. He had with Claggett though, the latter man, kind-hearted and soft-spoken, couldn't have been anymore Joe's opposite. "You look like you're getting ready to break wind. If so, please let me know so I can change positions."

Claggett shook his head and slammed a spidery, red paw down on the table, making some of the whiskey in the shot glasses slop over the sides. He opened his mouth to speak, but before he could get a word out, Mannion said, "If it's about Billy Lord, I—"

"Ah, hell, no—it ain't about Billy Lord. Nor Frank, neither. You tight-lipped old devil, Joe!"

The four other customers in the saloon as well as a young but tired-looking, scantily clad soiled dove sitting alone by the bar, a bare foot on a knee as she picked at a toenail, turned their heads toward the two lawmen.

"What the hell did I not say?" Joe asked. "I usually get in trouble for what I *do* say!"

"We been sitting here for over an hour an' you haven't mentioned one word about gettin' yourself hitched!"

"Oh." Mannion felt his cheeks warm a little. He lifted the shot glass and sipped. "I'd have gotten around to it eventually."

"I naturally heard. You're a favorite topic of conversation around these mountains, don't ya know, Joe? Wasn't I surprised when I wasn't overhearing a report about your latest effort at increasing the number of owlhoots you've planted on Boot Hill but that you went and got yourself married—in a church weddin' and *everything*!"

Again, Claggett slapped his spidery hand down on the table.

"Jeremiah, you're wasting good whiskey."

"And you married the lovely Jane Ford, no less. What'd you do, Joe? Conk her over the head and drag her down the aisle?"

"Somethin' like that." Again, Mannion felt his cheeks warm. Unconsciously, he covered his embarrassment by taking another sip of his whiskey.

"You know I'm just kiddin' you, Joe. It's nice that you

settled down, married you a good woman. Congratulations to you, old friend." Claggett reached over and clinked his shot glass against Mannion's.

"Thanks, Jeremiah."

"It's nothin' to get all embarrassed about, you know. Fallin' in love. Gettin' yourself hitched."

"I know," Mannion said. "I'm just not used to talking about it."

"What made you decide to pull the trigger?"

Mannion shrugged. "What can I tell you...?"

"You love her."

"What's that?"

"You love the gal. Go ahead and say it, Joe. The word ain't *poison*!"

Mannion brushed a fist across his brushy, salt-and-pepper mustache and gave a nervous chuckle. "All right, all right. What the hell?" He looked across the table to meet his friend's direct gaze. "I love the gal, Jeremiah. Purely, I do."

Jeremiah grinned. "See? That wasn't so hard, now, was it? Your tongue didn't turn black and fall off."

"Nah, hell. I might even get used to sayin' it."

"Where you livin'? I mean, since that hardcase son of Garth Helton burned your house down last year?"

"At Jane's San Juan Hotel, but I'm having a new house built," Mannion said. "I built the first one myself, but I don't have time to build this one. Besides, Jane wants something a little less, shall we say, humble than the one I was gonna throw together. We have carpenters building the new place where the old one sat and where I have a couple corrals and a stable. That's where Vangie spends most of her time, working with her horses."

Vangie, short for Evangeline, was Joe's seventeen-year-old daughter.

"She'll love the new place, I'm sure."

"I think she will."

"Gets along with Miss Ford...er, the new Mrs. Mannion...all right?"

"They're like two peas in a pod, Vangie and Jane. That's why I don't cotton to being in the same room with both of 'em." Joe snorted a wry laugh.

"Gang up on you, do they?"

Mannion stared across the table at his old buddy. Claggett's sparkling blue eyes had suddenly taken on a pensive cast as he sat back in his chair and gazed across the room at the papered wall behind the Del Norte marshal.

"What is it, Jeremiah?"

Claggett arched his bushy gray brows that still retained a few strands of brown here and there. "What's that?"

"Now don't *you* go gettin' tight-lipped. What're you thinking about?"

"Ah, hell, I don't know." Claggett ran a thick index finger around the rim of his now half-empty shot glass. "I reckon I'm sorta jealous, Joe. Startin' life over again... with a good woman." Before Mannion could respond, Claggett raised his hands, palms out. "Oh, I ain't complainin', though. I got Justy, and she purely fills that little, humble old cabin of ours. Don't know what I'd do without her, to tell you the truth."

"I have a sneaking suspicion she'd say the same thing about you." Mannion raised his shot glass and smiled, vaguely surprised that he could have a conversation about something so personal and not feel more than just a bit embarrassed.

The former Miss Jane Ford had changed him, sure enough. He'd even been wondering if it hadn't been Jane's influence that had caused him to bring Billy Lord to Fury alive when he could have very easily kicked the little devil out with a cold shovel, which was his usual way with criminals of Billy's low ilk.

Was that a good thing? If he'd punched the little snake's ticket, he could have been on his way to Forsythe now and gotten home to Jane and Vangie sooner.

"What'd we do without 'em, Joe?" Claggett asked, smiling pensively down at his own half-empty shot glass.

Mannion only smiled and turned his shot glass around on the table.

"Joe?" Claggett raised his voice and put some steel in it. "You be careful up around Forsythe. That's always been bad country and it's only gotten worse since a narrow-gauge railroad got laid up there to service the Forsythe Mine. You know as well as I do that Jasper Neal has a pretty loyal bunch in his tow, includin' his no-account son."

"I told you I'm not afraid of a tussle, Jeremiah."

"No, well, Neal's men aren't either. Jasper's the mastermind—if you can stretch the meaning of that term —of his outfit, and they likely want him back." Claggett finished his drink, slammed the glass down on the table, and winced at the creaking in his old bones as he rose. "I best get back and relieve Justy over to the jail. I'll keep an eye on that rapscallion since I can't sleep worth a shit anymore, anyway."

"I hear that," Mannion said, though he'd been sleeping far better since he'd hitched his star to the former Miss Jane Ford's wagon. "I'd best get some sleep myself."

"You can ride with Justy out to our place, Joe. Take my bed."

There were no longer any hotels in Fury.

Mannion set his hat on his head and adjusted the angle. "I'd just keep her up with my snoring. The livery barn with ol' Red is just fine with me."

Claggett clamped an affectionate hand over Mannion's shoulder. "Good night, Joe."

"Good night, Jeremiah."

Claggett turned to start toward the batwings then stopped and turned back. "Ride careful tomorrow, Joe." He arched his brows and dipped his chin severely. "You hear me?"

"I told you I don't mind a tussle." Mannion grinned. Suddenly, his expression sobered. "You keep in mind what I told you about Frank Lord being in these mountains, Jeremiah. If he hears I arrested Billy, he might come looking for him."

"What makes you think *I* mind a tussle?" Claggett wheezed a laugh, threw an arm up in a casual wave, and ambled out through the batwings.

Mannion shook his head and chuckled.

He didn't see the tight expression that overtook his friend's face as Claggett stepped down off the boardwalk and headed for the jail.

CHAPTER 5

"HELLO, DARLIN', I'M BACK."

The voice instantly drew Mrs. Joe Mannion, the former Miss Jane Ford, out of a deep sleep. A belly sleeper all her life, Jane rolled quickly onto her back and lifted her head from her pillow. "Joe?"

She frowned, blinking sleep from her eyes, as she looked around her large, opulently appointed bedroom on the third floor of her own San Juan Hotel & Saloon. She was surprised to find the room empty save herself.

"Joe?" she said again, sure that she'd not only heard his voice but had felt his large hand on her shoulder, pressing his fingers affectionately into her skin through the strap of her nightgown. "Joe?" she queried, louder, thinking he might have left the room to enter one of the other two rooms in the suite—the parlor or her office.

But the only response were the sounds of Del Norte coming to life on the street below the two long, recessed windows where the buttery, high-country morning sunlight streamed around the drawn velvet curtains—an amalgam of men's voices, barking dogs, the drum of horse and mule hooves, and the squawking and clattering of wagon wheels.

Del Norte in the southern Colorado Territory, abutted on three sides by the Sangre de Christo Mountains, the San Juans, and the Sawatch Range, was a loud frontier town. It was getting louder every day with more ranchers and cattle pouring into this fertile, mineral-rich land along with miners enjoying a second boom in the mountains and the whisperings of a railroad pushing up from the Topeka, Atchison, and Santa Fe Line running through Colorado Springs on the eastern plains.

Jane, a seasoned businesswoman who'd never been married until she'd married Bloody Joe Mannion six months ago, supposed she should welcome the progress of the ranching and mining boom as well as the railroad. As the owner of one of the largest establishments in town, she prospered as the town prospered. But she did not welcome such progress.

Pushing forty, she was comfortable with what she had. Pushing forty, she'd enjoyed the rollicking, challenging years—a single woman trying to carve out a niche for herself in the male-dominated world of the western frontier. She—a woman from back East, no less. A moneyed gal who twenty years ago had left that family money behind to carve out a life for herself in this man's dusty, smelly, loud, and bloody world beyond the Mississippi River.

She had no idea what had compelled her. An innate independence and defiance of society's norms, she supposed. In doing so, she'd been estranged from her family who'd wanted her to marry the son of a wealthy railroad magnate. She'd fled before the poor boy had gotten a chance to ask for her hand.

Well, she'd done what she'd set out to do. The San

Juan Hotel was one of the finest such establishments in the entire territory, and she was a widely respected businesswoman. And, unexpectedly, she'd even gotten herself hitched in the bargain.

Now, all she wanted was a quiet, simple life. A life with just her, Joe, and Joe's sweet and beguiling daughter, Evangeline. Soon, the three of them would live in the house Jane and Joe were building on the site of Joe's and Vangie's previous house, which had been burned by the vile son of an equally vile rancher and a blood enemy of Joe himself. Joe and Vangie would continue to live here in the San Juan with Jane until their house was completed in the fall.

Joe and Jane lived here in Jane's suite while Vangie had her own room just down the hall.

Joe...?

His presence had seemed so real that Jane felt compelled to call his name again, but she did not. Apparently, she'd only been dreaming he'd returned to her after riding out after a pair of killers the day before—the nasty little Billy Lord and his equally vile sidekick, Hector Hagness, who'd killed the liveryman, Cletus Alvarez, in cold blood because Alvarez had beat them at poker downstairs in the San Juan's gambling parlor—the Bear Den.

Jane rested her head back against her pillow.

She felt lonely.

It was an odd feeling for her. She'd once prided herself on her independence, at her ease with being alone. She'd filled the past twenty years of her life with so much work that she'd never had time to feel lonely. She'd had lovers over the years. While she'd enjoyed the relationships for as long as they'd lasted, she'd never loved any of the men she'd been with. When they'd become too much of a distraction, or maybe when she'd found herself growing too close to them, she'd ended the relationship.

Somehow, it had been different with Joe.

Improbably, she'd felt an instant attraction to the big, broad-shouldered, craggily handsome, taciturn man with his long, salt-and-pepper hair and long, salt-and-pepper mustache mantling his long, resolute mouth. His eyes were chips of granite, rarely betraying emotion. But when they did betray a little, a beguiling cast came to them, suggesting the depths of real, honest emotion the man himself tried so hard to conceal that the effort was almost heartbreaking to witness.

And there was *real* emotion, *real* feeling there. Almost too much for him to bear, Jane thought. It often surfaced...if just a trace here or there by way of a gentle caress or an intimate gesture...when they were enjoying the pleasures of each other's flesh in this very bed.

Most times, however, he funneled that emotion into anger.

But when Bloody Joe was with Jane or his precocious yet shy and retiring daughter, Vangie, it shown in his eyes as unabashed, unadulterated love.

Dammit, she missed the crazy bastard!

The former Jane Ford hated feeling lonely. She supposed that was why she'd managed to fight it off so thoroughly over the years. But now that she'd hitched her star to Bloody Joe's wagon, and he was gone, chasing after outlaws in the yonder mountains, she was not only lonely but worried.

Perhaps he'd returned late last night but had decided to remain at his jail house and office, locally jokingly referred to as "Hotel de Mannion," rather than come over to the hotel and awaken her when he knew that after working late almost every night, she liked to sleep in...sometimes till almost noon, when it was time to awaken the doxies to prepare for the midafternoon clientele. Midafternoon was when shifts changed in the mines and the miners came into town loaded into the beds of old prairie schooners or army ambulances, whooping and hollering and passing stone jugs.

The possibility that Joe was at his office called Jane to action.

Feeling like a silly schoolgirl with a schoolgirl's crush, she swept the covers away, dropped her feet to the floor, and began scrambling around the room, dressing in a simple skirt and blouse with a black belt, and high-heeled, pointed-toed, gold-buckled shoes. She pinned her long, curly, rust-red hair into a sloppy bun atop her head, letting several locks curl down against her cheeks, and then shrugged into a short, leather jacket against the chill that lingered this early in the year until noon or later.

She left her suite, smiling as she greeted a couple of her dozen or so doxies, recently risen from their mattress sacks and conversing desultorily and half-dressed in open doorways. She went downstairs and saw Joe's daughter, Vangie, sitting alone at a table at the back of the room, near the stairs, customarily separated from the other half dozen or so mid-morning dining or drinking clientele by several tables.

Separation from others was Vangie's way. It was well known she preferred the company of animals—dogs and cats but mostly horses—to that of other humans.

As lovely as she was—slender, brown-haired, brown eyed and with a disarming, heart-shaped face on the verge of striking young womanhood—the seventeen-year-old had turned away more than her share of would-be suitors—to the point that Jane was a little worried about the girl. Joe himself was not. After all, he was a notorious loner himself and did not trust those of his own sex around his daughter who, having been kidnapped and brutally savaged by Whip Helton and the firebrand's men, may have been innocent in the ways of many things of this world but no longer in the ways of men.

As Jane reached the bottom of the stairs, she saw that Vangie had a book open beside her plate of half-eaten eggs, bacon, and potatoes. Vangie, as usual, had her hair pulled back in a French braid, like her mother, who'd died by suicide when Vangie had still been a baby, used to wear. Also as usual, Vangie wore men's trail clothes—blue denims, wool plaid work shirt with a gold Spanish medallion (a birthday gift from her father) hanging around her neck and visible between the top two open buttons of her shirt. She wore pointed-toed riding boots, and a green felt, broad-brimmed Stetson rested on the table beside her half-finished glass of milk.

"Good morning, honey," Jane said as she approached the girl's table.

Vangie lifted her head quickly with a start, dropped her fork onto her plate, and splayed her right hand across the open book before her. That, too, was out of habit, for Vangie seemed a little embarrassed not only by her love for reading but by the content of what she read. A secretive child, this beguiling young woman. That every day she was becoming more and more of a "looker" could at the moment be attested to by the lingering stares of two cowboys standing sideways at the bar at the far end of the room, sliding their admiring gazes in Vangie's direction as they conversed.

One of them now pinched his hat brim to Jane and flushed before sheepishly turning away.

"Oh, good morning, Jane," Vangie said, flushing

sheepishly a little herself and glancing down at the open book before her.

"What are you reading?" Jane wasn't prying. She and Vangie often read the same books and enjoyed sharing their thoughts about them.

Vangie flipped to the title page which read up high in large, black letters: FRANKENSTEIN. Below, in smaller letters: *Or, The Modern Prometheus*. No author was listed.

"Again?" Jane laughed.

Vangie frowned and shook her head. "I swear it gives me nightmares, but it's got such a hold on me I was up till two in the morning! That's why I'm having breakfast only now. I did, however, go over and feed the horses, so they shouldn't be too put out with me. I'm gonna head over there and clean out their stalls and give them each a long ride soon."

Again, Jane smiled. That was Vangie—always putting her three horses first, Willow and Jack as well as the wild blue roan Joe had trapped and gifted her after the horse had fallen into the gunsights of area ranchers whose own herds the wild bronc had been badly disrupting. Joe had figured that slowly gentling the wild stallion, whom Vangie had named Cochise, would be a good way for his traumatized daughter to heal after her torment at the hands of Whip Helton, which included not only kidnapping and rape but the burning of her and Joe's home at the edge of town where her horses were still stabled and where theirs and Jane's new house was currently under construction.

Vangie closed the book then kicked out the chair beside her. "Sit and have a cup of coffee with me?"

Jane smiled then looked around. "No sign of your father, I take it?"

Vangie frowned, betraying her own concern. "No. I

sort of hoped he'd come in during the night and I just hadn't seen him yet, but..."

Jane shook her head. "He didn't."

"Oh, well. Not to worry too much, Jane. I'm used to living with ol' Bloody Joe and his odd hours."

"Yes, but I can't believe that little privy rat Billy Lord and his equally lowly accomplice, Hector Hagness, could be that much of a challenge for your father."

"Pa might be cagey, an' he was born with the bark on, for sure, but he's been known to be given the slip a time or two." Vangie chuckled as she lowered her head and looked around as though making sure she hadn't been overheard. "But don't tell him I said that, or he'll take the belt to me!"

She and Jane chuckled.

"I'm sure he'll be along soon." Jane sidled up to her stepdaughter, wrapped an arm around Vangie's shoulders, and gave her an affectionate squeeze. "I'm going to head out for some fresh air, pay a visit to Hotel de Mannion. He might've come in early this morning and fallen asleep in his chair."

"Could be. Let me know—will you, Jane?"

"I will, dear," Jane said, closing her jacket with her hands as she headed for the door.

Del Norte's hustle 'n' bustle was building momentum, Jane saw as she drew one of the hotel's two big, stout doors closed behind her. (Both cold-weather doors would be opened to the customary batwings once the morning chill had passed.) Already, dust swirled on the town's main drag and big Pittsburg freight wagons and ore drays passed, hauling goods and ore out of the mines deeper in the mountains. Smaller ranch wagons cut in and out of the slower traffic of the larger wagons, often evoking curses in German or one of the Scandinavian tongues from a peeved mule skinner, fists angrily pumping.

The cowboys from area ranches enjoyed hoorahing the burly, severe, taciturn Old-Worlders for whom English was still a chore.

Jane crossed the San Juan's broad front porch and descended the steps before swinging right and heading toward the jail, hoping she'd find her husband there while trying to ignore a suddenly nagging feeling that she wouldn't and may not for quite some time.

She was worried. She didn't like being worried any more than she liked feeling lonely.

CHAPTER 6

As Jane made her way along the boardwalks, returning greetings to passersby and hurrying past those, mostly men, whom she knew would want to strike up conversations with her, she blinked against the dust continuing to roil up from Main Street on her left. She was normally more congenial. But she was anxious about Joe. She was hoping against hope—for she was not a praying gal—that he'd made it back in one piece the night before and was merely asleep at his desk.

As she approached his office and jail house—Hotel de Mannion as it was known locally—two sudden cracks that could have only been pistol shots rose from maybe a block away, cutting through the street din and causing all heads to turn in their direction. Even a couple of dogs quarreling over a bone on the other side of the street stopped quarreling and looked around, ears raised. The gunfire had caught Jane up a bit, and she hesitated, frowning toward the north—the shots must have come from the All-Nighter Saloon, which lay a block away in that direction and was known for its less than respectable clientele.

She waited for a break in the traffic then crossed the street to the jailhouse's porch steps and stopped when the front door clicked and opened. She looked up, hoping to see Joe coming out to investigate the shots. But, no, she saw with some disappointment that it was Joe's young deputy, the aptly nicknamed Stringbean MacCallister, stepping out onto the porch resting a Winchester carbine on his shoulder and stopping just outside the jailhouse's front door. From behind the long faced, slightly bucktoothed Stringbean, who wore his sandy hair down over the collar of his chambray shirt, Jane thought she could hear loud though muffled voices, angry, arguing voices.

Stringbean had turned his frowning gaze in the direction of the gunfire but, seeing Jane standing at the bottom of the porch steps, he turned back to her and said, "Miss Jane—good mornin'. Loud one, sounds like."

Again, he glanced toward the All-Nighter.

"Yes, a rather boisterous morning. I suppose you'd better go have a look, but before you do—did Joe get back last night?"

"No, ma'am, I'm sorry to say," the young deputy said, pulling his weather-stained, cream Stetson down lower on his forehead. "Ain't seen hide nor hair of the marshal yet."

"That's a little odd, don't you think?"

"Well, the fellas over to the Come One, Come All said that snake, Lord, and his half-breed partner, Hagness, lit a shuck like their cayuses had dynamite with lit fuses stuck up their...er, I mean..."

"Yes, yes, I know. They galloped out fast. But they *are* just Billy Lord and Hector Hagness. Those two under-shot tinhorns couldn't have given Joe all the much trouble."

"No, you wouldn't think so," Stringbean said with a

suddenly distracted air, switching his frowning gaze back in the direction from which the gunfire had erupted.

"Don't you think someone should maybe—"

Stringbean cut Jane off with, "Here comes Rio, now. That musta been him poppin' off a coupla caps over to the All-Nighter. Looks like he's got Louis Chambeau in tow—another in a long line of clients here at Hotel de Mannion, I'm afraid. I hope the Chinaman over to Ida Becker's café can keep up with the vittles. Boy, the town council is really gonna squawk when they get Ida's food bill!"

Stringbean winced and shoved his hat up from behind to worriedly scratch the back of his head.

As he did, a fat, furry, black and white cat leaped out the open door behind him and onto the porch with an indignant meow. Buster belonged to Rio Waite, Joe's older deputy who lived in a crude log shack behind the jailhouse. Buster leaped onto the rail beside the deputy and set to work licking one front paw to clean behind his ears. In his black and white coat complete with a furry black bow tie, Buster looked nothing so much as an eternally tuxedoed fancy Dan with no debutante's ball to attend.

Now, however, as he cleaned himself, he curled his tail angrily.

"Poor Buster," Stringbean said. "There's too much noise back yonder for him to sleep." He hooked his thumb to indicate the office behind him.

"Yes, what is all that?" Jane asked, glancing as the short, stocky, pot-bellied Rio Waite approached at a slant from up the street, using his shotgun to shove a short, swarthy, hatless Mexican dressed in Spanish-style range garb along before him. The Mexican had a bloody patch on his right forearm, and his brown eyes were dark and dour behind his jostling, dark-brown hair.

"The punchers from two ranches have been goin' mano y mano every chance they get. Usually starts in Mrs. Baumgartner's House of a Thousand Delights till she and them two big ex-mule skinners of hers kicks 'em out. Then they continue the cursing and fisticuffs until it climbs to a big, dang head in the Three-Legged Dog. Dang near laid waste to the place last night. Me an' Rio had a heckuva time corralin' all fourteen of 'em an' hazin' 'em over here. They're in the basement cellblock, where Buster likes to mouse, but none of them from the Crosshatch an' the Kitchen Sink seem cat lovers, so Buster skedaddled. Rio wired the judge an hour ago, an' I ain't seen him since...till now."

Stringbean had turned his attention to the older deputy and his prisoner, approaching now from fifty feet and closing, swathed in the dust of a large, passing ranch wagon.

Both deputy and prisoner blinked their eyes and wagged their heads against the swirling cloud.

"Who you got there, Rio?" Stringbean asked.

"Jose Eduardo de Canenas," Rio said, enunciating each word precisely, stopping and glancing up at Stringbean, stretching his lips back from his large, tobacco-stained teeth. "I heard a commotion in the All-Nighter when I was headin' back from the Western Union office. I went in just as him an' some freighter from the Cloud Tickler Mine up by Winterset exchanged lead over a half-breed whore."

Jane sucked air through her teeth.

"How-do, Miss Jane," Rio said, pinching the brim of his weather-yellowed, shapeless hat.

"Rio."

Continuing with his story, sliding his gaze between Jane and Stringbean, Waite said, "Jose Eduardo de Canenas here appears to have been the better shot. He gave that mule skinner a third eye—one he couldn't see out of fer beans—while the mule skinner only gave Senor de Canenas here a burn across his arm."

"Oh, boy," Stringbean said. "Seth Vance is gonna be mighty piss-burn...er, I mean, *angry*," he corrected himself for the benefit of the lady in their midst, albeit one who runs her own saloon and brothel and had for years. "He's short-handed already, I hear, since he don't pay nothin' but pennies an' piss wat...or, I mean..."

"Oh, for Heaven sakes, Stringbean, but 'pennies and piss water! I've heard the expression before, and I didn't faint then, and I won't faint now!" Jane announced in exasperation.

Stringbean flushed.

Rio laughed as he shoved the Mexican on up the porch steps. At the top of the porch, he stopped, holding his prisoner by the back of the Mexican's shirt collar, then glanced from Stringbean to Jane and said, "Any sign of Joe yet? Either of you seen him?"

"No," both Jane and Stringbean said at the same time.

"That's what I came over here for," Jane said. "I was hoping he'd come in late and had fallen asleep in his chair, as he's done before when he didn't want to come over to the hotel and risk waking me."

"Yeah, Joe'll do that," Rio allowed.

"Well, he didn't do it this morning," Jane said. "Rio, I'm worried."

Still holding the Mex by his shirt collar, Rio turned full around to face the pretty, freckle-faced redhead. "I'll admit it ain't like Joe to take so long with a couple of tinhorns like Billy Lord and Hec Hagness, but you never know, Miss Jane. Those two might've forted up in some rocks and it's just takin' Joe a little longer than usual to lure 'em out. Or *shoot* 'em out, as the case probably is," the middle-aged, craggy-faced deputy added with a chuckle. "By noon lunch, he'll prob'ly be haulin' 'em both back to town belly down across their saddles, makin' Mort Bellringer a happy man."

Mortimer Bellringer was one of the growing Del Norte's two undertakers.

"Yes, I suppose you're right," Jane said, half-heartedly.

"I'd ride out an' look for him, Miss Jane." Stringbean glanced at the Mexican then tossed his head to indicate the half-full cellblock in the jail office basement behind him. "But we sorta got our hands full, if you know what I mean. An' I swear the trouble keeps comin' an' comin'. The marshal says he's gonna hire another deputy or two, so that should take the load off a bit."

"Yes, I suppose so." Jane swung around and began walking slowly, pensively, back in the direction of the San Juan. "See you fellas," she said. "Tell Joe when he comes in, I want to see his big ugly hide right away, will you?"

"Miss Jane?"

Rio's query caused her to stop and turn back to face the older deputy where he stood with the short, hang-headed Mexican atop the porch steps behind her. "You know they say cats have nine lives." He glanced at Buster sitting on the porch rail before him, staring down at the ground below, ears twitching, always on the lookout for mice. "But they say Bloody Joe has nine or ten an' maybe even eleven."

He grinned and winked.

"Yes," Jane said, feigning a smile as she turned back around and continued on her way, muttering under her breath, "But they also say he's gone through most of those..."

A rumble rose from ahead of her, to the south. She knew without really thinking about it that that would be the Rio Grande & Company Stage heading into town from Cimarron. While the rumbling grew until she could hear the distant bellowing of the jehu and hear the cracks of the blacksnake over the team's backs, she found herself being held up by a couple of businessmen wondering about the possibility of holding a meeting in one of the rooms Jane reserved for just such occasions at the San Juan.

So it wasn't until ten minutes later she found herself approaching the long, wood frame, clapboarded building housing the Rio Grande Line's office and the stage itself sitting in the street before the place. There was a scurry of passengers and porters and wranglers busy unhitching the team to lead it around to the barns in back. Lifting the hem of her skirt above her ankles so as not to drag it through the finely churned dirt, Jane stepped off the boardwalk, intending to avoid the commotion on the boardwalk ahead of her, and started to cross the street toward the Rio Grande.

As she did, a man's voice said behind her, "Good God —Jane, it *is* you!"

Jane stopped abruptly and swung around, frowning, to see a short, stocky, broad-shouldered older man in a three-piece cream suit standing in front of the stage, near the sagging tongue as the hostlers led the two wheelers off around the corner of the stage office toward the rear. Wearing a cream felt planter's hat, the man was perhaps in his late sixties, early seventies—bull-chested and pot-bellied, with rich cherry-hued cheeks that complimented his red-gray muttonchop whiskers and handlebar mustache with upswept, waxed ends.

Not much over five-and-a-half-feet tall, Jane guessed, he carried a cherry wood walking stick with a carved horsehead handle. In his free, kid-gloved hand he held a valise of the finest, butterscotch leather.

He regarded Jane warmly, and a sly, coyote smile—a familiarly warm but cunning smile that lifted the corners of his small, amber eyes and quirked his lips so that the ends of his fine, white teeth shone beneath the mustache.

Despite being short in stature, he owned a distinctly commanding air, even here, where he looked very much out of place—here on the dusty, smelly main street of the raucous mountain mining and ranching town of Del Norte. A rare, civilized visitor to the still mostly uncivilized frontier. In fact, the penguin-like dude couldn't have looked more out of place than a zebra in church!

Jane's eyes widened in shock. Bending forward slightly, she stepped slowly, hesitantly forward, sure she had it wrong. Or maybe she was seeing things.

But, no.

"Fa...Fa..." she tried. She stopped and tried again.

"Father?"

CHAPTER 7

MANNION HAD CRAWLED OUT OF THE HAY IN RED'S stall early that morning, when dawn had been a gray wash behind the eastern ridges and the birds had just started piping.

It was a long, rough ride into the high country where Forsythe lay, but Joe thought he could make it there and back to Fury in a day if he got an early start. He didn't want to worry his bride, Jane, nor his daughter, Vangie. After all, his decision to continue to Forsythe had been a spur of the moment one. There was no near telegraph to relay his plans to Del Norte. His delay in returning home would likely bring hell down on him from both women.

He might have been Bloody Joe Mannion, but he'd have rather wrestled a bull griz in a locked Concord coach than incur the wrath of either woman let alone the two together!

Also, he didn't want to burden Jeremiah and Justy with Billy Lord any longer than he had to. Billy had likely been lying about his plan to meet up with his older brother, but, under the circumstances of the Lord family's dark ties to Fury, Joe didn't want to take any more chances than necessary.

He knew he should take Billy back to Del Norte, but the little devil would only slow him down and he needed to get to Forsythe for Jasper Neal pronto.

However, remembering the rider riding hell for leather away from the Devil's Anvil gave him pause. Doubtful, however, the man had been one of Frank Lord's riders. Like Joe had figured at the time, he'd probably just been an outlaw—or possibly even a local cowpuncher—who hadn't wanted to risk getting mixed up in the melee he'd witnessed in the canyon beneath the Devil's Anvil.

Anyway, Mannion would return to Fury later that night then head south to Del Norte early the next morning.

He skipped breakfast and even coffee, saddled up, and rode out well before the sun was up. Climbing, he rode from early summer to early spring. Around Forsythe, dirty snowdrifts lingered in the deep woods and on the north sides of boulders and stone escarpments. The air was cool enough that Joe had stopped to unwrap his buckskin mackinaw from around his soogan and put it on, even lifting the wool collar up around his jaws.

The camp of Forsythe snaked around several deep ravines at the foot of Bighorn Ridge, which formed a horseshoe high and to the north and east around the village comprised mostly of tent shacks of all shapes and sizes and small, square log cabins, a few in the small business district boasting plankboard facades. At the edge of town was a depot for the new railroad though there was no sign of the train. At least, no sign of the train itself.

But the small town's streets were choked with people in skins and furs, of men of all shapes and sizes, including

many Chinamen and squared-jawed, fair-haired Scandina-
vians and Germans who likely toiled in the Forsythe
Mine, which had brought in the narrow-gauge railroad
and likely three-quarters of the recent uptick in
population.

Most of the cabins Mannion rode past as he and Red
threaded their way down the main street, Pine Street,
boasted facades announcing themselves as saloons,
gambling parlors, tattoo parlors, or hurdy gurdy houses.
Several announced more than one amenity in one place,
which was a little surprising given the diminutive size of
most of those squalid shacks.

The air was fetid with the smell of pigs and overfilled
privies, not to mention man sweat, and occasionally, the
cloying aroma of midnight oil, or opium, of which there
was plenty to go around in most frontier mining camps.

Mannion was halfway through town when he reined
up abruptly on the crowded street, which was too narrow
for the amount of traffic it saw. Three men stood on a
boardwalk fronting Rufus Fine's Saloon. Two were
leaning against awning support posts. Another stood
behind them and near the place's batwing doors in a long,
molting, deer hide coat, thumbs hooked behind his
cartridge belt.

All three were staring at Mannion.

All three were well-armed.

All three had mean, cow-stupid looks in their flat eyes
beneath the brims of their weathered Stetsons.

Mannion returned their stares with a stony one of his
own. The two leaning against the awning support posts
glanced at each other, exchanging some unspoken
communication, then swung around and strode past the
man in the deer hide coat and through the batwings. The

man in the deer hide coat continued to stare at Mannion, gimlet-eyed, for another few beats.

Then he turned stiffly, pushed open the batwings with a flourish, and drifted off into the saloon in which a young woman was laughing loudly and raucously as though at the funniest joke she'd ever heard.

Mannion clucked Red ahead and after another block of negotiating the thick wagon traffic—most of it ore drays from the local mines—swung the bay to the street's right side and up to a stone, tin-roofed building which a small sign over the front door identified simply as TOWN MARSHAL.

A roofed boardwalk fronted the place. On the boardwalk and standing to the left of the building's closed door stood a big, broad-faced man in a black suit and wearing a long tan duster and a broad-brimmed, tan Stetson. He wore a sweeping mustache over his thin upper lip. His expression was grim, his eyes hard, determined, as was the set of his knife-slash mouth beneath the 'stache.

He held a double-barreled shotgun with rabbit ear hammers up high across his chest as though he were ready to pull it down and go to town with the formidable-looking gut shredder at a moment's notice. Standing there, well over six-feet tall—well over Mannion's six-four, in fact—the man appeared as immovable as a mountain.

He wore a five-pointed deputy town marshal's star on the left lapel of his black frock coat, revealed by the pulled back duster flap.

"Cletus, how goes it?" Mannion asked as he stopped Red in front of the jailhouse's single, peeled pine pole hitchrack.

"Oh, can't complain," the stone-faced man said, tonelessly, not bothering to offer anything more. Not even the hint of a smile.

Mannion was neither offended nor surprised by the cool welcome. He doubted he'd ever exchanged more than two words at any one time with Cletus Booker, Forsythe Town Marshal Curt Bishop's lone deputy, though Mannion believed Bishop usually kept a night deputy or two on the payroll so he and Booker could catch a few winks now and then.

Forsythe had always been a raucous place from early spring to late fall and now with the coming of the narrow-gauge railroad and a population that appeared to have doubled or even tripled in size since Mannion's last visit, it was likely running off its leash most hours of the day than not.

Mannion swung down from Red's back, looped the reins over the rack, and stepped up to the boardwalk and the mountain of a man presiding over it. "What's the greener for?"

The door flanking the deputy suddenly opened and Town Marshal Curt Bishop stepped out, lighting a pipe. "What the hell you think it's for?" he said between puffs of blue smoke. "Didn't the federals tell you I got Jasper Neal locked up inside?" He lowered the match he'd been lighting the pipe with and grinned around the pipestem. "Or did they decide to let it be a surprise? Wouldn't put it past 'em one bit!"

Bishop was lean and weathered, his gray hair thinning badly in front. A thick salt-and-pepper mustache rode high atop his upper lip, beneath his long, thin, crooked nose that had been busted several times and either not set or not set *right*. He wore a pinstriped shirt and a brown wool vest. Two old Colts with worn walnut grips rode low on his hips.

"Nah, they told me, all right," Mannion said, poking his hat up off his forehead. "Them three back there try to bust him out yet?" He canted his head to indicate the three gents he'd exchanged the stink eye with back out front of Rufus Fine's Saloon.

"Jasper's boys, you mean?" Bishop said. "Nah." He grinned again, eyes twinkling delightedly. "They're likely waiting till you have him on the trail."

"Now, why did I think you were going to say that?" Mannion said, dryly.

"Want to come in have a drink, Joe? Rest your hoss and steel your nerves."

"Nah, I'll rest Red along the trail. Why don't you haul ol' Jasper out here and we'll get a move on? I wanna get back to Fury by dark if I can."

"I have a horse already saddled for him over at the livery." Bishop shuttled his gaze past Mannion to the livery and feed barn sitting nearly directly across the street from the jailhouse and where two big men in immigrant caps and wool coats, one red and one black, were repairing one of the two big stock doors near a dirty, melting snowdrift that had both men performing their task in ankle-deep mud.

"Weldon," Bishop called, "bring that beefy cayuse on over here now!"

Both toiling men glanced at Bishop, exchanged a few words, then the bigger of the two, wearing the red coat, stepped into the barn and came out a moment later leading a big foxy-eyed gelding. The liveryman waited for a couple of lumber drays to pass then led the big horse on over to the jailhouse. He tied the horse to the rack beside Red then, giving Bishop a two-fingered salute, returned to his onerous chore at the livery barn.

"All right, brace yourself, Joe," Bishop said as he turned and disappeared into the jail.

Presently, loud thumping sounded as well as loud complaints in a deep, guttural voice. The thumping and complaining grew louder until the door opened again and a big, shaggy-headed bear of a man—nearly as tall as Booker—came storming out onto the boardwalk, his hands cuffed behind his back—yelling, "If you think you're gonna get me to Fury without me first caving your head in, Mannion, you stupid son of a bitch, you got another thing—*oaff-ahhhh*!"

Joe had stepped forward and rammed the barrel of one of his two big .44s into Jasper Neal's belly. The man had folded like a barlow knife, knees striking the boardwalk with a thundering *boom*!

Neal's big, wart-bristling, shaggy-bearded face swelled and reddened until it was a mask of misery. He lifted his head and glared up at Mannion, "Oh, you bloody bastard, Mannion! When my boys kill you, they're gonna take their ti—" Neal stopped abruptly, eyes widening in exasperation when he saw the big .44 swinging toward him in a blur of fast motion. "Don't you...don't you da—"

Thunk!

"*Oaf!*"

Jasper Neal tumbled sideways to the boardwalk floor, out like a blown lamp. He looked like some wild animal collapsed there in his buffalo hide pants and beaded buckskin shirt under a heavy elk hide coat. Joe grimaced as he stared down at the man. Neal looked like something wild, and he smelled wild too. He was as whiffy as a bear den after the long mountain winter.

"Well, that's one way to skin a cat," Bishop laughed.

Mannion holstered the Russian and crouched over

Neal. "Help me here, Cletus. Let's get his hands switched to the front and get him on his horse."

Booker unlocked the big man's wrists, pulled his hands around to the front, and locked the bracelets over his wrists again. Mannion took Jasper by his feet. Booker took him by his arms. Together, they back-and-bellied him down off the porch and over to the big, foxy-eyed claybank. They hoisted the man up onto the horse and lay him belly down across his saddle.

"Tie his ankles to the cuffs," Mannion told the deputy.

As the deputy performed the task, Joe cast his gaze down the street to Rufus Fine's Saloon. The three men he'd seen earlier had been joined by one more—a thick-set man with a long, red beard. They all stood staring—or maybe glaring would be a better word, Mannion thought—toward where Booker was tying their outlaw leader's ankles to his wrists under the belly of the big clay.

Joe grinned and waved.

The thick-set man with the red beard raised his right, gloved hand and middle finger.

"That big fella with the beard," Bishop said from where he stood atop the boardwalk, "is Jasper's son, H.J. I can't believe H.J. loves his father. Christ, who could love a man like Jasper?" He scowled in revulsion at the big man who hung down the side of the horse with his cuffed hands hanging nearly to the muddy street. "But Jasper's the brains of the outfit. I use that term very loosely. The rest of 'em are likely lost little lambs without Jasper to plan their holdups and bank robberies. Dumber'n posts, each and every one of 'em."

"Yeah, they do look a little off their feed," Mannion said.

"I'll send Cletus with you, Joe. You may need some help on the trail back to Fury."

"Nah, you got your hands full here," Mannion said, untying both sets of reins from the hitchrack and taking a quick gander around the bustling town.

As he did, a gun barked in one of the buildings along the street to the south. A man yelled. A girl screamed.

Mannion turned to Bishop and smiled. "See?"

"Ah, hell," Bishop said. "The night's starting early." He glanced at his big deputy, who'd finished tying Jasper Neal. "Check it out, Cletus. I'll be right behind you, old son."

"All right, boss."

The giant of a grim-faced deputy picked up his greener from where he'd leaned it against an awning support post, broke it open to make sure it was loaded, then snapped it closed and headed down the street to the south. The folks milling and strolling along the boardwalks made way for the big, sullen man.

"See ya, Curt," Mannion said as he reined Red away from the hitchrack. He held the reins of his prisoner's horse in his gloved, left hand.

"I hope so, Joe," Bishop said, knocking the dottle from his pipe. He glanced in the direction of Jasper Neal's lost little lambs, winced, and shook his head. "I hope so..."

"Ohh." Jasper Neal stirred, shaking his big, shaggy head. "You hurt me, Joe. Ya hurt me *bad*!"

"Shut up." Mannion swung Red back in the direction from which he'd come and booted him into a trot.

The claybank lurched into a trot then too.

Jasper Neal bellowed loudly and miserably all the way back through town and well into the country where high rimrocks mocked him with echoes.

CHAPTER 8

JANE STOOD HANG-JAWED NEAR THE STAGECOACH'S LEFT front wheel, staring at the stocky, red-faced, impeccably attired man before her.

Yes, despite the graying of his hair as well as mustache and side whiskers and a deepening of the lines in his ruddy Celtic face and a bowing of his shoulders since she'd last seen him, almost twelve years ago—Jane decided that the man she stood staring at, as though in one of those crazy dreams just before waking, was none other than her father—John Van Nostrand Ford.

She strode forward now, boldly, feeling the old defiance...even rancor. She was a good inch or two taller than the penguin-like gent—from a very early age she'd seen him as a penguin, running here and there on his short, stout legs, throwing his fins out as he barked orders to the waiting staff or to his personal secretaries and accountants at all hours of the day and night with a cigar and brandy in hand, firing off cables to fellow businessmen overseas or on the other side of the continent.

But here he was on Jane's turf, and she felt a relieved superiority. She was even taller than he, she realized for the first time in her life! When dealing with commanding men like V.N. Ford, you looked for any advantage you could find. Even when you hadn't seen one particular one in twelve years.

Especially when you hadn't seen him in twelve years, because by then you might have forgotten what you were in for...

"What on earth are you *doing* here?" she asked with no little exasperation.

John Van Nostrand Ford, V.N. for short, lifted his deeply cleft chin as he threw his head far back, squeezed his eyes closed, and clapped his small, soft, kid-gloved hands together. "Ah, my dear, Janey, you haven't changed a bit. No tears for the old man you hadn't seen in well over a decade, no sentimentality at all. You just want to know what in holy hell brought the old rascal to your doorstep!"

"Indeed, I do!" Jane frowned suddenly, "Wait...it's not Nancy...Suzannah...Clayton...?"

"They're fine, dear. They're all fine."

"Mother?" Jane added, tentatively. She couldn't imagine anything bringing that old Irish war hatchet down. She loved her mother dearly, but Iris Ford had grown a tough outer shell, which was required by any woman married to the uncompromising V.N. An arranged marriage, to be sure. They'd both come from wealthy overseas merchant families.

"Your mother's fine, just fine...for now."

Again, Jane frowned. "What do you mean—'for now'?"

Her frown deepened when a man stepped around the far side of the stage to flank her father. Another impeccably attired man, obviously from the East Coast, as was Jane's father, of course. From the far East Coast—as far east as Boston, to be exact. Her father was a second generation, international shipping and trading magnate, though what he traded Jane had never been able to ascertain despite the number of times she'd inquired. She'd finally given up inquiring and decided it was something likely untoward.

Perhaps even illegal though men like V.N. Ford only recognized those laws that suited them and simply ignored the others, having the money to afford such a luxury when other men would likely be hanged or imprisoned behind the bars of some dingy federal prison for the rest of their lives. This new man, slightly taller but much younger than V.N., worked for him, of course. He smiled at Jane while blushing self-consciously before glancing at her diminutive father. He said, "Our accommodations have been arranged, Mister Ford, and our luggage is right now being hauled across the street to the San Juan."

He spoke with a lilting British accent. Likely an Oxford grad. Her father had been educated at Harvard.

The younger man, probably mid-thirties, glanced with another warm but unctuous smile at Jane, likely assuming that since the old man was such a handful, his daughter—especially the one who'd declared her independence and had headed West to fort up far, far away from the Fords of Boston—would be too.

"I own the San Juan," she said, suddenly feeling as territorial as any alley cat. She wasn't sure she wanted her father and his ilk under the same roof with her. Especially when she'd had no idea they were coming. No time to prepare herself physically or mentally!

One needed very much to do both for the highly discerning and trying V.N. Ford.

"We know," said her father and the handsome younger man flanking her father at the same time.

"Oh, I see," Jane said, nodding slowly, switching her gaze between the two men, both smiling like the cat that ate the canary. "You've done your homework. How much else do you know?"

Jane hadn't spoken with nor corresponded with her father in twelve years. That was when she'd last visited the family estate near Boston, twelve years ago—mostly to see her mother and siblings, nieces and nephews—and had refused her father's demand to settle there again permanently and to "give up this nonsense of making a name for herself as an independent woman of the West."

She was a Ford. She needed to live and marry as the Fords lived and married.

Not only had V.N., as she preferred to know him now rather than as "Father," gotten drunk but also enraged and had promised to write her out of his will and to give her a good "shellacking" with a bullwhip out in one of the several stables flanking their manor-like house on their wooded estate on the Charles River outside of Dover.

V.N. Ford might have had a temper to rival that of any to be found in any grog hall in County Cork, but, when riled, Jane could hold her own in a fight even against him. And she had. She'd retreated to her room, ignoring her entreating brothers and sobbing sisters, and locked herself in.

Early the next morning she'd had a servant summon a hansom cab, and she'd headed out to the train station and then had ventured back west, where she'd professed to live to the end of her days, with no further contact with the bullish V.N. or the rest of her family—all caught and impaired and made forever dependent by his controlling domination.

She had, however, corresponded with her mother. But knowing her mother, strong as she was, had never and *could* never keep secrets from V.N., she'd never told her where she was or what she was doing except that she'd become as successful as she'd wanted to be and was very comfortable and happy, indeed. She'd always left off from her correspondences any forwarding address.

She hadn't yet told her mother that she was married, not quite sure how to relay the news she'd married a notorious, rough-hewn western lawman—especially one with Bloody Joe's reputation! (She'd chuckled every time she'd thought about it.)

It wouldn't have been hard, however, for V.N. Ford to locate her, if he'd wanted. Jane had just never suspected he'd want to!

Now she was caught as flat-footed as she'd ever been in the presence of this penguin-like, blustering, intimidating man and, judging by that lingering coyote grin on his broad-featured, Irish mug, the old boy was enjoying every minute of her unease.

"Darling, this is J.L. Mosby," he said now, opening a small, kid-gloved hand to indicate the handsome younger man just now stepping forward to bow and click the heels of his dusty half boots together, like some minor lord in the king's court.

He extended a beringed hand to Jane. She sighed and gave him hers. He gave it a fishy squeeze and released it.

She looked up to see two more men flanking Mosby and her father. These were two impossibly large men who resembled overstuffed sausage casings in their three-piece suits and traveling dusters. One was blond and blue eyed, obviously of Viking blood. The other was dark, probably a Scot. Both had thick, soup-strainer mustaches and were looking cautiously around as though trouble were imminent. Grim-looking fellows, both of whom looked like they could pull up full grown trees by their roots and might even do so just to amuse themselves.

"Oh, those two are Thornbush and Nordstrom—your father's bodyguards," Mosby said with an offhand air. Obviously, V.N. couldn't be reduced to introducing the lower levels of his staff. He merely blinked, desultorily, before returning his bright, bemused gaze to his daughter once more.

"Shall we go over and take a peek at your I'm-sure fine establishment, my dear? We've much to discuss."

"Father," Jane said, frowning, feeling peeved. "Why on earth didn't you—"

"Janey, please, please, please! Let's not have a row right out here on the street!"

He'd said this loudly enough for everyone within half a block to hear, even above the low roar of passing wagons. Jane flushed, embarrassed. Suddenly, she was twelve years old again, and her father was calling her into his library for another scolding for playing out in the stables with the boys rather than practicing her violin lessons like a good, cow-towing Ford girl.

Passersby glanced at her, brows arched incredulously.

Who was the formidable Miss Jane Ford *taking* orders from?

Simply to get him and the dandyish Mosby off the street, she said, "Come! Right this way!"

She swung around, lifting her skirt again, and headed for the San Juan sprawling in all its western splendor on the opposite side of the street.

"Come on, gents! Come on, gents!" her father said, flapping his fins. "No dawdling now. Keep up with me!"

Ahead of her, Jane saw the stage line's half-breed porter, Kenny Two Owls, who wore a suit two sizes too small for his length of bone, pull his buckboard wagon up in front of the San Juan, just ahead of her. The back of the wagon was half-filled with accordion bags and portmanteaus, most of the luggage monogrammed with a JVNF. Near the wagon, Jane stopped suddenly and turned to her father, blinking against the dust and waving his planter's hat disdainfully at it, while two little dogs had come out from nowhere to bark at the heels of the two big men following him and Mister Mosby. One of the big men kicked at one of the dogs, who adroitly darted away, and the big man stepped into a pile of fresh horse plop and nearly fell.

The other big man grabbed his arm to keep him on his feet.

"Father, are you sure you want to stay here at the San Juan?" She glowered her embarrassment. "It is a, well, a..."

"Yes, it's a hotel and saloon," said V. N. Ford, scowling up at the big sign stretched across the large, rambling but handsome building's second-floor façade. "I can read, dear girl. It's a prerequisite for attending Harvard, don't ya know?"

Jane couldn't help giving her eyes a furtive roll. The man simply could not help but announce his alma mater every chance he got. He hadn't changed a bit in twelve years. In many more ways than in stature, he was a little, little man.

"It's a hotel and saloon," Jane said. "But what it doesn't say is...well..."

"Yes, it's a frontier brothel. I know that, too!" Her father scowled at her, cherry cheeks turning a deeper red in exasperation. "Is that what you mean, dear girl?" Quietly now, and with a tragic air of irony, he said, "Janey, you've never been able to shock me, try as you might!"

Jane laughed.

He really had done his homework.

She turned to Kenny Two Owls, who'd just finished setting the luggage down on the boardwalk at the base of the steps running up to the San Juan's broad front porch. "Kenny, please deliver the luggage to rooms fourteen and fifteen on the second floor. I'll take care of the rest."

"You got it, Miss Ford," Kenny said, and, fumblingly, grabbed two pieces of the unwieldy leather luggage and started up the steps.

"Right this way, gentlemen," Jane said, and started up the steps, smiling when she saw the big bouncer using a stick to scrape the dung from his black patent shoes.

There's more where that came from around here, she mused to herself. Much, much more...

CHAPTER 9

"KARL," BRING ME A BOTTLE OF POLLARD'S PRIVATE Stock, please," Jane yelled to the morning bartender, Karl Nordic, as she led her father and the handsome, dapper Mr. Mosby to a free table near the stairway running up to the hotel's second and third floors.

As she did, Jane noticed several of her half-dressed girls sitting at a table nearby, picking at their breakfasts and conversing in a desultory air, each looking up at their madam ushering the two obvious foreigners—at least, foreign to the West—across the carpeted room while the two beefy bouncers took up defensive, grim-faced positions to either side of the front door, thick arms crossed on their chests.

One of the girls, who called herself Miles City Nell, gave Jane a questioning frown. Jane returned to the girl— a tall, pretty blonde with a splash of freckles across her ivory cheeks—a dismissive head shake, then drew a chair out from the table she'd selected for its distance from other diners and drinkers and sat down.

"Pollards Private Stock," said V.N. Ford, his dismay causing deep lines to carve across his ruddy forehead, beneath the brim of his planter's hat, which he removed just now to run a gloved hand back through his thinning, gray hair, with little trace of its previous strawberry blond. "Janey, you know I drink only—"

"Father," Jane said, splaying her fingers down on the polished wood before her. "Even if I could get what you normally drink out here, I couldn't sell it."

She gave a stiff, castigating smile.

He was on her turf now, and he might as well be reminded of it until he got used to it.

Karl came with the bottle and three glasses, and Jane filled each of the glasses and slid one toward her father, one toward Mosby, and one toward herself. She drank half of hers down—she needed one hell of a bracer; it was not turning out to be a good day—then said, "All right, spill it, Father. Why have you come all this way without so much as a word that you were going to show up here in Del Norte?"

She noted that Mosby had opened a leather-covered notebook. He dipped a pen in a traveling silver ink flask and was busily scratching words onto the page before him, glancing quickly at Jane as he did so, moving his lips, repeating her words to himself.

Her father nervously adjusted his cravat while brushing a sleeve of his coat across the table, as though it wasn't clean enough to suit him.

"What's happening?" Jane said, sliding her exasperated gaze between her father and Mosby. "Is your secretary *writing down* our conversation?"

"Yes," Ford said. "That's all right with you, isn't it, Jane. My memory has gotten just awful, and I'll need something to review on the way back—"

"No!" Jane said, loudly enough that several of the mid-morning patrons turned incredulous looks at her.

"No, no, no," she repeated, less loudly than before. "This is not a business transaction, Father. I am your daughter. This conversation will remain personal and private."

She glanced at Mosby. "Mister Mosby, I mean no disrespect, but would you please give my father and me some privacy?"

Mosby looked at her hang-jawed. He'd placed a pair of pince-nez reading spectacles, connected to a pocket of his suit jacket by a slender black ribbon, on his long, fine nose. He stared over the top of them at Jane, scowling. A bead of blue-black ink was about to tumble from the brass tip of his pen onto the lined page before him.

He glanced at Ford, who sat sideways in his chair, one short leg crossed over the other, one arm resting across the back of the chair, the other hand slowly turning the glass of inferior scotch on the table before him. He'd removed his gloves. They sat in neat pile beside his glass and an unlit cigar he'd produced from a pocket of his coat.

He smiled ruefully at Jane then glanced at Mosby and then canted his head—a dismissive gesture.

"Yes, of course," Mosby said, a tad breathless. It had likely been a long trip for the fancy Dan. It would be a long trip for anyone much less one in the company of John "V.N." Ford. But now he was here in the rugged West with Ford and Ford's daughter, and how much could a man possibly endure?

He had a flush of consternation on his face as he gathered his accoutrements, stuffed them into a butter-scotch monogrammed valise of soft cowhide, turned away from the table then, remembering his untouched drink, turned back to grab the low-grade scotch off the table and strode to a table several tables away from that of his boss and Ford's insufferable, queen-like daughter.

He scraped a chair out from his chosen table with a loud, wooden squeal that seemed to express his deepest feelings on the matter of his banishment then sank into it and leaned forward over his shot glass, raising it very delicately to his trimmed-mustached mouth. He raised his upper lip as he sipped, so he wouldn't dampen the 'stache.

"Now you've got him in a snit," Ford said, leaning forward and encircling his as yet untouched shot glass with his arms. He smiled at his daughter—the expression was at once chastising and admiring. "My God, you're beautiful. You look just like your grandmother when she was thirty!"

"I'll take that as a compliment," Jane said, a little flushed. She was not accustomed to being complimented by her father. In fact, she couldn't remember the last time he'd done such a thing. She knew that how she'd responded hadn't made sense and knowing that made her flush even more deeply.

True to form, he had her flustered!

She sipped her scotch, which, to her, and most of her other clientele, was of the top-shelf variety. Only to someone like her father would it not be.

"You should take it as a compliment," he said. "It was meant as one." Finally, keeping his amber eyes on her, Ford lifted the shot glass to his lips, and sipped.

Jane arched a brow, finding herself falling into the age-old habit of awaiting his approval. "Well," she said, as he swallowed the "swill" and set his glass back down on the table, half empty.

He stretched his lips back from his teeth and drew a breath, pursing his lips and nodding slowly. "Not bad, not bad." Even if he thought it pretty good, he wouldn't have admitted it, of course. He'd leave her with "not bad" and leave it for her to interpret.

She remonstrated herself silently. Here she already was, letting him get under her skin again.

She threw back the last of her own shot, splashed more into her glass, then sagged back into her chair and crossed her arms on her chest. "What the hell are you doing here, Father?"

He looked down at his whiskey, nodding slowly, brows deeply ridged over his small eyes that always looked angry even when he smiled. He looked up at her, drew a breath, and picked up the cigar. "It's your mother."

"I thought you said they were all right...all the rest of the family."

"They are, they are." Ford clipped the end of his cigar and deposited the piece in the cut glass ash tray residing in the middle of the table. He snapped a lucifer to life between his soft, little thumb and index finger, poked the stogie into his mouth, and began lighting it, the flame climbing as he drew. Between puffs, he said, "There's just the little matter of...well, of..."

"Oh, for Godsakes," Jane said, riled again despite her silent personal entreaty to not let him get her dander up, which she'd often sworn had been the very reason he'd sire her nearly forty years ago. So he'd have a daughter to belittle and torment. "Out with it!"

Ford chuckled, eyes glinting delightedly, as he set the match into the ash tray, neatly beside the end he'd clipped.

He sobered suddenly as he took one more puff from the stogie then leaned down low over the table as though what he had to say was of the utmost confidence. "She's been a lunger for over a year now. Yes, consumption.

Caught it on an overseas trip to Italy. Whether she caught it on the ship itself or in Italy is anyone's..."

"How bad?" Jane asked, having a hard time imagining her mother, a tall, rugged woman who'd rarely shown any sign of weakness and hadn't allowed her children to show signs of it either. During Jane's childhood, one had to be nearly on one's deathbed to be allowed to take to bed at all.

"She coughs nearly all the time...spits up blood. She's miserable. The doctors, however, changed her longevity from one year to possibly five years, since I moved her out here."

Jane frowned. "Out here?"

"Yes, six months ago I moved her to Glenwood Springs west of Denver. I had a house built there, at the foot of Iron Mountain. It has its own mineral hot spring. Since she started sitting in the spring several times a day, some color has returned to her cheeks—some of the rosy color you no doubt remember. Her appetite has improved, as well."

Jane was slow to comprehend all she'd been told. Her mother dying...she and her father had moved out here to the Colorado Territory. They'd built a house...

They were here now in a territory—an entire region of the country—Jane had sort of appropriated for herself. At least in regards to the rest of her family. They were back East. She was out West. That was theirs. This was hers.

But they were here now, sharing this with her though she hadn't known until now.

"It's a lovely house, I assure you."

"I'm sure it is." Jane felt as though she were in a daze, which she guessed she was.

"Senators...western governors come to visit. I'm

taking the vice president hunting in the mountains this autumn."

"I'm sure they do. I'm sure you will." Jane felt badly about being unable to focus less on the fact that her parents were both here in the same territory than on the fact that her mother was dying.

What a monster she must be.

She felt angry, as though her parents had used the excuse of her mother's dire predicament to come and ruin the territory for her by their very presence in it.

Yes. A monster. Sure enough.

But then, the apple didn't fall far from the tree.

"Tell me about this husband," Ford said, turning the stogie as he puffed it, scrutinizing her closely through the wreathing smoke.

"Husband?" Jane asked.

"Yes, I heard you were married."

"Oh, yes...of course you did." Vaguely, she wondered if he knew how much she was worth. But of course, he did. He probably even knew how much she drank and how much she charged for her whores. How often she rode her horse in the country to clear her head of the daily clutter. Dress size. Shoe size. Sexual preferences, even. Sure. Nothing was out of bounds when it came to John Van Nostrand Ford's field of inquiry.

Whatever he wanted to know, he'd pay to know.

He'd probably had Pinkertons up here, inquiring about her, following her.

Suddenly, she felt the need for a long, hot bath.

She thought of Joe—so far removed from the world of John Van Nostrand Ford—and she hooked a devilish smile. "What don't you already know about him?" she asked, then enjoyed adding, "He's a wild-assed frontier lawman, Father. You've heard of Wyatt Earp. Joe's ten of him and then some. He's tall and handsome and he's quick to lose his temper. He'd rather shoot a man—especially killers and rapists, both of which are a dime a dozen out here—than bother to haul them in to his jail here in Del Norte, locally known as Hotel de Mannion."

"Yes, I heard he was rather savage," Ford said casually, through the cigar smoke wafting over the table.

"Yes. It was his savagery I was attracted to. I didn't want to believe it at the time, when I first started falling in love with him. But there you have it. It excited me. I was tired of 'civilized' men. Men who hid their own natural savagery in dark offices and behind vined walls. Lashing out only with pen and paper, numbers on a page, signatures on contracts. If Joe doesn't like you, he'll walk right up to you and punch you in the mouth."

"And that excites you."

"Yes, very much." She'd stuck the knife in, and she was twisting it now.

How dare they move out here?

"Your mother needs you." Ford tipped his square head back and blew a thick plume toward the stamped tin ceiling. He looked across the table at Jane, shrewdly. "Give up this crazy life, Janey. You know it's not you. Not really. You're only playing make believe in defiance of me, a man you've hated since you were old enough to feel the emotion."

He half rose from his chair and pounded the table. "Give up this crazy life, Janey. All right—you've proven what you're capable of. Come live with me and your mother before it's too late—before we're both gone—or you'll regret it for the rest of your life!"

He pounded the table again, harder. All eyes in the room were on them now.

Flushed, he sagged back down in his chair. "And I will, too," he added, breathless, sheepish.

"What?" Jane asked, confused. He'd never exposed himself like this before.

"Come live with us, Jane," he said softly, his voice uncharacteristically pleading. "That's all. Before she's gone. We both want it more than anything else in the world."

CHAPTER 10

"IF YOU DON'T SHUT UP, I'M GONNA TAP YOU AGAIN,"
Mannion said as he stopped Red and the claybank
roughly twenty minutes after leaving Forsythe, in a cold,
creek-threaded valley just south of Forsythe.

Ice remained at the edges of the stream. It clicked
and clattered against the current. Long fingers of dirty,
pine needle-peppered snowdrifts remained, as well. It
was late May on the calendar, but it was late March in the
mountains.

Mannion had halted the horses between two of these
drifts, both of which had formed rivulets trickling into
the creek. He'd stopped to give Red some air. He figured
he might as well build a fire and boil some coffee. He'd
eaten only bits of jerky from his coat pockets all day. He'd
eat some more and a stale white flour biscuit or two and
wash it down with the coffee, which he desired even
more than food.

"You're a bastard, Mannion. Purely black blood
runnin' through your veins. Cut me down, fer chrissakes.
You're gonna kill me, makin' me ride this way!" Jasper

Neal lifted his shaggy head to glare up at his captor. "I can't breathe!"

"I'm just so sorry you can't breathe, Jasper. Grieves me, it does. How impolite of me, not lettin' you breathe."

Joe chuckled as he tied both horses to a pine branch close enough to the creek that they could draw the cold snowmelt water at will. He walked over to the claybank, crouched, drew his bowie knife, and sliced through the stout hemp tying Jasper's handcuffed wrists to his ankles. Sliding the knife back into its sheath, he straightened, grabbed a couple handfuls of Jasper's elk hide coat, and gave a savage grunt as he pulled the man off the horse.

Jasper barked out a curse as he turned ass over teakettle to strike the ground on his back.

"Oh, you're a devil, Mannion!"

"Thank you."

Breathing hard and grimacing up at his captor, Jasper lifted his chin, dug his heels into the ground, arched his back, and shouted skyward, "Come fetch me from this madman, H.J! Oh, he's a bloody son of a bitch! *Kill him!* Take your shots, boys! Blow his goddamn head off!"

Jasper relaxed his body against the ground and smiled devilishly up at Joe. "They will, too. Might even be linin' their sights up on ya right now." He turned his head from right to left, looking around. "Oh, they're here, Joe. You can count on that. Just waitin' for the right moment to separate your head from your shoulders!"

"Nah." Mannion smiled down at the big, grizzly-like man. "They're holding back a good half-mile and more. When they come a little closer, I'll snuff their wicks for them. And then you know what else I'm gonna do, Jasper?"

"What's that, pray tell? I'm on the edge of my seat!"

"I'm gonna blow a hole through your head, too."

Jasper hardened his jaws. "You can't do that. You're the law! I'm a defenseless prisoner!"

"Who's gonna know, Jasper? You were resisting. Had to shoot you to save my own life. The federals'll understand. You're lucky I don't shoot you right now. In fact, I'm not sure why I haven't."

Mannion grinned as he pulled his Russian .44 from the holster thonged low on his right thigh. He clicked the hammer back and aimed down at his prisoner. "Maybe I just will. I'll dump your carcass on the trail for your lost little lambs to find. They wouldn't have any reason to keep gunnin' for me then, would they? Yeah, why don't I just go ahead and drill a big, ol' .44-caliber hole through that big, ugly skull of yours!"

"They'll avenge me, Joe!" Jasper bellowed, raising his cuffed hands as though to shield his face.

"I doubt they'd go to the trouble," Mannion said, keeping the Russian aimed at a large freckle on the big man's weathered forehead. "But you never know."

"Don't do it, Joe!"

Mannion narrowed one eye as he stared down the barrel. He drew his right index finger back against the trigger. For a couple of seconds, he thought he was going to do it. A few years ago, he might have done it. And then he'd kill those on his back trail, as well. Because they all needed killing.

The federals would have understood. Hell, he'd likely been sent for Neal because the federals didn't *want* Neal to make it to Gunnison alive and they likely knew they could count on Bloody Joe to make their jobs a whole lot easier. Back in the old days, though, Mannion wouldn't have cared if they'd understood or not.

"Dammit, Joe—don't you do it!" The outlaw stared fearfully up over the hands he held in front of his face. "That's cold, Joe. That's cold-blooded killin'! Dammit, Joe!"

Mannion eased the tension in his trigger finger.

He depressed the hammer, lowered the gun.

He wasn't sure why. Was it Jane? Or had he gone soft now in his later years?

He wasn't sure why he hadn't squeezed the trigger. But there was no getting around it. He hadn't. And he wasn't going to. Apparently, Neal would have to give him a better, more immediate reason to kill him.

He twirled the gun on his finger, dropped it into its holster, and secured the keeper thong over the hammer.

Jasper stared up at him, deep rungs of incredulity carved across his forehead. Slowly, cautiously, he lowered his hands.

"I'll be...I'll be damned..." He ran his tongue across his upper lip and gave a nervous chuckle. "Thought I was a goner there for sure. Thought I pushed you too far."

"Yeah," Mannion said. "Me, too."

He looked back in the direction of the trail. No sign of his shadowers.

He turned to peer into the trees and boulders behind him and scanned the ridges on either side of the canyon. No sign of them there, either.

Neal heaved himself into a sitting position, rested his cuffed hands atop his knees, spat dirt from his lips. He looked up at his captor, narrowed one eye, and canted his head back in the direction of the trail. "You can't blame them on me, Joe. They want me back. They *need* me back."

"No, no," Mannion said, lifting his saddle off Red's

back. "I don't blame them on you. Only natural, you bein' the brains of the outfit, they'd want you back." He dropped the saddle and blanket on a log then loosened the latigo of the saddle on Neal's mount. He glanced at his prisoner and gave a coyote smile. "If they get too close, though, Jasper, I *will* blow your head off. Just to make sure they don't get you."

Staring up at him, Neal made a sour expression.

"Nothing personal," Mannion said, and dropped the clay's saddle on the same log on which he'd dropped his own.

Joe chuckled then pulled a length of rope out of a saddlebag pouch and snapped it taut as he moseyed over to his prisoner. "Gonna tie your ankles then gather kindling for a fire. I need a good cup of hot mud."

"So do I." Neal looked speculatively, hopefully at Mannion as the lawman wrapped the rope around his ankles. "You'll give me some, won't ya, Joe?"

Mannion sighed in wonder at himself. "I don't know why, but I reckon I will."

What in hell has happened to me?

———

MANNION AND HIS PRISONER SIPPED COFFEE AND munched biscuits and deer jerky—yeah, Joe even shared his sparse foodstuffs with the old train robber!—long enough to give Red a good, twenty-minute breather. Then Mannion kicked dirt on the fire, saddled both mounts, and turned to his prisoner, who sat cuffed on the ground by the smoking ashes.

"It's up to you whether you ride sitting up or belly down, Jasper."

The prisoner gave a weak smile. "Oh, I reckon I'd like to try it sittin' this time, Joe."

"You gonna behave yourself?"

"You're gonna mistake me fer a church deacon."

"Anymore yellin' for those lost little lambs of yours to blow my head off, you'll be ridin' the way you were when we left Forsythe." Mannion stitched his brows and dipped his chin at his prisoner. "Comprende?"

Jasper winced. "Yeah, yeah—I got ya. I realize now how that was a mistake." He glanced quickly, hopefully toward the trail, looking for his pards, then turned back to Mannion and manufactured an innocent grin.

"All right, then."

Mannion untied the man's ankles then ordered him to mount the clay. When Jasper was astride the clay, Joe tied his ankles to his stirrups. Mannion mounted Red and, leading the clay by its bridle reins, headed back in the direction of the trail.

Once on the trace, Joe took a good look around.

Not seeing his shadowers but certain they were still shadowing him, he swung Red east and booted him into a trot, jerking the clay along behind.

He kept a close eye on his backtrail.

Maybe too close an eye on his backtrail.

When following a sharp, uphill bend in a narrow canyon he saw smoke puff atop an escarpment below and in front of him maybe seventy yards away. The bullet screamed past his right cheek to bark loudly into the stone wall flanking him on his right. The bark of the rifle that had fired the bullet belched a half-second later.

The bullet's loud meeting with the ridge wall spooked the usually unspookable Red. The bay pitched abruptly, front hooves clawing at the air, whinnying his disdain for nearly having had his head carved a third eye. Mannion hadn't been ready for the pitch. He reached for the saddle horn but his fingertips only grazed it before he went flying down the bay's left hip, striking the ground on his head and shoulders.

Bells of pain tolling in his ears, Joe looked up to see Red wheel and run back down the canyon in the direction from which they'd come. Another bullet blew up dirt in front of Joe, peppered his face with dust and gravel. Another plumed dirt just left of the first.

Mannion palmed his right-side Russian, extended it straight out before him and sent three quick shots caroming toward the escarpment where pale powder smoke was still wafting. He rose quickly, surprised to find that he was still holding the reins of Jasper's clay in his left hand. Jasper stared dubiously down at the mount, which was side-stepping nervously and whickering deep in its chest.

"Easy, now...easy, now," the outlaw tried to soothe the edgy mount.

Mannion swung around and, jerking the nervous clay along behind him, ran back around the bend in the canyon wall and down the hill just beyond it. He quickly tied the clay to a stout cedar then looked around for Red.

Mannion's Yellowboy was in the saddle boot. Red was gone. Cursing, he quickly replaced the spent cartridges in his right hand, top-break Russian with fresh from his shell belt then swung around to run back up the hill, both Russians in his hands now, and cocked.

"Don't leave me tied to this hoss, Joe—he's gonna bolt for sure!" the big outlaw pleaded, staring edgily down at the clay's twitching ears. The horse was snorting, whickering, and pawing the ground with its left front hoof.

"Then you'll have one helluva last wild ride, Jasper!"

Near the top of the hill, Mannion got down on all fours and crabbed until he could edge a look over the crest. Just as he did, more smoke puffed from the escarpment below. The bullet thumped into the dirt just inches to the right of Mannion's right arm.

"Damn!" he grunted, pulling his head down. "They're better shots than I figured them for!"

He aimed his right-hand Russian over the crest of the hill and fired two quick rounds at where he could see one of the four gang members hunkered down in a notch about halfway up the escarpment. He could see all four at different places along the side of that scarp. Their horses were likely tied somewhere behind it.

How in the hell had they gotten around him? Mannion wanted to know. They must know this country better than he did.

Three more bullets tore into the trail just ahead of him. He drew his head down again as dirt and sand peppered his hair. He winced and shook his head to rid it from his hair and spat it from his mouth.

"Sons of bitches!" he said.

He had just started to snake both his Russians over the crest of the hill to return fire when a large shadow slid across the ground to his left. Dread churned like bile inside him as he whipped around to see Jasper Neal standing over him, grinning. The big, shaggy-headed outlaw held a stout branch in his hands. Both hands were still cuffed. Only, the cuffs weren't connected to each other.

A few inches of broken chain dangled from each silver bracelet.

Somehow, the man had managed to break the chain. Then he'd freed his feet from the saddle stirrups. He'd probably been trying to pull those cuffs apart ever since they'd left Forsythe.

Mannion raised both cocked Russians but before he could get them aimed, Neal swung the stout branch with a fierce grunt. The branch slammed both Russians painfully out of Mannion's hands. The hoglegs flew off to thump onto the ground to his right.

"Gonna kill you, Joe!" the big outlaw roared.

He pulled the branch back behind his right shoulder again, gritting his teeth. Before he could swing it forward, Mannion drew both his knees toward his chest then rammed both feet against the big outlaw's crotch.

Jasper roared as he staggered backward down the hill, dropping the branch.

Mannion turned onto his side then heaved himself to all fours and crawled wildly toward where his Russians lay in the sage a few feet from the trail. He'd just gotten a hand on each piece when Jasper roared behind him, *"Oh, no, you don't, you son of a bitch!"*

The big man hurled himself on top of Joe. It was like having a bear throw himself onto your back. The man's sudden weight knocked the wind out of Joe who sucked desperately to get it back.

Suddenly, the stout branch lay across Mannion's throat, and Jasper Neal was pulling back on it, cutting off the lawman's wind. In the corner of his right eye, Joe saw Jasper grinning at him savagely, the man's swollen, red face knotted with bulging veins, his animalistic eyes glassy with savage delight as he drew the stout branch back taut against Mannion's throat.

Down the other side of the hill, Mannion heard the whoops and coyote-like yells of the rest of Jasper's gang. He could also hear the thudding of their horses' hooves. They were on the way, closing fast.

Joe stretched his lips back from his teeth. He couldn't breathe.

He raised his hands and wrapped them around each end of the stout branch, but in his current position he couldn't exert enough force to ease the pressure on his throat. Black motes danced in his eyes. He was starting to lose consciousness. At the same time, he heard the dreadful thudding of the four shadowers' approaching horses.

Dammit, why hadn't he killed Neal when he'd had the chance?

Now he was the dead one.

Jasper and his "lost little lambs" would likely kill him slow too. They'd brag about it across the entire territory and down into Arizona and Old Mexico.

Hell, a song would be written about the long, slow death of Bloody Joe at the hands of Jasper Neal...

Joe heard the pathetic, desperate raking of his throat as he gagged and choked while trying futilely to draw a breath. Automatically, as if of its own accord, his left hand left the stout branch, slid down to the sheath on his left hip. He wrapped that hand around the bone handle of his bowie knife, slid it out of its sheath, twisted his hand around it, angled the knife upward, and slid the curved front, razor-edged tip into Jasper's side.

Instantly, the branch dropped from the man's hands, relieving the pressure on Mannion's throat. Jasper screamed.

Joe drew a long, loud, raking breath then turned onto his side.

Neal had wrapped both hands around Joe's left one, trying to force the knife out of his side. Joe rolled over and onto Neal. He pulled the knife up out of Jasper's flailing hands and, using both of his own hands, swept the bowie across Jasper's throat, instantly opening the man's neck and causing blood to geyser.

The thudding of the oncoming horses had grown louder until now Joe could feel the reverberations of the pounding hooves in the trail through his knees.

"*Eee-haww!*" screamed a rider behind Mannion just as the four others crested the hill.

Guns barked loudly. Bullets plumed the dirt to either side of Joe as, scrambling off the side of the trail, he wrapped each of his hands around each of his Russians and rolled onto his back. The four riders were skidding their blowing mounts to halts just down the hill from the crest and swinging their rifles toward him.

Only Jasper's son—the thick, red-haired H.J.—got off another shot before Joe went to work with the Russians, blowing H.J. out of his saddle first and then following him up with the three others. The Russians bucked and roared in Mannion's hands.

The four tumbled from their saddles to hit the ground with loud groans, writhing, rolling, groaning.

Joe heaved himself up onto his knees and drilled another round into each man until all four lay quiet and bloody on the trail, the dust of their fleeing horses sifting around them.

Still raking air in and out of his battered lungs, Mannion heaved himself to his feet. He walked over and stared down at Jasper Neal.

The man was still alive. He stared up at Joe. He opened and closed his mouth until, faintly, he managed: "You...come by it honestly...Joe." Blood frothed on his lips.

"My name?" Mannion said.

Jasper Neal gave a brief nod.

"Oh, hell, I've grown soft, Jasper," Joe said, genuinely troubled. "You and your boys were way more work than they needed to be."

He finished the man with a .44 round through that big freckle on his forehead.

CHAPTER 11

IN FURY, TOWN CONSTABLE JEREMIAH CLAGGETT WAS nudged out of a deep sleep by a tug on his long beard.

"Sleepin'," he croaked out, waving his hand up near his cheek as though hazing away a fly. "Lemme sleep, honey."

He smacked his lips, drew a long breath, let it out slowly, snoring.

There was another tug on his beard.

Claggett groaned. "D-don't now...sleepin'..."

A soft, husky, intimate female voice said softly into his left ear, so close that Claggett felt the moist warmth of the woman's breath, only unpleasant because he wished to remain asleep, "I know you're sleepin', Jeremiah. But you ain't s'posed to be sleepin'. Not no more, honey. You wanted me to wake you at eight. It's eight. The sun'll be down in an hour."

The woman chuckled and gave Claggett's beard another playful tug. "Wakey, wakey, Constable Claggett!"

Claggett snapped his eyes open. He looked at the aging, tired-looking but still comely, full-bodied, round-faced woman resting beside him on a bed in the last hurdy gurdy house in Fury. Miss Kansas Montrose reached out again, closed the first two fingers of her right hand over Claggett's nose then pulled them away, sliding her thumb up between them. "Got your nose, Jeremiah!"

Claggett grunted out a laugh and looked at the clock on the wall to his right, above and beyond where Kansas —a big but still-pretty, heavy-breasted woman somewhere in her forties—lounged beside him on the bed, her cheek resting on the heel of her soft, pink hand.

Claggett had known the whore for over ten years. She'd come to Fury back when the miners and prospectors were still hauling gold by the bucketsful out of the creeks and canyons.

Kansas had remained in town after the boom because, not unlike Claggett himself, she'd had nowhere else to go. Her small cabin that served as a brothel was the last such establishment in town. She'd been considered past her prime by whoring standards even back then. Despite how long Claggett had known the woman, she'd never told him her age just as she'd never told him—or anyone else, for that matter—what her real name was.

Kansas might have been any man's for a price, but she retained an air of mystery about her. That's what Claggett liked most about her though he didn't mind her man-pleasing abilities one bit. She was a good talker, too. Maybe that's what he liked most of all. A man needed someone to talk to, especially as he got on in years.

"I'll be hanged if I didn't sleep for over an hour!" he said now, yawning and closing his hand over his mouth. He shoved the covers down and, sitting up, dropped his bare feet to the floor. "I have to get over to the jailhouse. Justy's all alone over there with that little Lord devil."

Jeremiah hadn't wanted to leave his granddaughter alone at the jailhouse, but earlier, after sitting up all night keeping an eye on Billy Lord, he'd practically been asleep on his feet. Justy had convinced him that if Billy's brother Frank came calling, her half-asleep grandfather would be little help. Besides, Billy had likely been lying about Frank's presence in the San Juans.

Since his old back couldn't handle the hard jailhouse cots, Claggett had headed for a nap over here at Miss Kansas Montrose's humble cabin just off the main street in Fury, between a boarded-up grocery store and barber shop. Of course, like he'd known he would, Jeremiah had had a little fun before falling asleep.

Now, feeling guilty for leaving Justy alone for longer than he'd intended—nearly two hours—and especially in light of the dark circumstances of them housing one of the Lord brothers, he rose, wincing at the creaking in his feet, ankles, and knees, and looked around for his duds.

"I don't think you have anything to worry about," Kansas said. "Four fellas from the Buckskin Ranch rode into town about forty-five minutes ago and they pulled up at the jailhouse. Been there ever since. That good-lookin' devil, Rance Hayward, is likely sparkin' Justy again."

"You don't say," Claggett said, moving to a window and peering through a gap between two buildings to his right. Sure enough, four horses were tied to the hitchrack fronting the jailhouse. "At least she ain't alone." He chuckled and shook his head. "Hayward's wasting his time. Justy's savvy to that alley cat's reputation."

Justy had grown right cautious about men, and for that Jeremiah was grateful.

He chuckled again. "I best get over there an' rescue poor ol' Rance from that wildcat I raised."

Claggett chuckled then turned away from the window too quickly. A sharp bayonet of pain stabbed out from his worn-out backbone to lance his left shoulder. "Ah, damn!" he cried, raising that arm and closing his right hand over that shoulder, trying in vain to press away the pain.

"What is it, Jeremiah?" Kansas sat up on the bed and cast a look of concern at the gray-bearded, old lawman. "Your back again?"

Claggett lifted his head and sucked a sharp breath through gritted teeth at the old injury—*injuries*, rather, including a good dozen or so spills from horses over the years starting when he'd punched cattle on ranches throughout the southwest—that continued to grieve him, making it nearly impossible to move.

"Yeah, damn back." Claggett raised and lowered his arm and tried to flex at the waist. "Froze up purty good on me." Stiffly, he turned toward the whore. "Can you do that thing you do, Kansas?"

"Sure, honey!" Kansas hurried down off the bed, heavy breasts jouncing behind the ancient, cream, see-through negligee she wore. She moved up beside the lawman, wrapped an arm around his waist, and led him over to the bed. "You lay down now, honey, and I'll smooth out those nasty knots."

"Ah, thankee, thankee."

Kansas helped Claggett onto the bed. He knelt on the edge of it and, climbing up beside him, Kansas helped ease him belly down against the rumpled sheets still a little sweat-damp from their tussling. She climbed on top of him, straddling his waist, and went to work gently with her hands.

She ran them slowly up and down each side of his spine, pausing to press the heel of one hand into the knotted muscles and bulging vertebrae, as though lightly kneading bread.

"Oh, yeah...yeah...that feels good." Claggett smiled as she worked, easing the pain. He chuckled and said pensively as he lay with his left cheek against the sheets, "Sure would be nice...ah, that's it, that's it, feels soo good...if you was to be able to do this all the time for me, Kansas."

He glanced up at her with a shrewd smile and a wink.

Kansas paused her ministrations to lean down, frowning curiously into his face. "Are you asking me to *marry* you, Jeremiah?"

Claggett suddenly felt as surprised as Kansas looked.

"Am I?" He frowned back at her. "Hmmm...I don't know. Maybe I am."

She curled a coy little smile at him then continued kneading his back. "'Hmmm' is right."

Jeremiah glanced up at her. "What if I was, honey? What would you say, do you think? I'm just thinkin' out loud, you understand."

"What would I say?"

"Yeah, what would you say? You know—if I was to go ahead and ask you?"

"What would I say? Hmm." Kansas paused but continued massaging the taut muscles in his back. "Jeremiah, what got you thinkin' about this? In all the years I've known you...been with you...you never once mentioned the idea of hitching our wagons together even once. What's come over you, honey?"

"What's come over me?" Claggett pondered on that, staring pensively down at the sheets. "I reckon it was Joe Mannion." He chuckled bemusedly. "Sure enough, it was Joe!"

"*Bloody Joe Mannion* got you thinkin' about *marriage?*" Kansas chuckled with great amusement. "How on earth...?"

"He got himself hitched, Joe did. Ohhh...that's the spot right there. Really work that area, will ya, Kansas? *Ohhh!* I'm feelin' ten years younger already. Sure, sure, Joe got himself hitched, all right."

"I think I remember hearing about that. Didn't he marry that lovely redhead who runs the San Juan in Del Norte?"

"Jane Ford, yes ma'am. One an' the same." Claggett smiled as Kansas, straddling him a little higher, worked the knotted muscles and sinews just beneath his right shoulder blade, which was where the trouble always seemed to start.

If he remembered right, it was a half-broke bronc in west Texas near the Davis Mountains just before the little misunderstanding between the States that sent him tumbling to the ground on the point of that shoulder, years and years ago now.

"She sure seems to have made him happy. I don't know—there seemed to be a glow about him yesterday when he rode through town. Joe usually looks so grim and businesslike, especially when he has a prisoner in tow." Claggett chuckled and shook his head. "Not yesterday. Has to be the redhead...marriage."

"A *glow* about *Bloody Joe Mannion?*" Kansas laughed.

Claggett grunted under the luxurious feeling of having those painful muscles untangled. "Yes, ma'am. There sure was."

"Maybe you just imagined it. Maybe you heard about him gettin' hitched an' you started feeling a little jealous, wondering what it might feel like to share your house with a woman again. Maybe you were the one feelin' the glow." Kansas paused in her work to frown curiously down at her patient. "How long's it been for you, Jeremiah? Since your wife passed, I mean."

"My dear Edith's has been dead these twenty years. The typhoid took her at forty, God rest her lovely soul." Claggett shook his head. "Never mind me, Kansas. I'm just talkin'. I got Justy, and she fills up that cabin out there in those rocks more than enough for this old rattlesnake."

"She's not the same as havin' a wife to work the knots out of your back, though, is she, Jeremiah?" Kansas leaned down and slid her face up close to Claggett's, smiling, making her brown eyes sparkle. "And to please you regular-like—you know, like a man should be pleased."

She planted an affectionate kiss on his cheek then resumed work on his back.

Claggett sighed.

"You're lonely, Jeremiah. As much as you love your granddaughter, you're a lonely man. I can see it in your eyes today."

"I reckon. I thought I was used to it. I guess hearing about Joe was what started it, an' seein' him yesterday lookin'...I don't know...younger, somehow." He glanced up at Kansas again. "I don't know...just thinkin' out loud. You don't have a man an' I don't have a woman. Just thinkin' out loud."

"I don't know," Kansas said, grunting as she worked a little higher on Jeremiah's shoulder, putting more effort into the massage now that the muscles were loosening, "I once had an old lawman—a deputy U.S. marshal I was makin' merry with right here in this very room—tell me that havin' a woman back to home could get a lawman killed."

"Pshaw! How so?"

"A woman'll make a man soft was how he told it. And bein' soft can lead to bad decisions and get a lawman drilled a third eye. One he can't see out of." Kansas laughed then leaned down again, slid her weary, fleshy but not un-pretty face up close to Claggett's, and narrowed an eye, ironically. "That's a direct quote."

She laughed and resumed work.

"Oh, hell," Claggett said, chuckling. "I'm not a real lawman, anyway. Not anymore. The little devil, Billy Lord, is the first prisoner I've had locked up in over a month. The one before that was Lester Kittleson and I only locked him up for a few hours because he punched Harvey Cartwright. Hell, I been wantin' to punch Harvey Cartwright ever since I first met the sidewinder. Ha!"

"Who hasn't?" the whore agreed.

Claggett slid a hand up and placed it on her supple right thigh. "Thank you, honey. I feel much better. I'd best get on back to the jail and send Justy home. I don't want her in town after dark. If trouble comes, that's when it will come, most like."

"All right. I'm glad you feel better." Kansas scuttled off Claggett's back to sit beside him on the bed, drawing her knees up to her chest.

When he rolled over and sat up, she leaned forward to sandwich his bearded face in her hands and once more slid her face up close to his. "I never had any plans to marry, Jeremiah. Didn't think it was in the cards for an old whore. But if there's any man I'd marry, that man is you, honey. If you'll have me. After all, I am the last whore in Fury."

They had a good laugh over that.

Then her brown eyes crossed a little as she gave Jeremiah a warm, intimate look. She kissed his sun-seasoned nose. "I'd be proud if it was you who made an honest woman of me while I'm still young enough to give you some enjoyment. You just let me know when you're serious."

She winked and again planted a kiss on his nose.

Claggett frowned, pensive, startled by the unexpected wash of feelings, of the sudden, unexpected fear of time's passing, of being alone. "Why, I think I am serious, Kansas. What do you say to that? Don't run away now, darlin'!" he laughed.

Again, the whore's eyes crossed as she sandwiched his face between her warm, soft, pink hands. "I say let's call a preacher up here and make it official."

Claggett felt his lower jaw sag in surprise. "Really? You'd marry this old reprobate?"

"Jeremiah Claggett, you're about the only man on this old earth I would marry. There's no better man anywhere. Now, you've asked me, and I'm gonna hold you to it!"

He'd be damned if she didn't seem serious. Imagine that. He was a good fifteen years older than she!

His old heart warmed.

"Imagine that!" Claggett laughed, took the woman in his arms, and kissed her with deep, genuine affection. She kissed him back, returning every ounce of his warmth.

When he finally dropped down off the bed, feeling years younger in both mind and body, he dressed, planted his big, old, battered hat on his head, gave his bride-to-be one more tender, parting kiss, and left to head back over to the jailhouse, whistling.

———

As he walked, Claggett saw four men file down off the steps of the porch fronting the jailhouse and step into the saddles of the horses tethered at the hitchrack. One was the darkly handsome Rance Hayward, who looked rather long faced as he rode down the mostly vacant main street between mostly abandoned and boarded-up business buildings. The three men flanking him were talking and chuckling among themselves.

Hayward wasn't joining in the banter.

"What's the matter, Rance?" Claggett said as the four riders approached. "She turn you down again?"

Hayward pursed his lips and shook his head. "That's one stubborn little filly you raised, Constable." He sighed as he passed Claggett and headed for one of the only two saloons that remained open here in Fury. "One stubborn filly."

Claggett chuckled as he approached the jailhouse.

He stopped at the bottom of the porch steps.

Justy sat before him in a scroll-back, hide-bottom chair, kicked back against the building's front wall, left of the door. She had her spurred, cowman's boots resting on the railing before her, crossed at the ankles. She had her arms crossed on her chest.

A wry little smile curled one side of her plump upper lip.

As beautiful as her mother had been, even in a wool work shirt, denim jeans, and weathered hat, she was a heart breaker. Long hair as black as her eyes, the late light glinting gold in both.

"You know, he's not really all that bad, honey," Claggett said.

"He's a man, isn't he?"

Claggett gave a dry chuff as he mounted the porch. He'd intended to go on into the jailhouse without saying anything more, but now he stopped and gazed down at her.

"You know, honey," he began, haltingly, "we never really talked about—"

"No, and I don't want to talk about it now," she said crisply, staring out into the street.

Jeremiah drew a deep breath. "All right." He drew another breath, let it out slow. "Go on home, honey. I'll take over from here."

"I want to be here."

"Everything will be fine. Billy's lying about his brother. You know that as well as I do. Frank keeps to New Mexico, Arizona. Likely too many bad memories in these parts."

"Just the same, abuelito, I—"

"Dammit, Justy, will you just this once listen to me!" Claggett uncharacteristically exploded. He suddenly realized he was clenching his fists down at his sides. The explosion had caught him off guard.

What had gotten into him?

Justy looked up at him, round eyed, wondering the same thing.

He ran the back of his hand across his mouth, drew another deep breath, and let it out slow. "Go on home, honey," he said, quietly. "I'm expecting a quiet night."

Slowly, keeping her dark eyes on her grandfather, Justy lowered her boots to the porch floor. "All right." She walked down the steps, untied her horse, mounted up, and galloped off into the shadows gathering west of town.

As Claggett moved heavily into the office and closed the door, he looked at the four cells lined up at the back of the office. Billy Lord sat on his cot in the cell to the far right, resting back against the log wall, one arm hooked behind his head. He stared up at the ceiling. His upper lip was swollen from its meeting with the butt of Justy's rifle.

"Expecting a quiet night—eh, old man?" Billy smiled. "We'll see."

CHAPTER 12

"YEAH, WE'LL SEE HOW QUIET THIS NIGHT TURNS OUT to be," Claggett's prisoner said again an hour later, after he'd awakened from a short nap.

With a big yawn, Billy dropped his feet over the side of his cot and smoothed his sleep spiked hair into place as he looked out the jailhouse's window right of the door. Beyond, the night-dark street was relieved by only a couple of oil pots burning near both still-open saloons so the drunken clientele, finishing up their night's revelry, didn't fall and kill themselves making their way to their horses.

It got good and dark this high in the San Juans on moonless nights. There were lots of stars, Jeremiah Claggett had noted when he'd sat out on the porch earlier, building and smoking a quirly and simply enjoying the fresh, cool, mountain air as well as reflecting on the prospect of being hitched again.

"Yessir, old man," Billy said, rising from the cot, running both hands brusquely through his longish, thin, yellow hair and sauntering up to the door of his cell.

"Might be quiet right now. Later, though...when Frank gets here...likely with all the boys in tow..." He grinned at where Claggett sat at his desk, running an oiled cloth down the barrels of his greener. "No, sir—ain't gonna be nearly so quiet, then."

He gave a devilish little chuckle, grinning. The scabs on his plump, girlish lips glistened in the light of a lantern hanging by a wire from the ceiling in the middle of the small office.

"Frank nearby, you think?" Claggett asked with a manufactured offhand air, as he continued to run the rag down the barrels of the old greener he'd been wielding for the past six years, ever since he'd started lawdogging to help makes ends meet for him and Justy after most of the color was plundered from the canyons.

"Oh, he's nearby, all right." Again, Billy smiled. "Hardville."

"Hardville, eh? That's a fair piece," Claggett said, not letting the kid rile him. "Besides, he doesn't know where you are. The San Juans are a big range."

"Yeah, but he was expectin' me. When I didn't show, he likely came out lookin' for me. That's how Frank is. He's my older brother, but we're closer than that. We're like this." Billy held up the crossed two fingers of his right hand. "He's got him a good tracker, Frank does. A big Apache named Three Moons."

"If you and Frank are so close, how come you're not ridin' with him?"

"Frank's bossy. You know how older brothers can be. Doesn't think I know a damn thing. That's why I ride alone. Leastways, I ride alone now since Bloody Joe took down Hec."

Billy bent his knees and drew his cheap, broadcloth

trousers up higher on his skinny hips. "That's all right. I'm a lone wolf. That's how I like it. Don't care for the company of other men. Even Frank. Oh, I like seein' him now an' then. Carousin' together like we gonna do in Hardville. But after two or three days—nah, I like to get back out on my own trail, only the stars for a blanket."

"Real independent, are ya?"

"Yep, that's me." Billy wrapped each hand around a bar of his cell door and frowned belligerently at the old constable. "Say, you're so ugly you'd make a freight train take a dirt track. But that granddaughter of yours—she sure did turn out purty. Even purtier than when I last—"

"We won't talk about Justy," Claggett said, crisply, turning his attention from the greener to the devil grinning at him through the cell door.

"All right, all right," Billy said. He looked away for a time, then, smiling again, he returned his gaze to Claggett. "You know why Frank never came back? You know—to get even?"

Again, Claggett looked at the young man. He was genuinely curious, so he said, "Why?"

"Because he said you were right an' we were wrong." Again, Billy smiled. "Imagine that. He said we weren't good folks, an' we had it comin'."

"That you did. Your family was a blight on this town."

"Maybe, maybe not."

"Oh, you were, all right."

"Frank—he's tougher than whang leather. You weren't expecting that, were you? Weren't expecting him to become what he is today?"

"No, can't say as I did," Claggett grimly allowed, slowly running the cloth down the greener's double bores. His voice was even, mild. But he felt a nervousness down deep inside him. He'd feared that one day that night would come back to haunt him, to haunt the town, but it never had.

Likely, it never would.

No, likely it never would. Billy was lying. Frank was nowhere near these mountains. Even if he was, he didn't know Billy was here in Fury, and there weren't enough folks left here for Frank to fiddle with. And Frank had it right. He and the rest of his family had had it coming. Especially after...

Jeremiah shook his head to dislodge the thought.

As though reading his mind, Billy said, "Sure is purty —Miss Justy. Even purtier than when—"

Claggett jerked an enraged look at him. "That'll be enough about my granddaughter!"

"I could talk about her all day. What's more, I could *look* at her all day."

"Did you hear what I said?" Claggett said, squeezing the greener in his knobby hands.

"Sure is mean, though." Billy gently fingered the cuts on his mouth. "For a purty girl."

Claggett resumed working on the greener, rubbing the cloth down the old, scarred, walnut stock. "She don't put up with no nonsense from hoodlums like you."

"Sure...is...purty, though..."

Ears burning with anger, Claggett dropped the oily rag and rose from his chair, glowering at the goatish little urchin behind the cell door. "I've had enough of that kind of talk. Remember what Justy did to you? That'll be nothin' compared to what I do to you if you don't shut up about her!"

Billy clapped his hands, laughing. He opened his mouth to speak but stopped suddenly and swung his head to the dark window. "Say, what was that?"

Claggett frowned as he turned his head to the window. "What was what?"

"I heard somethin'."

Claggett and his prisoner stared at the window.

"I don't hear nothin'," Claggett said.

"Sure enough," Billy said. "Lift the horn to your deaf old ears, old man. A good number of riders ridin' in fast!"

Claggett pricked his ears. After a few seconds, he could hear it too.

Sure enough, the thudding of several horses was growing louder.

The lawman broke open the greener, grabbed the two wads that lay on the coffee-stained desk blotter before him, and shoved them into the tubes.

"That old greener ain't gonna do you a bit of good, old man," Billy jeered the lawman as Claggett made his way from out behind his desk and moved slowly, frowning, his apprehension building, to the window.

"Oh, it'll do me *some* good," Claggett said, peering out the window and along the mostly dark street to his right, pulse quickening. He glanced over his shoulder at his prisoner. "If it looks like they're gonna get you, I'll blast you through them bars. Both barrels! If Frank still wants you after that, he'll have to mop you up and haul you out in a bucket!"

"That'd make Frank mighty mad!"

Claggett opened the door and stepped out onto the stoop. He strode to the top of the steps and stared to the west, the direction from which the hoof thuds were growing in volume. He removed the keeper thong from over the hammer of the old Colt holstered on his right hip, loosened the gun in the leather, then squeezed the greener in both hands.

His palms were getting warm.

Damn. Was he really going to have to face Frank Lord tonight? Part of him wanted to. A larger part of him did not.

"You're gonna die slow, old man!" Billy screeched behind him, making Claggett jerk with a start.

The constable cursed then stepped back to draw the office door closed.

"Better run an' hide, old man!" the little devil screeched behind the door.

Claggett stared to the west, nervously chewing his mustache.

The hoof thuds grew louder. They were accompanied by the jangle of bridle chains, the squawk of leather, and the slapping of saddlebag pouches. Shadows jostled out in the darkness beyond the dying town. The shadows grew larger as the thudding grew louder. Claggett heard a man say something. Another man laughed.

He squeezed the greener tighter in his gloved, sweating hands.

He started to raise it, inched a little closer to the edge of the steps, bracing himself.

The riders were approaching now—the horse-and-rider silhouettes of at least a half a dozen men. They were fifty yards away now...forty...thirty. They kept coming but did not angle toward the jailhouse but kept heading straight on down the street to the east. As they stormed past, the lead rider turned to the constable and said, "Evenin', Jeremiah! Ain't it a little past your bedtime?"

Relief washed over Claggett. It was like having a heavy log chain removed from his shoulders. He laughed as he lowered the greener and said, "Sure is, Tomer! What're you fellas doin' in town this late? It's a weeknight!"

"We're celebratin' Pete's birthday!" Tomer yelled over

his shoulder as he and the other riders galloped past the jailhouse, angling toward the lamplit windows of the North Side Saloon. "Got in off the range late an' gotta get up early, so we're gonna have to drink fast!"

The others laughed. The hoof thuds dwindled to silence as the Tincup riders checked their mounts down in front of the hitchrack fronting the saloon.

Claggett laughed and shook his head.

Lyle Tomer owned the Tincup Ranch four miles to the northwest. He might have owned the ranch, but he was like a fellow drover to the six men on his payroll and who were just now dismounting their horses and swiping their hats against their chaps as they stepped up onto the boardwalk fronting the North Side, about to give the saloon's proprietor, a Mex named Lope de Vega, a welcome inoculation of business.

Weeknights were especially quiet in the near ghost town of Fury.

Claggett turned, opened the jailhouse door, and stepped inside.

Billy was frowning through the bars. "What the hell happened?"

"Wasn't them, kid," Claggett said and laughed.

He'd just closed the door when the kid gasped.

He said, "Listen!"

Claggett frowned, pricking his ears. "I don't hear nothin'."

"That's because you're old and deaf as a post. Give it a minute." Staring through the bars of his cell door, a smile grew on the little devil's face.

A few beats passed and then Claggett's old ticker began quickening its pace again. Again, a rumble sounded to the west. Steadily, it grew in volume.

"That's him," the kid said after about a minute had

passed, smiling gleefully at the old lawman standing frozen with his back to the closed door. "That's Frank."

The rumble had grown to a low roar. Claggett could feel the reverberations of the oncoming riders through the floor beneath his feet.

Oily dread pooled in Claggett's belly.

The kid was still smiling at him, but Billy didn't say anything. He didn't have to. He saw the fear in Claggett's eyes.

The lawman opened the door two feet and peered out, holding the double-bore up high across his chest. The riders were just then storming into town—a black, jostling mass in the starry night. As they approached the jailhouse, oil from the pots burning to Claggett's left began reflecting in the eyes of men and horses and winked off metal tack and off the rifles several of the riders held across their saddle bows.

Claggett silently prayed that they, like the Tincup men, would ride on past him. He hoped maybe they were another crew of drovers or maybe pick-and-shovelers who'd just gotten off a shift and were heading to Del Norte or maybe some other place farther off to the east to stomp with their tails up.

Of course, he knew it wasn't true. Still, he prayed.

Keep ridin', he silently urged. *Ride on by, fellas.*

He was not surprised, of course, when they slanted toward the jailhouse, drawing back on their horses' reins —a little more than a dozen. A whole passel of gun-hung desperadoes in high-crowned, broad-brimmed hats, neckerchiefs, and long dusters.

Suddenly, the roar of the racing horses had diminished to blowing and stomping and the squawk of saddle leather.

And Claggett found himself staring through the two-foot gap between the door and the frame, feeling his knees turn to putty.

The men before him were armed for bear. Each man had at least two pistols holstered on his hips or thighs, and a knife or two, as well. Long guns jutted from leather scabbards or rested across saddle pommels.

Jeremiah noticed that the saddlebags on each horse bulged, likely from a recent take-down—a narrow-gauge train or a stagecoach, probably. The bags looked to the old lawman like rattlesnakes that had just eaten a squirrel or a gopher. Only half digested. The bulk of the digestive process would likely occur in Old Mexico, where he'd heard the bunch nearly always fled to let their trail cool.

One man sat his coal-black stallion a little ahead of the others, flanked off the black's left hip by a big, granite-faced Indian with two braids trailing down his shoulders. The Indian wore a big, round, silver medallion down his chest, over a calico shirt between the open flaps of his black leather duster. The gold-capped handle of a big bowie knife jutted across the Indian's flat belly.

Claggett returned his attention to the yellow-haired, yellow-mustached man on the black. A tall, broad-shouldered drink of water. Handsome, too, in a hard, mean sort of way. Bigger, meaner looking than Jeremiah remembered.

Frank Lord.

His cold, blue eyes sat deep in stony sockets, glinting in the guttering orange glow of the flickering oil pots. They were expressionless as was the rest of his face as he sat the stallion, staring at Claggett.

Claggett's heart drummed.

His gloved hands were slick as he squeezed the greener.

Finally, Lord lifted his chin as he said, "Been a while, Constable."

Not long enough, Claggett thought as dread churned in his bowels.

Billy squealed mockingly behind him.

The constable licked his lips as he studied the hard faces and dark eyes bearing down on him from ten feet beyond the bottom of the porch steps. The horses tied at the hitchracks down the street to Claggett's left danced and shifted, snorting, pulling at their tied reins. They, too, were nervous, glancing edgily toward the gang gathered in front of Claggett's jail.

Jeremiah cleared his throat and hoped his voice wouldn't tremble. "Ride away, Frank. Just ride away."

Frank Lord placed a fist on his hip and leaned forward a little. "You got my little brother in there, Constable?"

"I'm here, Frank," Billy yelled behind Claggett. "He's the only one here, Frank. Just a washed-up old scudder, deaf as a post!"

Frank frowned as he lifted his head and said, "That's no way to talk, Billy. I taught you to respect your elders. Now, you apologize to this man."

"*What?*" Billy was incredulous.

"I said apologize or I'm gonna let you rot in there!"

"Oh, come on, Frank!"

"Billy—I raised you better than that. After Pa died, I raised you better!"

Silence.

Then Billy's voice came, low and sheepish: "All right, all right." Claggett could hear the kid's boots shifting on the wood floor. Finally, the exasperated but cowed prisoner said, "Christalmighty, I *apologize!*"

Frank smiled.

A couple of the men around him chuckled and glanced at each other.

"Now, then," Frank said, keeping his hard, vaguely mocking gaze on Claggett. "Let's get down to brass tacks here—shall we, Constable?"

CHAPTER 13

"Now, I'm gonna ask you very politely to free my brother, Constable. Right here, right now. No fuss. You turn him loose, let him fetch his horse, and he rides on out of here with me an' my boys. We leave you alone. Billy belongs with me. I'm his brother."

"I can't turn him loose," Claggett said, half wondering if Frank could hear him above the loud thudding of his heart. "Mannion arrested him for murder. He'll stand trial in Del Norte."

He knew his words sounded preposterous, but he had to say them. Because they were true. He knew, however, that Frank Lord and his riders had not ridden all this way to listen to reason from a worn-out old man. They would not just turn around and ride back to where they'd come from.

Not without Billy.

Still, Claggett had to say them. He couldn't give in to Frank Lord. Especially, not after what he'd done. This was a personal as well as professional matter.

Frank canted his head a little to one side and

stretched his lips in a rueful half-smile. "Constable, you don't want to die here tonight."

Claggett swallowed down the dry knot in his throat or tried to. "I have a job to do."

"If you don't turn my brother loose, you're gonna die," Frank said matter-of-factly.

"Jeremiah, everything all right over there?"

The voice had come from Claggett's left. He turned to see Lyle Tomer and two of his men standing on the edge of the boardwalk fronting the North Side Saloon, staring this way. Light from the window behind them and from a near oil pot glinted off the dimpled beer schooners they held in their hands.

Claggett wasn't sure what to say.

Then it came to him. Because this was his fight, not Tomer's.

"Everything's fine, Lyle. I got it handled. Go back and enjoy your night."

"You sure?" Tomer said, incredulous, sizing up the dozen men sitting their horses in the street before the jail.

Claggett doubted Tomer or any of his men knew of Frank Lord. Tomer had established his ranch only two years ago, two years after the Lords had been kicked out of Fury.

"He's sure," Frank Lord said, keeping his gaze on Claggett. "Go back inside the saloon and enjoy your night, feller."

One of the men flanking Tomer said, "Come on, Lyle." Then he and the other man turned and strode back into the saloon.

Tomer stood staring toward the gang of riders and Claggett for another couple of seconds. "You sure, Jeremiah?"

Claggett turned to him as he squeezed the shotgun in his arthritic hands. "I'm sure, Lyle. Go on back inside."

"If you need help..."

"Lyle, I said I'm sure!" Claggett said, voice rising in anger as he returned his gaze to Lord.

Tomer held up his free hand, palm out. "All right."

He turned and followed the other two men back into the North Side. Claggett didn't like seeing him go, but this was his job, not Tomer's. He didn't want others to die for him. Especially when he knew he *should* let Billy go. A posse could run him down later.

But Claggett just couldn't do it. If Tomer stood and fought with Claggett against Frank Lord, he and his men would die as would anyone but a small army who stood against Lord's gang. There were no longer enough folks in Fury to fend them off.

No, it was Claggett's fight, all right. He might die tonight, but he'd take at least a few, including Lord, along with him.

"Turn him loose, Constable," Frank said, an impatient edge in his voice.

"Not gonna do it, Frank."

Lord sat up straighter in his saddle with a sigh. "Then, Constable, you're gonna die here tonight."

"Then so is your brother."

"What's that?"

"I said so is your brother," Claggett said, louder. He half-turned toward where Billy stood staring out through his cell door. "I'll give him both barrels."

"Frank!" Billy called, his voice breaking a little.

"Don't worry, little brother," Frank said. "He won't do it."

Claggett looked over his right shoulder at the outlaw

leader. "I'll do it," he said, aiming the shotgun at his prisoner. "Clear out, or I'll give him both barrels."

"Go ahead." Frank gave a knowing smile.

"What?" Claggett said, though he'd heard it loud and clear. He just hadn't expected Frank to call his bluff.

He wanted to be able to do it—to blast the kid through the bars. But he couldn't. Mannion could do it. Joe *would* do it. Claggett could not. He could not shoot an unarmed man locked up in a cell.

Even if that man was the devil, Billy Lord. Even if it meant his older brother would spring him and turn him back loose on the world.

He just couldn't do it.

It wouldn't save him, anyway.

Lord smiled again, cagily. He knew he'd called the old lawman's bluff.

"This ain't about my brother, is it, Constable?" Frank said.

Claggett's heart thudded. A toxic amalgam of frustration and fury was a tight, hot fist inside his head, pushing against the backs of his eyeballs.

Several of Frank's men looked at him, frowning curiously.

"It don't matter what it's about," Jeremiah bit out. "Your brother stays here with me."

"All right, then." Frank lifted his chin to call over Claggett into the jailhouse: "Get your head down, Billy. Looks like there's gonna be some shooting!"

Fear gripped Claggett but it did not temper his resolve. "Ride on out, Frank!"

Frank smiled, blinked slowly. "Not a chance, Constable."

He sat staring back at Jeremiah for nearly a full

minute. Claggett stared back at him, unblinking, feeling the weakness in his knees.

"All right, boys," Frank said.

Quickly, he moved his right hand toward the stag-handled Colt holstered low on his twill-clad right thigh. Claggett slammed the jailhouse's door closed just as a bullet punched through it and then another and another until a veritable fusillade rose from the street. He moved to the window as the glass shattered and bullets went screeching around the office and thudding into the log walls.

In the corner of his right eye, he saw Billy throw himself to the floor with a yelp and roll under his cot, covering his head with his arms.

Claggett crouched beside the window, keeping his head down and gritting his teeth against the flying glass, wood splintering from the window frames, and bullets.

After a minute of heavy firing, Frank yelled something Claggett couldn't hear beneath the cacophony. The shooting died quickly to silence.

"You all right, Billy?" Frank called.

Lying on the floor beneath his cot, Billy turned to look back over his shoulder. "So far, so good, Frank!" He looked at Claggett and gritted his teeth. "Kill this stubborn old bastard!"

"Hold on," Frank said.

"Gonna take you with me, Lord!" Claggett yelled then rose and shoved the double-bore out the broken-out window.

He aimed toward where Frank had been sitting the black just a minute ago. Only, while the black was still there, Lord was not in the saddle. The big Indian was holding the black's reins, smiling.

"What the...?" Claggett said, easing the tension in his trigger finger.

A deafening explosion sounded behind him.

He turned around to see the door slam against the wall and the tall, slender, broad-shouldered Frank Lord step through the doorway, catching the door with his right foot then swinging toward Claggett, aiming the big Colt at the constable, a grim smile curling his upper lip beneath his brushy yellow mustache.

"Damn fool."

Claggett had just started to swing the double-bore toward the gang leader when Lord lunged forward and swept up his right, black boot in a blur of swift motion. Jeremiah gave a cry of fear and exasperation as the double-bore discharged into the ceiling and then flew up onto his desk with a wooden clatter.

"Yes, Frank!" he heard Billy scream. "Get him, Frank!"

"Shut up, Billy," Frank said calmly, staring coldly down at Claggett with those bizarre, baby blue eyes set in deep, suntanned sockets beneath the broad brim of his cream Stetson. He holstered the Colt.

The outlaw's black-gloved, right hand rose to the back of his neck. Coming down, the blade of a black-handled stiletto glistened in the dull lamplight.

"Ah, Christ," Claggett groaned.

Lord's broad nostrils flared, and his jaws tightened, thin lips pursing beneath the brushy yellow mustache, as with a grunt he plunged the blade into Claggett's belly, just above the buckle of his cartridge belt.

"*Oh!*" Claggett cried, stumbling back against his desk.

He looked down in horror at the obsidian handle jutting from his belly. Blood oozed up around the blade. Suddenly, his knees buckled, and he dropped straight down to the floor.

Billy whooped and hollered. "That's it—make him die slow, Frank!"

Frank placed his left hand on Claggett's chest. With his right hand, he pulled the blade out of the constable's belly. The burning pain was almost as much as when the knife had first gone in. Blood gushed, ran down the constable's rounded belly to the floor.

Jeremiah fell back against his desk. He kicked and wailed. "*Ahhh...goddamn you to hell, Frank Lord!*"

Slowly, methodically, his face a stone mask, Frank cleaned the knife on Jeremiah's shirt. "I wasn't gonna come back. I was gonna steer clear. For her sake." He said that last with a sincere dip of his chin then glanced over at his brother jumping and hollering like a loco monkey in a cage. "If you'd only done as I asked an' turned him loose. I know he ain't much...but he's blood."

Outside, a man's voice rose from the street: "Got your back, Jeremiah!"

Claggett recognized the voice of Lyle Tomer.

"No," Jeremiah tried to yell, clutching his bloody belly and shaking his head as out on the street all hell broke loose in the form of gunfire, screaming and yelling. Horses whinnied, hooves thumped, rifles barked, and cocking levers raked.

"No," Claggett repeated, slowly shaking his head. "No...no..."

Frank Lord straightened and smiled down at him. He casually returned the pigsticker to the sheath behind his neck.

Clutching his belly, hearing the Tincup men dying on the street, Claggett watched helplessly as Frank strode past him, grabbed the ring of keys off his desk, and walked over to the cell in which Billy was yowling through the bars, jumping up and down.

That was the last thing Claggett saw before the pain swept through him, unbearably, and the world went dark.

He continued hearing the shooting and the yelling out on the street for another excruciating minute or two before that died too.

———

READY FOR SLEEP, JUSTY CLAGGETT TURNED DOWN THE lamp on the table beside her bed. As the glow died, she glimpsed another glow beyond the sackcloth curtains over the sashed window.

Frowning curiously, she parted the curtains and stared out. Her brows ridged more severely when she saw the red glow in the sky to the northeast.

"What in the...?"

Concern building in her, she moved out of her small bedroom and into the main part of the cabin she shared with her grandfather near their diggings southwest of Del Norte. She passed the lamp burning on the kitchen table —she always left a lamp burning for abuelito when he had to stay out late—which he seldom had to do anymore since Fury was practically a ghost town—and moved to the door, her cambric nightgown buffeting about her legs.

Her feet were bare, but she was too concerned about the glow in the sky to bother with the soft, doeskin moccasins she always left by the door for trips to the privy. She stepped out into the sage- and gravel-peppered yard in her bare feet, mindless of the prickling against her soles, and again cast her gaze to the northeast.

The glow was disturbingly large. It pulsated like some living thing just above the horizon. Like a fire.

A fire.

What else could it be?

The only thing that lay in that direction was Fury!

Justy gasped, spun around and, lifting her nightgown over her head, ran back into the house. She came out two minutes later fully dressed in her wool work shirt, black denims, hat, and leather boots, her Winchester carbine in her hands.

Her heart thudded painfully as, taking long strides toward the small stable flanking the cabin, she gazed again at the dreadful orange glow in the direction of town. Its size disturbed her. It told her that more than one building in Fury was on fire.

A glow that size meant several buildings were likely burning. While horrified, she wasn't surprised. The mostly abandoned town was dry as seasoned tinder.

She was ten feet from the stable when she stopped dead in her tracks.

A cold stone dropped in her belly.

She looked at the glow again, and her heart turned a flipflop in her chest.

"Frank," she said softly, dreadfully, instinctively knowing what had happened.

Sure, Frank Lord had come to get his brother out of abuelito's jail!

She pulled back on the stable door and ran inside. Five minutes later, she galloped out astride her grulla gelding, ducking under the door frame. Once in the yard, she neck-reined the mount toward the main trail to town and put the spurs to him.

"*Hy-yahh, boy—vamos!*" she yelled, leaning forward over the horse's glistening mane.

She galloped out to the shaggy two-track trail, turned the mount toward the northeast, and again spurred him into a hard run. It was too dark to ride that fast, but Justy threw caution to the wind. Terror was a wild stallion galloping inside her.

She felt her lips quivering as several horrific images played like a kaleidoscope inside her head as the cool night wind blew her long hair back from her face and basted her hat brim against her forehead.

Ahead, the glow grew larger and brighter until she could see individual tufts of dancing flames and see the glowing cinders rising skyward on thickening ribbons of black smoke.

Her terror grew as she closed the distance between herself and Fury. As the gelding chewed up the trail, the fire continued to grow, spreading across the trail ahead until it was obvious that several buildings on both sides of the street were fully engulfed.

She was maybe only a half a mile away from the conflagration when something large and dark bolted out from behind a small grove of aspens lining the mouth of a secondary trail and onto the main trail not ten feet away from her on her left. The gelding gave a frightened whinny and lurched hard to the right, nearly throwing Justy off the horse's left side.

The girl screamed. The horse whinnied shrilly.

Its rider hauled back on his reins, leaning far back in his saddle. As the big bay came to a skidding halt at the convergence of the two trails, Joe Mannion's voice yelled, "*Justy!*"

"Joe! You saw?"

"I saw! Stay here!"

Mannion and the big, snorting bay shot up the trail ahead of her, their single, jouncing form silhouetted against the building red flames beyond.

CHAPTER 14

MANNION SPURRED RED AHEAD ALONG THE MAIN trail, pulling his hat brim low to keep the wind of the stallion's ground-churning gallop from blowing it off his head. As he rode crouched low in the saddle, he cursed silently.

The fire grew brighter before him until he could see far enough into the business district to know that the conflagration had engulfed a good half dozen buildings at the center of the mostly abandoned town. It would engulf more quickly. Most of the buildings in Fury had been constructed of wood frame or logs. The wood was well-seasoned and most of the business buildings along the main drag had been built right up against each other.

The whole town would go.

Again, Joe shook his head and cursed. Mostly, he cursed himself.

Frank Lord had been to Fury to spring his brother. The brother Joe had left in Jeremiah's jail.

That had been the first thing Mannion had thought when, a couple of miles back along the trail from Forsythe, he'd spied the glow of the flames that had grown larger and larger as he'd approached. Of course, a town like Fury, without enough residents left to man a bucket brigade, could go up in flames with just a carelessly discarded cigarette or a broken lamp. Lightning strikes often set fire to towns in the mountains.

Mannion shook his head as the first shacks and stables of Fury slid up on both sides of the trail and he and Red shot straight down the main street. Justy Claggett, despite Mannion's admonition not to, following close behind on her grulla.

This was Lord's doing. Mannion knew it deep down to the marrow of his bones. He'd been a damn fool to leave Billy here.

Staring straight ahead along the street, his guts tightened. Two people were in the street before him. As he closed the distance between him and them, he saw that one was an old man, the other a plump woman in a pink wrap and nightgown, her lusterless brown hair liberally streaking with gray hanging down low across her shoulders.

Behind Mannion, Justy screamed.

Joe recognized the old man who lay with his head on the woman's thigh as she slumped over him, running a hand affectionately over Claggett's nearly bald head. The orange light of the fires raging on both sides of the street a half a block down from where the woman knelt over Claggett in front of the jailhouse shone in Jeremiah's open, unblinking eyes and in the dark-red patch of blood covering his rounded belly.

As Mannion reined Red to a halt, Justy reined the grulla to a stop to his left and leaped out of her saddle to drop to her knees beside her grandfather. She loosed a scream that Mannion would hear on his deathbed as she threw herself on her grandfather and wrapped her arms around his neck, lifting his head up off the woman's lap and sobbing as she hugged him.

"*Abuelito!*" she wailed.

Mannion slid his Yellowboy from its saddle boot and cocked it one-handed as he rode forward along the street, toward where a good many buildings were fully engulfed by flames. Just ahead, a dozen men—cowboys and miners, a couple of mule skinners Joe recognized—lay twisted in the street fronting the North Side Saloon and the Parthenon, both of which were nothing so much anymore than orange balls of roiling flames and falling timbers, cinders rising toward the stars the light from the fire had erased. Shotguns, rifles, and handguns lay strewn with the bleeding bodies, glistening in the light of the dancing flames.

Several of the bodies were broken and crumpled, likely trampled by galloping horses. Mannion could see three dead horses among the carnage.

A half dozen living men, mostly old-timers who'd originally settled Fury, milled among the bodies, staring in shock. Most were dressed in night clothes, a few in long nightgowns and night socks. A couple wielded shotguns. One man—small and wiry and bearded, the tail of his night sock brushing a shoulder—turned to Mannion, eyes dark beneath wrinkled brows. Slowly, he shook his head.

"Lord's bunch?" Mannion asked, just to be sure.

Slowly, the old fellow nodded.

"Which way they head?"

Slowly, the old fellow raised a hand to his shoulder and extended his thumb to indicate behind him, toward where the main trail became the trail leading out of the far side of the town.

Only death and burning buildings. The wind was

from the west, shepherding the flames east. Soon the entire town including outlying shacks would be engulfed. There was no stopping it.

The jailhouse wasn't on fire. Likely, the fires had started at the North Side and at the other saloon on the opposite side of the street. The men lying dead between the two saloons had likely come from both establishments to Claggett's aid only to be gunned down without mercy.

Such was the way of Frank Lord's savage killers.

The gang was gone now. The killers had freed Billy, punished Claggett for jailing him for Mannion, punished the innocent men from both saloons for taking the time and trouble to render assistance, and ridden on.

Mannion didn't need to check the jailhouse. He knew Billy Lord was gone.

He swung Red around and rode back over to where Justy was still sobbing over her dead abuelito. The woman on whose thigh Jeremiah's head rested was running a hand through Justy's hair. She too was crying.

"Frank Lord gutted him like a pig!" she screeched, glaring up through tear-filled eyes at Mannion, flaring her nostrils in fury. "He asked me to marry him—Jeremiah. Only a couple of hours before they rode into town and killed him."

The last words were choked out on a sob.

Mannion's guts were churning with fury as his heart was breaking.

He swung down from Red's back, walked over to Justy, crouched down, and placed a hand on her shoulder.

She turned toward him, her eyes on fire, her jaws hard, teeth gritted. "You killed him!" she screamed. "It was *you*! You killed him! You as good as plunged that pig sticker in his guts, Marshal Mannion!"

Joe leaned back, startled by the force of the girl's sudden fury.

She rose and let both hands fly, slapping his face. He did nothing to resist but merely stood there, letting her hands batter him until he could feel blood trickling down from his lower lip and his cheeks were burning. He had it coming.

When she stopped the attack, having worn herself out, Justy's face crumpled in agony once more. She lowered her head and sobbed, tears streaming down her cheeks. She slumped against Mannion. He wrapped his arms around her and held her tightly against him.

"You killed him," she sobbed into his chest. "You killed him..."

"I know," Mannion said, rocking her gently, his cheeks burning, lips bleeding. "I know."

Holding her, feeling her heart raging against his own, he choked out a strangled sob of his own and silently vowed revenge.

He spied movement straight ahead of him along the smoky street. The silhouette of a horse and rider trotted toward him from the west. The rider slowed his pace roughly a hundred yards away, came on a few more yards, then reined his mount to a halt.

He curveted the horse and stared along the street toward Mannion, the dancing orange light of the fire flickering faintly across him and his mount—a blaze-faced dun. The man just sat there, gazing toward Mannion. He was small and wiry. He wore a brown vest over a gray shirt, brown chaps, and a shapeless black Stetson.

A range rider, possibly. He'd come to town for a drink only to find the place ablaze. Odd that he was alone, though.

Or...could he be the same rider Mannion had spied galloping away from the Devil's Anvil...?

But then, a lot of men wore black hats and rode brown geldings.

The rider touched his spurs to his mount's flanks and rode ahead a little farther, sort of canting his head to one side, taking it all in—the fire, the carnage, the old man still resting his head in the plump woman's lap while she ran a hand affectionately across Claggett's nearly bald pate.

The rider checked his mount down suddenly. Just as suddenly, he reined the horse around so quickly that the horse pitched and whinnied. The rider touched spurs to its flanks, and the horse stretched into a ground-eating gallop back in the direction from which it had come.

The rataplan of galloping hooves dwindled quickly beneath the building roar of the flames.

———————

FRANK LORD RAISED HIS RIGHT HAND, GLANCED OVER his shoulder, and yelled, "We'll hold up here, boys!"

The gang leader checked down his coal-black stallion. Beside him his brother, Billy, reined in the paint horse he'd taken from the hitchrack fronting the North Side Saloon in Fury, just before they'd set fire to the place as well as the Parthenon across the street from it.

Just desserts, to Frank's way of thinking, for the customers from both places coming to Claggett's aid. He and his men had killed the barmen in both places, as well, when the aprons had voiced objections to having their places incinerated. Just desserts, to Frank's way of seeing, for voicing their objections.

Even if they hadn't voiced their objections, Frank

would have killed them. Frank was one of that rare breed of men who took satisfaction in killing and did it every chance he got with very little provocation.

He would not, however, have killed the constable back in Fury if the man had turned Billy loose. While Frank Lord was a cold-blooded killer, he was not a liar. No, when you dealt with Frank Lord, you knew you were dealing with a man you could trust while also knowing he would kill you for a look he took a mild offense to.

His father, old Delbert, had been notoriously untrustworthy. Frank's word was his bond.

The way he saw it, his family had deserved to be kicked out of Fury. But that didn't mean Frank would ever let anyone do anything like that to him again.

Another reason he hadn't burned Fury till now was because of *her*. What had it been about her, anyway?

He'd have spared Claggett for her. But the constable had offended him when he'd refused to turn Billy loose. That had offended Frank deeply. He hated nothing so much as not being obeyed. Not obeying Frank showed that you disrespected him.

Frank hated not being respected. He'd been disrespected for far too long, growing up. When his family had been kicked out of Fury in disgrace, Frank had vowed to start a new life for himself and his younger brother and their half-sister, Eloise. Frank had vowed to never be disrespected again.

He'd left Fury alone for her...and to remind him of how far his family had once sunk.

"What're we stopping for, Frank?" Billy said, taking a pull from the bottle he'd taken out of the North Side just before he'd stolen the paint horse.

Frank sidled his black up to the paint, grabbed the bottle out of Billy's hand.

"Hey!" the younger Lord objected.

Frank tossed the bottle into the darkness with a grunt. It shattered on a rock.

"Frank, that was half-fu—*owww!*" Billy cried as Frank smashed the back of his gloved right hand against his younger brother's mouth. Holding both hands to his mouth, Billy gave Frank an exasperated look. "What the hell was that for?"

Frank pointed an admonishing finger at him and gritted his teeth as he barked out, "You got a man shot tonight, you damn fool!" He turned his head sideways and called into the pack of men flanking him and Billy, "Shanaghy, are you gonna make it?"

"Yeah, I'm gonna make it, Frank," came a pinched voice.

"No, you're not."

"It ain't my fault!" Billy said with deep indignance.

"Yes, it is your fault. You let yourself get arrested!"

"That ain't so hard to do, Frank! Bloody Joe's one savvy law-bringer!"

"You're no damn good, Billy!"

"Don't say that, Frank—damn ya!"

"You owe me, boy," Frank said. "If you weren't my brother and my only full-blood kin, I'd have left you in that cell to wait for the circuit judge."

"But, Frank, I—"

"Shut up!" Frank yelled as he smashed the back of his hand again across Billy's face again.

"*Ow!*"

Frank reached over and pulled the old Colt from Billy's holster, flipped it around, snatched it by the barrel, and thrust it butt-first into his younger brother's soft, bulging belly. "Like I said, you owe me. Now, go back there and shoot Shanaghy."

"Frank!" came the pinched voice again from the rear of the pack of riders stoically sitting their saddles.

At least, most were sitting stoically. The man who'd been wounded, Walt Shanaghy, sat crouched in his saddle at the rear of the pack, holding one arm across the wound in his guts. The bullet had been fired by one of the would-be "heroes" from one of the two saloons in Fury. To either side of the wounded man sat Frank's two lieutenants, Lou Bronco and Bryce Sager.

"I can make it, Frank!" Shanaghy said. "I swear I can make it."

Frank looked at Bronco, then Sager. Both men shook their heads.

"You can't make it, Shanaghy, an' you know it. I saw you take that bullet. It's bad. You know the rules. No slowin' the rest of us down."

"I won't slow you down!"

"You're already ridin' behind!" Again, Frank shoved the butt of Billy's Colt against the kid's belly. "Take it. Earn your keep, kid. It's the right thing to do."

Billy turned to scowl back toward the rear of the pack. "Gee, Frank. You really want me to shoot Shanaghy?"

"Someone's got to." This from the big Apache, Three Moons, sitting his gray mustang directly behind Frank. "Those're the rules."

Shanaghy said tightly from the rear of the pack, "Shit, I've dug two bullets out of your hide, Three Moons. An' remember that whore that cut you in Tucson? I shot her!"

Three Moons sat straight-backed in his saddle, staring straight ahead, no expression on his flat-planed, severely chiseled features. "Mine were flesh wounds. As for the whore—I wanted to kill her myself. If I took a bullet to the guts, I'd have put my gun to my head by now and blown my brains out." He whipped around in his saddle to stare at the wounded man. "I thought you had courage, Walt."

A couple of the other men, sitting their snorting, blowing mounts, chuckled.

"Silence!" Frank intoned. "This is no laughing matter. That's a good man there, wounded!" He pitched his voice low and soft with gravity. "About to die..."

"Ah, hell!" Shanaghy said, tightly, where he sat with his head bowed over his saddle.

He was a beefy, baby-faced man with a heavy beard carpeting cheeks turned beet red by the Southwestern sun. He'd been a cow puncher till he'd been caught stealing his boss's beef and selling it to nesters. Good with a gun, he'd shot several of the men his boss had sent to hang him. That had been down in western Texas.

He'd fled north and met Frank, Three Moons, Ford, and Sager in a saloon in Ruidoso. They'd all gotten drunk and whored together, and the next morning Shanaghy had found himself one of Lord's formidable riders. That had raised Shanaghy's chin and thrust his shoulders proudly back, for Frank Lord had already acquired a reputation by then.

Shanaghy's voice now trembled defiantly, fearfully as he spoke. "Frank, I don't deserve to die this way!"

Frank turned to say, "I'm sorry, Walt. We've had a good time. I will always remember you with a smile and will pass a bottle in your honor tonight around the fire. But our paths fork here."

He turned back to Billy, "Hurry up. We're burnin' starshine, an' we got miles to ride yet."

They were heading for McCullough's, an outlaw road ranch up near Crystal Peak in the San Juan Range. There, in addition to enjoying good liquor and the bodies of some of the best whores in the San Juans, they would be outfitted with grub and ammo for the long trail to Mexico, where the gang cooled its heels between jobs.

In this case, their last job had been a mining payroll shipment east of Gunnison, along the Taylor River in Taylor Canyon. They'd wiped out the entire contingent of Pinkertons and stolen the strongbox containing the payroll coins. They'd left no witnesses and covered their trail, so while they were not expecting to be shadowed, Frank Lord was a man who took no chances.

Each of his men had a sizable bounty on his head. Frank himself had a fifteen-hundred-dollar reward on his own, offered by the Atchison, Santa Fe, and Topeka Railway. A few packs of foolish bounty hunters had formed in the past just to shadow and take him and the rest of his gang down for the lucrative bounties to be paid out by banks, railroads, or stage lines.

So far, none had succeeded. But only because Frank Lord was not a man to let his guard down.

Most lawmen veered far wide of his formidable bunch, and they were smart to do so.

"Ah, hell, Frank," Billy groaned.

"Do it," Frank demanded, tightly.

"Frank!" Shanaghy pleaded.

The wounded rider booted his horse up from the rear of the pack and checked it down to Frank's left. Crouched low in the saddle, he jutted his fleshy, sweat-streaked, bearded face toward Frank.

"Dammit, Frank—you an' me been through a lot together these past three years. I've never slowed you down yet and I don't intend to slow you down—"

A revolver's sudden thunder cut him off.

Shanaghy grunted as the bullet plunked into his forehead. He fell like a fifty-pound sack of cracked corn off the left side of his saddle to hit the ground with a heavy thud. His horse whinnied and lurched ahead with a start.

Shanaghy jerked, broke wind, and lay still.

Frank turned to Billy who sat his stolen horse, smoking gun in his hand.

"Damn," Billy cried. "I plum forgot what a windy bastard he was!"

Frank looked down at the dead man. The others sat in silent shock, holding the reins of their prancing horses taut.

Frank turned to his younger brother and with an admiring smile said, "Not anymore he's not."

The others laughed, tentative, afraid to get their leader's dander up.

"Gonna bury him?" Three Moons asked.

"No time for such frivolities," Frank said.

He called for two men, two of the lesser lights in the dozen-man bunch—a pair of Mexicans—to drag the body off the trail.

CHAPTER 15

MANNION USED HIS RIGHT FOOT TO DRIVE THE SPADE into the flinty soil. With a grunt, he pulled up a shovelful of dirt and gravel and tossed it up onto the heap he'd spent the last hour piling beside the grave he now stood five feet deep in.

The stars were fading as the light grew with the coming of a brand-new day.

A day that Jeremiah Claggett would not see.

It was still dark down here at the bottom of the grave. Mannion would fully see the growing light of day when he climbed out of it. However, that darkness at the bottom of the pit was all Jeremiah would see now until the end of time.

Mannion looked at the cold earth of the grave walls surrounding him and gave an involuntary shudder. He cursed again—cursed himself, cursed Frank Lord and his gang of kill-crazy coyotes and cursed the fate that had brought them together in the form of Jeremiah Claggett lying dead on the ground above Mannion, near the pile of raw earth Joe had mounded.

He surveyed the hole and, deeming it deep enough to

keep the predators from bothering his dead friend, he tossed the shovel up out of the grave then planted his gloved hand on the edge of the hole and, with another weary grunt, hoisted himself out.

He leaned down to brush the dirt from the knees of his black denim trousers and to grab his hat and set it on his head. He turned to where Justina Claggett and the woman whose name Mannion had learned was Kansas Montrose—not her real name, of course—sat on the ground a few feet from the grave.

Justy had chosen the gravesite on a slight rise behind the cabin, which sat in a horseshoe of a picturesque creek complete with a waterfall. Until only a few hours ago, she had shared the cabin with her grandfather, surrounded by forest, a creek, and the falls.

The girl was deeply grieved now.

So was Kansas Montrose.

Joe would be damned if the old scudder, likely having taken Mannion's own example, hadn't gone and proposed to the gal.

And then he'd been taken a knife to the guts.

The two women sat several feet apart, staring in mute shock and bereavement at the blanket-wrapped body of the old constable, the dawn breeze playing with their hair. They each had their knees raised to their chests, arms wrapped around them, forlorn casts to their gazes. The only sounds were birds, the breeze in the new spring leaves and branches, and the falls tumbling raucously with fresh snowmelt from higher up in the mountains, into the creek a couple hundred feet away, just east of the cabin.

Kansas Montrose had ridden with Justy and Mannion out from Fury, riding double on Justy's mount. The woman hadn't changed out of her nightgown and cream wrap. She hadn't wanted to leave Jeremiah. She'd found a blanket in the jailhouse, as yet untouched by the fire; it lay across her shoulders now.

Just before the sun had risen, Joe had seen the ominous glow in the sky, gradually fading. Now it was almost midmorning, and he was burning daylight. He'd wanted to lay Jeremiah to rest. That was the least he could do for his old friend, one of the few he had in this world.

"It's time," Mannion said to Justy. "Let's do what we're gonna do here. I should get moving." It had sounded harsher than he'd intended, but the urge to get after Frank Lord was keen.

He aimed to trail the gang. There were too many for him to take down alone, but he figured that if he planned it well, he had a good chance of killing Frank Lord before the rest of them turned him toe down.

It was the least he could do for his old friend.

Mannion's taking on the gang alone was not fair to Jane Ford, whom he'd recently married and was building a house for. It wasn't fair to his own daughter, Evangeline either.

But his getting Jeremiah killed hadn't been fair to Justy and the whore who called herself Kansas Montrose. Whatever she was, she'd obviously loved Jeremiah.

Justy, appearing worn-out and pale, eyes swollen from crying, looked at the blanket-wrapped body, and nodded.

There was no time for building a coffin. The blanket would have to do.

Heavily, the women gained their feet.

Mannion removed his hat. "Either of you want to say anything?"

The two women looked at each other.

Kansas shook her head. "What's there to say?"

The girl looked down at her grandfather. "I'm not good at words but I will say this..." She looked at Mannion and slitted her eyes and hardened her jaws with barely bridled rage. "I'm going to ride along with Joe Mannion and see that you are avenged, abuelito!"

Mannion looked at her, shook his head. "No, you're not."

"I am!"

"Nope."

"Dios mio, you owe me that!" She drew a breath, let it out slowly and looked down at her grandfather again. "Your turn."

Mannion dropped his own gaze to his friend, dead because of him. "I'm sorry, Jeremiah. I'm not much good with words, either, but I will say this." He shuttled his gaze back to Justy, put some steel in his hawk-like gaze. "I won't get your granddaughter killed too."

He set his hat on his head then crouched down over the blanket-wrapped body and lifted the dead constable up off the ground. He carried the body around the pile of dirt and gravel and lay it down beside the grave. He dropped his legs into the grave then reached up for the body and lay it down at his feet.

He climbed back out and, Justy burning holes of bitter hatred into his back, filled in the grave.

It took him nearly thirty minutes to get all the dirt and gravel back into the hole, but it, too, was something that needed to be done. When he finished, he turned to Justy sitting where she'd been sitting before.

"Best mound it good with rocks, keep the predators away."

He turned to the whore and said, "Don't let her follow me."

Kansas glanced at Justy then pursed her lips and nodded.

Joe walked over to where Red stood nearby, tied to a branch of the cottonwood. Joe untied the reins, swung up into the saddle. He looked down at Justy. She stared up at him, her face pale and drawn with grief, her Spanish-dark eyes bitterly defiant.

"If I see you on my backtrail, I'll tan your hide."

He neck-reined Red and rode away.

———

TWENTY MINUTES LATER, MANNION REINED UP ON A high hill just west of Fury.

A couple of hundred yards beyond lay what remained of the town. Not much. It had been reduced to smoldering rubble. The fire had scorched deep into the bunch grass, coyote willows, and sage brush beyond the town's peripheries before burning itself out. As it was late spring, the brush likely hadn't had a chance to dry out enough to burn.

Flames and thick, black smoke licked up from charred, black mounds of the log and wood frame buildings along both sides of the main drag and the small cabins, stables, and privies flanking it. A few of the cabins appeared to have been untouched by the fire though most of them had been or were still being consumed.

The acrid stench of the burning rubble was rife on the warm breeze. Mannion had started smelling it and seeing the rising smoke a mile back along the trail.

Surveying the ruins, he frowned suddenly.

He thought he'd glimpsed movement down there among the buffeting flags of smoke.

He reached back into a saddlebag pouch for his field

glasses, lifted them to his eyes, and adjusted the focus until the twin spheres of magnified vision became one. The thing he'd seen moving around among the rubble on the main street, obscured by the wasping guidons of heavy smoke, clarified into a horse and rider.

A smallish man in range gear—black hat and black vest over a gray shirt. He rode a blaze-faced dun. The same man Joe had seen in Fury the night before, before he'd suddenly lit a shuck.

"You again."

Mannion returned the field glasses to his saddlebags then clucked Red on down the hill at a gallop. By the time he had ridden into the burned-out town—now even the jail was only a smoking pile of glowing cinders around four scorched cells and a potbelly stove—the man again was gone. Joe peered through the billowing guidons of thick, acrid smoke.

Nothing but smoke issuing from the charred piles of wood on each side of the broad main street. The dead, Joe saw, had been dragged away by the living. The living who were now, no doubt, homeless.

"Hey!" Mannion called as he spurred Red into a forward trot, his eyes blinking against the sting of the smoke. "Who are you?"

Hooves drummed as the big bay shot straight down the main street. Red galloped through an especially thick fog of charcoal smoke. Joe couldn't see more than a few feet in any direction. After a dozen long strides, horse and rider emerged from the fog.

Mannion checked the bay down to a skidding halt and looked around. He was at the eastern edge of what remained of Fury.

Joe shuttled his gaze from right to left. He stared

straight ahead along the trail. The San Juans humped slate-gray to his right.

Nothing.

Suddenly, he picked up the distant drumming of hooves.

He swung his gaze left to see the horse and rider just then riding up out of a cedar-stippled canyon at the southern edge of Fury. The man in the black hat and vest and gray shirt was hunkered low in the saddle, casting cautious glances behind him, as the dun climbed a shelving, rock-studded scarp. Horse and rider crested the scarp then dropped down its far side, out of sight.

Joe cursed.

He considered riding after him but nixed the idea. Doubtful it was one of Lord's men. Why would one linger behind the others? No point in putting Red through a ride like that. Joe had bigger fish to fry.

He hardened his jaws at the thought of it. Unconsciously, he loosened the Yellowboy in its scabbard then clucked the big bay ahead along the trail and began looking for the tracks of the killers' horses.

CHAPTER 16

JUSTY GRABBED HER WINCHESTER FROM WHERE IT leaned against the wall by the cabin's open door and set it on the table with the lamp she'd left lit for her abuelito the night before still burning.

She grabbed two boxes of cartridges from a cupboard above the dry sink then pulled abuelito's pistol belt off the wall peg where she'd hung it when she'd removed it from his body.

She intended to kill Lord and his men with her grand-father's old Colt.

Justy had a feeling abuelito would smile in heaven at that.

She smiled now, bitterly, as she dug a thong out of a pocket of her denim jeans, gathered her long hair back behind her head in a queue, and wrapped the thong around it. She needed no distractions, including her hair. She planted one knee on a bench at the table where she and her abuelito had dined together, opened a box of .44 shells, and went to work thumbing the cartridges through the Winchester's loading gate.

Footsteps sounded behind her.

She glanced over her shoulder to see Kansas Montrose approach the cabin. She was still barefoot, and her hair hung long and disheveled, her eyes swollen from crying.

Imagine that, Justy thought. The old man had wanted to get married.

Funny he hadn't told Justy. She'd never even suspected.

She guessed there was a lot about folks, even those you loved most in the world, you knew nothing about.

"Justy," the woman said as she stopped in the open doorway, holding the old striped blanket around her heavy, bowed shoulders. "What're you doing?"

"Forget it." Justy cocked the Winchester then off-cocked the hammer and set the carbine back down on the table.

"The marshal, he said—"

Justy wheeled to her, eyes ablaze. "I don't give a good goddamn what Joe Mannion said!"

The whore's shoulders slumped further, and she lowered her head like a cowed dog. Slowly, she came into the cabin, pulled out a chair, and sagged heavily into it.

Justy pulled the old Colt from the cracked and worn leather holster and flicked open the loading gate. She spun the cylinder then slipped a cartridge into the chamber that abuelito had always kept empty beneath the old Colt's hammer for safety. Going after Lord's gang, she'd need all the chambers filled.

Besides, she didn't have a dick to blow off. She'd made the crack to the old man once, and his lower jaw had nearly tumbled to the floor in exasperation.

She chewed her lips to keep from bawling now at the memory.

"You'll die," the whore said, staring sadly down at the

table, tracing the flowered pattern in the oilcloth with her finger. "Just like your grandfather."

"So be it."

Justy slid the gun back into its holster, wrapped the shell belt around her waist, and buckled it.

She grabbed a sack of food from the table. Moving to the door, she pulled her battered tan Stetson off a wall peg and set it on her head. She pulled a canvas coat off another peg and draped it over her left shoulder. She set the Winchester on her right shoulder, glanced behind her at the whore and said, "Help yourself to whatever you find in here. I don't have time to mound abuelito's grave with rocks—will you do it?"

She didn't wait for an answer before striding off to the corral and stable flanking the cabin. She saddled the grulla, mounted up, and rode back around the cabin to the front.

The whore stood in the open doorway. "Dear girl," she said in quiet reproval, slowly shaking her head.

Justy looked at the falls tumbling from a ridge into the creek, sixty yards beyond the far side of the cabin, near a bend in the stream. A picturesque falls in the summer, after the waters had settled after the melt. A storybook falls. One of the main reasons her grandfather had chosen the sight for the cabin. Justy gave an angry grunt then turned her head forward and booted the horse out toward the trail that would take her to Fury, or at least to what was left of it.

She kept her head forward, her expression determined. But she had to fight her grief, put an end to the incessant sobs that kept bubbling up out of her throat and which had no place here on the vengeance trail.

When she came to the large black pile of smoldering ruins that was now Fury, she rode around the town, parts of which were still burning, wanting to avoid the smoke and cinders. Back on the main trail just east of Fury, she picked up the overlaid tracks of many horses—likely Lords' gang as well as Joe Mannion's.

According to Kansas and the men in town, when Lord's gang had left Fury in flames, they'd headed east along the main trail. That was all that Justy knew. Where they were headed, she had no idea. But she'd track them. She might not have known anything about hunting men, but she knew a thing about tracking and hunting animals.

One couldn't be all that different from the other.

She'd track Mannion tracking the killers. When the lawman ran them down, she'd find a way to kill the Lord brothers. She'd wait for Mannion to distract them. That would be her opportunity to avenge abuelito...

A careful hunter, she followed the tracks of her prey for several miles along the main trail. She knew she was following Mannion and Lord's gang because, except for a few remaining prospectors and cow punchers, hardly anyone ever used these trails out here around Fury anymore.

Around noon, she heard loud barking and screeching off the trail's right side. She turned to see buzzards swarming over something on the ground over there while several more traced lazy circles fifty feet in the air.

She rode to within twenty feet of the commotion then swung down and, because she did not want to alert Mannion that she was behind him, used rocks instead of bullets to frighten the carrion eaters away. Several of the ragged-looking, bald headed beasts held their ground, squawking and barking angrily, leaping challengingly forward, copper eyes bright with rage.

Justy tossed a few more rocks and when the last stubborn carrion-eater had flapped its broad wings and leaped awkwardly into flight, she walked over to stare down at what they'd been feeding on.

She'd started smelling the stench several steps back but now she raised her bandanna to her mouth as her eyes watered at the sickly-sweet smell of blood and death. Blinking the tears from her eyes, she stared down at the bloody remains only long enough to know that she was looking at a man's body.

Or what remained of it after the birds had found him.

Judging by the grisly carnage before her, they'd been feeding on him for several hours. There wasn't enough left to tell much about him, other than he wasn't Mannion.

One of Lord's men, maybe.

Justy grabbed her reins, swung back up onto the grulla's back, and resumed her hunt.

When her prey turned off onto a secondary trail that jogged off toward the hulking purple stone anvils of the San Juan Range, she swung the grulla onto the secondary trail, as well. The miles and the hours piled up.

She followed the trail through rugged country until she found herself in a hanging valley on the lower western reaches of the range. The valley was mostly in shadow now, as it was late in the day.

She stopped an hour later when, in the gloaming, she found a suitable place for a camp along a winding, rock-lined creek. It was well sheltered from sight by trees and boulders, so she thought she could build a small campfire and cook some beans and bacon. She was desperate to run down Frank and Billy Lord but she needed to sustain herself and the grulla.

Before making camp, she turned the horse around and gigged it back in the direction from which she'd come. Just ahead, the trail dropped down through a break in a granite wall. She stopped the grulla in this corridor of sorts and gazed down into the canyon beyond, looking for any sign of movement down there in that dinosaur's mouth of earth carved by an ancient river through bullet-shaped mounds of ancient lava and choked with aspens and firs.

As she'd ridden through the canyon earlier, following the tracks of the men she hunted, she'd had the uneasy feeling she hadn't been alone. She'd stopped several times to look behind her but had spied no one on her back trail.

Still, the uneasy feeling persisted.

Probably just nerves. She hadn't been this far from home in a long time. Not since the last hunting trip she and abuelito had taken last fall to fill their larder with elk meat for the winter. Not only was she farther from home than she was accustomed to, she was on the trail of some very dangerous men.

She hadn't expected to be scared. But now she realized from her rapid heartbeat and the tightness of the muscles between her shoulders that she was, indeed, scared.

What had abuelito said about fear?

Face it.

She reined the grulla around and booted it back into the trees and rocks until she came to the shore of the narrow creek bubbling over its stony bed. This side of the mountains hadn't seen much snow the previous winter, so most of the snowmelt had dropped down onto the plains, making for easier travel now when travel was usually almost impossible until June. There was a clearing along the shore, in a sort of horseshoe of rocks and budding aspens, with the ridge wall behind her on the other side of the stream.

She stopped here, unsaddled the grulla, piled the tack near where she intended to build her fire, then hobbled the horse so it could graze freely.

Chicken flesh rose between her shoulders.

She gave a shudder and, crossing her arms beneath her breasts, hugging herself as though chilled, she took another careful look around.

There were only the breeze-brushed trees, grass, and sage, birds flitting around the aspen branches, and a squirrel giving her hell from the top of a flame-shaped boulder. A pinecone dropped from a branch and landed on the forest floor with a soft thud.

She walked over to her tack, slid her rifle from its boot, walked back over to where she could peer through the trees back toward the trail she'd been following, and loudly levered a cartridge into the rifle's action.

"Who's there?" she called, tightly.

The only response was the sighing of the breeze in the tree crowns and the whirring sound it made as it came up against the bastion-like granite wall on the other side of the creek behind her.

"I know you're out there," she said. "Show yourself!"

She waited.

A few seconds passed.

Soft thuds sounded. She jerked with a slight start when she saw a horse and rider slowly moving toward her, weaving through the trees.

CHAPTER 17

"HELLO, THE CAMP," THE RIDER SAID AS HE AND HIS horse—a black with one white stocking—moved slowly through the trees.

He was an older gent in buckskins and a battered leather hat. He had a gray beard and long, pewter-colored hair hanging down from beneath the hat. He wore a big revolver over his bulging belly, and two big bowie knives were sheathed on his hips. His buckskins were badly bloodstained. Flies followed him as he drew to within fifty yards of Justy and kept coming, the buzzing of the flies growing louder.

"Uh-uh," Justy said, keeping the rifle aimed at the stranger, who was grinning as he cocked his head slightly to one side and narrowed one eye at her. "That's far enough. I got here first, and I prefer to camp alone."

Still grinning, the squat oldster said, "You campin' alone out here—eh, little girl?"

Justy loudly pumped a cartridge into the chamber and tightened her grip on the Winchester. "Not quite alone!"

The last word had barely left her mouth when she

heard the soft snap of a twig behind her. A long shadow slid across the ground on her left. Dread touched Justy.

She started to turn but made it only a couple of inches before thick, buckskin-clad arms snaked around her waist and grabbed her in a bear hug that punched the air out of her lungs in a single exhalation. The man behind her squealed a laugh and lifted Justy up off her feet, yelling, "Damn tootin' she's all alone, Silas! Just like we thought! An' she's a keeper, too!"

As the rifle barrel came up, Justy's right index finger inadvertently drew back on the trigger. The rifle thundered, the bullet caroming skyward. She screamed, "Let me go, goddamn you!"

She kicked at the man who held her taut against him. She swung her elbows savagely back behind her, trying to connect with no success with the man's head. She struck only his shoulders glancing blows. The sickly-sweet odor of dead meat left out too long in the sun and of unwashed male assaulted her nostrils as the man, hooting and hollering, spun her around in a complete circle.

As she spun around again, she saw the squat man ride up to her quickly. He ripped the rifle out of her hands and tossed it back over his shoulder and into the brush.

The rifle had no sooner thudded to the ground than the big man holding Justy suddenly tipped her upside down and sent her flying nearly straight down to the ground. She struck with a blow that made her ears ring and her eyes dim. It dazed her, caused the darkening grass and gravel of the clearing to pitch around her.

"Now, let's see what we got here, Gil!" the squat man said as he knelt down in front of Justy and with a single pull with both his gloved hands ripped her shirt wide open, causing bone buttons to fly in all directions.

"Whoo-hoo!" he hollered.

Regaining at least part of her senses, Justy hardened her jaws and delivered a hard punch to the man's left cheek.

"Why, you little catamount!" he raged and slapped her back.

Justy flopped back down against the ground, stunned once more.

Silas rose to his feet and grinned down at her though his cheeks behind his gray beard were red with fury. "Now, then, I'm goin' first, Gil. Age before beauty—ha! Hold her down, old son." He ran the back of his fist against the gash Justy had opened on his cheek. "Why, that gnarly little catamount opened up my cheek fer me!"

Again regaining her senses, Justy gave a cat-like scream and rammed her left foot into Silas's crotch.

He wailed and doubled over.

"Oh, shit, Silas!" Gil said.

Justy shifted around on her butt and with another enraged screech rammed her right boot into Gil's crotch, unable to connect as solidly as she had with Silas's oysters. It did the trick, though. Gil, too, doubled over with an indignant yell.

"Gutless bastards!" Justy screamed as she gained her feet and ran toward the black horse standing a dozen feet away, watching the violent happenings with its head down and a dubious look in its dark-brown eyes.

As Justy reached for the old Spencer repeater jutting up from the soft, brown leather scabbard strapped to the horse's saddle on its right side, the walnut stock angled back across the black's hip, the mount whickered and sidled away.

Justy's fingers slid off the stock and brass butt place.

"Dammit!" she cried then stepped toward the skittish mount again, and again reached for the rifle.

She got it halfway out of the scabbard. Running foot thuds sounded behind her. She heard a man grunting angrily as he ran toward her.

"Oh, no you don't!" Silas bellowed just before he slammed his short, lumpy bulk into Justy's right side.

She went down hard with another scream, Silas landing on top of her then rising to his knees between her spread legs. Gil was running up to her now too. Silas slid one of the savage bowies from its Indian-beaded scabbard and held it up for Justy to see—a good ten inches of razor-edged steel.

"I'm gonna ride you hard, you little bitch, and then I'm gonna cut your tits off, you little polecat!"

"I wouldn't do that," came another voice from farther away, from the direction of the creek.

Silas looked around, frowning.

So did Gil, who was standing eight feet to Silas's left.

"Where the hell did that come from?" Silas asked.

Justy lifted her own curious gaze and peered between her two tormentors to see a man standing in the fork of a slender aspen near the edge of the salmon-tinted water. He was short and bandy-legged. He wore a black Stetson with a tattered brim and brown, brush-scarred chaps and cracked brown vest over a gray shirt.

The man, somewhere in his twenties, had a weary, uncertain, slightly wayward look about him, and the carbine he aimed toward Silas and Gil appeared to be shaking slightly in his hands.

He said, "The girl don't seem all that interested in your attentions. Best clear out, I'd say."

"Mind your own damn business, sonny!" Silas said.

The man lowered the barrel of his Winchester slightly and triggered a round into the grass and gravel a foot right of Gil's right foot. Gil jumped with a yowl. The crashing report made the black horse back farther away, regarding the rifle-wielding stranger anxiously, twitching its ears.

"Told you to clear out," the stranger with the rifle said.

Silas and Gil shared a look. Justy sat up, holding her shirt closed across her thin chemise.

"All right," Silas said finally, holding his gloved hands up, palms out. "We're clearin' out." He glanced at Gil. "Go fetch your horse, Gil. I can see the stranger means business." He winked. The stranger with the rifle probably didn't see it.

"All right," Gil said, also holding up his hands. "Just gonna fetch my hoss," he told the stranger.

He edged away from Justy, moving tentatively, keeping his hands raised, toward where Justy could see a brown horse standing a good ways upstream of the stranger with the rifle.

"That's the right decision," the stranger said, sliding the rifle from Gil to Silas and then back to Gil.

Justy thought he looked nervous, not sure how to cover both men at the same time now that they were moving apart. The rifle-wielding stranger's nerves made Justy nervous, as well.

She glanced to her left to see Silas side-stepping toward the black. She glanced to her right to see Gil walking toward the brown horse, sort of twisted around at the waist, keeping his eyes on the nervous man with the rifle. Suddenly, Gil glanced over his shoulder at Silas. Silas looked at Gil, and nodded.

Justy held her breath.

Gil stopped suddenly, turned to face the stranger, and palmed the Colt out of the holster on his right hip. The stranger fired at Gil, but his bullet flew wide and plunked into a tree over Gil's left shoulder.

"Damn!" the rifle-wielding stranger said as he jacked another round into his rifle's chamber.

Gil triggered lead at the stranger while running toward the brush along the river. The stranger returned fire at Gil. Gil squealed, twisted around, and fell awkwardly in the brush while triggering another errant round at the stranger.

Silas was returning fire at the stranger now, too, whooping and hollering. The stranger had dropped down behind the bole of the aspen. He racked another round into his rifle's chamber, aimed through the fork in the tree, and fired.

Justy turned to see Silas leap up and howl as the rifle-wielding stranger's bullet tore into his right leg, just above his knee.

"You son of a bitch!" Silas yelled and fired awkwardly at the rifle-wielding stranger.

The stranger ducked again then lifted his head and fired another round just as Silas turned and ran limping toward the black. The stranger's bullet took Silas in the dead center of his back, punching Silas forward and down to strike the ground with a resolute thud and a groan.

Silas flopped around, groaning.

Justy looked at the stranger. He was looking toward where Gil was running off through the brush toward the brown horse. The stranger fired two more rounds at Gil, but his bullets merely blew up sand and gravel wide of the would-be rapist. The stranger cursed as Gil grabbed the brown's reins, fairly leaped into the saddle, then swung the horse around and galloped up stream, casting wary looks behind him.

"Damn!" the stranger said, lowering his rifle and

thumbing his battered hat up off his forehead, still watching Gil flee on the brown. "Doggone it, anyways!" He stepped out from behind the tree and looked at Justy. His faded red neckerchief danced in the breeze. "I been practicin'. I know it don't look like it, but I have been." He spat and shook his head. "I reckon it's different, though—shootin' airtight tins off tree stumps."

"Reckon." Holding her torn shirt closed with one hand, Justy pushed to her feet.

She walked over to where Silas lay belly down, groaning. The black had run off. Justy crouched to scoop Silas's Colt off the ground. She clicked the hammer back and aimed down at the back of Silas's head. His hat had tumbled off, and the top of his bald, pink head was flecked with lice.

Justy stared down at the wounded man. Her hand shook as she aimed the Colt.

She'd never shot a man before. Could she do it?

The Colt continued to shake in her hands.

She glanced over her shoulder at the stranger. He stood watching her, letting his rifle hang down against his leg in his right hand. He had a wary look in his eyes as he regarded the girl aiming the Colt down at the back of Silas's head.

Silas stopped groaning and lay still in the grass, sage brush, and gravel.

Justy was glad. She comforted herself with the thought that Frank Lord would be different. She wouldn't hesitate when the time came to kill Frank and Billy Lord. She wasn't sure why she'd hesitated to kill Silas. The man had threatened to rape her and cut her tits off.

Still, she had. She wouldn't hesitate when it came time to kill the Lord brothers, though. She was sure of it. She'd just now learned it wasn't easy to kill a man, even vermin like Silas. Still, she could and when the time came, she would.

She dropped the gun down beside the dead man. She glanced at the stranger again then turned toward where Gil had galloped upstream. Nothing there now but the dying, salmon rays of the setting sun glinting off the water. The shooting had caused the birds to grow silent though now a few piped again, tentatively.

Justy's grulla had sidled off during the shooting to stand regarding her from a good ways off in the brush, reins drooping to the ground.

Justy walked over and grabbed the horse's reins and led it back to where she'd plopped her tack and possibles down on the ground. The stranger stood regarding her as he had before, a strange pensiveness in his gaze, head cocked to one side, battered black hat shoved up above the tan line of his forehead.

"Thanks for the help," Justy said as she stooped to begin recovering her shirt buttons. She tried to keep her voice from quavering the way the rest of her was. "I was just gonna build a fire for coffee before I was so rudely interrupted. You're welcome to some. I tend to scorch it, but..." She stopped retrieving the buttons to add, "As long as that's all you want. I've plumb had my fill of men today."

"I'll fetch my hoss," the stranger said, then shouldered his rifle and walked downstream.

CHAPTER 18

FIFTEEN MINUTES LATER, JUSTY HAD REMOVED HER shirt, intending to sew the buttons back on later. She'd put on her only other one in her saddlebags—a green plaid work shirt similar to the one Silas had ripped the buttons off of. A girl needed few silk blouses when either picking and shoveling rocks underground or wearing a deputy town constable's badge in a near ghost town. She'd knotted her red bandanna around her neck and was gathering firewood when the stranger rode his blaze-faced dun up from the river and around the tree through whose fork he'd fired at Silas and Gil.

He came on slowly, looking Justy over with a queer expression on his somewhat hang-dog, slack-jawed face. He had some patchy beard stubble but probably didn't need to shave very often. He had something on his mind, but Justy didn't think it was lust. He looked...well, he looked troubled.

Did he feel guilty about killing Silas?

Justy dropped the load of wood she'd gathered beside a stone ring someone else had built and in which, judging by the scorched rocks, a good many travelers had built fires in over the years. Probably prospectors and wood cutters. Game hunters like Gil and Silas. And outlaws. Plenty of outlaws. This was outlaw country, indeed.

She dusted her pants off and said, "What's your name?"

"Me," the queer stranger said. "I'm, uh..." He paused to dismount the dun then turned to Justy as he loosened the saddle cinch. "I'm George. George Wilkes."

"I see." Justy didn't believe him, but she let it go. Many men in these parts had reasons for made-up names. "I'm Justy."

"George Wilkes" lifted his hat in a poor imitation of gentlemanly decorum and set it back down on his head. "Pleased to meet you, Miss Justy."

"What're you doin' out here?" She knew better than to ask strangers such questions in outlaw country but despite that she'd nearly been raped and had her tits cut off, she didn't find herself feeling afraid of this man. Just curious about him though she wasn't quite sure why.

Maybe because he seemed curious about her.

She dropped to her knees and set to work breaking up smaller branches for tinder and kindling to start a fire. As she did, she looked up at Wilkes as he set his saddle down in front of an aspen near the fire ring. "Me?" he said again as though there were anyone else here she might be asking. He straightened with a grunt and grinned. "I'm a bounty hunter."

"You're a bounty hunter?" Justy asked, unable to keep the skepticism out of her voice.

"Sure enough."

"A bounty hunter who can't shoot straight."

Again, he grinned in his off-putting way. "That's right."

"You new to the trade, are you, Mister Wilkes?"

"Oh, do call me George. And...nah, nah, I been huntin' thieves and killers for quite a few years now. I usually just take 'em down a little closer up. I'm better with my old hogleg"—he patted the holster in which his revolver sat—"than I am with the long gun."

Justy was blowing on fledgling flames. "I see." She looked up at him. "Who you after?"

"Same as you, I reckon. Frank and Billy Lord."

"Ah." Justy frowned. "How'd you get on their trail?"

"I followed Frank out of Hardville. Sorry I couldn't catch up to him before he burned your town." The man who called himself George Wilkes had draped a feed sack over his horse's snout and was rubbing the animal down with a scrap of burlap while the horse munched parched corn. Sweat foam bubbled up around the burlap as he worked at the soaked hide where the pad and saddle had been. "I assume it was your town. I seen you in it last night."

"You did?"

"I did." He grunted and gritted his teeth as he scrubbed the burlap over the dun's rump, and glanced over his shoulder at Justy. "Who was the old man I seen you so sad about?"

Justy turned her mouth corners down as she fed some small branches to the flames crackling in the fire ring. "My grandfather. He was the town constable. Frank Lord gutted him, left him to die slow though all he was doing was his job—keeping Frank's brother Billy locked up in his jail." She glanced up at Wilkes who'd stopped rubbing down the dun to stare sadly down at her. "It's Joe Mannion's fault," she said. "He was careless with my grandfather's life, but that's who Bloody Joe is. Only thinks of himself."

Was it really Joe's fault? Had she had no hand in it, herself?

"Mannion, eh? See him in town with you last night."

Justy frowned suspiciously at Wilkes. "Why didn't you show yourself?"

Wilkes shrugged a shoulder, glanced off, hesitating. "Seen it was a private moment. I circled around to get on Lord's trail."

"You were ahead of me and Mannion both. How come you were behind me? At least, I assume you were behind me...and behind them two, shadowin' me." She glanced into the gloaming now where Silas lay belly down in the sage.

Wilkes stared down at the flames Justy was building into a small but hot cookfire. He seemed perplexed, pondering with suspicious deliberation over his words. When he finally figured out what to say, he met her probing gaze. "I'm a man to watch his back trail, Miss Justy. I had to stop and reset a shoe on my hoss, ol' Chester. Took me awhile. Mannion got ahead of me."

Wilkes glanced at the dun munching cracked corn from the sack. "Spied you on my back trail...then them two. I let you three get ahead...since I didn't know what your intentions were, you see? This is outlaw country. Thought maybe one of you was after my hoss or my guns. You never know."

"Right."

"When I heard you scream, I moved off the trail to check it out."

"Well, I'm glad you did, George Wilkes." Justy straightened and dusted off her hands. "I'm mighty appreciative. I let my guard down. Damn silly."

She couldn't help castigating herself. How on God's green earth was she going to bring down Frank and Billy

Lord if she couldn't even prevent two vermin like Silas and Gil from nearly raping and killing her on her first day on the trail?

"Don't beat yourself up about it," Wilkes said. "It happens." He curled another smile. "Of course, not to me, but..."

"I know—you're a seasoned bounty hunter and I'm just a girl."

"Well, that much is plain, but there ain't no 'just' in it." Wilkes curled a wry half-smile.

"At ease, George."

He gave a snort then dropped to his knees and dug some trail gear and foodstuffs from a war bag. "I got fresh supplies including sow belly and coffee, even a can of peaches. I'll provide if you cook." That grin again. "I ain't had a woman cook for me in a month of Sundays."

———

AFTER THE MEAL, SINCE JUSTY HAD COOKED, THE MAN who called himself George Wilkes washed the dishes in the creek then returned them to his warbag. He yawned, stretched, and, since it was good dark now and they'd been hearing coyotes since the sun had set and the stars had come out, he said, "I reckon I'd best drag that carcass off. Might lure the wolves and wildcats in."

Justy glanced off in the direction Gil had lit a shuck then turned to Wilkes. "How bad did you hit the other one, you think?"

Wilkes winced. "Prob'ly only grazed him."

"He might be back, then," Justy pointed out. "We'd best take turns keepin' watch."

"I know," Wilkes said, a tad defensively. "I already had that one figured out, Miss Justy. Remember, I'm—"

"I know, I know. You're a seasoned bounty hunter."

He hooked that grin.

"You sure don't look like a seasoned bounty hunter, George," Justy pointed out. She was sitting on her saddle, sewing the buttons back on her shirt. She regarded the worn condition of his clothes, the hang-dog set of his features, the uncertainty in his eyes.

"What do I look like?"

Justy poked her needle through a button and drew out the needle and thread. "A saddle tramp. No offense."

"None taken. That's how I want to look. Keeps 'em guessin'."

"Yeah, well, you got me guessin'."

What sounded like a wolf howl rose from the buttes on the far side of the gurgling stream. Wilkes said, "I'll be right back."

He walked out into the darkness beyond where they'd hobbled their horses. Beneath the crackling of the flames, Justy could hear him grunting and the sound of a body dragging along the ground. A few minutes later there was a splash. Crunching footsteps sounded and Wilkes returned, a little breathless, brushing his gloved hands together.

"He'll be well downstream in a few minutes." Wilkes sat on a rock and began poking at the fire with a stick. "Make a nice meal for the carrion eaters." He chuckled.

"At least he'll have done some good on this earth."

Wilkes poked at the fire some more then looked up at Justy, the flames dancing across his face, which wasn't really unhandsome, just raw, and he could use a shave. "I'm sorry about your grandfather."

"So am I."

"You figure to get back at the Lord brothers for that?"

"I do."

"Suppose Mannion beats you to them?"

"I'll get my licks in." Justy looked across the fire. "I figure Mannion will distract them for me. While they're throwing down on him, I'll sneak around behind the Lord brothers and shoot them both in the back. I don't intend to kill them right off. I want them to see who shot 'em. And I want them to know *why* I shot them. I want them to crawl around some, begging me for mercy."

Wilkes poured himself a cup of coffee and blew into the steam. "You sure are determined."

"I am." She looked across the fire at him again. "You figurin' on riding with me?"

Wilkes shrugged and sipped his coffee again. "Don't see why not. Since we're headin' in the same direction."

"I don't know," Justy said, frowning at him again curiously. "There's something off about you, George."

"You can trust me, if that's what you're wonderin'. We'll split the reward if we get to Frank's bunch before Mannion does."

"Frank?" Again, Justy gave Wilkes a suspicious look. "Do you know him or somethin'."

"Hell, no." Wilkes gazed sheepishly down at his smoking cup. "I reckon I've studied on him some, though. Been trailin' him for quite a while." He shrugged a shoulder and looked at Justy across the fire. "Maybe in a way I do know him. Well enough to know his habits... well enough to help you take him down. And, believe me, you are gonna need help. Maybe not with Billy. He's just a whelp. But with ol' Frank and that big redskin, Three Moons, and Sager an' Ford."

Justy only grunted at that and started sewing the last button on her shirt.

Wilkes looked at her for a long time. Again, she had a hard time wondering what was going on behind those light-brown eyes of his. He looked downright...well...sad. Maybe guilty, though she had no idea what he had to feel guilty about.

At least, she found him no threat. And she supposed they might as well ride together. She wouldn't have admitted it to anyone, but after what had happened earlier, she felt a little off her feed. It was kind of nice to share the camp with someone.

Wilkes was a mystery, but he was sort of nice to have around and share the cooking duties with, at least. And it was true that she was going to need help bringing down Frank and Billy and as many of the rest of the gang as she could.

Suddenly, Wilkes lifted his eyes to gaze into the darkness beyond the fire.

"What is it?" Justy said.

"I heard something."

Justy pricked her ears and turned to look into the darkness over her left shoulder. She frowned and looked back at her trail mate. "I didn't hear—"

She stopped when one of the horses whickered softly. They were both standing stiffly, staring off into the darkness where Wilkes was still staring.

"See?" He rose, picked up his rifle, and stepped away from the fire.

Justy dropped the shirt and the needle and thread, grabbed her own rifle from where it leaned against a near tree, and rose and followed Wilkes out into the darkness. He stopped at the edge of the firelight. Justy stopped beside him. Her heart had picked up its beat.

"See anything?" she whispered.

"Hell, no. I been starin' into those flames too long. Gotta wait a minute, get my eyes used to the dark." He strode forward. "Wait here in case some circles around for the horses."

Justy stood watching the young, bandy-legged man, who looked more like a grubline-riding cow puncher than a seasoned bounty hunter, stride slowly off into the darkness. A minute later, there were thrashing and running sounds.

"Hold it!" George shouted.

A gun flashed. There was the quick metallic rasp of a cartridge being racked. The gun flashed again maybe fifty yards beyond Justy. There was a yelp. The running sounds stopped. They were replaced by the heavy thud and grunt of a body striking the ground.

There was the metallic rasp of the rifle once more. Walking sounds. The sounds stopped for a minute and then resumed again, growing louder as the walker approached.

Justy watched Wilkes's shadow take shape before her and then his eyes reflected the light of the fire behind her. She could hear him breathing, excited-like. He shook his head and grinned.

"Got him true that time!"

"The other one?"

"For certain-sure." Grinning, Wilkes walked past her. "This calls for another cup of coffee. Wish I had some whiskey!"

He seemed a little too proud of himself for a seasoned bounty hunter, Justy thought.

———

THEY EACH HAD ANOTHER CUP OF COFFEE.

Justy finished sewing the buttons on her shirt then strode off to tend nature. She brought her rifle just in case. When she came back, she checked her horse's hobbles. George was already asleep, his head lying back against the woolly underside of his saddle, hat tipped low over his eyes.

Justy kicked out the fire then rolled up in her own soogan. Despite her mental anguish over abuelito and her harrowing experience earlier, she fell fast asleep and slept well.

But very early the next morning she was lurched out of her slumber.

"*Please forgive me!*" a man's voiced exploded shrilly.

Justy sat bolt upright, heart pounding, and cast her gaze across the cold remains of the fire. As the plaintive wail echoed, she saw George Wilkes sitting upright, staring straight out before him.

He was breathing hard, panting, as though he'd run a long way. Sweat glistened on his cheeks in the starlight.

Both horses whickered.

George's plaintive wail echoed a few more times before dwindling to silence.

He turned his head slowly toward Justy. Even in the shadows she could see the sheepish expression on his face.

She stared back at him in the murky gray light of the false dawn, incredulous, her heart still pounding. She and George stared at each other for nearly a minute.

Wilkes gave a heavy sigh and lay back down against his saddle. He rolled onto his side, giving his back to Justy.

She lay back down, as well, frowning at the stars.

Forgive you for what, George Wilkes?

CHAPTER 19

"GOOD MORNING, RIO," JANE FORD SAID, PULLING HER chaise carriage up in front of Hotel de Mannion early the next morning. "Any sign of your boss?"

Rio Waite sat in a hide rocker on the jailhouse porch, his big black and white cat, Buster, perched on his left thigh, Sphinx-like, slowly curling and uncurling the end of his white-tipped tail. A steaming stone mug sat on Rio's other thigh, and a loosely rolled quirly dangled from the middle-aged deputy's mouth. He had his battered, colorless hat tipped back on his balding head.

Rio winced, shook his head. "No, can't say as there has been, Miss Jane. If we wasn't so galldang busy...or had us an extra deputy...I'd ride out my ownself and look for that old coyote. We got the judge showin' up soon, an' he'll have a whole passel of jaspers, locked up downstairs, to pass judgment on, so I don't see how neither Stringbean nor me can leave anytime soon. If we did leave the town in such a lurch, we'd likely get our hats handed to us by Joe his ownself when he got back!"

"Yes, if he's still alive," Jane said, grimly.

"Oh, he's fine, he's fine, Miss Jane. You know what I think he did? I think he..."

"Yes, you told me the other day."

Rio scowled. "I did?"

"You did. You think he rode up to Forsythe to fetch that prisoner the marshal up there was holding for the U.S. marshals in Gunnison."

"Oh, I did." Rio scowled again, worried about his memory. "Anyways...indeed, that would have delayed him some."

"I'm sure you're right. Thanks, Rio. Do be sure and send him to me, pronto, as soon as he shows his ugly mug, will you? I want to give him an earful. He has it coming!"

Rio chuckled as he ran his hand down Buster's back. Jane could hear the cat purring as he slitted his eyes and continued to curl his tail, enjoying the deputy's ministrations. "I will, Miss Jane. Don't worry about ol' Joe. He wouldn't like it that you're worried."

"I don't like it either. Good day, Rio."

"Goodbye, Miss Jane."

Jane shook the ribbons over the cream mare in the traces, and the carriage lurched forward along Del Norte's main drag, which was gradually growing busier now as the sun cast the top of its lemon ball above silhouetted western peaks. She was no longer as worried about Joe as she was angry at him. If he had decided to fetch the prisoner from Forsythe, he could have sent a rider from one of the several mining camps up that way to let her and his deputies know.

It was just like him, though, not to think about that.

Damned independent, was Bloody Joe Mannion. He probably hadn't got it through his thick head that he was married, and that his wife would be worried about him. His daughter, Vangie, was taking her father's absence in stride. After all, she'd been through it before. Joe Mannion was a man who came and went as he pleased.

But then, again, Jane had been that way too. Independent. She'd given that up when she'd married Joe. She thought he'd given it up when he'd married her. Apparently, he had not.

Anger flared hotter in Jane as she pulled up to the San Juan sitting on the street's right side, not far from the new opera house a moneyed gent from Leadville was building, on the sight that an old house and two of the town's original log cabins had once sat before being razed to make room for the new establishment that was being constructed of native stone as well as brick and iron that were being hauled up by mule train from Denver.

Several of the mule skinners could now be found in the basement cell block of Hotel de Mannion, having celebrated with a little too much gusto their arriving in Del Norte after the four-day-long, grueling climb from the eastern plains. At all hours of the day could be heard the din of incessant hammering of picks and shovels and the yells of the men currently digging the building's basement foundation and iron frame.

As Jane swung the carriage up to the boardwalk flanking the verandah of her own impressive, three-story, wood frame establishment, she scowled at the hive of activity on the next block to the south. She supposed she should be grateful for the opera house, for it would certainly increase business here in Del Norte. The San Juan would do nothing but benefit. But as Jane had told her mother in a letter, she was satisfied with her life—both business and personal—as it was.

Now she'd be satisfied if both sides of that life were

to settle more toward domesticate simplicity. Fat chance of that, however. Unless she accepted her father's offer, of course.

Which she would not.

She had not ruled out, however, visiting and assisting her ailing mother any way she could, in her parents new, most assuredly opulent digs in Glenwood Springs. She could travel to the mountain town, popular to tourists due to its healing natural hot springs, via stage and train. She could use a swim or two in one of those healing springs herself. Business and life with Bloody Joe Mannion was stressful enough itself; that stress had been compounded by the sudden appearance of her father, the uncompromising V.N. Ford.

Why was it she seemed destined to being pulled into the orbits of uncompromising men?

Her father had remained in Del Norte, forted up at the San Juan, awaiting his daughter's decision. In fact, he stood atop the broad veranda now, smoking his ubiquitous Cuban stogie, clad in a three-piece green suit owning a distinct metallic sheen, complete with coal-black beaver hat and black foulard tie. He stood there now like the Irish penguin he was, shoulders pulled back, chest puffed up, potbelly shoving out the green vest adorned with a gold watch chain, beringed fingers of his free hand stuffed into a pocket of the waistcoat.

He grinned down at his daughter like a cat that had just seen a mouse scurry under the boardwalk and was anticipating a feast. Jane sighed.

"Good morning, Father. Well, you wanted a tour of the land I've chosen to call my home, so, here I am." Jane patted the wicker basket perched on the overstuffed leather seat to her right. "I even had my chef pack us a picnic lunch. I know a very nice place to partake of one."

She glanced skyward. "Looks to be a nice day for such an outing, as well."

She'd thought that as long as she was going to have to endure V.N. Ford's company for at least half the day, she might as well make it as fun for herself as possible. Along with the fried chicken and all the trimmings in the basket, she'd made sure the cooks had placed a couple of bottles of the San Juan's finest French wine.

Of course, her father would deem it "swill," but Jane would enjoy it, anyway. She'd learned to put her father's judgments and arbitrary prejudices as well as his subtle and not-so-subtle belittlings out of her head.

Inwardly, she'd laughed. Who was she kidding?

"All right, then, my dear," Ford croaked out, crow-like, grinning, and twirling the walking stick in his right hand, "here we go."

As he started down the steps, free hand on the rail, his private secretary, Mosby, as well as his two impossibly big bodyguards, started down behind him. Both bruisers had sawed-off shotguns hanging from lanyards around their necks and arms, and silver-chased pistols were holstered on their hips with wide, black, bold-buckled, cartridge belts.

"Wait, wait, wait," Jane said. "Hold on. The old man is about as much as I can take. It's only Father and I, fellas" —she glanced at her father—"or I'm calling the whole thing off!"

Mosby said, "But, Miss Ford, your father is an important man. He is—"

V.N. Ford cut him off with: "Taking this jaunt solo with my daughter, fellas." He smiled at Jane then glanced over his shoulder at Mosby and the bruisers—one (Nordstrom) blonde and blue eyed, the other (Thornbush) dark and brown eyed, both with longish, wavy hair flowing down over their ears from their bowler hats, which, like the rest of their attire, they appeared stuffed into. "Stay here and have drinks and lunch on me." He narrowed an admonishing eye at his personal secretary. "Leave Jane's girls alone, Mosby. Especially that little brunette you've been giving the lusty eye."

He cackled delightedly as he continued down the porch steps. "Those sporting gals are far too sporting for you, I'm afraid, J.L.!"

Mosby flushed as he glanced at Jane then swung back around, hanging his head like a scolded dog. He turned back around at the top of the stairs and said to Jane, "Please, don't stray too far from town, Miss Ford. Your father really should have protection."

"Out here, this far off the beaten bath, Mister Mosby," Jane said as her father clambered into the carriage, "I doubt if anyone has even heard of the great V.N. Ford!" She laughed and glanced at her father, eyeing the fancy carriage with one brow raised in reluctant appreciation. "You ready, Father?"

He stuck the stogie in his mouth and dug a lucifer from a pocket to relight it. "Ready and raring, daughter! Ready and raring!" He glanced Mosby and the two bruisers regarding him dubiously from the top of the porch. "Don't wait up for us, gentlemen!"

He laughed as Jane shook the reins over the mare's back, and, after waiting a few seconds for an opening in the early morning traffic, turned the carriage out into the street, swinging entirely around and heading back in the direction from which she'd come.

As the carriage trundled south, V.N. Ford puffed his stogie and, squinting against the dust, turned his head from right to left and back again, wincing at a couple of burly miners in a pushing and shoving match, even this early in the day, out front of the Three-Legged Dog Saloon. He winced again at a butcher butchering a large elk with a seven-point rack out in front of the small, clapboarded Hogan's Grocery Shop. The butcher tossed scraps in chuckling delight to a snarling pack of strays.

"Good God," Ford said, turning to Jane. "What in the world do you see in this place, Janey? After what you *came* from? After what I and your mother *gave* you?"

"I didn't mean traveling out here and starting a new life for myself as an affront to you or Mother, Father. On the contrary, I owe you both so much for giving me a good, solid upbringing during which I was in wont of nothing. No girl could have been given more." Jane turned to her father with a rueful smile. "But it wasn't enough. Call me greedy, but I wanted more. More experiences. And I wanted power—the kind of power I never could have attained if I'd remained in the East and in your shadow."

V.N. Ford only glowered and shook his head, deeply confounded.

A minute later, Jane pulled the carriage up to the house she and Joe were building at what still remained the very edge of Del Norte, near a creek and surrounded by aspens. She pulled the carriage up in front of the house five carpenters were in the process of building. The frame had been erected and was currently in the process of being shelled in with large pine planks while at the same time one of the workmen—a middle-aged Mexican, Ernesto Gomez, was shingling the roof. Gomez waved his hammer at Jane, smiling around the nails in his teeth, and continued pounding.

"It's going to be a modified Victorian," Jane said. "Not large by your standards, but large enough for Joe and me and Vangie."

Ford nodded slowly, sucking in his cheeks. "The place I built in Glenwood is four times the size of this place."

Jane scowled her bewilderment at the man. "Why on earth at this stage of your life, without children at home and both you and Mother at the ages you are, do you need such a large place, Father?"

He turned to her and grinned, puffing the stogie. "Prestige, my dear. Prestige." He tapped gray ash off the end of his stogie.

Jane shook her head then drove the carriage around behind the house and over to the round breaking corral where Joe's daughter, Vangie, was riding her blue roan, mostly broke stallion, Cochise, in broad circles, occasionally stopping the horse then gigging him forward again, getting him ever more accustomed to the tug of the reins and the bit.

"Good to meet you, young lady," Ford said after Jane had introduced him to the pretty, warm-eyed brunette clad in blue denims, checked shirt, billowy neckerchief, and Stetson. Vangie worked with her horses nearly all day every day, occasionally taking them for long rides in the countryside. Her father and her horses were her life. Jane knew she couldn't wait until she was living out here, close to them again.

"Nice to meet you, Mister Ford," Vangie said, smiling and pinching the brim of her hat with her gloved right hand. Her eyes were a clear, sparkling brown in a heart-shaped, lightly tanned face. Having seen old tintypes, Jane thought she looked much like her mother, Sarah, dead by suicide when Vangie had still been a baby. "You've come a long way to visit Miss Jane. I'm sure she appreciates it."

Vangie slid her innocent smile to Jane, sure that the sentiment she'd conveyed had been true. She had no idea of the complexities of Jane's and V.N. Ford's relationship. Jane, also private, had never discussed it with her. She hadn't even discussed it with Joe, in fact.

Of course, Jane and V.N. Ford knew the truth. Smiles tightened on both their faces.

"Yes, well, it has been a long time," Jane said to fill the awkward silence.

Chancing the subject, Ford removed the stogie from his mouth and said, "You're a very attractive young lady, Miss Mannion. I bet the boys line up for you, don't they? Have any asked for your hand yet? Time's a wastin'!"

Jane drew a sharp breath through gritted teeth in horror at the old fool's remark. Vangie handled it with true, admirable grace, however. With even-toned equanimity, she said, "I have no plans to marry anytime soon, Mister Ford. I prefer life as it is, working with my horses."

Ford appeared flabbergasted. "But surely...surely you'll marry and have a family at some point. You know, there are several good schools out East that can prepare you for that. We sent Jane, of course, but—"

"And now she owns her own business," Vangie said, sliding a sly, knowing smile toward the redhead. A flicker in the young woman's eyes told Jane she suddenly understood the dynamic of the two people in the carriage before her. Of course, she would, having a father like the one Vangie herself had. "I'm thinking I might just do that, myself. I'm in no hurry, but I'd like to stake out a claim in life the way Jane has, own my own business maybe here...maybe elsewhere. I don't know. I figure I have a few years to decide. What I do know is that I don't intend to answer to a man. Any man. I've had to answer to ol' Bloody Joe long enough!"

She and Jane had a hardy laugh at that.

Vangie had dismounted, and the beautiful blue roan nibbled playfully at the young woman's ear, causing the lobe to flutter while strands of Vangie's hair brushed across his black muzzle.

Out the side of his mouth, Ford said to Jane, "A good example you've set, I see, dear Janey."

"Why, thank you, Father," Jane said out the side of her own mouth.

Vangie sobered suddenly and said, "Any word from Pa, Jane?"

Jane sobered suddenly, as well. "No, dear. I'm sorry." She glanced toward the purple line of the San Juans rising in the southwest. I do worry about him so. I know he's often gone longer than expected, but he hasn't since we've been married, so I can't help..."

"I know, you can't help worrying," Vangie said. "Believe me, it's been a way of life for me." She gave a shrug as she absently ran a hand along the roan's long, fine jawline. "I've learned to keep busy and not think about him overmuch. He's been gone a lot longer than this and came back in one piece." She gave Jane a reassuring smile. "He'll be back soon, I'm sure."

Jane nodded, returned the girl's smile with a resolute one of her own. "I'm sure, too. We'll stop harassing you now, young lady, and let you get back to that beautiful bronc of yours. You do truly seem to have taken some wind out of that cyclone."

"Not too much, I hope," Vangie said, turning to regard the shifty-eyed bronc. "He wouldn't be a cyclone without some wind in him." Her smile broadened as she slid that coyote gaze of hers, which reminded Jane of Joe's own similar expression, from Jane's father to Jane, and said, "You should know something about that, Miss Jane."

Jane chuckled and turned the mare around and shook the reins over its back. As the carriage rattled toward the main trail out from town, V.N. Ford glanced behind at the girl returning to work with the beautiful bronc, then turned to Jane and said stiffly, incredulously, "What did she mean by that last remark?"

"Never mind, Pa," Jane said, chuckling to herself.

Once around the sight of the new house, which had been the sight of the old one, burned to the ground by Whip Helton and his fellow curly wolves, she swung the carriage out away from town and toward a jog of low, wooded hills beyond. Among those hills wound a lovely creek. Jane thought maybe a picnic there along those serene waters might soften her father's hard, Celtic heart.

The sounds of the pounding issuing from Jane's and Joe's new house dwindled into the distance behind the carriage.

As the mare clomped along, Jane spied movement atop a bluff to her right, maybe a hundred yards away. She thought she saw a man step back behind a rock protruding from the top of the formation, lowering something in his hands—perhaps a pair of field glasses?

Trouble? Jane wondered and glanced at her father.

V.N. Ford was obliviously lighting the stub of his stogie as he rocked with the pitch and sway of the chaise.

Nah, Jane thought. Just market hunters looking for game, most likely.

She turned her head forward and clucked the mare into a trot.

CHAPTER 20

"HALLOO, THE CAMP!" FRANK LORD CALLED.

He and Billy and the other riders had just ridden around a steep, upward bend in the high-mountain trail. A covered wagon sat in a horseshoe of the creek thundering downhill through pines and firs, off the trail's right side.

A tall, lean man with a long, craggy face and a long, aquiline nose stood near a popping fire over which a coffee pot hung from an iron tripod. The man had heard the riders' approach even above the roar of the creek behind him, and he stood watching warily now as Lord, Billy, the hatchet-faced Indian, Three Moons, and the other riders including two Mexicans and a big Black man —Abe Galloway—angled their horses off the trail and into the clearing.

As the gang approached him, the tall, thin man, who had a thick crop of gray hair combed to one side, swallowed with apprehension. He turned his head sideways to regard the two obviously frightened young women standing behind him in colorful blouses and long skirts and knit shawls against the late-day chill. They wore colorful bandannas that held their chestnut hair back from their olive cheeks and large, brown eyes that were wide and deep now with the same apprehension as those in the eyes of the tall, thin man who was likely their father or perhaps their grandfather.

He was certainly old enough to be the latter. The taller of the two girls appeared somewhere in her early twenties while the shorter one, who was also plumper, appeared maybe seventeen or eighteen.

They both appeared to have some Gypsy blood, judging by their olive skin, dark hair, and colorful clothes. Gold rings dangled from the older girl's ears.

Fine female flesh, both, Lord was thinking not too far back in his lusty brain as his quick, cunning gaze shuttled around the encampment and roamed across the older girl's well-filled blouse. He'd bet, given half a chance and some freedom from the old man, she'd be a catamount in the mattress sack.

The old man and the two girls—there didn't appear to be anyone else around—must have stopped for a day or two to wash clothes and maybe bathe in the creek. Both girls had a fresh-scrubbed look. More colorful clothes including frilly underclothes and men's overalls, work shirts, socks, and longhandles hung from two ropes strung between four trees on the far side of the wagon, between the covered wagon and the rushing creek.

Both ropes dipped deeply with the weight of the still-wet, freshly laundered garments.

Around the encampment, the forest was thick and turning a deep blue green now at the end of a short, San Juan mountain day, chilly with the mountain spring. A few dirty drifts remained on the north sides of boulders and broad-boled pines; the rivulets they formed snaked off toward the creek.

Behind Frank a sheer, appreciative whistle rose. He heard Hank DePaul yell, "Look at them underfrillies on the wash line yonder, Frank!"

A couple of the other men laughed. T.R. "Frisco" Palin and Pete Drury exchanged a few lusty words. Palin chuckled.

Frank reined up several feet before the snapping, crackling fire over which steam curled from the mouth of the coffee pot. He stared down at the old man staring up at him warily. "I said halloo the camp!"

The old man gave a slight start, taking one-half step straight back. He held a long, double-bore shotgun down low across his thighs, his brown, bony hands squeezing the weapon so tightly that his knuckles had turned white.

The girls jerked with starts of their own and turned their wary gazes to each other. The older one put her arm around the shorter one's shoulders, comfortingly.

The old man had a stern, subdued dignity about him. He gave his spade-like chin a slow dip, blinked his piercingly blue eyes slowly, and said, "How-do."

Sitting his horse to Frank's right, Billy turned to Frank and laughed.

"Shut up, Billy," Frank said, keeping his eyes on the old man.

Billy scowled, indignant, but didn't say anything.

"What's your name, Mister?" Frank asked.

"I am Ezekial Storm, sir."

Storm's voice was low and rumbling, like the voice of a preacher, which Storm had been at one time before losing his faith in the wake of his beloved wife's death three years ago, after a long, grueling battle with cancer. She'd wasted away so that the coffin Storm had lowered into the grave had weighed practically nothing more than the wood itself.

"'Sir'," Billy said, grinning again, mockingly, shuttling his gaze between the old man and Frank. "I like that—'sir'."

"Shut up, Billy," Frank said again, tonelessly.

Again, Billy scowled, turning his mouth corners down in frustration.

Somewhere back in the pack, a man chuckled. Billy's cheeks colored in humiliation.

To the old man, Frank said, "I'm Frank Lord. This is my little, no-account brother, Billy."

Behind the old man, the youngest of the two girls gasped when she heard the name. She, like so many others, was likely aware of Frank Lord's reputation.

"Jesus, Frank!" Billy said.

"I said shut up!"

"All right, Frank! All right!" Billy gave an angry, frustrated groan.

Another one of the gang members laughed and Billy turned to see which one it was. He'd remember, by God. He didn't know what he'd do about it, but he'd remember.

Frank looked down at the shotgun the old man held across his thighs. "You plannin' on usin' that gut shredder anytime soon, Mister Storm?"

Storm looked down at the shotgun as though he hadn't remembered it was there. He lifted his head again slowly, blinking his watery blue eyes again, and said, "Why, uh...no. I don't reckon it'd be necessary." He'd said the words very slowly and the expression on his face didn't mesh with them. At least the last part.

"Then why don't you walk over and lean it against that tree? It's makin' me nervous. I hate it when I'm nervous."

Behind the old man, the older of the two girls drew a

slow, ragged breath so that her lush, bee-stung lips fluttered. Her brown eyes glazed with tears.

The old man stared up at Frank. His eyes took in the savage-faced riders flanking the outlaw leader and his brother. He, too, drew a deep breath, lifting his upper torso and showing his ribs through his white cotton shirt behind the open blanket coat he wore. He glanced behind him at the two frightened girls then turned and slowly walked over and leaned the shotgun against the fir that Frank had indicated.

"Why, thank you, Mister Storm," Frank said, good-naturedly. "Do you mind if we light and sit a spell? That coffee sure smells good. I bet those two purty girls over there can cook up a fine meal with all the surroundins, too, can't they?"

Standing by the tree where he'd leaned the shotgun, Ezekial Storm glanced at the girls once more. He turned back to Frank, gave his bony chin another cordial dip, and said, "Why, yes. Yes, they can. Don't know if we have enough to go around, but what's ours is yours."

He'd said the words automatically and with a nervous tremor in his voice.

"Don't know if he has enough women to go around, neither," said the resonant-voiced Abe Hucklebee sitting directly behind Frank, wearing his old Union kepi and bear fur coat. He wore a long, Union saber that angled down over his stout right leg. "But what's his is ours!" he said, louder, grinning at the men around him.

They all laughed.

Frank smiled. "What's the ladies' names?" he asked Storm.

Storm walked slowly over to stand between the fire and the two girls, both of whom appeared ready to cry.

He turned to face Frank and the other riders and said, "Magda and Josephine."

"Magda and Josephine," Frank said as he stepped down from his saddle. He turned to face the girls, doffed his high-crowned cream hat, and held it over his chest clad in a fox fur coat over his traditional suit and string tie. "My, my—two purty names to go with two purty girls, yessir!"

There was a loud squawk of leather and a few trail-weary grunts as the rest of the riders, including Billy, stepped down from their horses' backs.

"Fellas," Frank said, keeping his smiling gaze on Storm and the two frightened girls, "toss down what's left of that deer Kansas Jack shot yesterday, will ya?" He pulled a coffee cup from the war bag hanging from his saddle horn. "We're gonna have the girls cook us up a nice, big meal. I don't know about you, Mister Storm, but I sure am hungry!"

Frank headed for the coffee pot hanging over the fire.

Slowly, dreadfully, Storm turned his head to regard the two sobbing girls behind him.

———

WHILE THE GIRLS CUT UP THE HALF A DEER THE outlaws had provided and plundered their wagon for the "surroundings" Frank had ordered, Storm gathered firewood, built up the fire, and poured coffee until his pot was empty. He refilled the pot from the creek and hung it over the tripod to boil before adding a couple of bony handfuls from his Arbuckles sack.

He toiled silently, grimly, only occasionally looking around at the outlaws who'd essentially taken him and his daughters prisoner. They were terrorizing them and enjoying every minute.

When he'd refilled the outlaws' cups, he hung the pot back over the fire and sat on a log on the side of the fire nearest the wagon, as though forming a shield between these rough-hewn, savage men and Magda and Josephine. He draped his long arms over his bony knees. Frank, Billy, and the other outlaws sat in a semi-circle around Storm, saying nothing but grinning toward the wagon to and from which the girls hustled, albeit very stiffly, tears running down their cheeks, with pots and pans and then the spitted deer.

Frank smiled every time he saw Storm shuttle his eyes toward the shotgun leaning against the fir roughly twenty yards away from him before returning his tense gaze to the fire. As the light in the sky waned and the first stars appeared, the dancing flames were reflected in the bluing of the barrels of the man's ancient Stephens greener.

After the girls had served the meal and the outlaws and Storm had eaten, Storm taking each bite as though he were eating raw rattlesnake, the outlaws shoveling the food in as fast as they could, the girls took the dishes, pots, and pans down to the river to wash them.

Frank poured himself another cup of coffee and raised the pot to Storm.

"Another cup, Mister Storm?"

Storm looked up at the tall, broad-shouldered, blue-eyed, yellow-haired outlaw, and shook his head.

"All right, then—more for me an' the others!"

Frank chuckled and passed the pot to Three Moons, who filled his own cup before handing it to Lou Bronco who handed it to Bryce Sager, and on down the semi-circle of outlaws it went as they lounged back against their piled tack.

Their horses grazed on a picket line near Storm's two mules, near the wash strung on the ropes between the wagon and the creek. Earlier, when they were tending the horses, a couple of the men had played keep-away with a pair of one of the girl's under frillies until they'd torn it clean in two.

Frank sipped his coffee and sank back against his saddle, stretching out his long, lean legs toward the fire and crossing his ankles. He sipped his coffee, cleared his throat, and said in his overly jovial tone, "So, Mister Storm, what brings you to this neck of the San Juans?"

He took another sip from his steaming cup.

Storm looked at him from across the fire. "When my wife died, I bought a mining claim. The girls and I...we bought a wagon and headed up here from Denver. The claim is still a fair piece. We stopped to catch our breaths and to let the mules catch theirs."

"Prospectin', are ya?" Frank said, and took another sip of his coffee.

"That's right," Storm said, staring darkly into the flames. "Yes."

"Well, your daughters sure can cook a haunch of venison, I'll give 'em that. You oughta feed good, anyways, even if you don't find any color."

"Yes."

"What'd you do before you decided to come up here lookin' for gold? Don't mind me—just makin' conversation, ya understand."

Storm gazed into the fire for nearly a minute before lifting his eyes to the outlaw leader once more. "I was a circuit-riding minister of the Lutheran church. I used to preach in the mining towns here in the San Juans and over in the Sawatch."

"Preacher, eh?" Billy said, leaning back against his

own saddle beside his brother. He was grinning, eyes twinkling mockingly as he studied the grim-faced, long-boned, old sky pilot on the other side of the fire. "Why'd you have your daughters cook supper for us? Why didn't you tell us to go to hell?" he asked.

Storm looked at him without expression.

"You some kind of coward?" Billy asked. "Me? If I had a pair of daughters who looked like that, I'd tell us to go to hell!"

He snickered and looked around. The other riders regarded him with barely concealed disdain.

Storm turned to him. "All men are cowards in their own right. Besides, though I have lost my faith, I have not lost the worldly truths inherent in the scriptures. To quote one Peter, verse three, chapter nine: 'Do not repay evil with evil or insult with insult. On the contrary, repay evil with blessing, because to this you were called so that you may inherit a blessing.'"

"Ah, you're a blessed man, now, are ya?" Frank said.

He turned to look at the hatchet-faced, six-foot-five-inch Indian sitting to his left. The Apache wore a long buffalo coat and coonskin cap against the mountain chill. His braids hung down from beneath the cap, over each broad shoulder. Frank looked back at Storm. "Which daughter you gonna bless ol' Three Moons with?" His smile broadened. "Which one you gonna bless me with?"

Storm stared across the fire at him, eyes blazing, chest rising and falling heavily.

Frank turned to Three Moons. "I reckon we can just take our pick, then."

The flat planes of the Indian's copper face were expressionless as the flames danced in his dark-brown eyes and glinted off the porcupine quill necklace encircling his broad neck, where the buffalo coat gaped open near his throat.

"Let's go," Frank said, rising with a grunt.

"No!" Storm said, glaring up at him.

Ignoring the man, Frank brushed his hands together and strode off in the direction of the creek. "Sit tight, fellas. You'll get your turn."

"No!" Storm yelled, heaving himself to his feet and clenching his fists at his sides.

"Fellas," Frank called behind him as the big Indian followed him around to the other side of the wagon. "Tie Mister Storm to a wheel of his wagon, will you? If he kicks up a fuss, hitch his mules to the wagon and take him for a ride!"

Behind him, Billy laughed. That was Frank. There was no death brutal enough for ol' Frank.

Ahead of Frank, kneeling by the stream and cleaning the dishes, the girls turned toward him and the big Indian. They screamed so shrilly that their father, frozen in place by fear, would years later hear these screams over and over on his death bed and then again in hell.

CHAPTER 21

"Please forgive me! Please forgive me! Please forgive me!"

The agonized wail and its following echoes jerked Joe Mannion out of a deep sleep. Instantly, his rifle was in his hands. He loudly racked a cartridge into the action and looked around, peering into the weak gray light of the false dawn around him.

The stars were fading; the first birds were beginning to chirp.

Picketed in the deep shadows to Mannion's right, Red whickered. The cry had startled him, as well.

Joe had made his camp the previous night, just before dark, on a relatively flat shelf on a forested mountainside overlooking the trail he'd followed into these high reaches, on the trail of Lord's men. Beyond the trail roughly seventy yards below his encampment, a deep, forested canyon dropped away.

The trail had followed along the northeast rim of the canyon. Now as he squinted down the mountain and across the valley beyond the trail, he thought the cry had come from the rimrock on the other side of the canyon.

"*Please forgive me! Please forgive me! Please forgive me!*"

The cry echoed inside Mannion's head.

A man's voice. The voice of a very agonized man, indeed.

His heart still thudding, Mannion off-cocked the Yellowboy. Whoever the man pleading for forgiveness was, he was a long way away, likely a mile, a mile and a half as the crow flies but much farther than that by way of the trail that traced a broad half-circle around the darkly forbidding canyon, at the bottom of which a creek rushed, flowing from the snowier regions higher above.

Mannion had hunted enough human vermin here that he knew this country well.

He set the rifle down against a rock to his left and lay back against the woolly underside of his saddle.

Forgiveness, he thought. *Don't we all need that?*

I know I do.

What had he been thinking, leaving Billy Lord in the hands of Jeremiah Claggett when he'd known that Frank Lord was somewhere in the area? Of course, he'd known there was a good chance that Billy had been lying, only been trying to nettle Mannion, to give him a false complication that had needed thinking about.

Still, there'd been a chance the little viper had not been lying. Mannion should have taken him straight back to Del Norte where he and Hagness had murdered the liveryman then ridden back up to Forsythe the next day to fetch Jasper Neal. It would have taken extra time, and he hadn't had extra time, but he should have taken it, anyway. Now that he hadn't, Jeremiah was dead.

Mannion punched the pine needle-prickly ground beside him with the end of his right fist and cursed himself.

He sat up again and twisted around to stare out over

that dark canyon to that dark, fir-covered ridge on the other side. Who was over there? Who, like him, needed such forgiveness that his heart was breaking?

Again, Red gave a low whicker.

Mannion turned to see the horse, silhouetted in the gradually lightening darkness, craning his neck to stare across the shoulder of the slope beyond.

"What is it, boy?" Mannion whispered.

He pricked his own ears. After a short time, he heard the soft thud of a stealthy foot. Then another.

What the hell was that? Painter? Wolf? Some other four-legged hunter coming to inspect the two-legged interloper's camp, likely smelling the beans and bacon Joe had cooked last night for his supper?

Or maybe the two-legged kind of hunter?

Late the day before, as he'd been circling the canyon below, he'd spotted a man standing atop an escarpment high above him, glassing him. As soon as Joe had halted Red, the man had stepped back into the outcropping's shadow.

Damned suspicious.

But Mannion hadn't given the man much thought. He'd been too intent on Frank Lord's gang. He doubted the man had been part of the gang, sent to scout the gang's backtrail. None of Lord's gang would have glassed the trail right out in the open like that, silhouetted against the broad sky behind him.

This was outlaw country, stitched with men on the run. Likely a good many of those men considered Bloody Joe their enemy. The man who'd glassed him might have recognized him and decided to pay him something other than a social call...

At the very least, he might need a horse. Even from a

distance, a man who knew horses would recognize Red as some of the best horse flesh in the Territory.

Silent as an Apache, Joe slipped from his soogan. He didn't bother putting his boots on. He winced as he hoofed it stocking footed over to a tree at the end of the little flat he'd camped on. He dropped to a knee and peered around the tree and down the slope on the north side of his camp.

Again, Red whickered.

Joe winced and turned to the horse, placed two fingers across his lips. The bay gave his tail a switch in acknowledgment of the admonition.

Mannion edged another look around the tree. There was no movement down there for several seconds. Then a shadow rose from behind a deadfall and moved quickly to Joe's right. He heard the soft crunching sound of the man's footsteps as the man catfooted around the right side of the deadfall and then stopped for a second, crouched and listening, then started moving straight up the slope, weaving his way around trees and shrubs.

As he did, two more shadows took shape in the darkness down the declivity, moving up the slope toward Mannion, to Joe's left as he gazed downward.

Mannion pulled his head back behind the tree, and grinned.

Yep, he was being paid none too social of a call.

The three jaspers had likely waited all night at the bottom of the slope, waiting for dawn when they'd expected Mannion to start a small breakfast fire. When they saw the flames, they'd likely move in and try to shoot him.

Dawn was a good time for such a call. Just enough light for the stalkers to stalk by and to see their quarry. The situation was made even better when their quarry was distracted building a fire and then revealed fully in the firelight.

Mannion knew such tricks because he'd played a few himself, a time or two.

A dirty one, but then that was the life out here.

He waited, hearing the footsteps growing louder.

One set of footsteps fell silent. Then the other two stopped, one after the other.

A man whispered, "What about Mannion's hoss?"

Silence while the others thought it over.

Then a man said, "We'll shoot the sumbitch then shoot Bloody Joe before he even knows what happened!"

Mannion's mouth formed an *O* as he nodded slowly in realization that he'd had it wrong. These three were too stupid to have come up with any kind of effective bush-whack strategy. Essentially, they were committing suicide. Time to cull the herd...

Joe ratcheted back the hammer of his Yellowboy.

"What was that?" whispered one of the three men down the slope, roughly twenty yards from Mannion's position.

Joe rose and stepped out around the side of the tree.

"I'll tell you what that was, you damn tinhorns," he bellowed into the slope's murky shadows. "That was the sound of holy hell!"

He went to work with the Yellowboy, crouching and firing, the rifle thundering, flames lapping from the barrel, bullets screeching, dying men screaming then dropping and rolling.

Mannion stopped firing and stared into the shadows through the wafting fog of his powder smoke. No movement.

Then the man to his far right rose suddenly and went

running back down the slope. He was crouched forward, a definite hitch in his gait.

Mannion started walking down the slope, angling to his right, wincing against the pine needles chewing through his socks.

When he was clear of the deadfall and straight above the man he was following, he headed down slope, shadowing the run-limping man, hearing the man's fearful, painful sobs.

Joe stopped, raised the Yellowboy, and fired another round, the flames stabbing from the Winchester's barrel. He'd aimed low at his quarry. The man screamed as he threw his arms straight up in the air and then tumbled forward, rolled.

Mannion would have finished him, but he wanted a look at him, wanted to hear the damn fool's story.

He continued down the slope until he stood staring down at his quarry. Blood glistened in the growing light, low on the man's right side. He lay on his back and had both arms wrapped around his right knee, writhing and cursing and glaring up at his stalker.

Mannion smiled. "Hello, Harry."

"Go to hell, Bloody Joe!"

"You first, Harry."

Harry Winslow, a former saloon owner in Del Norte who'd set fire to his competitor's establishment and had spent four years in the territorial pokey, crossed his arms in front of his face as though mere flesh could stop a bullet. "Don't shoot me, Joe! We was just gonna fun ya, that's all!"

"That's all I'm doin', Harry. You havin' fun yet?"

"No!"

"I am."

Mannion shot Winslow in the head then turned and began tramping back up the hill in the graying light of full dawn. He didn't need to look at the other two dead men. He knew who they were. Most likely a couple of polecats Harry Winslow had owned his saloon with and who'd served some nights as card dealers, some nights as bouncers—when they weren't three sheets to the wind, that was. They'd likely been holed up here in the mountains after performing some two-bit robbery in one of the mining camps and were waiting for their trail to cool before heading to Denver to stomp with their tails up with their new-found wealth.

It was an old story in this country.

"Red, you ready for breakfast?" Mannion said as he reentered his camp. "I sure as hell am!" He felt better about himself now, having killed a man who'd needed killing without hesitating at all.

Red whinnied and stomped.

MANNION GAVE RED SOME PARCHED CORN.

He built a small fire and made coffee and sipped it while eating leftover beans and bacon from the night before. He needed to get on the trail because Lord's men were likely already stirring somewhere up the trail from him. Judging by yesterday's tracks, they were roughly two hours ahead.

Joe had a feeling he knew where they were heading. Or at least where they'd stop for a couple of hours. A prospector who'd gotten rich had used his wealth to build a notorious saloon and whorehouse called ROY MCCULLOUGH'S ROAD RANCH, which was what McCullough, a blustering Scot, had written in large, gaudy red letters across the wood, log, and stone rambling structure's second story.

So large that anyone could read the sign from a good mile, mile and a half away, and from farther away than that if you were perched on a ridge.

McCullough doubled as a sawbones. He'd once dug a bullet out of Mannion's backside when the lawman's trek after stage robbers had gone south after one of the men he'd been tracking the gang with had sneezed, and the gang had all come alive, grabbed iron, and started shooting.

That was when Joe had decided to forego catch parties and track the owlhoots himself. Besides, posse members, some not well trained in the use of firearms, often shot each other. Mannion still wasn't sure one of his own men hadn't shot him, and he had a feeling who it was though the bastard was dead now after being bit by a rabid fox he'd found early one morning in his outhouse.

Joe had shed no tears for Caleb Prince. McCullough had had a good laugh while he'd swilled whiskey and dug the bullet out of the notorious lawman's ass, but Joe hadn't minded. That was a painful, not to mention humiliating, place to get shot and he was damned happy and grateful as hell to have it extracted, the wound sutured damn near expertly closed.

At least, expertly for a big, blustering, drunk Scot who'd laughed as he'd worked.

That had been a big joke around Del Norte for a time and Joe had been relieved when everybody had seemed to have finally forgotten about it. Just thinking about it now made his ass ache, so he rid his mind of the ordeal, and saddled Red. He had a long ride ahead of him to McCullough's, which was two passes beyond his own current position, and he didn't need to be distracted by a sore backside.

He chuckled dryly at himself, stepped into the leather, and walked Red down the slope and onto the rocky, two-track mining trail below. He stopped on the trail and pondered that ridge on the other side of the canyon, again wondering, however fleetingly, who over there so badly needed forgiveness.

And for what.

Had he gotten a good friend killed?

He climbed deeper and higher into the San Juans until, following the steep trail up a sharp curve, with a rushing creek fairly roaring off the trail's right side, he came upon some poor bastard who'd been tied to the wheel of a covered wagon.

CHAPTER 22

"GOOD LORD, DAUGHTER," V.N. FORD SAID TWENTY minutes later. "Where are you taking me?"

He looked around anxiously. They were climbing a steep hill through an aspen forest. A shallow arroyo dropped off the left side of the trail; a shallow creek bubbled along its base, clear with snowmelt from up in the higher reaches of the Sawatch Range to the north of Del Norte. On the right side of the trail, a mountain rose, teeming with sun dapples and shadows and the piping of many happy spring birds.

Crows cawed up high on the ridge, where the long-dead body of what Jane assumed to be a cattle rustler or possibly a claim jumper still hung by a stout rope, from an arching bough of a fir tree. Jane had ridden up there one day on a whim, and had gasped when she'd seen the body, mostly a skeleton half-clad in torn trail clothes. Both skeletal feet were bare. Jane had assumed the man had kicked out of his boots when they'd hanged him.

Jane hadn't cut the man down or told anyone of his presence. Let him rest. It was a lonely place, but maybe he liked it up there, far from the fray. After all, he'd likely been there several years.

She couldn't help wondering now and then, however, usually late at night, if someone else somewhere in the world was thinking about him, wondering where he was and if he would ever return to them. A wife, perhaps. Maybe children. Maybe even just a fellow rustler.

No, she'd concluded. He'd likely been forgotten, up there where he twisted and turned in the arbitrary winds and breezes stitched with crow caws and owl hoots, serenaded from the ridges at night by wolves and coyotes. Jane didn't know why she thought about that man, that poor lost soul so often, but she did.

She thought about him now and brushed off the lonely feeling thinking about him gave her as she put the chaise up and over the hill and down the other side. "Almost there, Father," she said.

"You've taken me out here to shoot me, haven't you?" V.N. Ford said, chuckling ironically as he glanced down at the leather-sheathed rifle resting on the carriage floor beneath the seat. "That's why you didn't want Thornbush and Nordstrom along!"

"Don't give me any ideas," Jane said with a laugh.

As the chaise clattered down the rocky two-track trail, with the creek bubbling on her left, Jane frowned as a horse and rider appeared, moving through the aspens on the trail's left side and stopping his steeldust horse at the trail's edge. Two more riders appeared, ducking under branches and shoving them aside with raised arms as one of them drew his own mount, a long-legged buckskin, to a halt on the trail's right side while the other rider, astride a black Morgan, rode out onto the trail and turned the horse to face the approaching chaise.

He held up one black-gloved hand. In his other hand,

he held a Winchester rifle straight up from his right thigh. He opened and closed his hand around the long gun's neck, index finger curled through the trigger guard.

"Oh, dear Christ," V.N. Ford said, leaning forward to stare in dread at the three riders sitting in the middle of the trail before them. He was a long, rangy man with bushy, ginger hair, a tattoo on his neck, and fat silver rings hanging from his ears. He was dressed entirely in black leather, complete with leather coat with silver buttons, and a leather hat. "That's...Blade O'Riordan," Ford said, turning to Jane with darkness filling his fear-bulging eyes. He'd said the name as though Jane should recognize it.

"Whoa, whoa, whoa!" Jane said, slowing the running mare. She hadn't recognized the name, but she'd seen these three as trouble as soon as she'd set eyes on them.

The man to the left was big and square-headed and clad in a wolf fur coat. He, too, had a tattoo on his neck. He leaned forward in his saddle, grinning, showing a mouthful of gold teeth, at Jane and her father as the carriage drew within thirty feet and continued forward, the mare trotting now. The man to the right of the trail, also with a tattoo on his neck, had coal-black hair falling from a derby hat onto slender shoulders clad in a white silk shirt and red foulard tie between the open flaps of a fox fur coat. A long, mare's tail mustache was as black as his hair. He wore butterscotch leather pants stuffed down into the tops of high, black, gold-tipped boots.

"Whoa, there!" yelled the ginger-haired man with the thick silver hoops dangling from his ears, sitting in the middle of the trail and holding up one, black-gloved hand. He had a smarmy smile on his long, angular face, and his eyes were flat and hard. "We'd like to have a word with you, Mister Ford!"

"Dear God," Ford said under his breath. "And my bodyguards nowhere to be found..."

"Yeah, well, I reckon I'll have to do!" Jane said, giving the man ahead of her a brittle smile as the mare clomped toward him.

She'd taken both reins in her left hand. Now as the mare closed to within fifteen feet of the man in the trail, Jane lowered her right hand to the leather sheath secured to the bottom of the seat, just right of her right thigh.

It was a backup gun in case of trouble when she was taking a weekend ride by herself in the country.

She closed her hand around the gutta percha grips of the Sharps, 4-shot, .32-caliber pepperbox revolver. She withdrew the odd-looking, four-barrel popper, and raised it, clicking the iron hammer back and closing her index finger over the spur trigger.

She raised it quickly, extending it straight out from her right shoulder, and aimed at the man in the trail ahead of her and toward whom the mare kept closing at a fast walk. He'd just seen the Sharps glinting in the sunlight filtering down over the pines and aspens set far back away from the trail, and frowned. He started to pull his right, black-gloved hand down just as the Sharps popped, making a sound like a large branch snapping.

A ragged hole was punched through the black glove, in the middle of the man's hand. The bullet tore out the back of the hand, a little down from where it had gone in, and kissed the outside of the man's upper right arm.

His face crumpling in agony, he yowled as he dropped the Winchester and grabbed his right hand with his left. The black Morgan whinnied shrilly and sidestepped, curveting, its eyes growing wide and round as it saw the mare now lunging into a hard gallop straight for it. The Morgan sidled off the trail, head and tail arched, and gave another indignant whinny and crow hopped as the mare and the chaise brushed past it as Jane aimed the smoking pepperbox at the black-haired man on the trail's right side.

Again, the pepperbox spoke.

The horse of the man with the long, black hair was also backing away from the trail, turning anxiously, and the .32 caliber bullet caromed through the left-side tip of the man's mare's tail mustache before plunking into an aspen bole just beyond him.

All three hellions were cursing as Jane dropped the pepperbox onto the seat beside her and whipped the reins against the mare's back, yelling, "Let's go, Miss Annie—show me what you got, girl!"

"Good Lord! Good Lord! Good Lord!" intoned V.N. beside Jane on the buggy's seat, holding his planter's hat down firmly on his head with one pudgy hand. He craned a look behind then turned his astonished gaze on his daughter. "Here they come! I hope that mare has some bottom, or we're doomed!"

He cackled out an anxious laugh. "But you gave 'em the what-for, anyway, Janey! They weren't expecting that! And *I wasn't either!*"

Crouched low as rifles cackled behind them, bullets stitching the air between and around Jane and her father, Jane said, "There's more where that came, Father!"

"Ah, Jesus, I hope so. I dearly hope you're right...but you don't know who those men are. Hatchet men for one of my business rivals! Former street thugs from one of the nastiest gangs in Dublin!"

"Don't doubt it a bit!" Jane bit out as with a grunt she suddenly swung the mare off the trail's left side and through a break in the trees.

"*Get her!*" came an agonized wail from behind.

"Duck, Father!" Jane cried as low branches and shrubs plowed toward them.

Ford was slow to duck and one such pine branch swept his hat off his head.

"Hey!" Ford cried, reaching back with his hand.

"Forget it!" Jane cried back at him as men continued to shout, hooves drummed, and guns continued to pop behind them.

"That was handmade in Charleston!"

"You won't have a head to set it on if you don't forget it!"

The carriage plunged through a stand of willows lining the creek and then the mare and the carriage were in the creek, water rising around the mare's galloping hooves and the chaise's clattering wheels. The carriage clattered and pitched violently over rocks until two-thirds across the stream the right front wheel crashed into a large, pale, half-submerged boulder.

The chaise stopped so suddenly that both Jane and Ford were nearly thrown forward onto the tongue, both grunting loudly as the front dashboard punched the wind from their lungs.

"Oh, Lord God, help us!" V.N. Ford bellowed, his strawberry blond hair liberally streaked with gray blowing in the breeze around his large, jowly, granite-like head.

"Get out and run, Father!" Jane shouted, glancing over her shoulder to see two of the three assailants just then emerging from the willows to splash into the stream. She could see the ginger-haired man galloping behind them on the Morgan, holding his reins in his left, bullet-plundered hand, his rifle in the other, bellowing.

"Get them! Get that bitch, especially! I wanna kill her slow! *Get them!*"

"Jane, we're finished!" Ford cried, flinching as a bullet sliced across his right ear.

Kneeling on the carriage floor, Jane slid her Henry repeating rifle from the sheath. "Not just yet, Father! Get down from here and run while I slow them down!" she shouted so loudly that her voice cracked.

"All right, all right!" Ford wailed, clambering heavily, grunting and groaning, down from the wagon's far side.

On one knee on the wagon's floor, Jane racked a round into the Henry's breech. The first man, the black-haired man with the mare's tail mustache was within fifteen feet and closing, firing his carbine—jacking and firing, the shots caroming wide due to the fact he was firing from the horse not only galloping but negotiating the rocky bottom of the creek.

Jane had the advantage of a stationary position.

She put it to good use by lining up her sights on the approaching rider's forehead as he galloped right toward her. She squeezed the trigger and watched a large, round hole open up in the man's throat, right over his Adam's apple. He opened both hands from around the Winchester, letting it drop, and then tumbled ass over teakettle over the galloping Morgan's arched tail.

Jane turned to the other man riding left of where the black-haired man just now splashed into the creek. The man with the gold teeth and riding the buckskin had his own Winchester aimed at the back of V.N. Ford as the older man waded through the knee-deep water toward the opposite shore, throwing his arms out to both sides for balance.

"No!" Jane cried, knowing she didn't have a chance to shoot the bastard before he shot her father in the back.

The rifle in the man's hands roared, flames lapping from the barrel. The flames lapped high, however, on the heels of another gun report—this one from the far side of the stream, toward the willows through which the carriage had bulled through only two minutes before.

The man with the gold teeth gave a strangled wail as he lurched forward then tossed the Winchester high in the air. As he and the buckskin galloped past the carriage, on the passenger side, he slid down the buckskin's right hip and splashed into the stream. Water closing around him turned red. When his body floated back to the surface, Jane could see the thick blood streaming out of the hole in his chest. His open eyes did not blink as the creek turned him and ushered him off downstream, arms lolling out to each side.

Stunned, Jane turned toward the ginger-haired man galloping toward her, silver hoop rings jouncing along his jaws. He raised his rifle toward Jane, who, still puzzled by the gold-toothed man's demise, was slow to bring her Winchester up. A rifle barked, and Jane gasped, jerking with a start.

She thought for sure her ticket had just been punched, but no...it was the ginger-haired man falling forward across his buckskin's neck then rolling down the side of the horse to splash into the stream. He gave an enraged wail as, favoring his left arm, he rose from the water and swung around, raising his rifle toward yet another rider just then galloping into the stream.

That rider stopped, pumped a fresh cartridge into the breach of the rifle in his hands, snapped the butt plate to his shoulder, aimed, and fired again. That bullet plowed into the ginger-haired man's forehead, exiting his head beneath his right ear and spanging off a rock on the shore to Jane's left.

The ginger-haired man flew back into the water, floated back to the surface, and, like the man with the gold teeth, was turned by the current and carried off downstream, jouncing and bouncing off half-submerged rocks, his large, silver earrings glistening in the high-country sunshine.

Jane turned her exasperated but relieved gaze back to her savior. A few seconds before, she'd seen the long, chestnut hair blowing around slender shoulders in the wind. Now she watched, hang-jawed, as Vangie Mannion rode toward her, water splashing up against the handsome blue roan's withers and hips.

"Vangie!" she cried.

"Miss Jane!" Vangie thrust her left arm out, pointing back behind Jane toward the near shore of the creek. "I think you're Pa's been hit!"

"Wha—Oh, my God!"

Jane tossed the Winchester onto the seat then scurried down out of the chaise and into the creek. Sure enough, her father lay on the shore, opposite the side from which they'd entered the stream. He lay belly down against a rock, trying to gain his feet, digging the toes of his brown half boots of alligator skin into the sand and gravel at the very edge of the water.

"Father!"

Jane waded to him, the hem of her skirts drifting downstream in the water, and dropped to a knee. She raked his back and the backs of his legs with her eyes, seeing no blood. "Father, where are you hit?"

Ford lifted his head, shook his red, swollen face. "N-Not hit." Weakly, he pressed a thumb to his chest. "Tick...ticker. Brandy...pills...*pocket*!"

As Vangie rode the fine stallion up beside Jane and her father, and dismounted, Jane pulled a flat, brown, labeled bottle and a small tin from the coat pocket Ford had indicated. Ford took the tin and with fumbling fingers opened it, deposited one of the yellow gel lozenges under his tongue then pulled the stopper out of the brandy bottle. He tipped his head back and took a liberal swig.

Then one more.

Breathing heavily, but already looking better, he half-turned and slid down the rock to a sitting position. He looked at Jane and Vangie, both crouched over him, concern in their gazes.

He gave a feeble smile, drew a deep breath, and let it out slowly. "Thanks for the outing, Janey." He wagged his head. "You really know how to do 'er up right!"

She and Vangie shared a dubious look.

Then, to Vangie, frowning, Jane said, "How...did you...?"

Vangie canted her hatted head downstream, toward where, like some Western River of Lost Souls, the creek had shuttled the three, dead, would-be assassins. "Those three rode past the yard just after you and Mister Ford left. They had the look of trouble about them, sure enough, so I saddled Cochise and we shadowed 'em."

"Yes," Jane said, casting her gaze downstream. "They came by those looks honestly." She regarded Vangie again. "I sure am glad your impossible old man taught you how to ride and shoot!"

She turned to her father, whose heavy breathing was still slowing. He had a sort of dreamy look on his face as he raised it to take the sun. "As for you, V.N. Ford," she said sharply, "how long have you had a bad ticker?"

CHAPTER 23

JOE THOUGHT THE MAN WAS DEAD.

He'd ridden into the clearing where the wagon sat and dismounted and stood staring at the lanky, craggy-faced gent with a thick thatch of gray hair combed to one side. The man's eyes were open as he sat back against the wagon wheel, both hands tied with rope to wooden spokes. His long, lean legs extended straight out before him.

He wore high-topped, mule-eared boots. Bizarrely, a frilly woman's pantalette was hooked over each boot toe —one yellow and one red.

The man didn't seem to be breathing. He made no movement whatever, though he didn't appear to have a mark on him. The mid-morning breeze shifted the gray hair on his head, sweeping one thick lock down over one eye that seemed to be staring in death at nothing.

"Christ, partner," Mannion said. "Who the hell did this to you?"

But of course, he knew.

Who else?

The man's watery blue eyes suddenly rolled up to him.

"Christ!" Joe said with a start. He squatted on his heels and gazed into the man's eyes that had lost that distant glaze. "You alive, old son?"

"Untie me," the man said. "Untie me!"

"Easy," Mannion said, unsheathing his bowie knife.

He cut through the rope tying the man's left wrist to a wheel spoke, and then he cut the rope tying the man's right wrist to another spoke. The man gazed down in horror at the pantalettes hooked over his boots. He kicked around, yelling, "Gnaahhhh," trying to scrape the underwear off his boots, thrashing around until he leaned forward and used his hands to tear each piece of underwear off each boot and toss it away as though it were a poisonous snake.

He leaned back against the wheel, sank farther down toward the ground, closed a knobby hand over his face, and bawled. He bawled and kicked and punched his free hand against the ground beside him. He punched as though he intended to punch out a deep hole in which to bury his sorrow.

His face was a red mask of rage and unbearable heartbreak.

"Holy Christ," Joe said, staring down at the torn, castoff underwear. "What in holy blazes did they do?"

But just as he knew who'd been here, he knew what they'd done.

As he'd ridden into the camp, he'd seen the colorful underwear hanging on the line between the wagon and the creek. There were girls here. Or there had been girls here...

Mannion swung around, grabbed Red's reins, and stepped into the leather.

"*No!*" the tall, thin, craggy-faced man yelled behind him, flopping around on the ground and punching it with both fists now, kicking like a wild stallion. *"No! No! No!"* His voice cracked and then he rolled onto his belly, closed his hands over his head, and bawled.

He sounded like nothing so much as a mother cow with a calf turned cattywampus inside her.

Joe couldn't listen to it anymore.

He needed to get on up the trail. He needed to catch the Satan-spawn who'd turned this man's heart and soul to mud before they could do it again to someone else...

"Hy-ahh, boy!" Joe said, whipping Red's flanks with his rein ends. "Hy-ahh, boy! Hy-AHHHH!"

———

MANNION STUDIED THE ROAD RANCH FOR A GOOD fifteen minutes through his field glasses before he returned the glasses to his saddlebags, mounted Red, and rode down the ridge and into the yard. There were no horses tied to the hitchracks fronting the place, but there were a dozen or so in the corral flanking it.

Most of the corralled mounts were short but rangy, built for mountain speed.

Lord was here, all right.

Mannion put Red up to the hitchrack, dismounted, looped the reins over the rack, scrutinized the big building before him, and shucked his rifle from its scabbard. He racked a round into the chamber, shouldered the piece, and walked up the steps leading to the big, log front veranda. Many initials had been carved into the stout logs forming awning posts—even some hearts sandwiched, likely, between the initials of certain jakes and the whores they'd fallen in love with here at McCullough's.

For a few minutes or hours, anyway...

A little, pale-skinned whore in a red and black corset and bustier under a ragged blanket coat sat in a ladder-back chair to the left of the lodge's front door. She was peeling potatoes. Her narrow, sharp-featured face acquired a consternated look as she took in the big man in the high-crowned Stetson striding toward her. A yellow tabby cat sat beside a porcelain bucket of potatoes, to the right of her little, pale, naked feet.

The tabby looked up at Mannion and yawned.

The whore arched her brows and said, "You here for them?" She jerked her head to indicate the building behind her. Her upper lip was swollen and scabbed from a recent cut. A punch or a hard slap, most likely. She had many reddish-purple marks mottling her neck and an all-out bite mark just beneath one delicate ear. Mannion could see the lingering impression of a man's teeth.

"Yep."

The little whore hooked a lopsided smile. "Good luck."

Mannion touched two fingers to his hat brim then tripped the steel latch and shoved open the stout wooden door. It groaned on its hinges.

Mannion took one step inside and, holding the Yellowboy up high across his chest, peered into the big, cave-like room's cool shadows. The pent-up air smelled like stale tobacco smoke, whiskey, cheap perfume, sweat, and sex.

Three faces turned toward him with surprised expressions. Eyes blinked, reflecting the light angling through the windows flanking Mannion. One set belonged to McCullough, who was scrubbing a table to Mannion's left, near the long, plankboard bar. The big, dark-eyed Scot didn't say anything. He straightened and looked at Mannion and then, his lips slowly parting around the smoldering quirly he was smoking, turned his head toward where the two other people in the room sat on the room's far side, in dense shadows, between where two sets of stairs came down from a balcony ringing the second story and under a mounted grizzly head and a large oil painting of a yellow-haired young woman lounging on a red velvet fainting couch wearing only a pearl necklace and a dubious smile. Behind her, black horses toiled in a distant, green pasture.

Billy Lord sat with a plump, red-headed, freckle-faced whore on his lap and an open beer bottle on the table before him. The kid's pistol sat on the table beside the beer. He sat frozen, staring wide-eyed at Mannion. The whore stared at Joe, too, a weary half-smile curling her lips; the skin above the bridge of her nose ridged with a slow-building curiosity.

The girl was naked from the waist up, and she looked cold. Billy had been playing with her pink, pointed breasts until he saw Mannion. Now he stopped playing and scowled, eyes narrowing in disbelief at whom he was looking at—a man who couldn't be here. No way, no sir. Frank never let himself get followed.

Footsteps sounded from above and to Mannion's left. He turned to see a big Black man with a red sash and a cavalry saber appear on the second-floor balcony and at the top of the stairs on that side of the room. The Black man yawned big and stretched as he started clomping heavily down the steps.

"Dang near slept half the day—" He stopped when he turned his head to see the big lawman standing just inside the open front door.

Instantly, his mahogany hands closed over the grips of the two big Remingtons holstered on his hips. He left both guns in their holsters as he shuttled his gaze from

Mannion to Billy and said quietly, incredulously, frowning, "Is that...is that...?"

"It's *Mannion!*" Billy screeched as he leaped to his feet.

The redhead screamed as she slapped down hard against the floor.

Mannion snapped the Yellowboy's butt to his right shoulder, aimed quickly, and fired, satisfaction touching him when he saw the quarter-sized hole appear in the middle of the little vermin's forehead, punching Billy straight back over his chair, eyes rolling inward and back into their sockets, quickly showing only white.

The kid hadn't hit the floor before Mannion, levering a fresh round into the Yellowboy's action, ran ahead and to his right, throwing himself onto a table as the Black man on the stairs cut down on him with the Remingtons —*Pow! Pow!*—two rounds plunking into the table two or three inches to Mannion's left just before the table tipped to his right, and he and the table hit the floor.

Joe gained a knee, snaked the Yellowboy over the edge of the table and fired two rounds as the Black man fairly flung himself back up the stairs and onto the second-floor balcony, Joe's rounds chewing into the risers just beneath his running feet. One barked into the end of a heel, breaking off the spur which went zinging high up over the balcony rail before clattering onto the floor. The Black man hunkered behind the newel post on the left side of the stairs, and Joe plunked two rounds into the side of it, throwing slivers in all directions.

The whole place had come alive, running footsteps pounding, men yelling, women screaming, and doors opening in the balcony over Joe.

The newel post wasn't wide enough to fully cover the Black gent. Mannion shot him in the right shoulder poking out from the post's right side. The man howled as he twisted around on his butt to face Joe. Joe ejected the spent shell, seated fresh, and shot the Black man in the neck just after the man had hurled two quick shots at him through the balcony rail; both bullets plunked into Mannion's shielding table.

Thunder rumbled as though a violent storm were approaching.

And one was—only it was a man-made storm of half-dressed men running and leaping down both sets of staircases, howling and firing in Joe's direction. Mannion shot one and then he muttered a heartfelt, "Sorry, Jane; Sorry, Vangie," just as the howling horde descended on him a half a second after his Yellowboy pinged, empty.

He threw the rifle away and reached for the big Russian holstered on his right thigh.

"Don't kill him!" a man shouted from the balcony over the bar. In the corner of Joe's eye, he saw the big, yellow-haired, yellow-mustached Frank Lord, clad in only red longhandles and a big, cream Stetson, lean over the balcony rail to grit his teeth around a lit cigar in savage fury, glaring at Mannion. "*I want him alive!*"

Joe's Russian had just cleared leather when two men bulled into him, one with a cartridge belt and holster looped over one longhandle-clad shoulder. Joe went stumbling backward, dropping the Russian, shouting, "*You bloody sonso'bitches! Lord, I killed your vermin brother, but I wish I could have done it slow, like you did for Jeremiah!*"

"Jeremiah" quaked out of him as the two bruins slammed him onto the floor near a big, plate glass window left of the still-open door.

Bellowing like a poleaxed bull, knowing he was about to die but wanting to inflict as much damage as he could before he found himself shaking hands with ol' Scratch, Joe punched one of the two men and then another.

Somehow, with the howling horde converging on him, he managed to scramble to his feet, his big, left fist delivering a tooth-breaking upper cut to a near chin, evoking a howl. Then he was shoved brutally back once more...and through the plate glass window behind him.

Two men flew with Joe through the screeching rain of shattering glass. They landed on the broad veranda on either side of him, wincing and groaning, glass peppering them.

In mad desperation, Mannion scrambled to his feet once more, his long hair a silver-brown tumbleweed around his head, broken glass shining in it and in his mustache. Lord's men were spilling out the front door and the broken window. Joe swung at one but gave a startled "whoof" as his fist caromed through empty air, his intended target having just ducked the blow.

Joe wasn't so fortunate.

The man who'd ducked his blow hit him twice in the face and once in the belly.

Hard.

Mannion grunted, dazed, as he flew backward, struck the porch steps halfway down, and rolled violently the rest of the way to the ground. At the hitchrack, Red whinnied and pitched, pulling at his tied reins then dropping back down to both front feet and pawing the ground angrily as the half-dressed killers converged on his rider once more.

Again, in desperation, knowing he was a walking dead man, the enraged lawman scrambled to his feet once more. He roared like a bruin as he parried blows, dancing around, ducking, landing punches—mostly glancing blows—while the howling hoard landed solid blows of their own on his brows, nose, mouth, chin, ears, the back of his head, his belly...the small of his back.

Several times he reached for his bowie but wasn't able to unsheathe it before another blow staggered him.

Red continued to pitch and whinny, outraged.

There was little help for his rider.

Joe danced and roared until, finally unable to keep his feet any longer, for fatigue and agony weighed heavy in him, he dropped straight back onto his ass, dust wafting around him. Blood filled his mouth. Sweat dripped from his hair, pasted his shirt against his back.

The savage killers surrounded him, crouching, waving fists and showing gritted teeth—as well as a couple of missing teeth—between split, bloody lips.

Boots thudded above and behind them. Joe raised his bleary-eyed gaze to the broad porch fronting the lodge. Frank Lord stepped out, still clad in only his longhandles and hat, holding his vermin brother's body in his arms. Billy's long, thin, yellow hair hung down toward the porch floor. Offal from the blown-out back of his head dripped from his hair onto the toes of his brother's bare feet. Frank threw his head back and roared his sorrow at the sky in which clouds were gathering, piling up like oily rags, and a cold wind blew, moaning, as though a powerful storm were building in the heavens to match the one here on earth.

The men around Mannion turned to their heart-broken outlaw leader.

The big Indian, Three Moons, who'd gotten more than his share of savage licks in, turned to his boss. "Finish him, Frank?" he called, sliding a big Green River knife from a beaded sheath on his wide leather belt. He wore buckskin pants. That was all. His copper-red skin, crisscrossed with many old wounds including a couple bullet wounds, glistened in the high-country sunshine peeking wanly through the clouds. A porcupine quill necklace danced across his broad, scarred chest.

Lord crossed the porch and came down the steps with his brother's slack body in his arms. He sobbed and mewled like a gut-shot griz. He walked over. The men made way for him. He stopped in front of Mannion, stared down.

Slowly, he shook his head.

"Nope." Again, he shook his head. "Not yet." He turned to a wiry Mexican in a torn calico shirt over dirty cream longhandles. The Mexican had a split lip and bloody nose. One dung-brown eye was swelling. "Loco," Lord said, "saddle your horse and ride him over here." Lord smiled coldly down at the lawman on the ground before him. "*Dutch ride!*"

A victorious roar rose from the crowd.

Mannion was already too beaten up to feel much dread at the dreaded term, which meant for all intents and purposes to drag a man over rough terrain behind a galloping horse.

It was a hell of a way for a man to die, but it was Mannion's own damn fault. He'd gotten Jeremiah killed. Now it was his turn.

Joe stared up at Frank Lord. He grinned and slitted his gray eyes. "You go to hell! That little privy rat is already there, licking the devil's feet!"

"See ya there, Joe!" Frank laughed. "But I gotta feelin' I'm gonna be in a whole lot better shape than you!"

"That remains to be seen," Joe said, still all defiance despite that the short Mexican had already wheeled to tramp off in the direction of the stable and that Frank's men were crowded close around him, giving him no way out.

CHAPTER 24

"HOLD ON," GEORGE WILKES SAID, REINING HIS BLAZE-faced dun to a halt as he and Justy rode up a steep mountain trail that hugged a roaring creek.

Justy stopped her grulla then, as well, and frowned over at her trail partner. "What is it?"

George frowned as he looked around. "Heard somethin'."

Then Justy heard it, too—raking, thudding sounds. The sounds a shovel makes in gravelly ground.

She and George swung their gazes to stare up the slope on their right, toward the near side of the creek that moved so quickly the churning water was mostly white. It pounded over half-submerged rocks. A man stood up on the shoulder of the slope, raising and lowering a pick.

Justy and George shared a skeptical look. They gigged their horses up the steep, bending trail to see a covered wagon parked in a horseshoe of the creek, with brightly colored clothes strung from two lines and two picketed mules on the wagon's other side, between it and the creek. The man was to the right of the wagon and a little beyond it, toiling with the pick in the shade of a tall, broad spruce that was a vivid, almost sparkling blue green now in the midday light.

Two blankets lay on the ground near the man—two blankets that Justy had a pretty good feeling contained bodies. She could see a dirty bare toe peeking out from one of the blankets.

Her belly tightened.

The man was digging a grave.

Again, Justy and George shared another look then put their horses off the right side of the trail. As they did, the man—a tall, gray-headed scarecrow with his shirtsleeves rolled up his corded, brown forearms and a blanket coat draped over a nearby rock—glanced toward them. He dropped the pick suddenly and hurried over to where a long, double-barreled shotgun leaned against the spruce.

He hefted the greener defensively, curling his index finger through the trigger guard and then crumpling up his hawkish face in a suspicious glower at the two strangers. His eyes turned sharp.

Holding her reins in one hand, Justy raised both hands palms out in supplication.

George did the same.

Justy called, "We're friendly, Mister...if you are." She glanced at the two blankets forming the shapes of bodies.

The man lowered the greener a little, frowning, tentative.

Justy and George rode over to within ten feet of the man. Again, Justy glanced at the two blankets and said, "A passel of killers led by a cold-eyed devil with yellow hair been through here?"

The man licked dry, chapped lips. Beard stubble like steel filings carpeted his angular jaws.

"They have," the man said, hardening his jaws and narrowing his eyes.

"You have two dead?" George asked him.

The man nodded, said almost too softly for Justy to hear. "My daughters."

His voice was thick and heavy. The man's face was a mask of bitter agony. Justy knew the feeling. "I'm sorry, Mister..."

"Storm. Ezekial Storm," he said, removing one hand from the greener to brush the back of it across his cheek. "Murdered them both...after they ravaged 'em. They died, hard, screaming, while I sat tied to a wheel of the wagon over there. I didn't even fight 'em. I just let 'em tie me up, an' I just sat there...listening to them scream... listening to my daughters scream and cry and beg me for help. And when I didn't come, they begged the Holy Spirit. Only, He didn't come, neither."

Storm barked out a sob, produced a hanky, and blew his nose.

Just like his face, the man's voice was the epitome of bitter rage and eternal suffering. He must have seen the sadness in Justy's own face. His deep, fluttering voice said, "Good Lord, girl—what'd they do to you?"

"Killed my grandfather, burned my town...what was left of it after the boom went bust."

"Which town?"

"Fury."

"Rode through there, my girls an' me, just the other day. You know Jeremiah Claggett?"

"My grandfather," Justy said, narrowing her own eyes in fury. "The man they killed. Lord stabbed him, left him to die slow in the arms of a whore he'd asked to marry him only an hour before."

"We're on their trail, Mister Storm," George said.

"Awfully young," Storm said. "But I reckon you're not alone."

"You saw Mannion?" Justy asked.

Again, the tall, grave, roughly dignified man, who had the air of a preacher, gave a slow nod. "He freed me from the wagon, rode out like that big bay of his had tin cans tied to its tail."

"My grandfather was one of Joe Mannion's only friends," Justy said. "Joe got him..." She let the sentence die on her tongue and frowned.

Which one of them really got him killed—Joe or Justy herself? If she'd told Mannion the whole story, maybe...

She shook away the thought that made the bile rise in her belly.

Storm nodded slowly. "Should've known that was Bloody Joe. Never met him, heard his reputation. He's just one man, though. A little past his prime. Those devils that butchered my girls are devils—every man jack of 'em. Young devils. Man-beasts, more like. Devils meant for hell only. Let the devil choke on 'em...his own spawn!"

He squeezed the greener in both hands as he said, "I'm going after them too. I'm not a man-hunter by trade, but I'll ride along with you two, if you wait for me to finish burying my girls. Three pairs of eyes track better than one. Mine aren't as sharp as they once were."

He strangled out a sob as he looked over his shoulder at the blanket-wrapped bodies again.

Justy glanced at George. She didn't want to wait. She wanted to get after Lord before Mannion caught up to the bunch. She wanted to take Frank down when he was distracted dealing with Bloody Joe, who, knowing Joe's reputation herself, and, given the situation, would likely ride in shooting.

Again, she looked at the bodies and glanced at George.

He shrugged a shoulder and then she did too.

"We'll give you a hand, if you like," she said.

Storm glanced at the bodies again, turned his head back to Justy, and nodded.

He leaned his shotgun against the spruce and picked up the pick

---

WHEN THEY HAD THE GIRLS BURIED IN THE SINGLE grave, Storm did not recite the Lord's prayer, as Justy had expected.

He recited a prayer, all right—at least, it *sounded* like a prayer—but he recited it so softly that she couldn't make out the words. He spoke with is head down, eyes closed, barely moving his lips. When he finished, he looked up at the sky and said, "You help me, I'll help you...in the next world. Amen."

Justy's heart shrunk with an odd, dreadful feeling, a foreboding feeling, when the bereaved man dropped to his knees and raised his hands, high above his head, the wind making the pages of the open Bible at his knees flutter madly. He fairly bellowed at the sky, sobbing, tears dribbling down his cheeks and the chill wind of a coming storm tossing his thick, gray hair around his head—"*You will be avenged—the Dark One and I...we will avenge you! If there be no help in Heaven, there will be in Hell!*"

Thunder rumbled distantly but a fork of lightning flashed out of the still-clear sky directly above the raging Ezekial Storm, Justy, and George Wilkes.

Justy and George shared a puzzled, wary look.

Justy felt her heart suddenly beating much faster than before.

"*You will be avenged!*" Storm raged at the sky.

Oily clouds were piling high and quickly changing shape. Thunder pealed, making the earth pitch and leap. Justy could feel the reverberation beneath her feet.

Storm rose stiffly, set his bullet-crowned, black hat on his head, and donned his black frock coat and pulled a long black rain slicker on over the coat. He drew a deep breath and looked at the stunned Justy and George through watery blue eyes, and said deeply, quaveringly, "Let's get after those butchers and send them back to the hell they came from. It's hungry—the Dark One. The Beast!"

He glanced once more at the single grave containing his two daughters then turned to Justy again. "It's hungry." He turned and began walking down the hillock to his wagon.

Justy saw that he'd left his open Bible beside the grave, the violent wind tearing the pages, lifting the ragged pieces and blowing them away through the trees like dirty snow.

"Mister Storm!" she called beneath another earth-shuddering thunderclap.

"Leave it!" he yelled back to her.

She and George shared another look then followed the obviously crazed man down the hill. While Justy and George pulled on their own slickers against the coming storm and waited with their horses, both still touched with a feeling of deep befuddlement and dread—whom had they just thrown in with?—Storm freed one of his mules, saddled the other one, filled a war bag with trail supplies, and mounted.

Justy and George mounted then, as well, and the three unlikely trail partners, with Storm riding point on his beefy but sure-footed, brindle mule, his shotgun poking up from his saddle sheath, the tails of his long black rain slicker flying out behind him in the building wind, galloped up the steep mountain trail.

Thunder rumbled louder as the storm grew nearer, quartering out of the northwest. The day grew darker and the pines on both sides of the rocky trail, on the other side of the creek thundering just off the trail's right side, shook and danced and then began to sway madly as the rain, having spit at first, suddenly rifled down as though a dam had succumbed to Ezekial Storm's own bitter fury.

The riders found themselves in a canyon. The steep ridge ahead and up which the trail climbed, was a veritable waterfall of muddy water. Storm twisted around in his saddle to roar in his stentorian, bear-like roar, "Ride like hellfire or we'll be swimming for it!"

Elbows high, he leaned forward and batted the beefy mule's ribs with the heels of his mule-eared boots. In his long, black rain slicker whipping in the wind, he looked like nothing so much, riding fifteen feet ahead of Justy, as an enormous crow taking flight as he and the mule climbed the rise through the butterscotch wall of pouring, white-capped water shepherding driftwood and rocks down the rise.

"Let's go, boy!" Justy said when the grulla started to balk when it saw the wall of water tumble toward it.

She ground her spurs into the horse's flanks. The gelding snorted, shook its head, then laid its ears back and climbed. Justy leaned forward so she wouldn't be tossed back off the grulla's arched tail. The horse lunged through the water that rose above its fetlocks, and, slipping, sliding, and lunging, it finally gained the crest of the hill.

Storm was a jouncing, black silhouette ahead of Justy, dwindling into the distance through the shifting veil of rain. Justy stopped and turned to see George and his dun jouncing up the ridge behind her. George put his dun up beside Justy and, breathless, the rain pouring off the brim of his hat, said, "That fella means business!"

"Like anyone who crosses paths with Frank Lord!"

Justy gigged the grulla ahead.

After a ten-minute ride along a level stretch of trail, with the mountain-clad, storm-hammered forest climbing on her left and a steep canyon opening on her right and in which the creek snaked a hundred feet below, almost hidden by the torrent, she saw Storm stopped on the trail just ahead of her, at the lip of another decline.

Justy put her horse up beside Storm's mule and followed his gaze down into yet another canyon—a large, broad one. A sprawling lodge of wood and stone sat in the middle of it, in a clearing in the forest, off the right side of the trail. A stable and a corral flanked it; they in turn were flanked by the creek. On the left side of the trail, fronting the lodge, was a big cottonwood with a crown like a giant mushroom.

Lightning flashed, lighting up the darkly eerie hollow below. Justy thought she could see a few lamps burning wanly in windows.

"That'll be McCullough's!" Storm said. "A man like Lord would have stopped there, might be there, enjoying the pleasures of the flesh...as well as defiling it!" He turned his head forward and raised his elbows high. "Hy-yahh, mule—we have Satan to feed!"

The mule brayed and lunged on down the hill,

shaking its head in disdain at the hammering rain, crashing thunder, and brightly flashing lightning.

"Hold on!" Justy urged, but a thunder peel drowned her words.

The preacher quickly became a dwindling, amorphous black spot on the trail ahead and below her.

George, who'd reined up to Justy's right, turned his incredulous face to her. "'We have Satan to feed'?"

Justy gave her head a shake, a shoulder a hike. "Poor man's off his nut." She turned to George. "If Lord's down there, Storm's gonna ride right into him." She paused. "What do you think?"

George turned his head toward the sprawling lodge, stable, and corrals below. He winced, ran a wet, gloved thumb down a wet cheek. He looked reluctant.

"You know what?" Justy said, fairly shouting to be heard above the storm. "He's right. Come on, George," she yelled, putting the steel to the grulla and starting at a dead run down the hill. "We have Satan to feed!"

CHAPTER 25

EDGAR "HARD TIME" LAWTON, AKA GEORGE WILKES
(the name of his maternal grandfather), sat his blaze-
faced dun staring down the slope at the girl and the grulla
dwindling quickly before both horse and rider were all
but swallowed by the storm, revealed only sporadically
and briefly when the lightning flashed.

"Well, what're you gonna do, ya damn scaredy-cat?"
Hard Time asked himself, hating the fear he heard in his
voice. "What're you gonna do—just sit here and let the
girl do all the work?"

To think he'd once thought he was bold enough to
ride with Frank Lord!

Shame raked him until he gouged his gelding's flanks
with his spurs. The horse whinnied its agitation at the
sudden assault, the storm, and likely whatever hell lay in
wait down there at the bottom of the canyon, and lunged
off its rear hooves, bolting down the ridge after the girl.
Rain slashed at Hard Time, streaming down his face and
burning with the trail dust and sweat in his eyes.
Thunder clapped like cymbals, making his eardrums

rattle. He could feel the reverberations in the ground beneath the gelding's pounding hooves.

As though from far away, a girl's scream cut through the storm. A man's voice, similarly muffled, yelled, "Help! Help us! Over here!"

Hard Time had been following Ezekial Storm and the girl toward the sprawling building lying in the hollow at the bottom of the ridge. But now he saw the murky shadow of Storm halt his mule before man and mule suddenly headed off to the left side of the trail.

The girl followed Storm's sudden leftward course change on her grulla. Blinking against the rain, Hard Time checked his dun down, the horse's hooves sliding in the mud, and turned to follow Storm and the girl with his gaze.

Several shuddering lightning flashes, like a lantern's flames guttering in repeated strong drafts, revealed the sprawling cottonwood tree nearly directly across the trail from the road ranch's main building.

There were two people over there—a stout figure crouched by the tree's broad bole and another, more indistinct figure, someone in a sopping coat and rubber boots—reaching up toward a branch arcing out from the tree itself. Something big was hanging from the cotton-wood branch, maybe five feet up from the ground. As the lightning continued to flash, lighting up the entire sky at times, the thing that was hanging from the branch looked like nothing so much as a giant bird, one massive swing spread out to one side.

"Help!" yelled the man nearest the tree. "Gotta...cut him down!"

"What?" Hard Time heard Justy cry.

"Help!" screamed the girl leaping around beneath the

big bird that had somehow got caught up in the branch and was maybe hanging by one wing...?

Hard Time blinked and ran a soaked sleeve of his jacket across his eyes.

Was that what it was—a bird?

As Storm swung down from his saddle near the stout man nearest the cottonwood, Justy swung her horse hard left, toward the girl in a sopping coat and rubber boots.

"Oh, my God!" Justy cried as she fairly leaped from the still-running grulla's back.

Hard Time stopped his dun halfway between Storm and the stout man nearest the cottonwood and Justy and the girl, both of whom were now reaching up toward the ungainly bird hanging from the branch that arced out a good twenty feet from the tree. The bird appeared to have got hung up about ten feet from the tree's broad trunk.

Again, Hard Time blinked. He focused on the bird and just as Justy glanced over her shoulder at him and shouted, "It's Mannion!" Hard Time saw that it was true.

What he was staring at was no bird at all. It was a big man hanging upside down from the cottonwood branch by one foot. The other leg hung out to one side. The man's arms hung nearly straight out at his sides, making him look as though he'd been crucified upside down. What made him look so much like a bird was that outstretched leg and his arms as well as the long flaps of torn clothes hanging off his nearly naked body, appearing black and shiny between lightning flashes.

The man's long, thick, gray-brown hair hung straight down toward the girls reaching up for him, clawing at his shoulders, trying to get a grip on them, trying to break his fall when the stout man had finished cutting through the rope apparently tied down low on the tree's broad bole.

Hard Time was astonished that he knew right away what to do. The others had panicked, but he had not. Imagine!

"Hold on!"

Feeling proud of himself, Hard Time booted the dun over to the man hanging from the branch—the notorious Bloody Joe Mannion, no less! Hard Time wrapped his left arm around the man's waist, drawing him toward Hard Time and the dun, and turned toward the stout man crouching by the trunk, sawing away at the rope.

"Okay!" Hard Time yelled. "Cut him loose!"

The stout man continued sawing at the rope until the tall Ezekial Storm said, "Here!" Storm's right hand moved to his cartridge belt and then something shiny glinted in it. As the stout man stepped away, Storm crouched, raised and lowered his right hand twice, and Hard Time could hear him grunting beneath the storm's din with the effort.

With the first whack of the bowie knife, Mannion's body jostled against Hard Time. With the second whack, Mannion dropped free of the branch and would have dropped straight down to the ground if Hard Time hadn't tightened his arm around him.

"Help me here!" Hard Time bellowed, holding the long, heavy man upside down against his side and the side of the skitter-hopping horse. Mannion was sliding from his grip.

Justy and the girl, a tall blonde who wore a nightgown beneath a soaked coat, were already by his side, both girls grabbing the infamous town marshal. Grunting with the effort, they more or less gentled the big man down to the soggy ground.

"Is he alive?" Justy said, crouching over Bloody Joe, who did not appear to be moving.

Hard Time had come alive, buoyed by his quick assessment and handling of the situation of trying to get Mannion down from the tree without dropping and doing further damage to him. He slid down from the dun's back, fell to a knee beside the big man, and placed his hand on the man's chest.

He could feel a throb, however faint, beneath his gloved palm.

"He's still kickin' but just barely, I reckon!" Hard Time pronounced to the two girls, importantly, sliding his gaze between their terrified faces down which the rain streamed, glinting in the continued lightning flashes. The blonde's face paint streaked down her face in the rain, like ink.

Justy turned her frightened gaze over her shoulder to the roadhouse.

"They're gone!" the stocky man said, standing beside Storm. "They beat holy hell out of a couple of my girls, but they're gone and I hope they never come back! Mannion gave 'em a good fight, though—I'll give him that!" He spat to one side, returning the small folding knife he'd been using on the ropes to a pocket of his baggy denims. "I doubt he'll live long after what they done to him, but let's get him inside, maybe get a little whiskey into him, at least!"

He crouched at Mannion's shoulders and glanced at Storm. "Help me here!"

But Storm had turned to stare up trail, his tall, lean, rangy frame silhouetted against the lightning flashes. Thunder rumbled and roared between tooth-gnashing crashes that sounded like cannon fire.

"I'll help!" Hard Time said, crouching at the marshal's

feet. Mannion had only one boot on and the sock on that foot was nearly off. The other boot was badly scuffed and caked with mud.

Suddenly, Storm turned and as though waking from a trance, walked over, and sidled the stout man aside. "Here, here...let me. Show us the way!"

Storm and Hard Time lifted Mannion and began slogging through the mud toward the lodge, Justy and the blonde followed along behind. There were four or five more girls on the stoop of the lodge, hunched against the chill, pulling robes of various colors closed across their breasts. Sobbing and shivering, they were all bare-legged, barefoot, lifting their feet as they warded off the chill.

They'd obviously witnessed holy hell here. Hard Time didn't doubt it a bit. He'd seen what Lord had done to Fury. He wouldn't have believed it if he hadn't seen it himself. Guilt raked him, cored him like a hollowed-out Halloween pumpkin.

He'd had a hand in that, himself. In fact, he might as well have killed Justy's grandfather and set fire to the town. Lord never would have done it without Hard Time telling Lord where Mannion was housing his brother.

The stocky man, who wore a soggy apron, strode in his heavy, bandy-legged fashion toward the lodge, ahead of Hard Time and Storm carrying Mannion. As he did, he thrust an arm and pointing finger at the girls huddled before him. He bellowed in a thick, Scottish brogue: "Agness, Mary Beth, get upstairs and ready a room for Bloody Joe. By God, if he goes out tonight, we're gonna send him out in grand fashion. Hilda, you get my medical bag. Now, hightail it, you girls—don't just stand there sobbin' like the sky's fallin'! This is Bloody Joe Mannion we got here!"

The girls leaped to life and dispersed inside the lodge,

bare feet slapping on the puncheons. The stocky man led the way up the rickety stairs running up the wall on the room's right side, under a grizzly head, and Storm and Hard Time followed, the long, broad-shouldered body of Marshal Joe Mannion hanging slack between them.

Hard Time wouldn't be a bit surprised if the man had expired between the time he'd felt for a pulse and now, because he sure wasn't showing any signs of life. Now in the lamplight, Hard Time could see the man's face was swollen and cut dang near to shreds. Why, it looked like ground beef! His eyes were hidden inside swollen pouches of purple flesh. His arms hung slack, the tips of his bloody fingers lightly brushing the risers as Hard Time and Mr. Storm carried him up the stairs.

If he hadn't been beaten to a pulp and then dragged by a horse, Hard Time missed his guess. He'd seen such work before, usually on sheepmen in cow country and the occasional nester too stubborn to pull his picket pin. But this time had been Bloody Joe's turn, sure enough.

"Gypsy!" the stocky gent, whom Hard Time had decided was probably the lodge's owner, McCullough, bellowed over the second-story balcony rail, "bring a bottle of me best whiskey, my girl! That highlands Scotch on the top shelf!"

Hard Time and Storm followed two sniffing doxies into a room with red and gold paper covering its vertical pine plank panels and sparsely furnished with a rumpled bed, a single dresser with a cracked mirror, a single ladderback chair, and a washstand. They edged around the tight space between a corner of the bed and the dresser then eased Joe onto the bed right after the two sniffing doxies had pulled the covers down.

The bed sagged deeply beneath Bloody Joe's weight, the leather braces creaking.

Bloody Joe groaned and turned his puffy, chewed up face from left to right and lay still.

"Goddamn, those sonso'lowly dogs, anyway," McCullough said, running a fat, pale hand across his mouth. He turned to Hard Time and his brown eyes blazed with admiration. "You shoulda seen it, though. Joe came for blood, that's for sure. Killed three—includin' Frank's wee little rat of a brother, Billy." He grinned. "He couldn't get it up for Crystal. That's what he was doin' downstairs. The others laughed, includin' Frank. Hah!"

The Scot chuckled as he added, "Joe wounded one more before they converged on him. He fought 'em though. He fought 'em like an old wolf the younger ones turn on. I tell you, when they rode out later, Lord with his brother's body across the back of his horse, there wasn't a one that didn't feel like he'd just survived a cyclone. Hah!"

He slammed a hand down on the marble top of the dresser, giving Hard Time a start. As though the storm outside wasn't enough racket. He could feel the old building swaying with the wind, timbers creaking loudly. Lamp flames guttered badly, making mad fluttering sounds.

Justy moved up to the front of the bed, brushed gentle fingers down Bloody Joe's broken face. "Ah...Joe," she said in a whisper. She got low and slid her lips close to his ear. "It wasn't your fault. Not really." A tear rolled down her cheek as she ran her hand through his wet, muddy hair, smoothing it back against his head. "I only accused you because it was my fault. All mine. I should have told you...warned you. You did good, Joe. You tried. All alone, you blasted fool...you tried."

She straightened when the big McCullough sidled up to her, throwing up his hands and yelling, "All right—

everybody out. Everybody but me an' Gypsy." He turned to the tall blonde who'd been outside, helping the barman get Mannion down from the tree. She'd just entered the room now, still in her sopping coat and nightgown. She'd kicked out of her boots, and she was barefoot. She had a black eye and a torn lower lip; fear remained in her eyes. She gave McCullough the bottle she'd fetched from below.

"Everybody but me an' Gypsy out," McCullough continued. "Gypsy and I, we got our bloody work cut out for us, looks like. Out now, out now...get the hell out an' let us see if we can't save ol' Bloody Joe! At least so's he can have one last whiskey with me an' Gypsy Rose!"

The barman drew the blonde against him with one arm and bellowed out a laugh then took a deep pull from the bottle.

"Here we go!" he said, raising the bottle again and adding, "Here's to Joe!"

He took another pull.

A HALF HOUR LATER, McCULLOUGH CAME SLOWLY, heavily down the stairs. He was followed by Gypsy, who'd removed her coat. Her soaked nightgown clung to every curve, breasts jostling darkly inside it. She carried a wooden bucket of bloody rags in both hands straight down in front of her.

Justy sat at a table in the middle of the blood-washed room with its broken chairs and tables and smashed front window through which the mid-afternoon air came, rife with the smells of pine and sage and the cloying odors of the horses tethered to the hitchrack out front. The storm had passed but rain still dripped from the hulking building's eaves. The sun peaked out, a faded saffron, from behind the ragged edges of dark blue clouds.

Justy and Hard Time were finishing up the stew a couple of sullen but less badly abused whores had served after Hard Time and Ezekial Storm had hauled the two dead men from Frank Lord's bunch out to the barn.

Like the animals they were, the gang hadn't seen fit to even bury their own dead though, according to one of the whores, the savage outlaw leader had ridden away with his brother's body lying belly down across the bedroll and saddlebags of Billy's horse. Frank and the others had ridden off just as the storm had rolled in, his own voice rising with the loudening thunder: "*Die slow, Bloody Joe! Oh, you bastard...die slow and think of my little brother Billy whose life you cut short, you bloody bastard, Joe!*"

Ezekial Storm sat off in the shadows, tall and darkly clad and gray-headed, an old conversion Navy .44 revolver on the table before him, finishing his own stew and wedge of grainy brown bread. His odd blue eyes stared as though transfixed at the table before him. His shotgun leaned against his chair; his floppy-brimmed black hat was hooked over the end of the double barrels. The man's angular jaws moved slowly and slightly sideways, like a cow chewing its cud, as he stared.

McCullough and Gypsy stopped at the bottom of the stairs. The barman puffed up his big chest and large, sagging belly, and announced, "Alas, Bloody Joe is gone."

That single word, "gone," pierced Justy's heart like a bayonet blade. She studied the barman closely. "What?"

Hard Time jerked with a start, dropped his fork on his plate, and hipped around in his chair to regard the barman in disbelief.

"Couldn't save him," the man said, his voice heavy and thick. "We got his wounds cleaned and bandaged. He started to regain consciousness but only long enough to sort of whisper, 'Please, forgive me,' and then he drew a deep breath, let it out slow, and lay his head back against his pillow. Dead."

McCullough bowed his nearly bald head and recited the Lord's prayer.

Distant thunder rumbled. Birds piped. Out in the stable, where Justy had led her and Hard Time's horses as well as Mannion's baby and Storm's mule. One of the horse's, likely Mannion's own Red, whinnied forlornly, as though in grief for the departed. The rain continued dripping from the eaves of the sprawling building, and a mouse scuttled somewhere beneath the floorboards.

Justy couldn't believe it. Bloody Joe Mannion—dead.

It was her fault. All of it.

As McCullough trudged slowly toward the bar and Gypsy carried the bucket of bloody rags through a curtained doorway at the rear of the building, Justy turned her disbelieving gaze to the barman. "Are you sure?"

McCullough walked around behind the bar. "Quite sure, me girl. Quite sure." He was holding the bottle of Scotch Gypsy had fetched. It was half empty. He set it on the bar. He set two goblets down, half-filled each, nudged one with the other in salute, and threw back the entire glass. He set the empty glass down on the bar then grabbed a bowl and ladled himself a bowl of stew from the pot bubbling on the range behind the bar.

Ezekial Storm seemed not to have heard the grim news. He sat as before, chewing and staring. Suddenly, he set his fork down on his plate, cleared his throat, set his shotgun and hat on the table, and rose from his chair.

Slowly, drawing a deep breath, he strode toward the stairs down which McCullough and Gypsy had come, and rose slowly, clomping monotonously, into the shadows of the sprawling building's second floor.

Up there, a door closed, and a latch clicked.

Hard Time turned to Justy. He shrugged a shoulder. "Leastways, a Christian man can say a few words over him..."

He picked up his fork and resumed eating the last of his stew.

Justy stared up the shadowy stairs.

She slid her empty plate away from her and rested her head on the table. She closed her arms over it, shut her eyes, and let the heavy anvil of sleep overtake her.

She dreamed.

No, she remembered.

It was just a dream.

No. May the saints banish her from Heaven forever...

It was a memory...

CHAPTER 26

THE COOL, SPRING WATER TUMBLED OVER THE FALLS TO shower upon her head and shoulders and to stream down over her breasts that had been filling out, growing larger over the past year and a half, after she'd turned fifteen, so that the boys and men in Fury couldn't take their eyes off her.

Her abuelito, old Jeremiah, had noticed it and had encouraged her in his gentle way not to wear her shirts so tight.

Something inside her had made her enjoy those watchful, lingering gazes...and the brightness of passion that rose in them. She was not just a child from the rocks any longer, but a woman who could stir a man to heat, to want.

It gave her a strange, thrilling power.

The water tumbled over her, cool and sensuous and rife with the smell of minerals from deep within the earth's hot bowels. As she stepped back behind the falls, between the falling water and the slick granite wall of the ridge over which the creek tumbled from above, within a hundred yards of hers and her grandfather's cabin in

Edith's Gorge—named after her dead grandmother—
Justy soaped her supple body with the cake of lye in her
hand.

She ran the soap down and under each arm, ran it
lingeringly over each nubile breast, then lifted each finely
turned, long leg in turn, soaping her thighs and buttocks
and the long curve of her calves...then each small foot in
turn.

She set the soap on a natural stone ledge then stepped
forward into the tumble of water, closing her eyes as she
ran her hands down her fine body, rubbing the suds away,
smoothing her soaked hair back from her face. She
became aware that she was no longer alone by a strange
feeling of being watched, of being caressed by a male
gaze, that suddenly gripped her as well as the unmistak-
able snort of a horse.

She opened her eyes then stepped back from the
tumble of water with a scream.

A man sat astride a gray horse before her. A handsome man with long, wavy yellow hair and baby blue eyes
drawn up at the corners. One of the Lord brothers—the
oldest of the two who lived with their no-account father
and half-sister on a claim just outside of Fury. Frank Lord
was a handsome, devil-eyed man in his early twenties, six
or seven years Justy's senior. But that had not stopped
him from giving her the eye in town when she and
abuelito had happened to be in town, as well, both families stocking up on supplies.

Frank wore a red and black calico shirt with a red,
neck-knotted bandanna, tight, blue denims, and soft
leather boots. The first several buttons of his shirt were
undone, showing the long, strawberry blond hair running
down the center of his chest—probably all the way to his
hard, flat belly. Long, thick yellow hair hung down from

the low-crowned, flat-brimmed brown hat he wore, the chin thong of which dangled down across his broad chest.

Justy backed up against the stone wall behind her, half-turned, crossed her arms on her breasts and planted one bare foot atop the other, raising that knee to cover herself as much as she could.

"Frank Lord, how dare you!" she screamed.

Lord threw his head back and laughed. "Oh, I dare, darlin'! I do dare!"

He laughed again.

"May I join you?" he asked, letting his eyes roam across every inch of her.

"Get out of here!" she screamed. "I'll call abuelito!"

Again, Lord laughed. "Abuelito is in town, you purty little hothouse flower. I just left Fury, was gonna do a little fishin' in the high country...get away from my whinin' little brother an' slave-drivin' old man." He touched the cane pole jutting up from the same scabbard in which his old Winchester jutted, then lifted his hat and ran a hand through his thick, yellow hair.

He set his hat back on his head then hiked his right, black, silver-tipped boot over his saddle horn and dropped straight down to the ground with rakish aplomb, raising his arms. He swiped his hat off his head, let it tumble to the stony ground, and said thickly, raking her body again with his bright, lewd gaze, "With all your caterwaulin', you didn't answer my question," he said. "Mind if I join you?"

"Yes!" Justy raked through gritted teeth, her skin crawling.

Or...*was* it crawling?

Or did she feel a strange warmth inside her, one that she tried to suppress just as she denied that it was even there. She was terrified, but maybe she was as terrified at what she'd found herself suddenly feeling as she was terrified of the man who made her feel that way.

"Get out of here, Frank! This is private!"

Frank shrugged out of his shirt, tossed it to the ground, and unbuttoned his pants, laughing, keeping those bright, dancing blue eyes on her, tracing the curve of her hips with his penetrating gaze, nearly as physical as a man's hands. "Darlin', you're bathin' outside. Nothin' private about that!"

"I'll tell my grandfather—you Lords are already pariahs!"

"Par...*what?*" Lord laughed as he kicked out of his boots.

"Get out of here, Frank—I'm warnin' you!"

"Warn away, sweetheart," he said, as he sat down on a rock and peeled off his denims. Once the pants were on the ground with his hat, shirt, boots, and gun belt, he jerked the sleeves of his longhandles down his arms and then, looking at her with a defiant, goatish grin, began peeling them down his legs.

His long, pale, muscular legs were carpeted in fine, red-blond hair that glinted like liquid gold in the sunshine penetrating the canyon.

Justy's heart raced and bucked.

Her mouth was dry.

Her knees were like warm mud.

Try as she might, she could not keep from watching him peel his longhandles down his legs before rising from the rock and tossing them down with the rest. He gave a loud, wild whoop and then jumped into the falls, letting the water tumble over him not four feet away from her. Beyond him, his horse, who'd drawn water at the pool around the falls, sauntered away, grazing.

Lord was like a wild animal—a wolf or a grizzly. He was so close that Justy could smell the half-feral scent of him. The smell of sweat, horse, and cigarette smoke. She tried to close her eyes but they came open several times of their own accord and she couldn't help watching him, in fleeting spurts, with horrific fascination.

She'd never seen a man naked before.

Finally, while he hopped up and down, whooping and hollering and scrubbing his man's body with his hands, tilting his head back to take the full force of the falls on his face, she gave a strangled cry of disdain and revulsion then brushed past him, quickly gathered her clothes, and ran barefoot across the clearing to the cabin, from the tin stovepipe of which a thin skein of pale smoke issued.

"I'll be right there, my pretty!" Lord screeched jeeringly at her.

"No!" Justy screamed back, meaning it.

Yes, she meant it.

She ran into the cabin, slammed the door, and pulled her grandfather's spare pistol out of a drawer. She threw herself into a corner by the dry sink, and, holding her ball of clothes against her naked body, shivering with cold and anxiety, aimed the Colt at the door with her other hand. The gun was too heavy for one hand so she released the clothes, let them rest against her bare breasts, and held the gun in both hands, aimed at the door.

The gun quivered as she shook.

Her mind was in such turmoil she didn't know how much time had passed before there was a loud whoop and the drumbeat of hooves, growing louder. The horse galloped around behind the cabin. She glimpsed horse and rider in a window above and behind her, to her right. He would tie the horse out of sight of the main trail leading into the yard.

"No," Justy ground out through gritted teeth, desperation clawing at every bone and muscle. "No...please, go away...leave me *alone*!"

Footsteps rose. From the sound, she tracked him as he came around to the front of the cabin. She saw his shadow through the crack beneath the door. She stared at the door and her heart turned a somersault in her chest. She had not lowered the locking bar through the iron braces in the door. The board leaned against the wall.

Why had she not locked it?

But then she knew.

When he opened the door and came in, clad in only his longhandles that clung wetly to his skin, she lowered the gun. He dropped the clothes and hat and gun belt he held in his hands then, staring down at her, his expression suddenly humorless, he peeled out of the longhandles, breathing hard, eyes shimmering. She watched him and did not turn away even as he walked toward her, his goatish male lust obvious, jutting before him.

She was not sure how much time had passed since he'd entered the cabin to when she heard the clatter of her grandfather's buckboard as it swung off the main trail and onto the trail that led to the cabin.

Frank cursed and looked up from where he'd been nuzzling her throat, their sweating bodies sticking together. He rose from between her spread knees and, staying low, edged a look out the front window. He laughed as the clatter of the wagon and the thuds of the mule's shoes grew louder as her abuelito approached the cabin.

Frank turned to her, laughing. "'Fraid it's time to say goodbye, milady." He gathered up his clothes and hat and gun belt.

He stepped onto a chair and then scurried quickly out the open window above Justy, in the wall to her right. At nearly the same time, Justy heard abuelito drive the buckboard around to the stable flanking the cabin.

The wagon stopped and abuelito yelled, "Hey, there—you! Frank Lord, you stop right there, damn your vermin hide!"

Wild laughter and the thuds of an instantly galloping horse.

"Damn you, Frank—you stay away from my granddaughter or there'll be hell to pay!"

Justy leaped at the thunder of abuelito's double-bore.

More laughter and hoof thuds dwindling into the distance.

Justy leaped again as abuelito triggered the second barrel of his double-bore.

Silence.

Justy lay on the old horsehair sofa, holding a moth-eaten trade blanket up tight against her breasts, covering her nakedness.

Her grandfather swore under his breath. He spat and then there was the crunch of footsteps as he made his way around the cabin to the front door. She saw his shadow beneath the door.

He stood there for a long time. She could hear him breathing—a faint rising and falling, a wheezing sound.

Slowly, he turned the knob, pushed the door inward.

His eyes swept the room, stopped when they found her.

He stood staring grimly in at her.

Slowly, she turned away from him in shame, giving him her naked back...

Justy jerked her head up from the table when a thundering voice that could belong only to Bloody Joe

Mannion yelled from the second story, "Somebody bring me a pot to piss in!"

JOE HAD NO IDEA HOW MUCH TIME HAD PASSED SINCE that first awakening after his beating and the hanging by Lord's gang, before he woke again and rose heavily from the bed.

He stood over the porcelain thunder mug and relaxed his bladder, which he'd awoken yet again to find so achingly full that he thought the seams of the poor organ would burst. He filled half the bucket before he finished. With a bare foot, he slid the bucket under the bed, sat down, and leaned back against the papered wall on the bed's far side.

When he heard someone coming up the stairs, he grabbed a pillow and lay it across his privates.

Heavy boots barked in the hall. Two quick knocks on the door then the door opened, and McCullough stuck his round, bearded face into the room, and smiled.

"Ah, you're up again!"

Mannion scowled at him, badly disoriented. He felt as though he were half in a dream. Half awake, half dead-out. He remembered waking, evacuating his bladder, even eating some food. But he wasn't sure how many times.

"How long have I been here?" he asked the barman. His voice sounded foreign to him, far away. But then, the rest of him felt far away, foreign, too. It was as though he'd crossed through some invisible portal into a strange land—strange because it looked like the land he'd passed from, strange because, in some inexplicable way it looked and *felt* far different from that land.

The brain scrambling he'd received from Lord's men must be the culprit.

"This is your third day here, Joe."

McCullough stepped into the room. He held a bottle in one hand, two glasses in the other. "You gonna stay awake for a while?"

"I'm all slept out...for now, anyway." Mannion ran a hand down his face. Each time he'd done that in the past three days, he'd noticed the swelling had gone down more and more around his eyes and mouth. His cracked lips were healing much faster than normal.

Frighteningly fast.

His strength was returning, as well.

Frighteningly fast.

By how quickly he'd healed, he felt as though he must have lain in this room a good month, recuperating. But it had been only three days...

McCullough looked at him a little dubiously, a little apprehensively, scrutinizing the lawman's face, which, by rights, should still look much the same as it had three days ago—like fresh soup scraps scraped off a cow's carcass. Joe didn't want to look in the mirror above the dresser behind the barman. He feared what he'd see there. It was enough just to feel it with his fingers.

Inexplicable healing. At least, inexplicable in any *normal* way. In any rational, *earthly* way. There was no way to explain the fast abatement of the almost unbearable pain that had raked nearly every inch of him when they'd first cut him down from the cottonwood.

Surely, he'd had some broken bones. All healed now, or nearly so. He still had some aches and pains, but nothing like three days ago.

McCullough set the bottle and the glasses on the nightstand beside the bed. He pulled a chair out from a small table next to the dresser, turned it to face the bed, and slacked his considerable weight into it. Breathing heavily with the strain of leaning forward against his considerable paunch, he pulled the cork from the bottle and half-filled each glass.

He handed one to Mannion, knocked it with his own.

"To the Good Lord's healin' of ya, Joe." The barman threw back the whole glass, puffed his cheeks out, and shook his head. His brown eyes watered. "I have to admit, if only to you, Joe, me boy, my faith was on shaky ground till the preacher come up here an' laid hands on you...or whatever in hell he done."

"Is that what he did? Laid hands on me?"

"I don't know. I didn't see. He was the only one here." McCullough refilled his glass. "What do you remember?"

Joe closed his eyes against the remembered voice in his head, muttered into his ear, the man's voice deep and resonant and pitched with foreboding, the kind of chilling presentiment that made a man's inside writhe. "Your soul for revenge, Joe. It hungers. The Dark One..."

He squeezed his eyes more tightly shut when he heard the prayer Storm had spoken into his ear. He couldn't remember the words, but he knew by the tone that—what?

A hand nudged him.

Mannion snapped his eyes open with a start, relieved to see only McCullough sitting there, not the long, craggy, eternally sad and, yes, somehow malevolent face of Ezekial Storm. Joe threw down half the whiskey then rested the glass on his bare chest.

"What do I remember?"

"Yeah."

"I saw Sarah."

McDougal frowned. The barman didn't know about

Sarah. Joe's wife. Dead by suicide when Vangie had still been a baby. She'd taken her own life because she'd been overcome with depression in the months after Vangie's birth and Joe had been too busy taming yet another town to lend comfort where it had been needed most—in his own home.

"My wife...Sarah. I saw her...out in our yard in Kansas. A windy day...sunny...she was hanging clothes on a line, her apron fluttering, hair blowing. She laughed as she stooped to pick up clothes that were blown off the line, had to run after them. She looked up at me suddenly, as though I were looking down at her from a window on the second floor of our house. Only it wasn't her looking up at me. It was the face of a giant crow."

McCullough swallowed, licked the underside of his dry upper lip. "A crow, ya say..."

"A crow. Its eyes sent a chill into me. I can still feel it." He shuddered and drew the bedcovers over his bare legs and chest. He looked into McCullough's dark, grave eyes. "Tell me I've gone nuts. Something, anything..."

McCullough stared back at him. Finally, he smiled. "You're just a fast healer, Joe. That's all. Storm...he's the one who went nuts. Crazier'n a tree full of owls."

Mannion looked down at his glass. "Maybe. Maybe so..." He threw back his drink then turned back to the barman. "Where's Storm?"

"Gone. Right after the squall blew itself on to the southeast. The girl and the younker, George Wilkes, waited till the next morning. I warned 'em the canyons would be overflowin'...no way across without drownin', fer sure."

"That damn kid," Mannion said tightly, giving his head a single, angry wag. He remembered through the fog of agony glimpsing her crouching over him when he'd first been hauled in here, mostly unconscious. He should have known she'd follow him. He should have lain back and given her the ass-tanning he'd promised. He'd been too intent on Lord to keep much of an eye on his backtrail.

He turned to the barman now and frowned. "Who's Wilkes?"

MacDougal shrugged both shoulders. "Never seen him before. Tight-lipped fella. Rode in with the girl, rode out with her."

"They left yesterday?" Mannion said.

"Yesterday mornin'," McCullough said with a nod.

"What time is it now?"

"Last I checked, almost three."

"I'm a day and a half behind them."

"They probably got held up by the floodwaters. Storm, too, if he didn't drown."

Mannion leaned forward, wrapped his hand around the barman's thick wrist. "Where are they headed? Lord's bunch?"

MacDougal shrugged a heavy shoulder. "Mexico. They outfit here then turn south, through the Black Range and then the Chiricahuas. But first they pay a visit to the lumber camp over by Morning Thunder Peak. Frank's got a half-sister who works over there. Eloise." The barman traced a circle in the air just off his left ear with his index finger. "Soft in the head. Cooks an' whores over there."

McCullough smiled, shook his head. "You sure gave him the what-for, Joe. Killed Billy outright. Frank left sobbin' with the kid laid belly down over his horse."

"So I did kill him. I was worried I only dreamed it."

"Killed two more. I dragged 'em out to a ravine. Wolves been howlin' at night. MacDougal grinned. "You best go home, now, Joe. Frank'll be through here again next year. You can get him then...with help. I warned Storm. I warned those kids to go on home."

Mannion shook his head. "Justy never will."

"I heard about Fury, the old constable."

Mannion squeezed the barman's wrist a little tighter. "Roy, tell me somethin'."

"I'll try."

"Do you believe in the devil?"

"Oh, yeah." MacDougal pursed his lips, nodding. "It's God I didn't believe in...till that preacher called you back from the dead."

"He's no preacher," Joe growled, flaring a nostril.

"Who is he, then?" When Mannion didn't respond but just stared off into space, the barman scowled and said, "Joe, you don't seem all that grateful. By God, man, you were dead..."

Mannion drew a deep breath, let it out slow. Maybe he should be grateful. At least, old Storm had given him another shot at Lord.

He threw the covers back. "Fetch me some clothes, Roy," he said. "My guns!"

CHAPTER 27

LIGHTNING STILL FLICKERED AND THUNDER DRUMMED when Ezekial Storm had left Roy McCullough's Road Ranch not long after the lawman, Mannion, had opened his eyes with a gasp and had stared up at him, his hard gray orbs opaque as isinglass.

As the lawman's eyes had rolled back into his head—heading for sleep this time, not death—Storm had smiled grimly and left the room.

It needed feeding...

McCullough had told Storm he should wait for the canyons to drain on the lee side of the storm, but the voice in Storm's head would not let him dally.

The voice was a combination of Storm's late wife's voice and the voice of the rattlesnake slithering around inside his head—if a rattlesnake could speak in a human tongue, that was. If such a thing could happen, and Storm wasn't sure about anything anymore, the snake would sound like the half-snake, half-human voice in his head, behind a background of distant rattling, castigating him with:

"How dare you consider waiting, Ezekial! Did your

daughters not wait for your help...in futility? Did you not stand frozen in your boots while the laughing and goatish Frank Lord and the Indian walked away to assault them? Now, since the killers left you alive to be tortured by what you did...or did *not* do...you must finally *act*, Ezekial! You must hunt down and murder Magda and Josephine's murderers so your daughters' souls may rest in peace!"

Now, on the morning of his second day out from McCullough's place, Storm sat atop a rise and studied the torrent of water flowing down a canyon from a steep ridge above and to his right, the crest of the ridge obscured by low clouds and pine forest. What had been a shallow creek was now a raging river tumbling downward at nearly a forty-five-degree angle, flowing from Storm's right to his left, filling up the canyon at the base of the rise.

Storm chewed his bottom lip, considering.

No, he and the mule wouldn't make it. They couldn't cross here.

He decided to follow the creek's shoreline farther down the mountain and hope to find a less risky place to ford the swollen, raging waters that pounded and thundered, throwing up white rooster tails in the canyon below and before him. To that end, he swung the nervous mule off the trail's left side and booted it through ferns and hock-high, green spring grass, descending the steep grade through the fragrant conifers, mountain blue birds and nuthatches flitting around him. He passed a trio of ravens sitting on a half-devoured elk, eyeing him sharply, warningly, as they continued to peck at the exposed ribs. The hindquarters had been completely severed and hauled away, likely by some stalking puma, leaving the rest to the lesser lights on the carrion-eating food chain.

As Storm passed the carnage, his eyes watered at

the stench of death. He brushed the tears away automatically and kept moving down along the east side of the hammering waters, looking desperately for a way across.

Although desperation pounded away at every sinew inside him and made his hands squeeze the mule's reins until his fingernails nearly cut through his gloves, he did not betray that desperation to the world. If he were to meet another rider out here, that other would see merely a lanky, black-clad, gray-headed figure sitting the beefy mule straight-backed, his long, craggy, hook-nosed face as hard as weathered granite.

Finally, the slope leveled. A clearing opened around the former preacher. The water was still moving quickly through the deep bed before him, swirling in places and lapping noisily against the shore on both sides. But it was no longer white. Now it was a fast-flowing sheet of deep blue, a hundred feet wide, black where the shadows of ridges angled over it.

In contrast to the pounding torrent above, it was ominously quiet but for a constant, low sucking sound with a faint rushing sound farther downstream.

Storm booted the mule up close to the edge where the water lapped against the rocks. The mule stiffened, shook its head, and gave several anxious brays. Something large and black swept down over Storm's right shoulder.

The raven lighted on a branch of a cedar to his right. The raven turned toward him and cawed, golden eyes bright with mockery.

"Do it, Ezekial! Cross over!" cawed the raven over his wife's admonishing voice. "This is no time for cowardice!"

"You know I can't swim, Natasha," Storm grunted out.

The raven turned those bright, mocking eyes on him again. CAW! CAW! CAW!

The jeering laughter was too much. Storm batted his heels against the mule's ribs. The mount took half a step forward, shook its head.

"Go, dammit, Yeroshka!" Storm bellowed, smashing his heels harder against the mount's broad barrel.

The mule lunged forward and into the water.

The water rose to nearly its withers.

The mule continued forward, and the water swept up and over Storm's hips. The current caught the mule and rider and swept them downstream, the mule braying and pawing desperately at the water. It couldn't touch bottom. As it fought forward, lolling this way and that, Storm slid off its back, his legs floating straight out behind him as he clung to the horn.

His hat tumbled down his shoulder and into the stream, floating along beside him as though trying to keep up.

"Oh, Lord! Oh, Lord!"

Storm closed both of his gloved hands around the saddle horn, terror consuming him as the current tugged him and the mule downstream while the mount fought desperately to cross to the other side. The poor beast's eyes were barely above the level of the inky black water. It kept its black snout above the surface and Storm could hear the *chuff-chuff-chuff* and as it fought for air, flailing its hooves so violently that Storm could sometimes see the front ones nearly breaking the surface of the stream several feet beyond Yeroshka's head.

They were halfway to the other side when an especially strong current grabbed them. With a screeching, otherworldly cry of grave terror, the mule swung sharply to the left. Storm gave a horrified cry as the violence of the animal's sudden movement caused his gloved hands to slip free of the horn and he spun out away from the mule, turning circles in the water along with the terrified mount, as they both were swept with dizzying quickness downstream so that the rocks and shrubs and occasional cedars and cottonwood saplings passed along both shores in a blur of fast motion.

The roaring grew louder on what was Storm's right and then his left and then his right again as he continued to spin in the swirling current. When he found himself facing downstream, an especially large knot of horror tightened inside him, caused his heart to leap into his throat, squeezed it so that he could feel it hammering against the underside of his tongue. He saw the downward curve of the stream and the rocky chasm with the stream continuing maybe fifty feet below and beyond that descension.

The roaring sound was a falls!

The knowledge raked across his brain as he stared over the panicked form of the mule ten feet away from him, between him and the falls, and the falls just beyond it—a hundred feet away and the gap closing fast. He swung himself around to face the shore and flung his arms forward, kicking desperately with his legs, his clothes weighing him down, impeding his progress.

CAW! CAW! CAW!

The raven caromed over him, looking down with those bright, jeering eyes, laughing at him.

"Can't even ford a simple stream to avenge your poor daughters, you simple fool!"

CAW! CAW! CAW!

Storm could hear his wife's voice in his head: "Ezekial, your daughters' souls will never be at rest. Knowing that you did nothing to help them—NOTHING—in their hour of need but stand frozen to the ground in fear for your own life. And yours will never rest, either!"

He gave a hoarse, animal wail as he watched the mule, lying on one side, its snout pointed up, its eyes so round they showed nearly all white, dropped over the smooth downward curve of blue-back water and was suddenly gone. Only three seconds later, Storm saw the beast again, falling straight down along the tumbling white, striated sheet of water below him, its bulky body somehow forming an S curve, stirrups and reins rising, Yeroshka's legs still thrashing as though trying to swim in midair.

And then Storm felt the stream drop away from beneath him as it opened its watery jaws to release him.

He flew straight down the falls in a sitting position, arms thrown out to his sides, legs up before him, bent knees pointed at his chest. He looked up and thought that anyone seeing him fall from above, as he'd watched the mule fall from above, would have seen his descent much as he'd seen that of the mule—all white-eyed horror and disbelief at the grim and improbable predicament the stream of his days had led him to.

CAW! CAW! CAW!

The raven flew down beside him to jeer into his own eyes with its small, bright, gold ones before giving its broad, black wings a powerful downward thrust and then rose up and away from him as though to mock him with its powers of flight a second before he plunged into the pool at the bottom of the falls.

Down...down, he went...the water falling from above hammering on top of him.

His ears...his mind...filled with the stream's own hysterical laughter.

His boots touched the stony bottom of the turbulent

pool and then he waved his arms, fighting for the surface against the downward thrust of the water plunging down around him. Finally, he turned himself slightly and swam up at an angle until his head broke the surface maybe twenty feet out away from the roaring white cascade of the falls.

Several currents tugged at him until one seemed to out tug the others and he found himself angling toward the right side of the stream as he faced downstream, turning as the hands of the floodwaters grabbed and tugged then released then grabbed and tugged once more...until he found himself heading straight toward the smooth, branchless bole of a long-fallen tree jutting straight out into the stream from the rocky shore. He was moving so quickly toward it he wasn't sure if he should duck under it or grab it.

Grabbing it might cave in his chest and break his arms.

He had no choice but to try for it; who knew if and when another possible lifeline might show itself farther downstream?

The bole grew and grew before him until he could see the knots and ants milling inside striations of the brittle grain and bits of remaining bark.

When he was ten feet away from the tree, he thrust his arms straight up and hooked them over it.

WHAM!

It hammered against his chest, knocking the wind out of him.

He hung there, the water pushing against his legs, threatening to rip him off the bole and continue to cast him downstream.

He drew a breath, making strangling sounds. He drew another, and another, until he thought he had a good enough hold on the bole, and enough strength, that he wouldn't come off it. He *couldn't* come off it!

Indian war lances of agony impaling his chest, he winced as he crabbed along the bole to his right, making for the shore from which it jutted, having been pulled up by its roots. He could see the tangled ball of webbing root maybe fifteen feet beyond the rocky embankment.

Groaning, crying out against the pain in his arms, shoulders, and chest, he inched along the bole to his right. Finally, he gained the shore. Several stubby branches extended from the bole here. Slowly, painstakingly, he climbed them, pulling himself up with his arms, pushing up with his feet...until, with one last groan and burst of energy, he heaved himself up out of the clinging stream and over the bole and onto the rocks at the top of the bank.

He lay, soaked and cold and shivering, half-conscious. For how long, he didn't know.

He only knew he'd tried to cross the stream in the midmorning of his second day on the trail out from McCullough's Road Ranch. When he opened his eyes and looked up, salmon light carpeted the rocks and slanted across the shadowy forest beyond him. He glanced to the west. The orange ball of the sun was impaled by the jutting black church steeple of a ridge crest.

Shivering so violently he could hear his teeth clattering, he turned back to the forest.

Hope rose inside him.

A small cabin hunched there—an age-grayed box of tin-roofed, hand-adzed logs slouched along the slope just beneath where the forest began.

CHAPTER 28

LEADING THE PAINT HORSE ACROSS WHICH SPRAWLED the dead body of his poor, misbegotten brother Billy, killed by the notorious and aptly nicknamed Bloody Joe Mannion (that would go on Billy's tombstone), Frank Lord passed the tilting signpost into which the name PEGASUS LUMBER had been burned, and stared straight ahead along the old logging road he and his gang had started following not long after they'd left McCullough's Road Ranch just ahead of the storm.

The camp was a small sprawl of cabins to the left and a long, low eating hall built of logs to the right. Behind the eating hall were three barns and several corrals in which milled the big, beefy mules, still with their coats shaggy from the long mountain winter, the lumber crew used to haul the logs they cut on the surrounding plateaus down to the lower reaches, on big, lumbering drays.

A two-track trail led up a slight rise beyond the barns and corrals to the larger building of vertical pine logs that housed the mill with its giant saw, silent now in the growing dusk.

Smoke issued from the two tin chimney pipes poking up out of the eating hall's roof of corrugated tin. The crew would be eating supper now, as it was late in the day and the sun was angling westward. Long, bulky shadows slid down from the forested ridges and hanging canyons that cupped the camp in the palm of their giant, collective hand. Silver mountain sage and blond needle grass was all that grew down here, on the floor of the plateau; spotted with lingering snowdrifts clinging to the north sides of shallow ravines, the prairie stretched away in all directions, undulating as it rose toward the forested higher slopes, several of which showed the broad scarred areas of slash where acres of pines and aspens had been cut.

A slight wind gusted as Frank led his nine-man procession into the camp. The wind caused a hay hook to slam every few seconds against the face of the barn beyond the long, low eating hall he was angling toward. Two mules and a cream-colored Concord wagon—a former stagecoach outfitted for a private carriage, most likely— were tied to one of the two, long hitchracks fronting the hall. In ornate red lettering, the words PEGASUS LUMBER ran across the side of the carriage above the doors. Across the doors, in somewhat smaller letters, was the name H. Leroy Hamm.

"Halloo, the camp!" Frank called in his sonorous baritone.

The hall's front door, set above two wooden steps, was closed. There were four curtained windows in the front wall, two on each side of the door. Burlap curtains were closed over all four, but through the curtains could be seen the shadows of men seated on long wooden benches fronting a long, wooden table twenty feet from the front door. Through the windows and the closed door could be heard the loud roar of raucous conversations—the jubilant albeit weary conversations of men who toiled many hours outside in all manner of weather and lived for nothing more than a good meal, a few drops of grog or whiskey, and a mattress dance or two with a big-assed whore at the end of the toilsome day.

"I say," Frank called between gloved hands cupped around his mouth, "halloo, the camp!" He'd dropped the reins of Billy's horse, which snorted behind him, turned its head to sniff the blanket-wrapped body draped across its saddle, and gave a peevish chuff. It stomped one front hoof.

It was one thing to contend with the little viper when he'd been alive. It was another matter to carry him when he was dead and beginning to bloat and smell.

The door opened and a slender, medium-tall, brown-bearded man wearing a red knit cap and flannel shirt and suspenders stuck his head out, scowling angrily at the intrusion. "Who the hell are you?" he said, casting his incredulous gaze across the nine men before him.

"Probably just some tinker, Daniels. Send him on his way and sit down to hear my toast!" came a man's voice from behind the slender, bearded man.

Daniels gave a single, angry, dismissive wave, glaring at Frank, then slammed the door.

Frank could see through the curtained window right of the door a man standing at the end of the long table. He was short and impeccably dressed, standing out in the crowd of bulky, bearded men around him. What appeared a woman—and a pretty one at that, clad in furs —sat to the fancy Dan's right. Her thick hair spilled onto her fur-clad shoulders as she smiled adoringly up at the foppish gent. She also raised a glass.

A beer glass.

They were all raising beer glasses.

The woman's glass looked too big for her beringed, little hand. Her lovely face betrayed some strain.

The foppish gent said loudly, "My toast this evening is to all of you—the men of Pegasus and for all the hard work you do. This has been a record year for profits for Pegasus Lumber, and I and the missus and Mister Daniels, your devoted superintendent, have only you and your hard work to thank. Salute to you all, my good men, then down the hatch!"

"*Salute! Salute! Salute!*" roared the beefy, bearded men sitting at the long table, facing the foppish, bespectacled gent in a three-piece suit, facing them on Frank's right as he gazed through the window.

As one, they all tipped their raised beer schooners back.

The one called Daniels stepped forward, away from the door and into Frank's field of vision fronting the window, and said, "We couldn't have done it without you, boss." Louder, to the men at the table, he bellowed, "A big round of applause for the boss, you mother-lovin' scoundrels—er, with apologies to Missus Hamm!"

Ribald laughter.

The beefy mill workers set their glasses down and gave a loud, raucous round of applause for the bespectacled, suited gent, who hung his head as though with great humility. The pretty woman—she resembled a blooded mare in a corral of burred-laden, broomtail broncs in there—smiled up at the man, her husband (and a moneyed one, at that, for sure) as she joined in with the beefy, whistling mens' applause.

POW! POW! POW!

As the Colt in Frank's hand bucked and roared, flames lapping skyward, the din in the eating hall dwindled quickly. All heads turned toward the window. Boots thudded inside the place. The door scraped open and Daniels, the dark-bearded man in the red stocking cap, swept through it, a double-barreled shotgun in his hands.

"What the hell is going on *now*? I told you men to *git!* This is mill business!"

"Sounds to me like mill business is kissin' the boss's ass," Frank said. "Send Eloise out here."

The heavy, single, dark brow over Daniels's eyes ridged severely. "*What?*"

"Send Eloise out here. Eloise Lord. I'm her brother, Frank."

When he'd heard the name "Lord" and "Frank," Daniels's face blanched a little. Uncertainty washed into his angry gaze. "There's no Eloise here," he said, finally, incredulously. "Now, ride on!"

"She works in the kitchen!" Frank said. "I know she's here. I been here before. Besides, where in hell else could she be?" Frank looked around at the vast, mountainous country beyond the yard that was slowly being consumed by purple shadows sliding down from higher plateaus and stony ridges.

The wind was turning colder. It had the smell of snow in it.

Quick, angry footsteps sounded from within the eating hall. The door behind Daniels opened wider and the dapper gent stepped out onto the stoop, the salmon light of early evening glinting in his glasses. "Just what in holy Christian hell is going on out here, Daniels? I was just about to unveil the plaque for—"

He stopped abruptly when another head appeared in the doorway behind him and a young woman pushed out onto the stoop between Daniels and the man who was obviously the camp's head honcho, H. Leroy Hamm. The dandy and his wife had probably ridden up from Denver or Colorado Springs to mingle with the crew, as though they were all one big happy family.

The girl was tall, pale, and rail thin, with a round, freckled face, thin lips, and a long, pale nose set beneath a ruffle-brimmed dusting cap. A checked gingham apron hung straight down against her legs over the shapeless sack dress she wore.

Her hair, poking out from beneath the cap, was the same stark yellow as Frank's, her eyes the same odd, baby blue. They were now wide and round with foreboding. Her mouth shaped a small *o*.

"Frank! What are you *doing* here?" she said, as flabbergasted as the men standing to each side of her.

Frank raised his left fist to his mouth and nose, squelching a sob. He shook his head, cleared his throat. "It's brother, Billy, Eloise. He's..." His voice cracked but he turned his head slightly to glance at the paint horse standing ground-reined behind him and finished with: "He's gone."

"What?" Eloise said, taking one step forward. "Billy's...*gone?*"

"Gone!" Frank croaked out through a sob.

The eight men flanking him glanced around at each other, but none said a word. This was how Frank got from time to time. You had to let him be or God help you...

The dapper little man in the black, three-piece suit and red cravat had had enough. He scrunched his face up in disdain as he stepped forward and said, "What is the meaning of this? This woman has work to do. Back," he said, giving Eloise's pale arm a hard tug, turning her around and pushing her toward the door. "Back to the kitchen at once! You will serve dessert shortly, and I want that cream freshly whipped!"

He jutted his arm and pointing finger straight out before him into the hall of beefy lumbermen staring toward him in hang-jawed incredulity.

"Unhand her, damn you!" Frank raged, thrusting out an arm and admonishing finger. "You touch her again and I'll blow you out of those shoes, you little termite!"

The little man turned slowly around, a look of disbelief on his little, mustached mouth. "What did you just call me?"

Frank leaned forward over his saddle horn. "Termite," he repeated, enunciating the word very carefully. "I'm pulling my sister out of here, *Termite*, and her an' me is gonna find a proper place to bury our brother."

"She won't be goin' anywhere," Daniels said at last, apparently buoyed by his boss's show of bravery. He turned to Eloise and gave her a hard shove through the door. "Get moving!"

Eloise gave a little yelp as she stumbled into the eating hall, twisting around and casting Frank a frightened, sad, befuddled look over her shoulder. As she did, another woman stepped into the doorway and walked out onto the stoop, close beside the dapper, little H. Leroy Hamm.

Instantly, Frank felt a warming down deep in his loins, and his tongue grew thick.

"What's going on, Leroy?" said the woman, a little brunette ensconced in her fox fur coat, with a little red fox head resting on each shoulder.

Each head resembled a tiny fox, sound asleep on each shoulder. The woman wore little, black, pointed toed boots, which stuck out beneath the hem of her spruce green velveteen skirt that cast a golden sheen. Her face was so delicate and cherubic and downright intoxicating, with pouting little brown eyes and plump little pouting red lips, that she could have been fashioned from china, or painted on a china tea server.

Frank couldn't tell much about her body inside all those clothes, but he could imagine what it looked like, all right—stripped naked, creamy and supple and snuggled down in a nice, warm, feather bed, clad in only a thin, silk sheet. He thought he could smell her from here —pure femininity.

He moved around uncomfortably in his saddle.

Three Moons rode up to sit his pony to Frank's left.

He'd smelled her, too, and his black eyes fairly smoldered in their deep, red sockets as they swept over her like the gaze of a hungry jaguar.

Bronco and Sager rode up to sit their horses to Frank's right—Sager in his Stars and Bars, gold button shirt under his long, buffalo hide coat, the old, ratty, gray Confederate kepi on his head. He and Bronco had smelled her too.

Sager whistled his appreciation, gave a loud rebel yell.

Three Moons turned to Lord, his eyes dark and wide and round as 'dobe dollars. "A man gets lonely out here, Frank. As long as we been ridin'."

Bronco laughed. "We're only three days out of McCullough's."

"Still, though," Three Moons said, his eyes riveted on the little brunette pressing herself close to the dandy, stepping ever so lightly on the dandy's foot and canting her head against his shoulder.

Frank imagined her canting her head against his own shoulder.

The dandy didn't deserve such a creature as that. He likely had no idea what to do with that. No idea at all.

Hamm and Daniels had obviously seen the expressions on the faces of the three men sitting their mounts before them. Their own expressions were deeply indignant, downright enraged. They knew the danger, though. They'd seen the guns bristling on the men and horses.

Daniels stepped forward and showed his teeth in an angry grimace but kept his voice low as he said, "You men get the hell out of here now!"

"What's going on, Boss?" came a deep, husky male voice behind the three gathered on the stoop just outside the doorway.

A big, beefy man stepped out from behind Hamm, the woman, and Daniels. He walked a few feet out into the yard between the eating hall and Frank and Three Moons and Bronco and Sager and the rest of Lord's gang. He was followed by one more man and then another... and then others came, moving in the opposite direction as they stepped out of the eating hall. Finally, they formed a semi-circle around the gang.

There was a good dozen of them.

They were all big and bearded and wore wool shirts or buckskin tunics, denim or canvas trousers, the cuffs stuffed down into high-topped, lace-up, cork-soled boots. Some were bare headed. Others wore wool caps like Daniels. One man—an especially large, gorilla-like man— wore a bowler hat with a red feather sticking up out of the band.

A few were wielding hide-wrapped bung starters, likely used for breaking up fights. Nothing rowdier than a hungry bunch of wood cutters. A few more held chunks of cordwood. Daniels was the only one armed with a gun.

The first man who'd sauntered out of the shack held a large chunk of split wood. He stood maybe six-three. Bare headed, he was bald as an egg with a dark-red beard but no mustache. Fine red freckles mottled his broad, pale, sun- and windburned face. Blue eyes were set close together on either side of a wedge-shaped nose. One of those eyes was a little cloudy, and an old, healed, pink scar angled down through the brow above it to continue several inches into the man's cheek below it.

He tapped the wood in his open palm, threateningly. As he did, the thick, chorded muscles in his bare forearms writhed like snakes.

"If the boss says you go, then you go," he said, and tapped the wood in his big, open palm again. He spoke with a heavy German brogue; spittle flecked his lips.

Frank gave a laugh and grinned down at the men. "What the hell you talking about? Daniels there is the only one with a gun. Go on—tuck your tails in and go back to your meal like good little wood cutters." He canted his head to see through the open door flanking Daniels, Hamm, and Hamm's pretty wife. "An' send my sister out here. We got family business."

"You men leave!" pronounced H. Leroy Hamm, nudging Daniels aside and stepping forthrightly into the yard, extending his arm and pointing a finger to the west. "This is Pegasus property. You are trespassing. Leave this instant and I do not want to have to say it again!"

"Leroy..." the women said warningly behind him, staring anxiously up at Frank, plump red lips stretched a little back from her perfect, little teeth as white as porcelain.

Daniels, squeezing the shotgun in both hands up high across his chest, and looking none too thrilled at the prospect of having to use the two-bore gut shredder against nine better armed men than he, gave a dreadful wince.

"Oh, hell, you prissy fool!" Frank said in disgust.

He pulled his Colt from the holster thonged on his right thigh and shot H. Leroy Hamm through the chest, just above his waistcoat and through his red cravat.

The woman screamed as Hamm staggered backward and into Daniels, who removed one hand from the shotgun and wrapped it around Hamm, crouching to catch the fool, eyes darkening with exasperation and stone-cold fear.

"Get them!" bellowed the big, bald German as he ran toward Frank, who shot him as casually as he'd shot H. Leroy Hamm.

Guns erupted around Frank, and Daniels was the next to go, just as he rose from his crouch and took the shotgun again in both hands. He gave a screeching cry as he flew backward into the woman, knocking her down onto the stoop with a scream that was nearly drowned by the thunder of Lord's gang's pistols and rifles, his men shooting as their horses danced testily, noses in the air, bits drawn back taught against their teeth lest they should bolt.

Pale smoke wafted in the darkening air as the big bruisers dropped like ducks being shot off a millrace, cursing, grunting, wailing.

In seconds, all were down. Half were still moving but another fusillade, smoke and flames lapping from barrels slanting down from the backs of the gang's skitter-hopping ponies, rendered all dozen or more wood cutters still in death or shivering as they gave up their ghosts.

Silence descended.

Silence, that was, save for the sobbing and grunting of Hamm's wife who lay pinned beneath the body of Daniels, who lay belly up atop the pretty lady, his dead eyes glinting in the light of the flickering lamplight issuing from the dining hall's front windows. His shotgun lay slack against his chest, arms thrust out to both sides.

Frank spied movement inside the shack.

He looked through the open doorway to see a tall, slender figure in a dusting cap walking slowly, dreadfully toward him. Eloise was silhouetted against the lamps behind her. She had both hands drawn across her mouth in horror.

She stepped into the open doorway, looking around slowly, then slowly lowered her hands from her mouth and gazed up at Frank sitting his stocky black stallion before her, twenty feet away, a half dozen large bodies lying twisted in death between them.

"Frank," she said, voice pitched with shock and dread. "What have you gone an' done *now*?"

Frank holstered his smoking Colt. He looked at his sister, hiked a shoulder. "I just wanted to tell you about Billy, sis." He slid his raptorial gaze to the woman still half-pinned by Daniels but was giving a valiant try at working herself free of the body, sobbing as she did.

"But now," Frank said, swinging down from his saddle, tossing his reins up to Three Moons, and stepping forward. "Now..." He pulled the sobbing woman to her feet and then tossed her over his right shoulder and stepped through the open doorway, swinging wide of his gaping sister. "Now, I think I need comforting!"

He marched up to the cluttered table, used one arm to clear a big swath at the right end, where H. Leroy Hamm had been standing and toasting his men, and then threw the woman down on the table before him. With three or four savage grunts, he stripped her naked while she writhed and kicked helplessly, then went to work removing his gun belt, laughing between the woman's pale, bare knees.

Eloise moved forward, drawing the door closed behind her with a click. She moved out onto the stoop, looked around again, and, hearing her brother's savage grunts through the door behind her, looked up at the men before her and said in a tone of quiet disgust, "He hasn't changed a bit, has he? Still a man-child, Frank."

She moved to the horse flanking her brother's stallion and held her work-roughened hands out, fingers splayed. "Oh, poor, poor, dear, sweet Billy..."

CHAPTER 29

Ezekial Storm woke with a start, jerking his head up off the pillow, which was merely a scrap of burlap crudely sewn and stuffed with hay.

Storm looked around, trying to get his bearings.

He ran a hand down his face, blinked, then slowly the humble cabin swam into shape around him, and he remembered where he was—in the shack he'd spied after he'd fought his way out of the stream. He'd been so cold and exhausted he'd practically crawled to the place. Apparently, it had been recently occupied; dry wood was neatly stacked beside the potbelly stove, and a fresh supply of canned goods stood in a pyramid on one of the shelves above the plankboard counter.

The cabin was maybe ten feet by ten feet, if that. But the potbelly stove had gotten it so warm that Storm had fallen right to sleep after he'd eaten a few bits of deer jerky he'd found in a pouch on a shelf near the airtight tins and had crawled onto the cot outfitted with the pillow and several striped trade blankets.

He turned to the window right of the door, but the shutter was closed over it, as they were closed over the three other windows in the place—two in the front wall, two in the rear wall. Storm rose, feeling weak and dizzy with sleep. He'd been so exhausted the night before that he hadn't even pulled his boots off. Now he rose to his lanky six-foot-five, having to stoop to keep his head from brushing the ceiling beams, and stumbled to the front door. The bangs of his thick, gray hair danced across his eyes until he swept his hand through the unruly mass and threw it up onto his head. He tripped the latch, pulled the door open, and stepped out onto the stoop.

He gave a disgusted chuff.

Deep shadows filled the valley around him and stretched out from the opposite ridge to angle over the fast-moving stream seventy yards away. Salmon and saffron light angled through gaps between the surrounding ridges, making the stream shimmer in places and turning silver the wings of the large hawk swooping low over the water's surface, looking for fish.

Storm had slept well over twenty-four hours.

He hoped he hadn't slept any longer than that. If he had, he likely would have wet himself, which he hadn't. His bladder was full, however. He turned to his left, opened his fly, and gave a deep sigh as the stream started, hesitating painfully at first before the old organ relaxed and gave him release. He had the urge to saddle his mule and set out after Lord's bunch. He was nearly two days behind them now. At least, there was only one trail out here—one that led to a lumber camp, he knew, because when he'd been circuit riding, he'd stopped at the place to deliver sermons in the eating hall. They hadn't been well attended, as he remembered.

Storm had no idea why Lord's gang would be heading for the lumber camp. Maybe they weren't. Maybe they were headed elsewhere and would simply pass the place and ride on. Eventually, Storm thought, the gang would likely swing south and make their way over steep passes as they headed to Mexico. He remembered having seen bulging saddlebags on the backs of the gang's horses, which meant they'd likely done some recent pillaging and plundering...and raping and killing, no doubt, as was their way...and might think the law was looking for them. In that case, they'd likely head to Mexico, and enjoy themselves down there south of the border until their trail cooled.

Then they'd return north and continue to ravage the defenseless.

Not if Storm had anything to do about it.

Storm and the Beast. The Beast must be fed.

What could possibly be more appetizing than Frank Lord's bunch?

When Storm had finished his business, making a large puddle just off the edge of the stoop which had been deeply eroded by others, Storm tucked himself in and buttoned himself up. He'd just finished with the last button when a rifle cracked in the far distance, and echoed.

Storm jerked his head up. He turned to gaze past the front of the cabin to his right and up the forested mountain. The shot had come from up there. High up there.

The shot might have been fired by the man who owned the cabin, if it was owned and lived in by one man. Storm thought it was. The man who lived here might have gone up the mountain to hunt. The single shot might mean he'd killed something. He might be returning soon.

The thought left a sour taste in Storm's mouth. He was a solitary man even at the best of times but now, at the worst of times, he did not want to share his shelter with another.

If the man came, Storm would make do and leave early the next morning.

He had to feed the Beast.

He opened the shutters over the cabin's two front windows then went back inside and closed the door. He used an ax stuck into an upright log beside the stove to chop up a neat pile of kindling then returned the ax to the chopping block, built up the fire in the stove, and set a pot of coffee to boil. His clothes were still wet from his ordeal in the stream, so when the coffee boiled, he filled a cup and sat in front of the fire, a blanket from the cot draped over his shoulders.

He was still chilled. Chilled to the bone. He felt as though that frigid stream was running through his marrow.

Outside, shadows gathered.

Night bugs ratcheted and a hunting nighthawk screeched.

Inside, Storm had lit a single lantern hanging over the eating table behind him. The mantle was badly soot-streaked, so the light was murky, the cabin filled with as much dark as light.

Storm took a sip of his coffee and made a sour expression as he swallowed. The coffee was fine. It was what he heard outside that soured him.

Men talking, horses clomping.

Tack squawking, bridle chains jangling.

The thuds of the slow-moving horses grew steadily louder.

Storm cursed. A gun belt with a badly worn holster hung from a post of the cot flanking him on his left. A Colt Navy that had been converted to fire metallic cartridges jutted from the holster. There were only three such cartridges in the cracked, weathered cartridge belt.

Storm rose slowly and, crouching beneath the rafters, made his way to the cot and pulled the Colt from the holster. He flicked open the loading gate and slowly turned the cylinder.

Four chambers showed brass.

Storm slipped two of the cartridges from the shell belt and slid them into the Colt's empty chambers. He flicked the loading gate closed, spun the cylinder, and pulled his old cap and ball revolver from the waistband of his trousers. He slid the older Colt, which had no doubt gotten fouled in the river, into the holster. He slid the newer Colt with its more dependable metallic cartridges into the waistband of his pants. He hoped that if one of the men approaching the cabin was the one who lived here—he'd decided that only one lived here as there was only one cot and not enough supplies for two men for any length of time—he would not notice he'd switched the Colt in the holster.

He stooped to peer out the window right of the door and jerked his head back to one side when he saw three riders ride down out of the black mass of the forest flanking the cabin.

"Hello, the shack!" called one of the riders, beneath the loudening clomps of the approaching horses. "We're friendly if you are! Sure could use a cup of mud and a place to sleep. We got fresh elk liver, if you're hungry!"

Storm narrowed an eye as he watched the men approach from a hundred feet away. Light from the rising moon shone on the gold buttons of the man's tunic sewn from a Confederate flag and which shone between the open flaps of his long, black duster. Moonlight shone on the cream-colored but badly weathered cavalry kepi he wore atop his shaggy head.

Storm drew a sharp breath, pulse quickening.

He'd seen that tunic and that worn hat before.

He'd heard the man's deeply Southern-accented voice before.

"Gonna take this one for a nice long ride!" he'd yelled on the other side of the covered wagon to another man, the one in the tunic called Bronco. "Gonna break her in real good for ya, Mister Storm!"

He'd whooped loudly. His whoops were nearly drowned by Josephine's screams.

"I said—*hello the shack!*" called the Southerner again, in a peevish tone. "I see ya in there. We got grub if you're hungry! Come on out an' be sociable!"

Storm crouched before the window. He grinned and raised his hand in a congenial wave. He moved to the door and opened it, brushing his right thumb against the satisfying bulge of the converted Colt behind his blanket. He ducked out onto the stoop. He didn't think his three guests could see him clearly, as the light behind him likely silhouetted him against it.

"Sure, sure...that sounds fine as frog hair split four ways!" he said, deepening his voice a little and putting some amusement in it, disguising it. He waved again, grinning—a simple, lonely man of the mountains enthused about the prospect of visitors. "Nothin' better than fresh elk liver. I heard the shot up on the mountain!"

He saw the bloody burlap bags tied behind the cantle of each man's saddle. One was the big Indian the others had called—what? Three Moons. They'd field dressed the elk and cut it into thirds. A smaller bag, also bloody, hung down from the saddle horn of the shaggy-headed man with the Stars and Bars shirt and whose name just then popped into Storm's head. One or two of the others that horrific afternoon had called him Sager. Bryce Sager.

Apparently, the rest of the gang was holed up somewhere not far ahead. Probably the lumber camp. These three had been sent back to hunt for game, which the wood cutters had likely hunted out of the mountains right around the camp itself.

Storm grinned and waved—yeah, a poor, lonely soul touched with cabin fever. "I'll put on a fresh pot o' mud while you put your critters up. Plenty of feed in the barn!"

The men glanced at each other dubiously. Sager said, curtly, mockingly, "You do that," and booted his mount around behind the cabin. The others followed suit, both men glancing back over their shoulders at the crazy old, stoop-shouldered man in the doorway.

Snow stitched the cold wind that had been picking up since sunset.

Storm had donned his floppy-brimmed, black hat by the time the three men had tramped back to the cabin and stomped in, shivering and cursing the cold.

"I don't know why we had to ride up here when it's damn near summer down below!" complained the blond man with a blond, soup-strainer mustache. He wore two revolvers in shoulder holsters. Storm could see the bulge beneath his duster.

The blond man stood near the fire, just right of Storm, who'd taken a seat in a hide-bottom rocker angled close to the stove. The light was behind him. He'd found a pouch of chopped tobacco and had packed his corncob pipe and was smoking it now, the pipe and smoking further disguising his face. He held the trade blanket up high around his neck. He was still cold down deep in the marrow of his bones. He had a feeling the ice would thaw soon. He grinned around the stem of the pipe as he took another drag and blew it out at the stove, the fire glowing bright orange around the gaps in the small, square, dented door.

"It's that sister of his," Sager said. He and the other man, the big Indian called Three Moons and who'd mewled like a grizzly when he'd been mauling Storm's daughters, were preparing supper at the table. "Always has to pay her a visit, Frank does. Pass her some jingle though I hear she does just fine for herself—on her back!"

He and the other two laughed raucously.

A glance over Storm's shoulder told him Sager was slicing the big slab of fresh elk liver while Three Moons was cutting up a couple of wild onions he'd washed outside the cabin with water from his canteen, and two big potatoes. They must have stocked up on supplies at McCullough's before they'd left, shy of three men. At least, shy of three living men. According to the big, Scot barman, Frank Lord had ridden away with his dead brother Billy, wailing.

Storm glanced over his shoulder again at Three Moons, who wore his hair in two braids pulled forward over his shoulders. The silver medallion he wore glinted in the lantern light. He was big—a whole head taller than Sager, and the high, flat planes of his face set beneath deep, inky black eyes told of ancient savagery.

He worked adeptly with his big bowie knife.

He caught Storm's glance and narrowed his fierce eyes at him. "What're you looking at, old man?"

Storm jerked his head forward with a startled grunt. "Oh, nothing...nothing." He stuck his pipe back in his mouth, puffing. Apprehension touched him.

It tugged at him again when the Indian said, "Say... haven't I seen you before?"

"Who, me? Hah! Oh, no." Storm grinned tensely around the pipestem, rocking and puffing.

"You seen him before, Jack?" he asked the man standing to Storm's right, warming himself in front of the stove.

"The old man? Hell, no." Jack didn't give Storm another look. "He's just an old man."

"How 'bout you?" In the corner of Storm's eye, he saw the big Indian nudge the ex-Confederate.

Sager laughed. "Where'd we have seen him before? Like Kansas Jack said, he's just an old man." He turned to Storm and raised his voice. "How long you lived out here, old man? Way off the beaten path. Hell, you're a good mile, mile and a half from the logging road!"

"Me?" Storm said, rocking and puffing his pipe. "Oh... I don't recollect. An old man gets foggy in his thinker box... 'specially after so many years livin' out here..."

Again, he grinned around the pipe in his teeth.

"Yeah, well, just the same."

The Indian gave Storm another suspicious stare. Storm glanced over his shoulder to see the man walk over to the cot, slip the old cap and ball from the holster, and carry it over to the door. He opened the door, tossed the old Navy out into the yard with a grunt. The gun thudded, bounced, clacked off a rock. The Indian closed the door.

"There," he said. "Just in case."

Sager and Kansas Jack laughed. "You're gettin' as senile as the old codger," Sager said. "An' you ain't even thirty."

"I am thirty," the Indian said, grabbing a cast iron skillet off a shelf.

"Oh, you are," Sager said, scooping up a handful of the wild onion and dropping it into the pan with a good-sized chunk of butter from a tin on the table. "All right, all right. I had it wrong." He chuckled to himself.

"Say..." That was the Indian behind Storm.

"Say what?" Sager asked.

The Indian walked around the table and stopped and turned to Storm. He crouched and canted his head to one side. "Take off your hat, old man."

Storm tightened his teeth around the stem of his pipe.

"Hey, old man," Three Moons said. "Take off the hat." He moved his right hand—big and red-brown and to which bits of wild onion clung—to the Colt jutting from the wide, brown belt wrapped around his waist.

Storm turned to him. He continued to grin around the pipe. Slowly, he reached up out of the fold of the blanket to his hat. He grabbed it by the crown, removed it, and let it drop to the floor.

The Indian's dark eyes widened.

His right hand tightened around the staghorn grips of the Colt in his buckskin holster.

Storm was already bringing his own Colt up from behind the blanket, grinning. He extended the Colt, clicking the hammer back. The old gun roared. The big Indian was punched back against the door, raising his own Colt straight above his head and firing into the ceiling. Slivers rained down, and he dropped the gun. He stood there, slowly sliding down the door, a dark-purple hole in his forehead, just above the bridge of his nose.

He stood staring at his killer in mute shock, moving his lips but not saying anything. As he slid down the door, the back of his head painted a thick line of blood and brains down the gray, vertical pine boards. His right elbow clicked the latch, the door swung upon, and the Indian swung out to tumble onto the stoop, making gurgling sounds in his throat. His high-topped, rabbit fur boots scissored and jerked as though he were trying to run even as the Beast snatched him from this earthly world where he'd caused so much grief and torment.

Kansas Jack stood staring in shock at the hard-dying Indian, giving his back to Storm.

Storm shot him through his spine.

As Kansas Jack screamed and went running out the door that Three Moons was propping open with his now-unmoving form, Storm turned to where the ex-Confederate, Sager, was awkwardly staggering to his feet, screaming, tripping over the bench he'd been sitting on while trying to slide his six-guns from his holsters. He was panicking, likely not a familiar emotion for one so venal and usually confident in his malevolent pursuits.

He'd been caught with his pants down, as the saying went.

He'd locked eyes on Storm, and the horror in them told the older man Sager now knew who he was...and what he'd become.

Did he see the Beast perched on his shoulder, lifting its feathers in the breeze through the door in its owl-like form, small eyes showing gold in the satisfaction of partial fulfillment of its vengeance quest?

Storm's own eyes glowed, turning bright red as he heard again Sager's rebel yell amidst the horrific screams of his dying daughters. Sager's revolvers were just clearing leather, having been caught up in their holsters by the keeper thongs and then the flaps of his long duster. He'd gotten his left booted foot caught up with the bench, and he fell now with a yell as the bench went over with him, pinning his left leg to the floor.

"No!" he cried, staring up at Storm who stood over him now, casting a long, slender death's shadow over Sager's own terror-bright eyes.

Storm aimed the Colt and fed the Beast, who gave a ratcheting cry of unadulterated satiation then spread its wings, lighted from the tall man's shoulder, flew through the door, the tips of its broad swings brushing the frame, then disappeared into the silent, moonlit darkness where the carrion eaters were already howling their anticipatory delight.

Storm set the gun down on the table and picked up the skillet in which the fresh elk liver resided with wild onions, chopped potatoes, and thick chunks of butter. He went over and set the skillet on the stove, swirled it.

"Feed thyself. Feed the Beast."

CHAPTER 30

"HELLO, DARLIN', I'M BACK."

The voice instantly drew Mrs. Joe Mannion, the former Miss Jane Ford, out of a deep sleep. A belly sleeper all her life, Jane rolled quickly onto her back and lifted her head from her pillow. "Joe?"

Mannion smiled and sat down on the edge of the bed. "Hi."

"You're..." Jane looked around incredulous, certain she was dreaming. Morning sunlight shone around the edges of the curtained windows. She placed her hand on his shoulder, pressed her fingers into flesh. It was him. It was really him. "You really are back, aren't you?"

"I'm back," he said with a sigh. He removed his high-crowned black Stetson and tossed it onto a chair, ran a hand through his thick, longish hair. "I'm back."

"A tough one?"

Mannion turned to her, nodded grimly. "Real tough. Tougher than the last. Tougher than any of them."

Jane frowned, feeling the old anger. "Why didn't you send someone to let me know...to let your deputies know...that you'd be gone longer than expected?"

"Darlin', don't be angry. This was a tough one. Especially tough."

"How so?"

"It's changed me."

Again, Jane frowned. "How so?"

Mannion looked off, pensive, his craggy features drawn. Morning sunlight shone in his gray eyes. Behind the light, there was a darkness in them. "I'm not sure."

She studied him for a time, pensive. Then her frown deepened, and she said, "Oh, Joe, come here!"

She hooked her arm around his neck and drew him down to her. He smelled like sweat and horse and saddle leather, but she didn't care. She pulled his head down to hers and closed her lips over his own, feeling the masculine scratching of his mustache, probing his teeth with her tongue. She moaned with the ecstasy of having the big brute home, of holding him again in her arms. The big, middle-aged, hard-eyed berserker who had two soft spots deep inside that rugged hide of his—one for his daughter, certainly, and, just as certainly, a soft spot for the former Miss Jane Ford, as well.

Her anger at him dissipated. She felt only love now. It fairly swelled her heart so that she could hardly breathe around the thick lump in her throat.

"Oh, Joe," she said, pulling her lips back from his. "Oh, Joe, you're home now and everything's all right now —isn't it?"

He turned to her. The look of consternation on his face, reaching far back into his eyes, had her worried. "I don't know," he said. "I want it to be, but..."

"What? What is it, Joe?"

Mannion just stared down at her. His eyes were on hers, but his thoughts were far away. Almost as though he'd retreated so far inside himself he could never fully be present here in Del Norte again...ever be fully with *her*, his wife, again.

"What is it, Joe? What's happened?"

Mannion rose. The big Russians holstered on his hip and his thigh bobbed as he moved to the window, parted the curtains, and stared down into the street.

Jane rose up on her elbows. "Joe, what is it?"

For a long time, he stared down into the street. She could hear the passing traffic, the occasional laughter and shouts of men.

"Joe..." she said, the fear inside her growing.

Finally, he released the curtain. Shadows closed over the bed, around Jane. He turned to her. But his face did not belong to Joe Mannion. The face turned toward her was the face of a giant crow, its beady eyes turning sharp and bright as it opened its giant beak and filled the room with: "CAW! CAW! CAW!"

Jane lifted her head from the pillow with a wail, turning onto her back and sitting up, her breasts rising and falling sharply, heavily, behind her thin cotton nightgown. She turned to the window against which heavy wings fluttered and several crows cawed loudly beyond it, the din dwindling as the birds flew away, leaving only the sounds of the town's mid-morning traffic.

"Oh, good heavens!" she said with a relieved sigh.

Just a dream. Nightmare, rather.

She was alone.

Of course.

She stared at the window for a long time, thinking. Finally, she tossed the covers back, stepped into her slippers, grabbed a powder blue robe off a wall hook, walked to her door, and went out into the hall. She crossed at an angle to her father's suite and knocked.

Her father's deep, pugnacious growl rose around a

mouthful of food: "Come in, but if I don't know you, you're gonna get four barrels of buckshot in your guts!"

"Oh, my God," Jane said through an eye-rolling sigh. She stepped to one side just in case her father's bear-like bodyguards got over eager with their sawed-off, double-barreled shotguns, which they'd both seemed to have gotten better acquainted with after her and her father's close call the other day with his three would-be assassins whom she and Vangie had sent down the River of Lost Souls. "Father, it's your daughter. Have the hellions stand down, please."

V.N. Ford chuckled, muttered something too quietly for Jane to hear. Then: "Come on in, Janey. Have a cup of coffee with your beloved old reprobate of a father!"

Jane twisted the knob and poked her head into the room. Both bodyguards, flushing with chagrin, had lowered the shotguns they both wore on leather lanyards around their necks, and, first the blond one and then the dark one, filed through a door to Jane's left.

The dark one closed it.

V.N. Ford sat in a plush-covered armchair at the end of his big, four-poster bed. He was still in his robe and striped silk pajamas, slippered feet propped on the ottoman before him. A breakfast tray steamed before him over the arms of his chair. He was buttering a slice of toast. A fat stogie smoldered in an ashtray beside his three-platter breakfast of eggs, potatoes, and biscuits flooded in sausage gravy.

"My God—you even smoke while you eat?"

"A potpourri of flavors." Ford closed his eyes, dreamily. "Nectar of the Gods, my dear."

Jane stepped forward, crossing her arms on her chest. "Well, you keep eating...and smoking like that...you'll be seeing one of them soon."

Ford canted his head to one side and grimaced. "You're so much like your mother, I don't know whether to kiss your cheek or tan your ass!"

"Father?"

"What?" he said, grumpily, and chomped nosily into his buttered toast which he'd also slathered in dark-red strawberry jam.

"I'm going with you. I'm going to help you and Mother. I don't know for how long, but when you catch the stage back to Glenwood Springs, I will, too."

Ford dropped his fork and knife with a clatter and stared at her in shock. "Good Lord—what made you come to that unexpected conclusion?"

Jane sucked her bottom lip. "The man I married is not who I thought he was. At least, not anymore. He might be dead. For Vangie's sake, I certainly hope not, but I think we would have heard by now. The man I thought I knew when I married him wouldn't have been gone this long without sending word. He's either changed...and changed drastically...or he's not who I thought he was. I'm tired of waiting."

Ford smiled broadly around the stogie he was puffing. "Jane Ford waits for no man!"

Jane laughed. "Men wait for Jane Ford!" she repeated her old refrain. "I need to get my life back, and maybe that starts with coming home...at least to help you and mother in Glenwood Springs." She frowned, puzzled, shook her head. "Whoever would have thought Jane Ford would ever need her father to get her head straight?"

"I would!" Ford said and threw his head back and laughed.

Jane chuckled, turned to the door, and went out.

———

MANNION WOKE WITH A START. "JANE!"

His heart thudded as he lifted his chin from where it had sagged down against his chest and thumbed his hat back up on his forehead.

Only a dream.

Nightmare, rather. In it, when he'd finally ridden back into Del Norte, she was gone.

He drew a deep breath of the early evening air and looked over to where his hobbled bay cropped grass along a little creek murmuring through aspens. He and the horse had been so exhausted after the long ride from McCullough's that he'd stopped, unsaddled Red, and dropped down in the prickly needles beneath a pine, pulled his hat down over his eyes, crossed his arms on his chest, and fell nearly instantly asleep.

Now he heaved himself to his feet, walked over to the placid, slow-moving stream, and stared down. He flinched and turned away when he saw his own reflection in the calm water. He forced his head back, his eyes down to the mirror of the stream. He fell to his knees, kept his eyes on the image of himself in the water. He raised his gloved hands to his mouth, touched his lips.

Where before there had been open cracks oozing blood, those cracks were all but closed. He remembered feeling both eyes swelling shut even as he'd taken on the howling horde inside McCullough's. He remembered the dragging, the sharp fingers of the ground tearing at him, ripping his clothes, shredding them, ripping them off until the man they'd hanged upside down by one foot had been damn near naked.

Naked and beaten and broken and torn, a six-foot-four-inch, two-hundred and twenty-pound welter of bruises and broken bones sliding around against each other in his chest, causing such agony as to render him mostly, mercifully, unconscious.

He hardly remembered being cut down, carried upstairs.

He remembered dying and visiting Sarah; only Sarah had been a crow, mocking him.

Storm had called him back.

He should have let well enough alone. But, no. Mannion had the man to thank for somehow summoning him back to this world, for laying hands on him, healing him, so he could finish the job he'd started when he'd drilled the forty-four round through Billy Lord's head.

Storm had called him back. Healed him.

At what cost?

What had the man done to him? Whom had he summoned to help him restore Mannion's body if not his soul, so he could complete his quest to annihilate Lord's bunch?

He shuddered.

"Crazy damn business," he muttered, feeling a chill deep inside himself.

Whom had Storm summoned? What had Mannion had to exchange for life?

Again, he shuddered then doffed his hat, lowered his head to the stream. As he drank of the cool, minerally waters, he jerked each glove off in turn then used his hands to cup the water to his face. It stung only a little when it touched the lingering cuts and welts. He could have sworn that when he straightened and the water had settled into that placid mirror once more the lingering blemishes, too, were gone.

He gave another shudder.

Damn near healed.

But at what cost? What had he been forced to surrender?

He gave a dry snort at that. Hell, whatever it was he'd likely given it up long ago. Might as well stop thinking about it, worrying about it. Most folks didn't know. They wouldn't see him any differently than they'd seen him before. His life would go on like always unless, of course, Lord's bunch extinguished it once more and Storm wouldn't be there to call him back...

Next time, he'd best let him go even if it was only to a place where a crow pretended to be Sarah, mocking him.

The urgency to continue moving chewed into him. He set his hat on his head. It was the only article of his former wardrobe that had survived the beating and dragging. Now as he stood and looked at himself in the stream, he saw himself, the man he'd been before he'd arrived at McCullough's, only now he wore the dissonant amalgam that the girls at McCullough's had thrown together for him—baggy, old denim trousers, cream chambray shirt under a brown leather vest, neck-knotted green bandanna, flannel-lined canvas coat, and a pair of brown boots that were about one-half size too small. One girl had found an old pair of moccasins under one of the beds. Who would have worn a pair of moccasins into McCullough's and then for some reason had left without them, Mannion had no idea. He'd almost taken them, but then nixed the idea. He was accustomed to boots. The moccasins might have distracted him when the chips were down, so he'd left with the boots despite the slight pinch in the toes and heel.

He touched the grips of his holstered Russians. He still had his guns. A girl had found one revolver as well as his Winchester amidst the ruins of the saloon; another girl had found the other Russian in the yard. Mannion and McCullough had carefully cleaned the weapons downstairs over coffee and Scotch whiskey, with the solemnity of two soldiers on the eve of battle. The girls had watched from where they'd been gathered, resembling brightly plumed birds in their gaudy, frilly underclothes and hair feathers, at a table near the bar.

One had hummed what had eerily sounded like a death dirge while she'd painted her toenails.

Now Mannion tightened Red's cinch, mounted, and rode on, following the only trail out here—the only main trail, anyway—a logging trail that he knew from previous visits to this neck of the San Juans led to a the Pegasus Lumber Camp. The storm had long since scoured away the sign of Lord's bunch as well as the sign of Justy and the mysterious young man she rode with, but Mannion knew from the information he'd gleaned from McCullough that he was on the right path.

If he didn't find Lord at the lumber camp, he'd swing south and hope to overtake the gang before they made it into Arizona.

He pushed himself and Red hard.

He was still riding after nightfall when a soft whistle sounded from the darkness of a forested slope off the trail's left side. Mannion checked the dun down and listened to the quiet night beneath the horse's weary blowing.

The first whistle was answered by another one a little farther up the slope.

Mannion's blood warmed. Could be a couple of Lord's men watching their backtrail.

Joe closed his hand over the Yellowboy's stock. As the barrel cleared leather, he dropped to the ground. He released Red's reins.

"Stay, boy!"

He drew a deep breath and catfooted it up the slope, wincing at the pinch of his too-tight boots.

CHAPTER 31

STAYING LOW BUT MOVING QUICKLY AND RELATIVELY silently, Mannion made his way up into the trees that started roughly thirty yards up the slope from where he'd left Red ground-reined below. He had no spurs, or he would have removed them. Kind of silly to wear the damn things when Red didn't really need them save when an especially prickly situation presented the need for an instant, lightning-fast run. Spurs were just plain noisy and not worth the trouble.

Whoever was moving around on the slope above him, maybe fifty feet away to Mannion's left, hadn't removed his own spurs. The man was moving around slowly up there, his soft, crunching footsteps joined by the faint rings of jingle bobs. Joe thought the man was moving down the shoulder of the mountain, away from him.

Suddenly, the chinging stopped.

A soft whistle.

A return signaling whistle rose from lower on the slope to Joe's left. Footsteps came from the same direction—faint, slow, crunching footsteps growing louder as whoever was over there approached.

Mannion dropped and rolled beneath a cedar, holding his gloved right hand over the Yellowboy's brass breech. His breathing was strained from the hard climb; he consciously controlled it, forced the air in and out of his mouth. The slow footsteps grew gradually louder until Mannion could see a shadow moving on the downslope over his left shoulder. There was no moon yet, and the surrounding high ridges blotted out most of the stars, so all he could see was a moving silhouette in the darkness, growing gradually larger as the person approached from that direction.

Finally, Mannion heard the person breathing.

He moved up from Joe's left flank to pass at a slant before him and maybe ten feet away. The man stopped just ahead and to Joe's right. Mannion could make out the silhouette of a tall, lean man in a hat and holding a rifle. He could see the barrel poking up from in front of the man's right shoulder.

The man whistled. Like the others, the whistle was supposed to sound like something a bird would make, but no bird Joe had ever heard had ever made a whistle like that. No seasoned outlaw would make it, either.

As the answering whistle came from the upslope on Mannion's right, Joe cursed under his breath, crawled forward, then took the Yellowboy in both hands. He swung it fiercely from right to left, the barrel about three inches above the ground. The barrel crashed into both ankles before him, slicing both feet out from under the person they were attached to.

The girl screamed and struck the ground hard on her right hip and shoulder, losing the rifle in the process. A hat tumbled to the ground; long hair flew.

Mannion dropped his own rifle, crawled forward, and climbed to his knees. Justy rolled onto her back and Joe could see the gleam of her white teeth between stretched-back lips.

"I warned you!" Mannion shouted.

"Get your hands off me!"

"The hell!"

Mannion rolled her brusquely over so her pert, round butt was staring up at him, ensconced in skintight, black denims. Holding her down with his left hand and knee, he opened his right hand, raised that arm, and swung arm and open palm down until the palm resounded with a sharp *crack!* against the girl's ass.

Justy screamed.

Mannion raised the arm and hand again, brought them down.

Crack!

Again, the girl screamed.

Crack!

Scream.

Crack!

Scream.

Then: *"Go to hell, you son of a bitch!"*

Jaws hard, gray eyes bright with fury, Mannion bellowed, "I told you what was gonna happen if you followed me, and I'll be damned if I don't keep my promises!"

Crack!

"Owww! *George!*"

Crack!

"*George!*"

Mannion heard running footsteps growing louder. In the corner of his right eye, he saw the silhouette of the other scout approach, crouched over a rifle.

Ignoring the kid, Mannion brought his hand down again across Justy's butt, evoking another scream followed by a spew of epithets Mannion hadn't heard since he'd sent a bevy of Irish mule skinners to Hotel de Mannion for drunk and disorderly though their brand of drunk and disorderly had entirely redefined the term.

"Hold it!" ordered the kid.

Crack!

The kid loudly racked a round into his Winchester's action. "I said stop it, dang ya! One more an' I'll...I'll..."

Mannion removed his left hand and knee from Justy's back and pulled away from her. He grabbed his hat, which had tumbled off his head during the one-sided melee, and set it on his head. He climbed to his feet and walked forward, toward the short young man standing before him, aiming the old-model Winchester at him.

"Or you'll what!" Mannion raged.

He grabbed the rifle out of the kid's hand and tossed it off in the brush.

"Hey!" the kid cried, indignant, looking toward where his rifle landed with a thud.

Justy climbed to her feet, her long hair falling around her shoulders in tangled wings, her white teeth showing again between her stretched lips. "Goddamn, you Mannion!" she screamed, crouching forward, holding both hands against her tender backside. "He was my grandfather!" Her lips twisted and her voice quavered as she added, "My *abuelito!*"

She ran forward like a bull from a chute. Mannion raised his hands to counter an attack, but it wasn't an attack she had in mind. Instead, she threw her arms around his neck and thrust her face against his chest, crying. "He's gone and he's not coming back—my abuelito!" She stared up at him, ambient light glittering in her tear-filled eyes. "It's all my fault. All mine! Not yours! I should have told you!"

She lowered her head, bawling, and dropped to her knees. She looked up at him again, tears glinting as they rolled down her cheeks. "I should have told you...what happened"—she lowered her face again, bawling, tears dribbling onto the ground—"between Frank and me..."

"Ah, hell, Justy." Mannion sunk to his knees, placed a comforting hand on her back. "It's all right."

She looked up at him again, and suddenly her expression changed to grief, to befuddlement. The skin above the bridge of her nose wrinkled. She shook her head slightly. "Joe...how do you live...?"

She looked at him closely.

"Joe?" said the kid, his own voice suddenly curious. He glanced at Justy. "You mean...*Mannion*...?"

"Si, si. I mean Joe Mannion." She straightened and leaned forward, placing her hands on the lawman's face. "How do you live? How do you live? Dios mio! Storm really did call you back from the dead. As bad as you were beaten, I didn't think you would...could...*stay alive!*"

She regarded him as though a miracle.

He wished he could regard himself the same way.

Justy ran her fingers across his lips, across his nose which had surely been broken. "You not only live, you..."

"Oh, I'm thriving," Mannion said, dryly. "Speaking of Storm—have you seen him?"

She continued to stare at Joe in amazement. Finally, his query clarified in her mind, and she shook her head quickly. "No."

"We figure he might've died in a one of the flooded canyons. He didn't wait for them to clear." The kid, too, kept his astonished gaze on Mannion's face, for he, too, had seen the condition the lawman had been in when he and Storm had hauled him into McCullough's.

"Maybe," Mannion said, but since the man had—with

or without help—brought Mannion back from the dead, he'd likely find a way—with or without help—to get himself across those flooded canyons.

To Justy, he said, "What about Lord?"

"He's at the lumber camp." She jerked her chin. "Just over the next ridge. We're camped above. We have a good view of the camp. Join us? We have food, coffee."

Mannion nodded, glanced down the slope up which he'd come, and whistled softly. It didn't sound much different than these two younkers' whistles but then he wasn't trying to. Presently, hoof thuds sounded and the big bay took shape on the downslope. Red came up to Mannion, blowing, rippling a wither and stretching his long snoot toward Justy and the kid. Leading the bay, Mannion followed Justy and the kid up the mountain through the trees.

Where had Mannion seen the kid before?

The question vexed him.

It was only when he'd unsaddled Red and tended the mount and picketed him with the other two horses and sat by the fire that Justy had built up after they'd entered the camp, that the answer dawned on him. Sitting back against his saddle, Mannion looked at the kid sitting back against his own saddle while Justy stirred bacon and beans in an iron skillet over the fire, and said, "That was you in Fury. The night of the fire. I saw you again the next morning."

Hard Time stared back at him, color rising in his cheeks.

"Why'd you run?"

Hard Time stared at him, two veins forking in his red-mottled forehead. He glanced at Justy, who'd turned to him now with mute interest, brown eyes dancing in the firelight. Hard Time looked back at Mannion and said, "You're so smart, Mannion, you figure it out."

"What do you need to be forgiven for, Wilkes?" Mannion said, tapping the edge of his tin coffee cup.

Hard Time sipped his coffee and shook his head. "It's not George Wilkes. That was my grandfather on my mother's side. It's Hard Time. Leastways, that's what I've been called most of my life. Come by it honestly too. Hard Time Lawton." He turned to Justy again, ironically pinched his hat brim. "How-do, senorita." He turned to Mannion. "Marshal."

Mannion didn't say anything. In his mind's eye, he saw again the black hat and the brown horse of the rider who'd galloped away from him and Billy Lord that early evening near the Devil's Anvil. He stared across the fire at Hard Time Lawton. Hard Time stared back at him.

"You told Frank," Mannion said.

The statement so startled Justy that she dropped the plate of beans and bacon in the fire. She cursed as the food sizzled and steamed. "Shit!"

She turned her incredulous gaze to the young, nondescript man known as Hard Time then sank back on her boot heels as the food continued to steam in the fire, the hiss dwindling slowly.

"Why?" she said quietly, in astonished disbelief. "Why would you do that?"

"Me, I've been a big fan of Frank's don't ya know? I've followed him and his bunch, watchin' 'em, admirin' 'em for their big guns and big reputations, the way people sorta turn white when they ride into a town. Big men, Frank's bunch. Oh, I've studied 'em...followed 'em, sure enough, though I reckon I got myself believin' I wasn't really *followin'* 'em. What kind of useless fool would do something that stupid? No, I got myself believin' that we just sort of *happened* into each other."

Hard Time sipped his coffee. He had a casual, ironic air but Mannion saw that the hand holding the cup was shaking a little. Hard Time lowered the cup, smacked his lips together and returned his gaze to Justy sitting back on her heels, staring at him. "I got myself believin' that I might one day ride with ol' Frank an' those two lieutenants of his, Lou Bronco and Bryce Sager, the Black fella with the saber, Abe Galloway, and the Apache tracker, Three Moons. Big, big men..."

Again, he sipped his coffee, stared at the ground. Absently, he swiped his free hand across his chaps, worrying a thread had come loose from its stitching. The fire snapped and crackled, bits of bacon and beans sizzling on a rock forming the ring when the flames found it. The flames slid across the underside of Justy's hat brim, cast a dancing orange glow across her face, flickered in her eyes that stayed glued to the man called Hard Time.

Slowly, she said, "You thought that..."

Hard Time turned to her, again with that casual air. But his right hand was shaking.

He smiled as he said, "I thought that if I told Frank where I figured Bloody Joe Mannion was taking his dear brother, Billy, he'd invite me to throw in with him, Frank would." Hard Time's sardonic smile grew. "I'd be one of Frank's mean-eyed gang of cutthroats, respected and feared throughout the land. Hell, I could see my own face penciled on a wanted dodger hangin' in some Western Union office, my name"—he thrust up a hand in the air before him—"in big, bold letters. Not only my name, but the big, thousand, maybe *two*-thousand-dollar bounty on my head!"

He chuckled, wagged his head.

He raised his cup with his shaking hand and took another sip of his coffee. He lowered the cup, smacked his lips, and returned his ironically smiling countenance to Justy. "Imagine being so feared...so respected..." He drew a deep breath, let it out slow, keeping his gaze on Justy. "So, yeah, I told Frank I figured Bloody Joe was heading to Fury."

He swirled his cup, smiling down at it, just telling another campfire tale. A doozy, this one. He threw back the last sip, tossed the drags into the fire, and returned the cup to the canvas war bag open beside him. He sighed deeply, said, "Well, it's been a long day. I do believe it's time for me to get some shuteye."

He kicked out of his boots with a grunt. He didn't look at Mannion or Justy. He stretched, yawned, drew his blankets up around him, punched his saddle with a gloved hand, and rolled onto his side. He placed his hat over the side of his face and gave another, long, weary sigh.

Just the end of another long day. He was ready for sleep.

Mannion and Justy stared at him in funereal silence.

After a long time, Justy turned to Joe. "I burned the beans."

Mannion turned to her. "That's all right. I'm not hungry anyway."

Justy returned her gaze to the still figure of Hard Time lying under his blankets, right cheek resting against his saddle, battered black hat covering his face. His chest rose slowly as he breathed.

"I'm not either," Justy said.

Joe sipped his coffee. It had gone cold. He tossed it over his shoulder with a splash in the brush, shoved the cup into a saddlebag pouch. "I'll check the horses," he said, and rose with a grunt.

He walked out into the darkness beyond the slowly dying fire, tended nature, and checked the hobbles on each of the three mounts. He walked around slowly, making sure they were alone. He stared down into the night-choked canyon where the lumber camp sat, maybe a half a mile away. He couldn't see much from this distance, maybe a few dimly lit windows.

He'd hatch a plan for killing Frank and the rest of the gang in the morning, when he was fresh. He was near the end of the trail. So was Frank Lord.

His body felt good. Strangely good. But his spirits were bleak, indeed.

When he returned to the fire, Justy had lain down beside Hard Time, curled herself against him from behind.

She held him tightly as he sobbed.

CHAPTER 32

MANNION WAS A LIGHT SLEEPER, ESPECIALLY WHEN ON the stalking trail.

Sometime during the night, he heard a stirring, and opened his eyes, one hand automatically sliding toward his pistol belt coiled beside him. The fire had burned down to a few glowing red coals, revealing a shadowy figure rising on the other side of the fire from Joe, over where Justy had bedded down with Hard Time Lawton.

"Come on," Justy whispered.

"What?" whispered Hard Time, poking his hat brim up off his forehead.

"Shh." Justy extended her hand. "Come."

Hard Time stared up at the girl for another couple of seconds then reached up and gave her his hand. She helped him rise. "Take your bedroll," she said.

He looked at her again then stooped to pluck his blankets up off the ground. Mannion watched the two silhouettes pad off into the night beyond the camp, hand in hand, causing Red behind him to give a low whicker and a nervous stomp.

"Go back to sleep, boy," Mannion said.

He rolled onto his side, closed his eyes, and let sleep overtake him.

Soon, the groaning of the two lovers awoke him. They were trying to keep their voices down, Mannion could tell, but it wasn't working. A strange, dark passion had overtaken them both. They sounded like a pair of wildcats toiling together out there in the wild darkness maybe fifty feet from the camp.

The groaning and grunting and sighing rose to a crescendo, then silence descended over the forest once more.

Red gave an incredulous snort, stomped his foot again.

Mannion looked up at the stars. It would likely be dawn soon. He slept for another hour, until the birds woke him. He'd just lifted his head up from his saddle when footsteps sounded from the darkness relieved by the gray wash of the false dawn that had started to fade the stars beyond the arrow-shaped, black crowns of the pines above him. He turned to see Justy walking toward the camp, tucking the tails of her shirt into her denims, her long, black hair dancing about her shoulders. Pine needles clung to her shirt.

She turned her head toward Mannion and stopped.

Her face acquired a sheepish cast and then she continued walking toward the fire ring.

"Morning," she muttered as she dropped to a knee and began crunching up pinecones and small twigs for kindling.

"Morning," Mannion said. "How'd you sleep?"

She gave him a sharp look then continued crunching up the kindling and turning back to the ring, her hair sliding down to cover her face. Mannion gained his feet, stomped into his left boot, then his right while tucking his shirttails into his baggy denims.

He turned to her and said, "If you're riding with me to the lumber camp, and I know there's no way I can stop you save hog-tying you both," he said, glancing toward where Hard Time was just then approaching the camp, head bowed as he buckled his cartridge belt around his lean waist, "this will likely be your last day on this side of the sod. You do realize that—don't you?" He looked at Hard Time again. "Both of you."

Hard Time stopped, looked at Mannion, then turned to Justy. His soogan was rolled and tied and clamped under one arm. They shared a look and then Justy loudly broke a branch over her knee and said, "If you're riding with Hard Time and me to the lumber camp, Marshal Mannion," she said firmly, dropping the broken branches onto the flames she'd coaxed to life with the tinder, "this will likely be your last on this side of the sod."

She turned to Mannion, tucking a thick wing of her long hair back behind her left ear. "You do realize that—don't you?"

She smiled.

Mannion drew his mouth corners down. "Figured as much."

She reminded him so much of his own, half-wild daughter, Vangie, that a tear damn near came to his eye.

Damn near.

He turned away to feed the horses while the two younkers made breakfast.

———

AN HOUR LATER, FRANK LORD OPENED ONE EYE suddenly, then the other.

He turned his head to stare up at the ceiling as gray dawn light bled around the curtains over the two windows of the room in the half-story above the dining hall at the Pegasus Lumber Camp. The second story was where the cooking staff resided, or *had* resided. At the moment, there was only Frank's half-sister, Eloise. The fat German cook named Herman Wolfe had run off into the night right after Frank and his men had killed all the woodcutters, the camp superintendent, and the owner of Pegasus itself—H. Leroy Hamm.

Frank had taken a couple of casual shots at the big man's figure dwindling against the gloaming, but he didn't think he'd hit him. He could have sent men after him, of course. But what was the point? The big German would likely die out there among the sage and rocks, torn apart by wildcats or wolves.

Curled against his left side, the woman moaned, dug fingers into the thick, strawberry blond hair matting his chest. She slid a knee over his left one. "What is it?" she said in a small, sleep-husky voice.

He glanced over to see her snuggling against his side, eyes closed, smiling luxuriously. He was a little surprised to find her still there. But then, why should he be? After the night's wild coupling after he'd carried her upstairs from the dining table, she'd become as docile as a kitten. Even with her man and all his men lying dead in the yard between the dining hall and the small cabins where the woodcutters had bunked.

Or maybe *because* of all that carnage.

What the hell was her name? Had she told him? Yeah, yeah...she had. Frank just couldn't remember. That was all right. He had more important things on his mind...

She looked up at him, frowning. "What is it?" she repeated.

"Not sure," he said, scowling up at the ceiling. "But a fella don't get this far in life without having a sixth sense about things, my darlin'." He turned his head to one side and planted an affectionate kiss on her forehead though he felt no affection for her whatever.

A man like Frank Lord felt no affection. Never had.

Or...maybe once...

He thought about that now but the strange feeling that had just come over him while he'd been rising from sleep nudged him back to the moment. He threw the covers back, rose, and began gathering his clothes from where he'd tossed them last night in a near-frenzy to get after the comely wife of H. Leroy Hamm again, whom, after having such a good time the first time downstairs, he'd kept for himself.

At least, in the short term. He'd send her to the others soon, after he'd tired of her. Which wouldn't take long. It never did.

He stumbled around, dressing. He was still hungover from all the busthead he'd drank the night before and well into this morning. A couple of his men had found a still out back as well as several shelves heaped with crock jugs of busthead. And busthead it was too! That was all right. The pain helped dull the pain of losing his brother, useless as Billy had been. Still, he'd been family. He and Billy had been all the family Frank had left.

Frank buttoned his shirt as the woman pushed a pillow up against the headboard and lay on her side against it, curling up becomingly. She let the sheet slide down to reveal nearly all of her small but well-rounded, alabaster body.

Good Lord—did the girl never get any sun at all?

"You going to take me to Mexico with you, Frank?" She smiled as she lay with her two hands pressed palm to palm beneath her right cheek. "Leroy never took me anywhere. At least, never out of the country. I think I'd like Mexico just fine." She broadened her smile and blinked slowly, alluringly.

"You think so—do you?"

"I think so," she said in her kittenish purr, blinking again, slowly. "With the right man..."

What the hell was her name again?

Gwen? Gwyn? Guinevere?

Something crazy like that. Not of this world...

"Sure, sure," Frank said, stomping into his boots and grabbing his hat off a chair. "We'll talk about it later."

"You'll protect me won't you, Frank?" she said, suddenly leaning forward as he walked to the door and pushed it open, sudden fear in her voice. "I'm a girl who needs protection!" she called as he strode quickly down the short hall toward the stairs.

He rolled his eyes.

She was already getting on his nerves, H. Leroy Hamm's wife was.

The stairs dropped down into the kitchen where Eloise was toiling, washing dishes with more hot water bubbling on the range. Her face and hair were soaked with humidity. She looked at Frank, looking pale, drawn, and weary.

"What the hell are you doin', sis?" Frank said, adjusting the set of his pistols on his hips and heading for the door leading to the main eating hall. "You got no one left to cook for. Stop that! We're goin' to Mexico!"

"Someone has to clean up this mess, Frank," Eloise said in her mild, thin voice behind him. "I can't just go and leave it like this."

"Leave it!"

Frank laughed as he pushed through the swing door and crossed the room, noting the crock jugs, glasses, tin cups, and overfilled ash trays littering the room's three, long tables, where his men had reveled the night before, on the lee side of the blood bath. Frank stopped before the door, frowning, and pulled both pistols holstered on his hips. He clicked the hammers back then drew the door open and stepped tentatively out onto the small stoop fronting the building.

As he did, he noted three horses galloping into the camp from his left, fifty yards away and closing fast, manes dancing in the buttery light of the sun that was peeking out from between two tall, eastern crags. Had it been the hoof thuds that had awakened him as it had the others in his bunch, all of whom were now surfacing in various stages of dress, bleary-eyed from sleep, from the cabins on the far side of the yard, a hundred feet away from the dining hall?

"Who the hell's that?" said one of them, Loco Santiago, cocking the Winchester in his hands. He wore pants and leather leggings but no shirt, his sombrero hanging from its neck thong down behind his back.

He and the others stared at the oncoming mounts, as did Frank.

Frank felt a tightening in his loins when he saw no riders on any of the three horses. At least, not *upright* riders. No, the three riders riding in on the three mounts appeared to lay belly down across their saddles, wrapped in their own bedrolls.

As the horses galloped up between the dining hall and the six shacks on the other side of the yard, Frank said, "Did Three Moons, Sager, and Kansas Jack come back last night?"

Lou Bronco, standing outside the shack nearly directly across the yard from Frank and tucking his shirt-tails into the back of his pants, shook his head darkly. "Nope, can't say as they did, Boss."

Frank had sent the three men out for game to tide the gang on their long trek to Old Mexico.

"That's their horses, though," said another man as all three mounts came to a stop in the yard between the dining hall and the bunk shacks.

All three mounts whickered and sidestepped, glancing behind at the cargoes on their backs. Cargoes whose smell they didn't seem to care for one bit.

Holding his cocked Colt barrel up, Frank glanced across the yard at Lou Bronco. "Check 'em," he said, knowing full well whom Bronco would find lying across the mounts' saddles.

But he had to check.

He slid his eyes to the horses' backtrail, narrowing it cautiously.

Who was back there?

Bronco winced in distaste at the potentially grisly task then stepped forward, heading for the first mount in the group—Kansas Jack McMichael's strawberry roan. Bronco walked around in front of the roan to the mount's right side, crouched down, and carefully parted both sides of the end of the blanket. Bronco drew a head up by its hair, scowled down at the face.

Frank saw a brown nose and brown cheeks and part of a blond-mustached mouth.

Bronco turned to Frank with a revolted grimace. "Kansas Jack."

Frank jerked his head to the second horse in the bunch—the rangy pinto belonging to the proud South-erner, Bryce Sager.

Bronco walked over, parted the blanket on the horse's near side, and glanced over his shoulder at Frank. The man's look said it all.

He turned to the last horse in the group—a big gray mustang. He turned back to Frank and didn't say anything.

"Check it," Frank said.

Bronco gave a fateful sigh and walked over to the big mustang. The horse had turned to stare toward the cabins on the far side of the yard. Bronco steadied the prancing horse by grabbing the cheek strap of its bridle then crouched to open a fold in the blanket wrapped around the big man lying belly down across the saddle.

Three Moons, of course. Who else?

Bronco opened a fold, frowning at the thick, gray hair. He lifted the head by the hair, revealing a long, thin, sun-browned nose.

Bronco's disbelieving scowl grew more severe.

Three Moons had a long, thick wedge of a beak, as copper as it was brown.

Bronco lifted the head higher, his curious scowl turning more curious. The eyes opened suddenly. They were bright and blue, not the inky black of the Indian's eyes. They stared up at Bronco, wide and jeering.

Bronco screamed and stumbled straight back away from the mustang, which gave a start of its own.

The blanket opened even wider and the man parting it...from *inside* the blanket...brought up the long, double-barreled shotgun he'd been holding up close against his right side. He took the long double-bore in both hands and grinned more broadly, showing his large, horsey teeth as he leveled the shotgun at Bronco.

The left bore blossomed rose red flames and white

smoke and made a sound like that of an of an angry God
smashing a boulder against a mountain.

Ka-BOOOOMMMMM!!!

CHAPTER 33

JOE MANNION'S EYES WIDENED IN SHOCK AS HE watched the man standing near the big gray mustang fly back away from the horse in two equal halves.

Joe sat astride Red's back off the corner of one of the bunk shacks facing the camp's dining hall. Most of Lord's men stood thirty to fifty feet away from him, facing the three horses that had galloped into the camp with what appeared blanket-wrapped bodies lying belly down across the saddles.

Now as he watched in grim fascination the man who'd obviously been shotgunned, torn in two bloody halves flying back against the dining hall's front wall, painting it red, Mannion raised his Winchester high above his head, giving the start-the-dance signal to Justy and Hard Time perched on the roofs of two bunk cabins above and to his right.

Lord's gang was down to eight or nine men, including Lord himself, and now as Justy and Hard Time cut down on them with their carbines from atop the cook shacks, Mannion rammed spurless heels into the bay's flanks. Red lunged forward as Joe took the bay's reins in his teeth and commenced triggering the Yellowboy, aiming straight out from his right shoulder at the gang twisting toward him, astonished expressions on their wide-eyed faces.

Several fell from Justy and Hard Time's bullets while two others went dancing and spinning as Mannion's own Yellowboy, fired as he stormed the group from the west side of the camp, added its own raking barks to the melee, evoking its own bitter, agonized screams.

The three horses carrying the three dead men—er, two dead and one right sporting fellow, rather—galloped away, whinnying fiercely.

As they did, Mannion saw none other than Ezekial Storm standing at the center of the billowing fog of gun fire, extending two long-barreled revolvers straight out before him, shooting and shouting, "Search not for Satan, for you are *heeee*!"

He blew the head off one of the men trying to rise after being shot by either Justy or Hard Time, bellowing, "Feed the Beast, yelleth the Dark One. *Feed the Beast!*" He shot one more man who'd already been wounded, and yelled, "Divine Providence, brothers! Go forth, He sayeth...and the sinners shall perish while the saints languish in the darkness of their own bitter hearts!"

He looked around in the sudden silence that had fallen over the yard, swinging his pistols to-and-fro, searching with childlike eagerness for another target.

Mannion had halted Red at the opposite side of the camp from where he'd galloped in. Like Justy and Hard Time standing atop two cabins ahead and on his left, he'd stopped shooting. Lord's gang lay in bloody heaps before him, surrounding Storm, who staggered around, inspecting the bodies, looking for any sign of lingering life he might extinguish with lunatic glee.

Finally, Storm turned to Mannion. The gray-headed old scarecrow thrust his smoking revolvers straight up above his head, barrels aimed at the lightening sky, and smiled like the madman he was. "Saints and sinners," he said, showing his yellow, horse-like teeth between thin, chapped, spread lips. Raising his voice, he brought one of the Colts down to thump the butt against his chest. "Saints and sinners we are, devils we are"—he thumped himself again—"who feeds the Beast inside us and in our worldly ignorance deems Himself holy above all others!"

As he grinned at Mannion, his head jerked violently to one side, spilling brains down his shoulder.

The report of the rifle that had hurled the killing bullet sounded ahead of Mannion and to his right. He swung his head toward the open window in the upper half-story of the dining hall. At the same time, Justy shouted, "*Lord!*" and dropped to a knee atop the shack nearly directly across the yard from the dining hall's front door.

She pumped two rounds into the window from which the gang leader had fired.

The rifle disappeared from the window, the man wielding it screaming, "My eyes! My eyes!" Wild thumping sounded from behind the window, a woman screaming "Frank! Frank! Oh, *Frank!*"

There was a crashing sound. Again, the woman screamed.

Joe swung his right leg over his saddle horn and dropped straight down to the ground.

"Wait there!" he shouted at Justy and Hard Time then took off running to the dining hall's half-open front door.

He kicked the door wide and looked around, making his way toward a door at the back of the cave-like, wooden-floored room. He bulled through the door and looked around, swinging the Yellowboy this way and that, looking for a target. There was only a thin young woman standing at a steaming, sudsy sink, doing dishes and singing softly to herself, apparently oblivious of the foofaraw around her.

Smelling smoke, Mannion turned to the plankboard stairs rising to the half-story above. Smoke billowed down it, rife with the smell of kerosene from a shattered lamp.

Joe strode quickly to the stairs, automatically thumbing shells from his cartridge belt and through the Winchester's loading gate. He aimed the Yellowboy up into the smoky shadows as he climbed the stairs slowly, one step at a time. Above him, from somewhere in those shadows, the woman screamed again, shrilly. Wild thumping. Then suddenly a flickering light grew in the murk at the top of the stairs and a man-shaped figure appeared. Mannion drew a bead on Frank Lord's head but held fire when a pillar of billowing flames was suddenly hurled toward him.

Again, the woman screamed. As the column of flames flew down toward Mannion, he saw the dark body of the woman ensconced inside those flames. It was as though she wore a nightgown of roiling fire!

Joe threw himself against the rail to his left. The screaming, burning woman flew past him, the loud dragon breath of the flames all but drowning her dying wails.

Mannion raised the Yellowboy and fired up into the murk at the top of the stairs. He pumped another round into the breech and held fire.

Lord was no longer above him.

The loud crash of breaking glass sounded from above.

Above the loudening breath of the fire now overtaking the kitchen, Joe heard Justy and Hard Time yell from down in the yard. He swung around then leaped over the rail and into the kitchen as flames crawled up the walls and across the ceiling.

"Get out! Get out!" he called to the girl who'd been obliviously doing dishes.

She was still there, Mannion saw in hang-jawed horror. She was still doing the dishes, singing softly while flames engulfed her.

As the flames licked toward him, red snakes slithering across the floor, Joe ran back through the door, across the main dining hall foggy with building smoke, and outside. He stopped when he saw Justy and Hard Time standing in the yard before him, surrounded by dead men including Ezekial Storm.

"I got fifty cents I can pink the left leg," Hard Time said as he pumped a round into his carbine's action.

"I'll raise you a quarter and call his right one," Justy said, also pumping a round into her Winchester's breach and raising the rifle to her shoulder.

Mannion turned to follow their aiming rifles to the half-clad figure of Frank Lord limping badly as he ran away to the east. Thick yellow hair bounced on the outlaw leader's shoulders as he fled through the rolling sage beyond Pegasus Lumber, the hills brightening now as the lemon orb of the sun rose above the eastern ridges. Lord's wash-worn red longhandle top had been scorched black by the fire. Tendrils of smoke rose from it as it did from Frank's scorched hair.

Mannion turned back to Justy and Hard Time as they stood side by side in the middle of the yard, drawing their index fingers back against their long guns' triggers.

Red flames stabbed from the barrels.

"Saints and sinners," Mannion said, sliding down the

front wall of the burning dining hall. He lowered his Yellowboy as the rifles before him barked and Frank Lord screamed.

Joe sank to his butt on the stoop and leaned back against the door frame. He dug his makings out of his coat pocket and commenced building a smoke. "Saints and sinners," he said, wearily, amusedly, dribbling the chopped tobacco onto the wheat paper troughed between his fingers. "Saints and sinners..."

He snapped a lucifer to life on his thumbnail.

"We all do feed the Beast," he said, touching the flame to the quirly's tip, drawing the smoke deep into his lungs.

Again, the rifles belched before him. Justy howled victoriously. Hard Time laughed.

Out in the sage to Mannion's left, Frank Lord sobbed and begged for mercy.

CODA

MANNION DIDN'T EVEN KNOW WHAT DAY IT WAS WHEN he rode into the southern edge of Del Norte a week later. All he knew was that, judging by the shortness of the shadows, it was high noon or thereabouts and it was a day on which the stage rolled into town.

The Concord coach owned by the Rio Grande & Company Stage Line was there now, parked before the line's main depot building on Main Street's east side, opposite the Rio Grande Hotel.

Joe was flanked by Justy Claggett and Hard Time Lawton, both of whom had accompanied him out of the mountains though neither had told him, if either had had any, of their plans. They seemed to have taken to each other and maybe, on the lee side of all the hell they'd both gone through in recent days, that was enough.

For now.

It might have been enough for Mannion himself at their young ages, though of course he couldn't know for sure. He'd been their ages one hell of a long time ago. Lifetimes ago, it felt like now. He might have had Ezekial Storm's dark hands "laid on him," as the saying went, his aches and pains somehow dissolved—at what cost, he didn't know—but he was still a man with a heavy weight on his shoulders.

You couldn't go through what Mannion had gone through, being the man Joe was, without those travails weighing heavy. All he knew for sure was that he was far different from the man who'd ridden out of Del Norte more days ago than he'd been able to keep track of, on the trails of Billy Lord and the half-breed, Hec Hagness.

Justy and Hard Time were conversing in light, jovial tones, having grown easy with each other on the long trek out of the mountains, when Mannion suddenly reined in so suddenly ahead of them that both nearly ran their horses into Red.

"Whoa, whoa!" Justy told her grulla, drawing sharply back on her reins. "What's the matter, Marshal Mannion?"

Joe only vaguely heard her. His eyes were on the person—woman, more specifically—who'd just stepped out of the Rio Grande office. A tall, slender redhead in a red felt traveling dress with a red waist coat trimmed with white. Mrs. Joe Mannion wore a matching felt hat on her pretty head, trimmed with faux green berries and flowers in front. She stepped to one side as a stocky, older gentleman stepped out of the building behind her and then another man, a younger one just as nattily dressed as the older man, stepped out, as well.

That the older man—clad in a light-brown coat and vest, white necktie, and cream slacks, with a light-brown bowler on his head—was Jane's father Joe could tell right off. Father and daughter couldn't have had dissimilar builds but there was something in the old lion's face and in the fire in his expressive eyes, windows to the soul, sure enough, that told Joe there was no mistake.

Then Joe saw Vangie as well. She'd been standing up the boardwalk a ways, in the shadows, as the two pullers had been harnessed to the rest of the team on the far side of the coach from where Joe sat Red, staring at the small group on the boardwalk surrounded by toiling wranglers and porters arranging the travelers' luggage in the coach's rear boot.

Vangie was dressed as she usually was—for work with her horses. Her tan Stetson sat on her brown-haired head, the chin thong dangling across the open neck of her black and gray plaid work shirt. She looked sad. She spoke to Jane, and Jane said something back to her, taking the girl's right hand in her own two white-gloved ones, squeezing. Mannion could see their lips move but he couldn't hear what they said above the low roar of the street enmeshed in the midday hustle and bustle.

Still talking to Vangie and the older man who could only be Jane's father, Jane glanced toward Mannion, glanced away, then returned her gaze to him quickly.

Her eyes widened, and she stopped speaking.

She released Vangie's hand as she held Joe's gaze with her own.

Mannion sat on Red's back, staring at his wife who was slipping away from him just as fast as she could. He could tell that from over a hundred feet away. He could tell it in her eyes and in the traveling clothes she wore, the two steamer trunks he recognized as hers just then being hefted into the coach's rear boot.

Joe knew he had to do something fast to stop her.

But he did not.

He sat Red in the street to the south of the Rio Grande depot, staring, feeling sad and forlorn and as lonely as he'd ever been. He wanted to boot Red on ahead and tell Jane not to go, that he loved her, that he'd do better in the future, that he'd be a better man...in the future...but he knew it would do no good.

Still, that's what he should do.

But he did not.

When the older gent who was her father thrust out a short, thick arm and kid-gloved hand to indicate the coach's open door, Jane turned her gaze away from Joe and stepped up into the carriage, holding the hem of her billowing skirts above her ankles. The older gent and then the dapper younger gent followed her inside. Two more passengers followed them into the coach and then the door was closed by a porter and the driver's yell caromed out over the street from the boot at the front of the carriage—"*Headin' out—clear the way or get your raggedy asses runover!*"

The black snake cracked over the team's back, the carriage lurched forward, and dust streamed from its rear wheels as it pulled out into the street and lurched into more and more speed, heading toward the far side of town and the open country beyond—toward the Sawatch Range jutting its several slate-gray peaks and shoulders beyond. Jane stuck her head out the right rear side window and, holding her hat on her head with a gloved hand, turned to face Mannion.

Her brown-eyed expression was unreadable.

The team pulled the coach around a bend in the street, and she was gone, the hustle and bustle of the midday street filling in behind her.

Rio Waite was standing beside Vangie now on the boardwalk fronting the Rio Grande office. Both were looking at Mannion.

Slowly, Vangie shook her head. Joe could see tears running down her cheeks.

He rode forward. Vangie and Rio Waite stood watching him, dark expressions in their eyes.

Behind him, Justy and Hard Time exchanged curious glances then shrugged and booted their own mounts ahead.

A LOOK AT BOOK FOUR: TO MAKE A MAN

In this 4th book in bestselling author Peter Brandvold's exciting new Bloody Joe western series, Del Norte Town Marshal "Bloody" Joe Mannion and his junior deputy, Henry "Stringbean" McCallister, run down an especially violent as well as beguiling outlaw in the pretty form of Mathilda Calderon. The senorita is just one pretty girl, but she fights like a leg-trapped puma, leaving Mannion with an arm full of buckshot and Stringbean hurting where a man just shouldn't be attacked, gallblastit!

Senorita Calderon is wanted not only for aiding and abetting the commission of a federal crime but to testify in a court trial against her boyfriend, the notorious border bandito and revolutionario, Diego Hidalgo, who stole three Gatling guns from the U.S. Army, wiping out a dozen soldiers in the deadly process. Hidalgo and three members of his gang were captured by the Army. The U.S. Marshal for the Southwestern District has sent three deputy U.S. marshals to retrieve the senorita from Del Norte and to escort her to Tucson. The marshal believes she will not only identify Hidalgo as the leader of the gang who stole the Gatling guns but will also testify as to the guns' whereabouts.

COMING SOON

ABOUT THE AUTHOR

Peter Brandvold grew up in the great state of North Dakota in the 1960's and '70s, when television westerns were as popular as shows about hoarders and shark tanks are now, and western paperbacks were as popular as *Game of Thrones*.

Brandvold watched every western series on television at the time. He grew up riding horses and herding cows on the farms of his grandfather and many friends who owned livestock.

Brandvold's imagination has always lived and will always live in the West. He is the author of over a hundred lightning-fast action westerns under his own name and his pen name, Frank Leslie.